Praise for *Death of the Mantis*

"Assistant Superintendent Kubu is back! In *Death of the Mantis*, a killer stalks the Kalahari Desert—and it's a page-turner from start to finish. Michael Stanley's enthralling series, with its very likable Botswana policeman, is a must-read for anyone who enjoys clever plotting, terrific writing, and a fascinating glimpse of today's Africa. Kubu—*Death of the Mantis*—Michael Stanley: the perfect mystery trifecta for any crime fan."

—Charles Todd, *New York Times* bestselling author of
A Matter of Justice

"*Death of the Mantis* is the best book yet in one of the best series going: a serious novel with a mystery at its core that takes us places we've never been, thrills and informs us, and leaves us changed by the experience. I loved this book."

—Timothy Hallinan, author of *The Queen of Patpong* and
A Nail Through the Heart

Praise for the Detective Kubu Novels

"[Kubu is] the African Columbo. . . . Like the first book to feature Kubu, *A Carrion Death*, this is a smart, satisfyingly complex mystery. A."   —*Entertainment Weekly*

"If you have yet to discover the charm of Detective Kubu and his extended family, and the lure of Botswana's unique landscape, now is the time and this is the book."   —William Kent Krueger

"A brilliant sequel to *A Carrion Death*. Suggest to fans of the No. 1 Ladies' Detective Agency series, who will appreciate Kubu's laid-back style and happy home life, and to Henning Mankell fans, who will respond to the complex plots and palpable sense of place."   —*Booklist* (starred review)

"Stanley offers a lot more action 'out bush,' while delivering a tale every bit as evocative in its sense of a place and the people who live there."   —*Times-Picayune* (New Orleans)

"A complex mystery that should appeal to both history buffs and armchair travelers."   —*Christian Science Monitor*

"A dramatic opening. . . . More smart than bloody . . . with clues that will have readers flipping back chapters to check alibis and opportunities. . . . Kubu himself is a marvelous creation, as well-considered as the plot. This is a marvelous debut."

—*Boston Globe*

"Delightful. . . . Plot twists are fair and well-paced, the Botswana setting has room to breathe and take shape as its own entity, and Stanley's writing style is equal parts sprightly and grave."

—*Los Angeles Times Book Review*

"Kubu follows in the literary footsteps of Christie's Poirot and Conan Doyle's Holmes—[a] brilliant male detective with a love of classical music, a palate for good food and fine wine, distant but compassionate, who solves crimes with reason and resolve. . . . This is a deliciously satisfying first mystery. I want seconds."

—*Milwaukee Journal Sentinel*

About the Author

Michael Stanley is the writing team of Johannesburg natives Michael Sears and Stanley Trollip. Sears lives in Johannesburg and teaches part-time at the University of the Witwatersrand. Trollip was on the faculty at the universities of Illinois, Minnesota, and North Dakota, and at Capella University. A full-time writer, he divides his time between South Africa and Minneapolis, Minnesota.

DEATH OF
THE MANTIS

DEATH OF THE MANTIS

A DETECTIVE KUBU MYSTERY

Michael Stanley

HARPER

NEW YORK • LONDON • TORONTO • SYDNEY

HARPER

DEATH OF THE MANTIS. Copyright © 2011 by Michael Sears and Stanley Trollip. All rights reserved. Printed in the United States of America. No part of this book may be used or reproduced in any manner whatsoever without written permission except in the case of brief quotations embodied in critical articles and reviews. For information address Harper-Collins Publishers, 10 East 53rd Street, New York, NY 10022.

HarperCollins books may be purchased for educational, business, or sales promotional use. For information please write: Special Markets Department, HarperCollins Publishers, 10 East 53rd Street, New York, NY 10022.

FIRST EDITION

Library of Congress Cataloging-in-Publication Data is available upon request.

ISBN 978-0-06-200037-8

11 12 13 14 15 OV/RRD 10 9 8 7 6 5 4 3 2 1

In memory of Salome Comley (1954–2010)

She left too soon.

The peoples of Southern Africa have integrated many words of their own languages into colloquial English. For authenticity and color, we have used these occasionally when appropriate. Most of the time, the meanings are clear from the context, but for interest, we have included a glossary at the end of the book.

For information about Botswana, the book and its protagonist, please visit *www.detectivekubu.com*.

⊞ CAST OF CHARACTERS ⊞

Words in square brackets are approximate phonetic pronunciations. Foreign and unfamiliar words are in a glossary at the back of the book.

Banda, Edison	Detective sergeant in the Botswana Criminal Investigation Department (CID) [Edison BUN-dah]
Bengu, Amantle	Kubu's mother [Ah-MUN-tlé BEN-goo]
Bengu, David "Kubu"	Assistant superintendent in the Botswana Criminal Investigation Department (CID) [David "KOO-boo" BEN-goo]
Bengu, Joy	Kubu's wife [Joy BEN-goo]
Bengu, Wilmon	Kubu's father [WILL-mon BEN-goo]
Gobiwasi	Elderly Bushman [GOB-i-WOSS-i]
Haake, Wolfgang	Namibian geologist [Wolfgang HAA-kuh]
Helu, Philemon	Detective sergeant in Namibian police [FILL-eh-MON HEY-loo]
Khumanego	Bushman [Ggoo-muhn-AY-go] (gg = guttural sound like clearing one's throat)
Krige, Joseph	White Namibian [Joseph KRI-gguh] (gg = guttural sound like clearing one's throat)

Lerako, Phinda   Detective sergeant in the Botswana Criminal Investigation Department (CID), based in Tsabong [PIN-duh Luh-RAH-koh]

Mabaku, Jacob   Director of the Botswana Criminal Investigation Department (CID) [Jacob Mah-BAH-koo]

MacGregor, Ian   Pathologist for the Botswana police

Monzo, Tawana   Game ranger at Mabuasehube [Tuh-WAH-nuh MON-zoe]

Muller, Henk   Executive in Namibian junior mining company

Ndoli, Thebe   Office manager of Mabuasehube ranger station [THE-beh n-DOE-lee]

Piscoaghu   Mysterious man in Hukuntsi [PIS-koh-ah-ggoo] (gg = guttural sound like clearing one's throat)

Robinson, Cindy   American journalist

Serome, Pleasant   Joy Bengu's sister [Pleasant Sé-ROE-mé]

Sibisi, Bongani   Professor of ecology at the University of Botswana [Bon-GAH-nee See-BEE-see]

Tau, Lekang   Detective in the Botswana Criminal Investigation Department (CID), based in Tshane [Leh-KANG TAU (as in COW)]

Vusi, Peter   Head of the Mabuasehube ranger station [Peter VOO-zee]

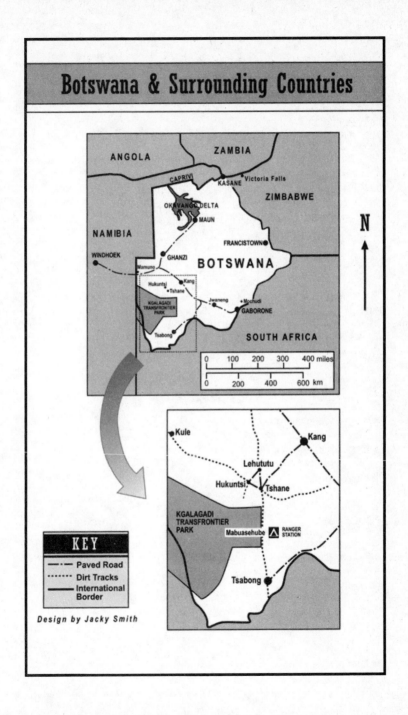

Botswana & Surrounding Countries

Design by Jacky Smith

❖ PROLOGUE ❖

Sixty Years Ago

The desert glowed in the dawn light. The Bushman boy woke from a deep sleep, still tired from the exertions of the last days. His father was already up, standing like a sentry, watching the sun creep above the horizon.

"We must go on, Gobiwasi," he said. "We will reach The Place today. We must travel while it is still cool. Here, chew on this as we go." He handed the boy a chunk of *Hoodia*.

For the boy it had been a journey of heat, of sun, of exhaustion, as he tried day after day to keep up with his father. But he had offered no complaint, and now felt the thrill of discovery ahead. Today *he* would be at The Place! Very few people had ever seen it or even knew about it! He gathered up his few belongings, gnawed the root, and tried to match his father's easy pace.

After about an hour his father stopped and pointed silently ahead of them. Gobiwasi could see what appeared to be small hills on the horizon. He looked up at his father, and the man nodded. Then they set off again.

At last they came to the hills—a group of *koppies* rising out of the desert. They passed between them until they came to one in the center of the group—a solitary hill with a rocky cliff facing them to the east, steep slopes to the west. It was uniformly high north to south, showing caves and recesses from bottom to top in the cliff. They rested in the dappled shade of a scrubby acacia and ate and drank a little. Then Gobiwasi's father said it was time.

First they went to a large overhang in the center. There his father pointed out paintings of ancestors: men and women dancing, thin-legged, watched by *gemsbok*, eland, and springbok—gorgeous and strange representations that left the boy awed and a little afraid. Low down on the right, a lion, teeth unnaturally large, with a black mane and a long tail, seemed to growl at him.

Then they climbed to a cave many yards off the ground. The walls were black with soot, and on the floor lay a human skeleton, bones picked clean. Spread around it in a spiral were the contents of a hunting bag—spear, bow, delicate arrows, knife, cord, sandals that looked as if they would fall from the feet at the first step, leather-topped hollow root for holding the arrows, and several horns that Gobiwasi knew had contained poisons. To one side was a toy bow with small arrows—a child's precious possessions. And two necklaces of cocoons containing pieces of ostrich egg shell that rattled in dance. A Bushman's entire life lay on the floor. The boy wondered whose life.

They climbed farther, Gobiwasi scared of the height, afraid of slipping and falling. His father scampered up to the topmost cave, almost perfectly round at the entrance and perhaps five yards deep, and waited there. When the boy joined him and had caught his breath, his father took him by the hand and led him past a crowd of people, watching from the walls. Red people and brown people. Adults and children. Animals watched too, and a strangely shaped white fish that Gobiwasi did not recognize.

For the next few hours his father told him about the spirits and about the ancestors, visiting different caves and pointing out important paintings. Then they climbed down, and his father showed him a hidden spring at the back of a small cave, from which they drank.

On the second day his father said they must fast. No food and just a little water during the day. Gobiwasi must purify himself. For that night he would come to know the spirits of The Place. Gobiwasi was excited, scared, wanted to know more. But his father would say nothing, and they spent the day resting in the shade.

When it was dark and before the moon rose, they climbed to the very heart of The Place. In the dark it was difficult, but the man knew the way, and they went slowly. "You must remember the path," he said. "You will need to find it again a long time from now." After a while they came to an open place and rested. His father gave him some white powder to swallow, and then he collected a bunch of very dry grass from the previous summer or perhaps the summer before that. "We will need fire," he said.

At last they came to a huge dark mass with a gaping crack, as if split by lightning or a supernatural power. They squeezed through the crack into the deep dark inside. It was cool, and Gobiwasi thought he heard whispers. It is the spirits, he thought, his heart in his mouth. Is this what my father meant? His father sat, put a wood block on the floor, and rolled the firestick between his hands. After what seemed an eternity, the grass flared.

Suddenly the cave became the night sky. Blinking lights set in darkness. Lights of beauty that searched, probed, judged. He saw the light flicker on his father's face, saw that his eyes were tight shut. He heard voices in his head, knew his father heard nothing. He cried out.

Then it was over. The flame died. The lights were gone. The beauty was gone. The voices were gone. He felt his father's hand dragging him through the crack in the cave wall, skinning his knees in the process. The pain brought him back to his senses. He cried out, gulping the cool night air, and feeling a terrible thirst.

"We will go now to the spring. You can drink. Then we will eat a little *Hoodia*. Then you will sleep and dream. For the spirits have accepted you."

Gobiwasi looked up at the stars and thought they were close enough to touch. They are watching me, he thought, and watching over me. Then he went with his father.

When Gobiwasi had drunk his fill, his father said, "You have met the spirits. You have seen their home. The Place is very sacred and very secret. You must take nothing. You must tell no one where to find it except your own oldest son when his time comes. And you must tell no one what you have seen here tonight, not even him. Do you swear this?"

Gobiwasi nodded. "I swear."

After that his father showed him the ancestors in the sky, bright-eyed and clearly seen. They spoke of these and other things, until Gobiwasi fell into a drugged sleep.

At dawn he woke with his head full of vaguely remembered dreams. His father was already up and motioned Gobiwasi to join him on a flat rock facing the east. Together they watched the great sun slowly lift itself from the desert to scorch another day.

Part I

Hõũŋhõũŋ haŋ //xΩm //ke: //ke :ja //khabo,
ti ε: i ka //khabo-ã

A presentiment is also like a dream
which we dream

One

It was so hot the jackal couldn't stand still on the sand. It must be well over a hundred degrees out there, Vusi thought, watching the jackal trotting toward the shade from the birdbath where it had been drinking, shaking its paws comically when it stopped momentarily to sniff the wind. Vusi turned back to the others. Where the hell was Monzo? He'd be the first to complain if anyone else was late, but he had no problem keeping his boss and three colleagues waiting for a quarter of an hour. He was probably picking a fight with someone or causing other trouble. There's always one on every team, on every one of my teams anyway. Vusi frowned.

"Let's start." He wanted to get the meeting over before the extra bodies in his office drove up the temperature. The windows were closed against the heat, and a desk fan was laboring to keep the office bearable. There wasn't much to discuss anyway. The meetings existed because Monzo complained that he wasn't being kept informed. That's because no one likes him, and so no one talks to him, Vusi thought sourly.

"We need the aerial species-count numbers for the quarterly report. Who's got those?" Silence. It was Ndoli, the office manager, who answered. A slender man with rolled-up shirtsleeves and inkblot patches under his armpits. "Monzo will have them."

Vusi sighed. Well, of course. It was Monzo's job. He did the statistics and drafted the damn report anyway, coaching Vusi on the presentation to the Kgalagadi Transfrontier Park Steering Committee. Monzo was good at what he did, when you could focus him on work. They weren't going to get anywhere without Monzo, damn him!

Vusi used his handkerchief to wipe his damp face. Why didn't they have air-conditioning anyway? This was the main Botswana office of the Transfrontier Park after all. Ten thousand square miles to manage! He looked out of the window again. The jackal had reached the shade of an acacia tree and was lying, panting. He's hot too, but he doesn't have to deal with Monzo and the director of Wildlife Conservation, Vusi mused unsympathetically.

"Where is Monzo anyway?" Vusi asked no one in particular. "He's twenty minutes late now. I'm a busy man. We're all busy!" He glared at the others as though they were to blame for Monzo's rudeness.

Again it was Ndoli who answered. "He said he was going to check up on the Bushmen. He drove out that way this morning."

"Why? What's it got to do with him? Why did you let him go?"

Ndoli rubbed his chin. A group of Bushmen had moved close to the park boundary a few weeks ago. No one knew why, perhaps not even the Bushmen themselves.

"He was worried they'd poach in the park." He didn't bother with Vusi's last question. Monzo never asked permission for his escapades. A month ago he had gone off on a "field trip" to the middle of nowhere, supposedly after poachers, and hadn't returned for five days.

"So what? Maybe they kill a springbok. Is that going to ruin the statistics? We don't want all the trouble the Central Kalahari people had. High-court challenges, Survival International, speeches at the United Nations." Vusi felt his blood pressure rising. He thumped his fist on the desk. "I'm in charge here!" His staff looked at him silently.

Vusi lost his temper. "Well, get out there and find him!"

He pulled a file across his desk and pretended to study it, indicating that the meeting was adjourned. No one would argue about looking for Monzo in the suffocating heat. They simply wouldn't do it.

Why must I work with people like this? Vusi asked himself. When will I get a promotion out of here to the head office in Gaborone, or at least to Tsabong? He heard the chairs scrape back as his staff left. He glanced up, avoiding their eyes, and found the safety of the window instead. The jackal had gone. He looked down again, and a bead of sweat dripped onto the file.

Oddly, it was Ndoli who became concerned. As much as he disliked the man, he had a sneaking admiration for Monzo's manipulative abilities. Certainly, Monzo would be capable of keeping them waiting, but he'd do it for a reason or to make a point. Here there was none. And why didn't he answer the two-way radio? Ndoli had tried several times to raise him. No one had heard from Monzo since he set off to check on the Bushmen. Hell with him, Ndoli thought, he deserves whatever he gets. But, unable to concentrate on anything else, after an hour he cursed loudly, causing everyone in the communal office to look up. He grabbed a bottle of drinking water and opened the outside door. Waves of heat invaded the office like a live thing, gobbling the less fiery air inside the room. He forced through the barrier of heat, slamming the door behind him.

His vehicle was parked under shade cloth with the windows open, but the driver's seat was still too hot for his bare legs. He had to perch on the edge of the seat so that his shorts protected him.

The dirt road was nothing but a track leading from the Wildlife offices at Mabuasehube through thick Kalahari sand, and he had to use four-wheel drive, sometimes low range, to battle through it, avoiding slowing lest he sink in and be unable to move again. Maybe that's what happened to Monzo, he speculated. But why doesn't he answer the radio? Maybe he's driven out of range. As he drove, his shirt used captured sweat to glue itself to his body, while his face and arms suffered convection roasting from the open windows. The discomfort made him furious. Monzo better not be sitting under a shady tree drinking beer!

After half an hour, he was starting to wonder if Monzo had gone another way. But around the next bend, he saw Monzo's vehicle, off the road on the higher, harder verge. He pulled in behind it and went to investigate. Monzo's Toyota HiLux 4x4 *bakkie* was not locked, but nothing appeared to be wrong. Ndoli walked around the vehicle and saw a set of footprints heading away from the road. He followed them for about fifty yards, until they disappeared as the sand merged into the ubiquitous calcrete limestone of the Kalahari. Circling around for a few minutes, he spotted the prints continuing into the desert sand.

Soon the prints disappeared again. As he searched for them, he came to the top of a *donga*, a steep ravine cut by an ancient stream through the gray calcrete. The soft rock at the edge was crumbling.

Ndoli looked down. At the bottom of the *donga*, some fifteen feet below, Monzo was lying on his back, not moving. Next to him squatted a Bushman. Two others stood and watched. When they saw Ndoli, there was consternation; then they waved and shouted to him.

Ndoli let out an exclamation and scrambled down the scree slope. A few moments later he was kneeling next to the prone game ranger. One of the Bushmen was trying to pour water from an ostrich shell into Monzo's mouth, but the liquid appeared merely to be running over his face. Grateful for his first-aid training, Ndoli felt the throat and found a faint pulse. He thought he detected shallow breathing, so he spread fine Kalahari dust on his palm, held it to Monzo's nose, and was relieved to see it move. Next he felt for injuries, but found no obviously broken bones. But the back of Monzo's head was a mass of congealing blood; he must have sustained a vicious head blow when he fell into the *donga*. And he would have sunstroke as well.

Ndoli turned to the Bushman. "When you find?" he asked slowly in Setswana.

"Soon." The man shrugged. It was obvious that his knowledge of Setswana was limited.

"Move him?"

The man shook his head. "Give water."

Ndoli wondered if it was safe to move the injured man,

wanting to get him out of the sun. It would be difficult to do carefully even with the Bushmen's assistance. Monzo was large, big-boned and overweight. After a moment he decided not to try and pulled off his damp shirt, using it to protect Monzo's head and arms from the marauding sun. Then, asking the Bushmen to wait, he went back to his vehicle and radioed for help.

Vusi was not overcome by sympathy. What was Monzo doing wandering around in the desert and falling into *dongas* anyway? Serves the bastard right! But, of course, it would create more work for Vusi and difficulties for his staff. How typical of Monzo! Perhaps he would be rid of him for good. But he shook his head to dispel such uncharitable thoughts. The man was in critical condition. He was suffering from heatstroke and dehydration in addition to concussion from the bad head wound. He had not regained consciousness, and the doctor who had seen him in Tsabong thought his skull might be fractured. Now he was being taken by helicopter to the hospital in Gaborone. And whose budget will pay for all that? Vusi fumed.

He heard the outside door open. Ndoli must be back. He went out to the main office and found the manager looking tired, hot, and depressed.

"What took you so long?"

"I stopped at Monzo's house to tell Marta about the accident."

Vusi paused. He should have done that himself. "I want a report on what happened," he snapped.

"I don't know what happened. The Bushmen found him lying in the *donga* with his head bleeding. I told you everything on the radio."

"Did you get their names? The Bushmen?"

Ndoli shook his head. "They're not going anywhere. I'll recognize them when I see them." He wondered if that was true. There was something generic about the small, yellow-brown people and, if they wanted to, they could vanish into the desert in a few hours.

"But what was he doing there? How did he fall into the *donga*? It was broad daylight!" Vusi winced, thinking of the blinding sun.

"Maybe he was looking for the Bushmen, or discovered the *donga*, wanted to take a look, and got too close to the edge. It was very crumbly. Perhaps it broke under him. He's heavy enough."

"Maybe. How long will it take to get him to Gaborone?"

"Should be there. They left well over an hour ago."

Vusi was silent. An unpleasant thought had occurred to him. Perhaps Monzo *had* found the Bushmen and had picked a fight with them. Maybe he got a rock in the back of his head and a shove into the *donga* for his trouble. Still, Bushmen weren't aggressive. They were peaceful people. They had tried to help. But Monzo could make anybody mad. Perhaps there had been a struggle and Monzo fell. Well, they would know what had happened soon enough, once the man regained consciousness.

Vusi's thoughts were interrupted by his radio phone. He grabbed it and listened for a minute. Then he thanked the caller, disconnected, and turned to Ndoli who was waiting in the doorway. "Monzo died on the way to the hospital. God rest his soul."

Ndoli nodded and walked away, the talk in the office suddenly stilled. Vusi scowled. There would have to be an investigation. Intuitively he knew that while his difficulties with Monzo were over, his real problems were just about to begin.

Two

Vusi stopped his car in the sandy track leading to the last in the row of comfortable homes that the Wildlife department supplied to its staff members at Mabuasehube, courtesy of a large grant from the European Union. White plastered walls, roofs of thatch, and even lawn and small gardens fighting the desert sand, the dryness, and the heat.

Ndoli had offered, but this was a duty Vusi felt obliged to handle himself. He knocked quietly, and Monzo's wife, Marta, let him in and offered him a seat. She folded herself onto the couch and started comforting a small boy. Vusi felt the first pang of regret at Monzo's death; the boy could not be more than six. Vusi took in the short, busty woman sitting opposite him on the threadbare sofa. She looked good in a dress with traditional touches, and large loop earrings framed an interesting face. Behind her on the wall were two faded prints, and to the side was a table holding mounted photographs and a crude carving of a woman's head, perhaps done by one of her boys. The room was tidy and clean despite the kids, and clearly the center of the home.

He wondered how to begin. Marta looked composed; she had not obviously been crying, but she wouldn't have seen Monzo after the accident. Perhaps she doesn't know how serious his injuries were, Vusi thought. Also some women don't show their emotions. "Mma Monzo," he began. "I have some news. I'm afraid it's not good." She nodded and sent the boy outside to play with his brother.

"He died?"

Vusi nodded. "I'm very sorry. He was a wonderful colleague and friend, really. He never regained consciousness, you see. He wouldn't have felt any pain." He wondered what would be an appropriate reaction if she started to sob.

But Marta just shook her head. "Your wonderful colleague and friend was a lousy husband, Rra Vusi. Well, actually, he wasn't a husband at all. You'll find out when you check his records. He never married me. I discovered he already has a wife somewhere in South Africa. I'm his mistress. Isn't that what you men call us? They're his children, though." She nodded to the boys playing in the yard. It looked like a game of hide-and-seek, but the younger one had forgotten to hide in time, and a quarrel looked imminent. "I suppose now I go with nothing but the two kids. When must I leave?"

Vusi was horrified by this development. Another problem, a scandal! The paperwork to determine insurance and pension payouts! How like Monzo. Causing trouble from the grave. He pulled himself together.

"No, no, Mma Monzo, that is, er . . . you can certainly stay for the moment. No rush to leave the house. It will take us time to get a replacement for your husband . . . I mean Monzo. And there will be some money, I'm sure. You'll be the common-law wife and, of course, these are his children. We're definitely on your side. You mustn't worry."

She gave him a strange look with a mixture of emotions. Then she folded her arms, lifting her generous breasts, and smiled.

"Thank you, Rra Vusi," she said. "You are very kind."

The detective was taking his time, Vusi thought with irritation. The man settled himself into a chair and glanced around the office, peering at the wall calendar. He looked relaxed despite the two-hour drive from Tsabong through the sand and heat. A Bushman of indeterminate age, wrinkled and wizened, leaned against the office wall. Detective Sergeant Lerako had brought him, but hadn't introduced him. Ndoli sat on the edge of his chair, looking uncomfortable.

"I understand that Monzo went to meet some Bushmen," Lerako said at last. "Have you had any problems with them here?"

"Certainly not," Vusi replied. "No problems at all, as far as I know." He looked at Ndoli for confirmation, but was met by silence. "Why?"

Lerako ignored the question and turned to Ndoli. "Exactly what did Monzo say to you when he left?"

Ndoli shifted in his chair. "He said he'd had a report that the Bushmen were poaching in the game reserve. Said he was going to put a stop to it one way or another."

"What did he mean by that?"

Ndoli shrugged. "He was angry. I guess he meant to chase them off."

Lerako turned back to Vusi. "Did he say anything like that to you?"

"No," he said flatly. "What's it matter why he drove out there anyway?"

Lerako folded strong arms across a broad chest. His neck spread from his head to his heavy shoulders. He looked like a bodybuilder. And he didn't smile.

"In homicides, people found at the scene are often involved. There were Bushmen at the scene."

"But this was an accident! He fell into the *donga*!" Ndoli exclaimed.

"We have to consider every possibility. I'll want to know where everyone was that morning. Another fact is that most murders involve family, or friends, or persons who knew the victim."

"Murder? That's ridiculous!" Vusi had an uncomfortable feeling that he was losing control of the situation. Where was I yesterday in the morning? he wondered. I was late. Monzo had already left when I got in.

"You can't think one of us was involved!" Vusi said. "We're a team."

Lerako ignored him and changed tack. "Who benefits from Monzo's death?"

Vusi swallowed, hesitated. "Well, he had a wife and family. Marta and the two boys. There will be pension and insurance benefits for them. Little enough to bring up two young children, I'm sorry to say."

Ndoli looked at his boss sharply, but Lerako appeared not to notice. "How much?"

"I can't say yet. It depends on certain things . . . Perhaps fifty thousand pula."

"I need to see the place where he was found. Will you take me?"

"Ndoli will do it," said Vusi, firmly. The day was already hot. "He's the one who found Monzo with the Bushmen anyway. He can tell you about it."

Lerako nodded. Turning to Ndoli, he indicated the Bushman. "I've got a tracker with me. He may be able to help if we can't find these Bushman suspects. I'll get my stuff, and we'll meet you at the vehicle."

When they had gone, Ndoli turned to his boss. "Do you know Marta wasn't Monzo's wife?"

"Yes, I know. Just a technicality. Nothing to worry about. I don't think we should bother the police with it."

"He had another woman too. Not the wife. More a pay-as-you-go."

Vusi winced at the term. "So what? We need to get this over with. It *was* an accident, wasn't it?"

Ndoli nodded and went to join the detective. Vusi was left wondering why he felt guilty and a little scared.

It was hardly a pristine crime scene. There were scuff marks and footprints everywhere. Monzo had been strapped to a stretcher, carried out of the *donga* at a point where it was less steep, and driven to a spot where the helicopter could land, so the whole area had been trampled. The entire staff must have been here milling around, Lerako thought with dismay. Anything could have happened at the edge of the *donga*. He dumped the evidence bag he had carried from the vehicle and turned to Ndoli. "Tell me how it was."

Ndoli hesitated, looked down, and then met the detective sergeant's impatient look. "Well, the vehicle was back up there where we parked"—he indicated the location vaguely—"and Monzo was over here." He pointed at the precise spot. He remembered the scene perfectly, and it was clearly marked by the efforts to get Monzo onto the stretcher. What else should he say? "I'm not sure what else you want to know, Sergeant Lerako." Lerako was an odd name. He wondered if it somehow matched the man's personality. He had no intention of asking, though.

"Why did you move it? Monzo's vehicle?"

"Why abandon it out here? We thought it was an accident." He looked down at the glaring sand. "I still think it was an accident."

"All right. Go on."

"Well, I stopped when I saw Monzo's *bakkie*. Then I followed his footprints. I lost them once or twice, but eventually they led me to the edge of the *donga*." He pointed to a position above them at the top of the steep incline. "Monzo was lying down here, and one of the Bushmen was squatting next to him. The other two were standing over there. I thought he was dead. When I got to him, one of the Bushmen was trying to give him water. Why would you do that if you were trying to kill him?"

Lerako ignored the question. "Did you notice footprints? Were there any up there except for Monzo's? Any down here except for the Bushmen's?"

Ndoli frowned. He'd just assumed the ones at the top of the *donga* all belonged to Monzo. Once he'd spotted the ranger lying crumpled below, he'd forgotten about footprints. Now, with all the prints from the rescuers, it was unlikely that anything could be identified. He shook his head, feeling foolish.

Lerako made him describe the scene exactly and then nodded. "I see it," he said. "Wait. I'll call if I need you." Puzzled,

Ndoli did as he was told, finding a thorn tree with a thick canopy nearby. If only there was a breeze!

Lerako photographed the scene and then started walking upstream from where Monzo had fallen. The tracker walked with him, a few paces to his right. Here there were no footprints. Only the tracks of buck—springbok judging by the size—and some old hyena spoor. Nothing recent. Their eyes scanned the ground. From time to time one of them would stop for a closer look before moving on.

Ndoli wiped sweat off his face with his sleeve wondering what on earth the policeman hoped to find. The sun didn't seem to bother him. His clothes looked fresh despite the oppressive heat and the journey from Tsabong. By comparison, Ndoli's khaki uniform already felt like wet rags.

About fifty yards from where Monzo had lain, Lerako stopped and bent over for a careful look. He called the tracker over and pointed something out before walking back for his evidence bag. Then he retraced his tracks back up the river, yelling for Ndoli to join him. When he caught up, Lerako pointed to a chunk of calcrete, a convenient shape to hold. It was partially covered with a russet stain. There was no doubt about what that was. Even after a day and a half of drying in the sun, there were several flies.

"That's what killed your friend," Lerako said. "Someone smashed his head with that. Then threw it here, probably from the top of the *donga*." He shook his head. "It's very unlikely he'd kill himself falling down that slope. Break a few bones, yes. Bash his head, yes. But smash open his skull, no. And why fall anyway, in broad daylight?" He didn't mention that the doctor in Gaborone felt a deep skull fracture was unlikely from such a fall. He turned away, took pictures from different angles, and then pulled a latex glove onto his right hand and carefully lifted the rock into a plastic bag.

He turned to the tracker and said slowly in Setswana, "Find tracks. One hundred yards all 'round. Here and up there." He pointed to the top of the *donga*. The tracker nodded and set off upstream, examining the ground closely.

Lerako turned to Ndoli. "We may as well wait in the Landie. Then we'll go and find your Bushman friends. I suspect they know a lot more than they told you. What do you think?" Ndoli started to answer, but Lerako was already walking back to the vehicle. Clearly he wasn't really interested in Ndoli's thoughts on the matter.

Three

When the phone rang, Assistant Superintendent David Bengu—Kubu to his friends and even some of his enemies—was contemplating how his life had changed. He was holding a desk photograph taken at Tumi's christening. The baby, of course, was the center of attention, resplendent in a blue, green, and gray dress, which a neighbor had hand made for the occasion. Tiny curls were threaded with crimson ribbons. It was completely over the top, Kubu felt, smiling approvingly. More suitable for a birthday party. Their neighbor also had a baby, and suddenly she and Joy had become firm friends. We've changed our social status, Kubu mused.

Tumi was being held by Kubu's mother, Amantle, who had a wide, although not very toothful, grin, and behind her stood Kubu's father, Wilmon, his usually impassive face cracked into a smile. A scatter of gray invaded the hair around his ears, a sure sign of advancing age in a black African man. *Honest* was the first adjective that came to Kubu's mind about his father; *warm* was the one for his mother. He hoped Tumi would inherit both those qualities.

In the picture Kubu stood next to Joy, his wife and lover, and now, against the odds, the mother of his child. The two of them luxuriated in the pleasure of presenting the first grandchild. Unusually for an amateur photo, all the participants had their eyes open and their smiles natural. Tumi would be the cause of both.

Kubu's pleasant recollections were spoiled by the harsh ring of the phone. How often that happens, he thought—a moment of peace banished by the telephone.

"This is Assistant Superintendent Bengu."

"David? This is Khumanego. Are you well?"

"Khumanego!" The name unpeeled years. "What a surprise! Are you in Gaborone? It would be wonderful to see you."

"I'm in Lobatse. I work here now."

Khumanego! They had been friends at primary school in Mochudi even though Kubu was two years younger. They had made an odd pair: the Bushman youth and the share-farmer's son, one short and slender in the manner of his people, the other big and already overweight.

Khumanego's parents, part of a small nomadic group roaming through southern Botswana, had sent him with great sadness to distant and unenthusiastic Christian relatives in Mochudi for good schooling. To prepare him for a different future, they had said. But Khumanego had confided to Kubu how unhappy he was. He disliked his relatives and town life, missing his people and the desert desperately. But it was school he hated the most. He was the only Bushman in the school, and the teachers regarded him as a backward child from the bush, incapable of learning anything but the simplest concepts. The cane was always close to hand.

Both Khumanego and Kubu were teased and taunted by the other pupils, Khumanego for his small stature and poor Setswana, and Kubu for his fatness, bookishness, and ineptitude at sports. Mismatched with their classmates, the two boys drew together and became friends.

It was Khumanego who had shown Kubu the desert, how to love it, and how to understand it. It was he who had drawn a circle in the scorched sand and shown Kubu that a superficial look reveals only sand and a few pebbles, bits of dried grass. But on closer inspection, some of the pebbles are, in fact, curious succulents, and what looks barren is actually teeming with life.

Kubu began to think of the desert as a metaphor for the world—superficially everything is as you expect. But if you look beyond the obvious, you see what others do not, and by observing things properly, you understand them better. He started looking for the "why" rather than the "what" in people too. That had set him on the path to becoming a detective.

"David? Are you there?"

"Yes, yes. I was just thinking of the times we spent together. You remember that trek we took into the desert?"

"Yes, I remember."

"You live in Lobatse now? I thought you wanted to go back to your people? Back to the Kalahari? You didn't like towns and electricity and what you called funny clothes."

"That is what I wanted. But what of the future? My parents were right. The world is closing in like a pack of hyenas circling. You can't seal yourself in a time capsule and hope to escape. So now I'm an advocate."

"You became a lawyer?"

"No, not that sort of advocate. I work for my people. Making sure they are heard. Making sure that when the great desert is gone, taken from them, they know their traditions, and have rights and money and a way of avoiding the fate of most other aboriginal peoples when the hyenas take their lands."

Kubu was surprised, shocked. A bitter Khumanego living in a large town? What had happened to the boy who was happiest alone in the Kalahari? Who knew all would be well when he was back there? "But the Bushman people had a great triumph! The High Court ruled your people had the right to live freely in the Kalahari. Surely that pushed the outside world back?"

There was a long silence before Khumanego answered; this time it was Kubu who thought he had lost the connection. And when Khumanego did answer, his voice was tired.

"Yes, a great triumph, as you say. I worked behind the scenes for that, David. You won't find my name on the reports. It's the elders who speak, as it should be, but someone needs to be between them and all the interest groups pressing for their own ends. That's my job. But in the end, how many people went back? Turned their backs on the comforts of the camps set up for them? And the promises—maybe empty, maybe not—of schools and medical care? How many?"

Kubu didn't know. Not all, he supposed. Perhaps not many, judging by Khumanego's tone. "What is the answer then?"

"The answer? Perhaps there are answers. Perhaps not. One can't give up."

I owe this man a lot, Kubu thought, and yet I don't know him at all. I remember an intense and enthusiastic boy. An older friend even than the friend who called me a jolly hippo, and I became Kubu forever. Kubu felt a sudden pang of loss for that friend, and a pang of a different type of loss for Khumanego.

"Is there a way I can help?" Surely Khumanego had not called to chat after all these years.

"Do you mean that?"

"Of course."

"I can't talk on the phone. I need to see you privately. And not at a police station."

The Criminal Investigation Department was not a police station, but Kubu doubted that fact would satisfy Khumanego. He checked his watch. Just about ninety minutes to lunch. Time enough for Khumanego to drive from Lobatse.

"Do you drive?"

"Yes," Khumanego answered.

"Then we can meet for lunch—a light one, mind you, because I'm on a diet. I've put on a few extra pounds over the years." He hesitated over this understatement. A lot more than a few pounds had attached themselves to his frame since he was ten years old. But then, of course, his frame had increased quite a bit too. "Do you know where Game City is? From the Lobatse road, you'll see Kgale Hill on your left and Game City is a big shopping center a bit further on before you reach the city. There's an excellent coffee shop that serves snacks on the upper level. I'll meet you at twelve thirty."

Khumanego said he would find it and said good-bye.

Kubu was still turning the strange telephone discussion over in his mind when Edison Banda walked in clutching a forensics report. He waved it excitedly at the senior detective.

"We were right, Kubu! They were poisoned!"

Kubu leaned back in his chair, causing a protesting creak. Who was poisoned? It took him a moment to recollect the case. The forensics report had taken weeks! Two students from the University of Botswana had been found dead at a campground in Sekoma, collapsed outside their tent, faces horribly contorted. They'd been on their way back from a field trip to collect samples of plants in the Kalahari. The locals had immediately suspected witchcraft.

"What's it say? Why did it take them so long?"

"Well, we had to send samples to the Poison Information Centre in Cape Town. They were able to do it the quickest. Then Ian MacGregor was sick, so . . ."

"Never mind that. What killed them?"

"Bushman poison bulb. Just as we guessed. Apparently it's a member of the amaryllis family. Very poisonous indeed. Remember there were samples of it in their collection? I'll bet anything you like that they knew the Bushmen use it as a hallucinogen. So they decided to try it out on their last night alone. But they took much too much."

"But they were senior students! Of botany. Surely they'd know better?"

Edison shrugged. "They were students," he said, as though that explained everything.

"Could it have been deliberate?"

"You mean a suicide pact?" Edison shook his head. "Two young guys. No note or motive. Doesn't make sense."

Kubu hesitated. "Two men. Could there have been something going on between them?" That might be a motive for suicide. Homosexuality was illegal and deeply frowned upon in Botswana.

"One had a regular girlfriend here. I talked to her after they died. She was very upset. They wanted to get married. He was saving for the *lobola*. The other didn't have a girlfriend, but played the field."

"What about murder?"

Edison was not to be shifted. "By whom? What for? Nothing was stolen as far as we can tell, and no one knew them in Sekoma. The local police asked around the campground. No one saw anything suspicious."

Kubu thought it over. The kids had enjoyed a few beers—not drunk, but perhaps enough to make them irresponsible. Try out a Kalahari traditional drug. A big mistake. A fatal mistake.

"Have you told the director?"

Edison looked sheepish. "I thought I'd try it out on you first. Maybe we can see him together."

"He won't bite off your head," said Kubu, although he thought it likely Mabaku might do exactly that. Edison had been out of favor with the director of the CID for some time. Kubu sighed, clambering to his feet to share the news with his boss. This is what our work here is almost always about, he thought. Not solving puzzling crimes but rather picking up the pieces after a drunken knifing, a domestic brawl, or two kids who threw away their young lives on a stupid experiment.

"Okay," he said. "Let's go and talk to Mabaku."

Khumanego was more than half an hour late. Kubu drank water with lemon and then, growing desperate, ordered a salad with as much in the way of cheese and avocado as the chef could find. Joy had assured him that salads were healthy, that he would lose weight, and that he would feel full at the same time. The salad-lunch diet had lasted a week, and so far Kubu had no evidence to support any of these three contentions.

He had finished the salad when Khumanego arrived. When Kubu saw him, he had to suppress a smile. Khumanego was no more than four and a half feet tall—a diminutive figure wearing ill-fitting clothes he must have bought in the boys' section of a supermarket, his narrow yellow-brown face sticking out from a blue shirt. His trousers were too long and overlapped his shoes. On most people, Kubu thought, they'd be shorts.

Khumanego muttered about traffic and parking by way of apology. Kubu responded that neither were significant problems in the Kalahari, and his friend nodded but didn't smile. Although Kubu made it clear that he was paying, Khumanego ordered only an open sandwich of bacon, lettuce, and tomato, and a glass of water. Kubu felt it would be rude to let him eat alone and, having satisfied the requirements of the salad diet, ordered the same sandwich. While they ate, questions bounced to and fro filling in the intervening years. Kubu explained how he'd got his nickname at high school and that all his friends still called him that. Khumanego laughed, enjoying the humor around their size contrast. "They should call me Mongoose then," he joked. But then he sobered and recounted how he'd returned to his people before finishing high school.

"You know how hard it was, David," he said. "I couldn't take it anymore. But when I got back to the desert, I didn't fit there either. I'd lost the ways of my people. I couldn't track a wounded springbok, and I was no longer able to make myself invisible to animals. People found my ways strange; they were uncomfortable with me. I had become a stranger in my own land." He shook his head.

"It was a terrible time, David. I had waited for so long to be a Bushman again. A Bushman in the desert. With my friends and family. Going to where we could find game and plants.

Moving or staying as living dictated. But it wasn't like that anymore. Everything was being fenced for cattle. We weren't allowed to hunt freely; we had to get permits and often had to pay bribes for them. The government was moving my people to settlements on the edge of the Central Kalahari Game Reserve. They said it was for our own good; that there would always be water there, and permanent homes, and schools for the children. But in the end they were just camps, places where we could be forgotten. Then foreigners came from overseas, to help us fight the government, to win back our rights, they said. But they didn't understand us either. Maybe they made things better, maybe worse."

Khumanego paused after this uncharacteristic torrent of words. Kubu just nodded, and Khumanego continued. "David, who could we trust? Who was right? What was right? I saw what was happening to our people. They were confused, not understanding what was going on. Pulled this way and that. Puppets in other people's games. My parents had been right; what they feared had already arrived."

Kubu responded that he had been fortunate to go to Maru a Pula high school in Gaborone, where he too had been unhappy at first, bullied because he was different. But after some time he had found friends. He started to sing in the choir and enjoyed cricket, becoming the school's official scorer. He told of his love of detective work and how it linked to what Khumanego had taught him in the desert. And, with a broad smile, spoke of meeting Joy and the miracle of his little girl, now three months old.

Khumanego asked after Kubu's parents, around whose modest house he had spent many hours playing. He was delighted to hear they were still alive and in good health. But when Kubu asked after Khumanego's parents, he replied, "My mother is living in one of the new settlements."

"And your father?"

Khumanego just shook his head. "He died," he said simply without elaboration. "After that I felt a responsibility to guide my people through the barrenness of the political landscape— things they know nothing of and certainly don't know how to deal with. I felt I had to guard their interests."

Eventually there was a lull in the conversation, and they agreed on coffee, Kubu recommending the cappuccino.

Then, at last, Khumanego was ready to come to the point.

"Do you know about a man who died at the Kgalagadi Transfrontier Park a week ago? His name was Tawana Monzo."

Kubu remembered a report crossing his desk. "Yes, it was an interesting situation. He fell off a cliff into a dry riverbed or something like that, didn't he? Worked for Wildlife? Initially it seemed to be an accident, but the doctor who signed the death certificate was wide awake. Does some pathology work, I think. He felt that the skull had been fractured with a weapon rather than in a fall."

Khumanego nodded slowly. "The police have made up their minds that it was murder. The investigating officer found a sharp rock near where the body was found and claims it had Monzo's blood on it."

This was news to Kubu. Khumanego seemed very well informed. Kubu concentrated on spooning the foam off his cappuccino as he waited to discover where all this was leading.

"The officer walked up the riverbed in a direction where there were no footprints and found the weapon. How did he know to look there? After that he went with a park official to where the Bushmen are living and questioned them about who attacked the man, who pushed him off the cliff, who found him. He thinks the three men with Monzo when he was found are the most likely suspects. He told them it would be better to admit it immediately rather than wait till they were caught out." Khumanego paused, waiting for a reaction. When none came, he said with a new intensity, "Don't you see, David? He's already decided it's the Bushmen. It's all starting again."

"Who is the investigating officer?" Kubu asked mildly.

"They say his name is Detective Lerako. Detective Stone Wall! That's what his name means, and that's how he behaves!"

Kubu knew the man—fair but not imaginative. It was true; once his mind was made up, it was hard to shift Stone Wall. "What do you want me to do? It's not our case. It'll be handled out of Tsabong."

"I want you to make sure it's fair. You know our people. We don't kill; human life is sacred. To survive in the desert everyone has to contribute, to support. Those three men found Monzo injured and tried to help him; did help him. Why would they want to kill him anyway?" Khumanego paused. "David, I know those men myself. I work with them and they are from my group. We are brothers. They are like me."

"You had brothers?"

"All children in a group are brothers, David. These men would never kill another human. I was with them a few weeks ago. Still traditional. Still following the old ways in the desert." Khumanego stared at Kubu, challenging, pleading.

"And now they've been arrested! They're being held in Tsabong. It's crazy! This Monzo had an unlucky accident, and now it's being turned on these peaceful people! To get rid of them."

Kubu was already worrying about how he was going to explain all this to Mabaku. He could hear his boss asking him how come he had so little to do that he had time to interfere in another detective's case. He sighed and hoisted himself to his feet.

"All right, Khumanego. I'll look into it. I'm not promising anything, but I'll see what I can do."

Four

"The answer is no!"

"But, Director!"

"No buts, Kubu. You're not going to stick your nose into another detective's case. Lerako does things by the book. He's not going to arrest anyone without good cause."

"I've known my Bushman friend for over twenty years. I trust him, and he vouches for the men Lerako has arrested. He knows them like brothers and says they would never kill another human being. Lerako must've missed something, jumped ahead of himself."

Jacob Mabaku, director of the Criminal Investigation Department, snorted. "Known him for over twenty years, you say? Close friends, you say? That's bullshit! You've barely seen him since you left primary school!"

Kubu looked down in embarrassment. How did Mabaku know these things?

"Director, it's true that I haven't seen Khumanego for a long time. But people don't change. He and I were very close at school. He was the one who showed me how to see things that others didn't. It was really because of him that I became a detective. I owe him for that."

"Then take him out for a drink or dinner or something! You are not going to get involved in a case in Tsabong. It's under control. You've enough to do right here."

Kubu looked at Mabaku. There was no give in his face. How am I going to tell Khumanego? he wondered.

"Yes, Director. I'll tell Khumanego that the police aren't interested," Kubu said as he turned to leave.

"Bengu!" Mabaku's voice stopped Kubu in his tracks. It was a long time since Mabaku had used his last name. "Bengu, if you undermine my authority or the reputation of the police in this matter, you'll spend the next few years as the detective in Tshootsha or Hukuntsi!"

"Yes, Director. I'll tell Khumanego that I'm too busy to help." He walked out of Mabaku's office, closing the door gently behind him.

Tshootsha or Hukuntsi! I'll starve to death if I go there, Kubu thought. If I don't die of boredom first. He walked back to his office, depressed. I shouldn't have raised Khumanego's hopes. I should've realized that Mabaku wouldn't let me tramp on another detective's turf. Khumanego is going to be very disappointed. But then again, I won't have to leave Tumi and Joy.

◀▶ ◀▶ ◀▶

Kubu was still depressed when he left work and drove home. Khumanego hadn't taken it well when he told him of Mabaku's decision.

"I told you, David! All the police want to do is persecute the Bushmen. Another government effort to stop us living how we have always lived! Why don't you put us in cages and show us in the zoo? That's about all we seem to be worth in this country."

Kubu had tried to console the irate Bushman by reiterating how solid Detective Lerako was. Khumanego was scathing.

"I've checked him out. He's traditional. Typical *Motswana*—regards Bushmen as lesser beings. Doesn't know their language. Doesn't know their culture. My friends have no chance."

Kubu was unable to pacify Khumanego, even when he promised to try to review the case when the paperwork came through to Gaborone.

"You watch, David! They're guilty already. They don't need a trial—just send them to jail." Khumanego had put the phone down so hard that Kubu's ear hurt.

As Kubu drove home that evening, he was so preoccupied with disappointing Khumanego that he didn't consciously notice the other vehicles, or the pedestrians who sprinted through the moving traffic, or the taxis, which used any lane, including the sidewalk, to get ahead. He didn't even see the livestock, which were clustering around the roads because of the grass growing in the ditches after the recent rain.

His spirits lifted marginally as he turned into Acacia Street. At least his other four loves would be there—his beloved Tumi, his wonderful wife, Joy, Ilia, the rambunctious fox terrier, and of course, food and wine. Today, his fifth love, being a policeman, had let him down.

He stopped in front of the gate and, true to form, Ilia was there, jumping up and down, barking a delirious greeting, stump tail wagging furiously. The moment he opened one half of the wire-mesh gate, Ilia hurtled out and tried to jump into Kubu's arms.

"Down, Ilia. Down," Kubu said halfheartedly. Ilia paid no attention and continued to bounce off Kubu as he opened the second half of the gate.

"Car!"

Ilia immediately jumped into the car and sat on the passenger seat, tongue out, panting furiously. After Kubu had driven up the short drive, turned the engine off, and walked back to close the gate, Ilia was much calmer, just getting between Kubu's feet rather than imitating the *pronking* of a springbok.

Kubu smiled, expecting Joy to meet him on the steps of the brushed concrete veranda, but he was disappointed.

"Hello, dear! I'm home," he called, as though Ilia's welcome wouldn't have alerted her.

No response.

"Joy! Where are you?" Still no response. She must be occupied with Tumi, he thought. Then he heard the baby cry. He went into the house, put his briefcase on the couch, and walked to the small room at the back—Tumi's room—painted with cartoon-like animals on the wall and a bright yellow sun on the ceiling. Joy was changing Tumi's nappy. Tumi was complaining loudly.

"Hello, dear." Kubu leaned over and kissed Joy's cheek. Joy looked at Kubu and frowned.

"Let me get you a drink," he said. "You look as though you need one."

He walked to the small kitchen and took a box of inexpensive but acceptable South African sauvignon blanc from the fridge, and poured her a large glass. Kubu was embarrassed to serve box wine, but the financial realities of having a baby and Joy working only half time had taken their toll. Bottles were rare these days, usually only when there were guests.

He always started the evening with a steelworks. He poured two tots of Kola Tonic into a large glass, added a tot of lime juice, and splashed on a liberal portion of Angostura bitters. Next he filled the glass with ginger beer. Only then did he add ice. He despised barmen who started with ice then added the liquid ingredients. They never mixed properly.

"I'll be on the veranda," he called.

A few minutes later Joy arrived carrying Tumi, who was now quiet.

"You hold her," she said.

Kubu smiled as he took his treasure—the baby that was never meant to be. He rocked her gently, delighting in the small hands that clutched his fingers. He pulled a face, and Tumi smiled. "We're so lucky, my dear. Tumi is perfect."

Joy didn't respond, but took a large gulp of wine, closed her eyes, and put her head on the back of the chair.

"Tough day?" Kubu asked.

Joy nodded.

"How was work?"

Joy still didn't respond.

"Well, I had an awful day. Remember my old Bushman friend, Khumanego? I told you about him. We were friends at school in Mochudi. Anyway, he called. Spoke to him last about ten years ago, I guess. He's now an advocate for the Bushmen, advising them about the relocation plans of the government, helping their teams in the law cases, and so on. He's become a sort of urban Bushman. It's a strange mix. You should see him! His little body in Western clothes, all too big. Quite funny actually." He took a big mouthful of his steelworks, swilling it around his mouth to get the most benefit from the tanginess of the ginger beer.

Joy's head was still laid back, eyes closed.

"Anyway he called and asked for help. Some of his friends have been arrested for murder in the southern Kalahari. He swears they would never kill anyone—against Bushman values. He thinks the police are out to get the Bushmen because they're easy targets. I spoke to the director. He told me to mind my own business—that the situation was under control. It was embarrassing to tell Khumanego that I couldn't help. I'd all but promised."

Joy opened her eyes and sat up. She took another drink, this time more of a sip than a gulp.

"Kubu, dear, please don't go out of town unless it is absolutely necessary. You're going to have to spend some more time with Tumi. I'm really struggling. I'm tired the whole time. When I thought we couldn't have a child, I went to work at the crèche to be with kids. But now they're too much. Too many questions, quarrels, demands. And I don't have the patience I used to. It's the broken sleep. I always wake when Tumi cries. I don't know how you sleep through it."

"My darling, you know I'm always happy to help. Wake me during the night, and I'll give her a bottle." He tickled Tumi under the chin. Joy sighed. She'd tried to wake Kubu many times. It was easier to deal with Tumi herself.

Kubu asked if she wanted another glass of wine, and she nodded. A few minutes later he returned, two glasses in hand. He handed one to Joy and raised the other. "To the best mother in the whole world! Thank you my dearest." Their glasses touched with a clear ring. They had learned long ago to hold their glasses at the bottom to get the best sound. "Tonight, let's go down to Wimpy. You won't have to cook, and they're having a special on T-bone steaks."

Joy nodded. Wimpy was fine, and they could take the baby.

The next morning, as Kubu walked into the office a few minutes late, Edison pulled him aside and said quietly, "The director wants to see you. Right away."

"I'll get myself a cup of tea then go and see what he wants."

"I think you'd better go right away. He's been into your office several times, looking like a thunderstorm."

Kubu wondered what was on the director's mind as he knocked on the door and pushed it open.

"About time! Why are you late again?" Kubu recognized Mabaku's voice of anger. Before he could answer, Mabaku had pointed to a seat. Kubu sat quickly and tried to look as nonchalant as possible.

Mabaku just stared at him for what felt like an eternity. Kubu didn't even want to wriggle in the chair to make it more comfortable.

Mabaku started quietly. "Kubu, yesterday I told you not to get involved with your Bushman friend." He paused and raised the level. "And when you made a snide remark about the police not wanting to help the Bushman people, I told you not to be clever." Kubu nodded. Mabaku jumped to his feet. "When I tell you not to get involved, I mean DON'T . . . GET . . . IN-VOLVED!" Each of the last three words was accompanied by a loud crash as his fist hit his desk.

"But, Director . . ."

"You can't sneak around and try to embarrass me into changing my mind!"

The whole of the Criminal Investigation Department was now privy to what was happening in the director's office as his voice echoed through the building.

"I will not have you subvert my authority! What do you think you were doing?"

Kubu didn't move. He was stunned.

"But, Director . . ."

"What do you think you were doing?" Each word was uttered like a separate sentence.

"You've always been fair to me, Director. What have I done? I've never let you down before."

Mabaku glared at Kubu.

"Cindy Robinson!"

Kubu frowned. "Director, I don't know anyone by the name of Cindy Robinson."

"Bullshit! If you don't know her by name, you certainly know who she is!"

"Cindy Robinson?"

"At eight oh five this morning, I got a call from a Cindy Robinson—an American reporter. She's been working on a series of articles on the Bushmen. But now she smells news. Why are the Botswana police persecuting the endangered Bushman peoples *again*? she asks. How can the Botswana police hold three Bushmen in Tsabong on a charge of murder without any evidence?" He paused still glaring at Kubu. "She's heading to Tsabong right now. Someone tipped her off. Well? Do you deny it?"

"Director," Kubu said quietly, "I'd never do that. I never spoke to anybody at any newspaper, let alone an American newspaper. I promise." He paused, then anticipated Mabaku's next question. "And I didn't suggest it to anyone else either."

Mabaku sat down and rubbed his chin.

"Then it must have been your Bushman friend. He's using you, Kubu. Good friend indeed! He set you up."

Kubu flushed. The director had to be right.

"I'll call him right away. Tell him to back off."

"Too late. This Robinson woman is writing an article—backing off won't help. I've changed my mind. You'll have to go to Tsabong. Tomorrow. Make sure that Lerako is on top of everything. That it's all up front and transparent. Keep me informed."

But Kubu wasn't going to leave it at that. He wanted Mabaku on his side. "Director, do you remember the Maauwe and Motswetla case?"

"Of course I remember it. It was a disaster for the whole country. Going to trial without the two Bushmen having any idea of what was going on. Outrageous. Convicted of a capital crime with no adequate defense. Embarrassing. Made us look like racists." Mabaku paused in his tirade. Kubu said nothing.

"You think it could happen again?" Mabaku stared at Kubu.

"I don't know what to think, Director. Lerako is solid but unimaginative. If he's satisfied with the evidence he's got, he won't look any further. But why would my friend Khumanego come to me after all this time unless he was very concerned? Let me help Lerako. You can remind him of the Maauwe and Motswetla case and say you are making sure everything is in order. We can't take the chance of this blowing up in our faces."

Mabaku stood up and gazed out of the window at Kgale Hill, which formed the backdrop to the Millenium Park office complex, where the CID was housed. None of its resident baboons was visible. Neither man said anything for several minutes.

"All right," Mabaku said pointing his finger at Kubu. "But it's still Lerako's case. You are his backup, checking all the facts. I'll tell him that it's nothing personal, but the government can't afford another scandal. I'll make sure he knows he's still in charge."

"Thank you, Director. I should only be away a few days. None of my cases here are so urgent they can't wait."

Mabaku wagged his finger at Kubu. "Make sure you don't stir things up. Check back with me before you say or do anything that runs against Lerako. And don't talk to that reporter woman."

Kubu nodded and left with a mixture of emotions. He felt Khumanego had let him down, and he knew Joy would be upset that he'd be away. And Lerako was a tough man, hard to deal with. But Kubu was intrigued. If the Bushmen were innocent—as Khumanego averred—then who was behind the killing? Lerako wouldn't have missed obvious clues, so it was a puzzle. And Kubu loved puzzles.

Five

Joy had reacted very badly to the news that Kubu would be away for several days, and the atmosphere was still strained the next morning.

Breakfast was rudimentary. Joy again had not slept well, and Tumi was very demanding. Joy sat breast-feeding the infant as Kubu helped himself to two bananas and a cup of tea. Joy accepted tea, but didn't want to eat. Kubu made himself four sandwiches: two were savory, with cold meat and mustard, two were sweet—for dessert—with strawberry jam.

He filled a thermos with water and ice, collected several cans of ginger beer, packing it all in a cooler, and took his luggage to the police pool car. He'd tested the air conditioner the day before, so he was confident he'd have a comfortable journey.

Preparations finished, he went inside to say good-bye to Joy and Tumi.

"I have to go, dear," Kubu said brightly.

Joy turned around, tears running down her face.

"Darling, what's wrong?" Kubu sat down next to her and put his arm around her shoulders. Tumi sucked contentedly at her nipple. Joy just shook her head.

Kubu pulled her closer, but she resisted.

"You've got to go," she mumbled. "I'll be all right."

"I'll call you every evening, and I'll be back in no time at all."

He leaned over to kiss her, but she turned her head. Kubu was gripped with uncertainty. He'd never felt so isolated from Joy. Not once since he'd met her.

"Go!" she said. "Drive carefully."

Kubu turned and walked out to the veranda, down the steps and to the car. Out of character, Ilia didn't dash around barking loudly. She lay on the cool veranda floor, head between her paws, and watched Kubu leave, moving only her eyes.

When he'd told Khumanego that he would be visiting Tsabong after all, Kubu was surprised—and not entirely pleased—that Khumanego asked to come along. With some misgivings, Kubu agreed. Khumanego could be his translator, and it was a chance to clear the air over the reporter. It meant a detour to pick him up in Lobatse, but it wasn't far out of the way.

As he drove, Kubu mulled what was happening to his marriage. He had to keep working and be on top of his job, but he loved Joy and Tumi with all his heart. He'd been ecstatic when Tumi was born, but ill-prepared for what he perceived as Joy's distancing herself from him. All his life he'd yearned for a family. Now he felt his dream was slipping from him. He was glad to reach Lobatse and find Khumanego waiting for him.

However, the trip began in a tense atmosphere aggravated

by the usual traffic problems around Lobatse and Kubu's worry about Joy. Khumanego admitted that he'd contacted the reporter. He had met her previously to help with her research and had called her when Kubu had said he wouldn't help. Kubu corrected that to "couldn't," but the Bushman just shrugged. The effect was the same. Perhaps he had overstated the case, Khumanego admitted, but what was he to do? It was the last card he had to play.

"You don't have any idea how we react when a Bushman is imprisoned for murder," Khumanego said quietly. "You know about the Maauwe and Motswetla case, but it is only the Bushmen who really feel it. You know the story. Several men including Maauwe and Motswetla were desperate for food in the midst of a drought in 1995. They saw a stray ox and killed it. The next day the owner challenged them and was killed. How did he die? Who was responsible? We don't know. It's what happened afterwards that's important.

"Maauwe and Motswetla were Bushmen. The police arrested them, beat them, and forced them to sign confessions written in a language they didn't understand. They only spoke a Bushman dialect, not Setswana. And they were illiterate. Then they went to trial. They had no money, no education, nothing. How could they understand what was going on?" Khumanego gazed out the passenger window into the distance. Kubu let the silence be.

"So the government appointed lawyers for them. It was a sham. They never consulted the accused, never spoke to anyone about the case, and then they let the confessions stand. Maauwe and Motswetla never spoke in their own defense. Of course they were found guilty." Khumanego paused. "Then came the clemency hearings. Nobody was asked to vouch for them, and a letter they sent, asking for better lawyers, was never put in their files. It was hidden away. So the court found no grounds to be merciful and sentenced Maauwe and Motswetla to be hanged. But no one knew when, not even their families. It was all secret. Then in January '99—almost two years later—by luck someone saw a little notice in a newspaper that the execution was going to take place the following day." Suddenly Khumanego swung round to Kubu, agitated. "Nobody was told, David! Nobody. Not their wives, parents, friends. Nobody.

"There's a human rights group in Gaborone—Ditshwanelo. They applied for an urgent injunction to delay the execution, and amazingly they succeeded. Eventually, thanks to the efforts of many people around the world, a mistrial was declared. The government appealed and won the right to retry. That was at the end of 1999, nearly five years after the initial incident. The government kept dragging its feet, and six years later nothing had happened. But Maauwe and Motswetla were still in jail. They'd been there for ten years! The government tried everything to make it difficult for them. At first Ditshwanelo lawyers weren't even allowed to see the two. When the courts forced the government to allow visits, there were always warders within earshot, so there was an atmosphere of intimidation."

Khumanego looked away and continued more calmly. "That's our wonderful government, David, the model of democracy in Africa! Protector of all its citizens. It's a farce. It despises the Bushmen and will do anything to get rid of us, to get rid of our culture. The only good news is that the courts eventually said enough was enough and freed Maauwe and Motswetla, never to be tried again. What you would call a victory. But the two men are lost souls. Bewildered by ten years in jail and a system that failed them. That's why I'm going to Tsabong, David. This smells of another case of injustice. Another effort to get rid of my people."

Kubu thought for a moment, then said, "I know that happened, Khumanego. But things have changed—for the better. The government is concerned about the Bushmen now. Perhaps because of the outside pressure or perhaps because of changes in the ministers. And the police have new leadership. That couldn't happen again."

"We'll see."

Kubu found he had nothing more to say. The affair *had* been a disaster, and Botswana had lost face in the eyes of the world.

They drove in silence for some time until they came to Jwaneng, bypassing the town on the left and the brooding diamond-mine dump on the right.

"And how much of *that* wealth did my people see?" Khumanego asked, coming to life once again and pointing at the huge pile of tailings. Kubu just shrugged; Khumanego obviously didn't expect an answer.

As they reached the verges of the Kalahari Desert, Khumanego's mood improved. As more red crept into the gray sand, he spoke enthusiastically of life in the area, the edible and medicinal plants he spotted, and how once this land had plenty of game if you knew how to find it. At one point he asked Kubu to stop so that he could speak to a small group of Bushmen who eked out a living by being a tourist attraction in a small camp near the main road. The Bushmen squatted on their haunches and talked. The conversation was prolonged, and Kubu was hot and hungry by the time it was over. But when he asked Khumanego what it was all about, he merely shrugged and said, "They see things. They watch things. The tourists laugh at them. But they are all right."

Near noon, they stopped at a roadside cafe and bought some more sandwiches. The sun glared down at them, and they cowered in the stuffy cafe. Kubu grumbled that the bread was stale and the meat tough, but Khumanego ate without complaint. At least they had cold drinks from the cooler in the car.

When they returned to the Land Rover, it was boiling. Although Kubu had forced it as far as he could under the branches of an acacia tree, the back window remained in the sun, and heat streamed from the open front windows.

Once they were under way again, Khumanego suddenly became talkative. "David, you have to understand about my people. People don't understand. Even good, smart people like you. You think we want too much, that we should be happy to join with everyone else, to be the same. Some of us want that. Some want to be the same. But others want to be as we were, to have what we had, not more, not less. Is that unreasonable?"

Kubu thought about it. "It depends what it means, Khumanego. This is one country after all, and the laws must apply to everyone. But the laws must be fair. Fair to your people, in particular. I know that hasn't always been the case."

Khumanego shook his head. "More than that. We had land before. Land that wasn't ours, but it wasn't *not* ours. Do you understand? It's not about ownership—that is an alien concept for us—Bushmen don't own anything. It's about the right to use. We believe that nobody owns the earth. The earth is there to be shared. Not horded. Or claimed. Or fenced. We must use the earth so it can sustain all that lives on it. That is why we never kill more than we can eat, or harvest so much that the next person will find nothing and starve. That is what we must fight for today—the right to use as we have always used. We are at a point where we must stand up for ourselves, or just be swept away like sand."

Kubu could see that his friend was struggling to explain, trying to control the intensity of his feelings.

"We have to fight to keep the government from taking our culture, from making us empty of who we are. Making us nothing."

They drove in silence for a while, each with his thoughts. At last Kubu spoke quietly. "Your people are lucky to have you arguing for them, Khumanego. Don't give up."

Tsabong was a helter-skelter of houses seemingly randomly scattered over the flat sands. They clustered around a dry pan, which would occasionally flood the nearest ones after heavy rain. But the pan meant that water was accessible below the surface.

As Kubu drove down the main street, recently tarred, he spotted a gas station and pulled in to fill up. The attendant shook her head. There was no gas today. Perhaps down the road. Perhaps not.

Kubu thanked her and drove on. At the next station they were in luck. There was a buzz of activity as cars fueled while supplies lasted. After Kubu paid, the attendant gave him directions to the Mokha Lodge, the usual lodging for government employees, and they weaved between the houses until they reached it. When they turned into the sandy car park, Kubu didn't know whether to be aghast or delighted. The entire outside of the hotel was painted a bright burned orange—a bold statement in the desert sands. Then he spotted the window air-conditioning units and decided the hotel would be quite satisfactory.

Khumanego settled for a modest single room. He liked small rooms, perhaps surprisingly after the openness of the desert. But he felt that he fitted a small room. For once, things were the right size. He unpacked his overnight bag, thinking how much more he carried now for a few days than he would have living full-time in the desert. He wondered how long he would have to stay in Tsabong this time and whether Kubu could save his friends from jail. He ground his teeth, trying to keep feelings of worry and anger at bay. Then he washed his face and headed to the Sand Dune bar to meet Kubu for a quick cold drink. They would visit Lerako next. Kubu would just introduce him as interpreter, and he was to keep his mouth firmly shut. The Bushman role, he thought bitterly.

Khumanego found the bar, opening onto the heat of the veranda. Behind the counter was a small two-door refrigerator containing beer, soft drinks, and a few bottles of inexpensive South African wine. The counter was decorated by a small vase of purple plastic flowers, which partly obscured a large dispenser of free condoms mounted on the wall. Khumanego shook his head in disbelief.

A black woman was sitting on one of the bar stools, drinking what appeared to be soda water. Her hair hung in braids around a long face. Oakley sunglasses clasped her ears and balanced on the top of her head. She was wearing blue running shorts and an orange tank top stretched over broad shoulders and generous breasts. Strong legs descended to running shoes and white socks. Khumanego was amazed to see her, and embarrassed. But there was nothing he could do.

She was bound to recognize him. He walked up to her and held out his hand.

"Cindy, what a surprise."

For a moment she looked down at him quizzically, and Khumanego realized that she might not have recognized him after all. The invisible Bushman. All look the same. "Khumanego!" She mispronounced his name using a hard k. "Great to see you! What are you doing here?" The two sentences revealed her Southern U.S. accent.

Khumanego didn't answer her question, but indicated Kubu, who was sitting at a table watching this exchange. "This is Superintendent David Bengu of the Botswana CID. He's come to help us." He glanced at Kubu's surprised face. "David, this is Cindy Robinson. She's a freelance journalist from the U.S."

Cindy offered Kubu a smile, walked over, and firmly took his hand as he struggled to stand. "So you've come to sort out this mess with the Bushman suspects, Superintendent? Something to do with my call to the director of the CID perhaps?"

"*Assistant* Superintendent. I'm here to assist the local CID people, in case they need extra help."

"And do they need extra help, do you think?"

"I'm sorry, but I can't comment on the case at this point. Our investigations are continuing."

Cindy laughed, a loud, attractive laugh. "You've been watching American TV, Mr. Bengu! Don't worry, I won't quiz you about the case. But we're the only guests here tonight. Shall we have dinner together? Here or somewhere else if you like. It's not much fun being alone in Tsabong."

Kubu hesitated, obviously uncomfortable. "I'm not sure if it would be appropriate . . ." he began, but Cindy interrupted. "Look, just dinner. You off duty, and me off the record. Promise."

"Of course," said Kubu after a brief pause. "Khumanego?"

Khumanego wasn't happy about it at all, but it would be rude to refuse. And he might need Cindy's help again one day. "That would be nice," he said.

"Great! See you later then. I'm going for a run now. See you here at around six?" With that Cindy swallowed the soda water, pulled the sunglasses over her eyes, and headed out into the heat.

Detective Sergeant Lerako met Kubu in his office while Khumanego waited outside. Lerako had made a point of firmly closing the door on him. Yet he was more amenable than Kubu had expected.

"You're welcome to talk to the suspects. Use your own translator if you like. See what you can get out of the bastards."

"What have you got so far?"

"Nothing. They deny everything. They say they were in the area and came on this man lying in the *donga*. Tried to help. But of course that ignores all the other evidence. I suppose you've reviewed it. We checked for a hundred yards in all directions. There were no footprints, except for the Bushmen's. Unless the murderer could fly, nobody else was there. And there was the ongoing animosity between Monzo and the Bushmen—they'd had run-ins before—the murder weapon in the riverbed, and the fact that they were all there when Ndoli arrived. Much too much of a coincidence. I don't believe in coincidences."

"You sound like Director Mabaku. He's not strong on coincidences either. Did any of them say they saw the man fall? Or just that they found him?"

"They found him."

"And the murder weapon? What was it exactly?"

"Hard chunk of calcrete. It's limestone and absorbs fluids. So there was enough blood on it and in it to test. Got the results back this morning. Human blood all right. I was spot-on." He hesitated.

"But?"

"No fingerprints."

So that was it. Lerako's case had just become much weaker. There was nothing to connect any of the Bushmen directly to the murder. "Is it possible it was an accident after all? He slipped and hit his head so hard on a piece of protruding calcrete that it broke off and fell too?"

Lerako shook his head. "Too far away from the body. It must've been thrown." He might be battling for evidence, but he wasn't going to give up on his murder.

Kubu didn't rub it in. "Well, let's see if I can get anything more out of the suspects," he said.

Kubu interviewed the three Bushmen together. Normally he would have seen them separately, trying to get contradictory stories, trying to catch them out. But Lerako had tried that to no avail. Kubu wanted the three men to feel that this was a more sympathetic meeting, that they were witnesses rather than suspects. Khumanego had introduced the three—Dcaro, Gai, and N!xau—but Kubu wasn't sure that he could remember their names let alone pronounce them. He addressed them as a group through Khumanego.

"What were you doing when you found the man lying in the *donga*?" he asked.

"They were looking for food!" Khumanego replied at once.

"Please ask *them*, Khumanego."

Khumanego gave Kubu a quizzical look, but then turned to the Bushmen and spoke. After a few minutes of discussion he turned to Kubu and said, "They were hunting."

"What were they hunting for?"

"Anything they could find. They say they caught two spring hares. They fished them out of their burrows with hooked sticks."

"Did any of them hear anything or see anything before they found the man?"

Again there was discussion, but when Khumanego reverted to English he had nothing to add. They had discovered the man lying in the *donga* unconscious, and that was all they knew.

Kubu sighed and started from the beginning. Where was their camp? When had they left it? Where had they gone? How long until they discovered Monzo? What did they do then? How long until Ndoli had appeared? It took a long time, but the answers seemed natural and consistent. At last he got up and indicated to Khumanego that they should leave. But Dcaro had a question. He spoke to Khumanego for almost a minute. Then Khumanego turned to Kubu.

"Dcaro says that they have done nothing wrong. That they tried to help the man who was hurt. That they are sorry that he died but it wasn't their fault. He wants to know when they can go back to their people. He is worried that they are starving. There are only a few men left to hunt." All the Bushmen looked at Kubu expectantly. He thought for a few moments. There was really no case against them. They should, in fact, never have been arrested. His instinct was that they should be released immediately, but he remembered Mabaku's warning. He should at least go to where the body had been found, and check the suspects' story with the other members of their band tomorrow. He sighed. "Soon," he said. He saw the hope fade from their faces.

Khumanego said little on the way back to the hotel. Kubu explained that he wanted to visit the band, and Khumanego nodded. "I understand," he said. "They're guilty until they prove themselves innocent." But he said it as a matter of fact, without rancor.

It was six when they got back, and Cindy was already in the bar. Kubu excused himself to have a shower before dinner, leaving Cindy and Khumanego alone. When he returned almost half an hour later, he found Khumanego with an orange juice and the reporter drinking a beer. Khumanego looked uncomfortable. Serves him right, Kubu thought. Teach him to try to use reporters. "Let's get some wine," he said. "And some dinner. I'm starving. I've had nothing all day except some cereal—with awful skim milk—and a few sandwiches on the way here."

They settled at a table in the hotel restaurant and studied the menu. Kubu battled to choose between the restaurant's famous (so the menu trumpeted) Hunger-Buster rump steak and the Ranch House oxtail stew. Bulk versus taste. Eventually he settled for the oxtail with a side order of chips. Cindy ordered the Mongolian beef-and-vegetable stir-fry, and Khumanego the goat stew. Kubu then ordered a ginger beer—a steelworks seemed highly unlikely—and the wine list. The waiter shook his head. There was no wine list. They did have wine, but he didn't know what it was. Kubu sighed, and thinking of the red meats, asked for a red. The waiter said he would try to find one. When the drinks came, the wine was a generic cabernet from a big South African producer. Kubu consoled himself with the ginger beer while the wine breathed. Gasped would be a better word, he thought, given how warm the bottle was.

"So, Ms. Robinson," he said turning to the reporter, "what brings you to Botswana?" As if I didn't know, he thought sourly.

"Please call me Cindy. May I call you David?"

Faced with that, Kubu was forced to relax. "Call me Kubu. Everyone else does. It means 'hippopotamus' in Setswana."

Cindy smiled. "Hippopotamus! Don't you mind?"

Kubu chuckled. "I don't actually respond to anything else. The nickname goes back to my school days. It just stuck right away."

She laughed. "Well, Cindy isn't my real name either, but I'm not going to tell you what is. Not now. Let's try the wine."

Kubu poured. Khumanego wanted only a taste, but Cindy was happy with a full glass. "Let's toast new friends," she said holding up her glass. Kubu thought she was laying it on a bit thick, but was happy to clink, and swirl, and sip the wine. The cabernet actually wasn't bad. He took a mouthful.

"You asked what I'm doing here, Kubu. I'm a freelancer, writing articles for a variety of U.S. newspapers. I studied anthropology and journalism at college, but journalism won out. I was more interested in current issues than in how things were in the past. My interest in anthropology today is social—looking at how cultures are evolving now rather than historically."

"So you think cultures should change? Move with the times?" Khumanego interjected.

"Not that they should. I just think they do. But sometimes they are forced to change in unnatural ways by people or governments with ulterior motives."

"And you think that's the case with the Bushmen in Botswana?" Kubu asked.

Cindy shrugged. "That's what I came to find out. And to write about."

"How long have you been here?"

"Two months. Of course, when the issue of the three Bushmen being arrested here came up, it stopped being article stuff and became news. So I came down here and filed a piece on the wire service. I think you'll have someone from Survival International down here soon also. That should make for an interesting dinner discussion!"

Kubu was beginning to feel uncomfortable with the way the reporter was steering the conversation. But he was saved by the arrival of the food. They settled down to eat. At some point Cindy asked the waiter for another bottle of the wine. Since he now knew where to find it, he returned with alacrity. But Kubu was drinking slowly. He felt the need to be on his guard with this confident young lady.

She turned her attention to Khumanego. "So where does it go from here? The future of your people, I mean, not the future of the three suspects in jail. We agreed not to talk about that."

"You're the anthropologist. Why don't you tell me? What happens to cultures—old indigenous cultures—when another culture becomes dominant? Especially if the new culture despises the older one?"

"Well, it can be preserved. Sometimes outside pressure is needed for that. And a change of attitude."

"You have to preserve a base. A position you don't give up. That you defend. That's the only hope. If there is any at all." Khumanego got up. "I'm tired. It was a long trip. And this isn't an academic discussion for me. I'm going to bed." He turned to Kubu. "I'll see you in the morning. Good night, Kubu."

Cindy pouted. "I guess I said the wrong thing."

"He's sensitive. That's understandable, isn't it? The way things are."

She nodded. "I'm sorry. Let's have dessert. I'm going to have the fruit salad and ice cream. What about you?"

Kubu would have liked to escape, but that would be rude. He forced himself to have a stack of cinnamon pancakes with ice cream. They had the desserts and then finished the wine. Cindy talked about herself and living in Atlanta. Kubu started to relax.

Cindy smiled. "Kubu. It really fits you, you know. Personality as well, I think. I'll tell you my given name now if you like. But you must promise not to laugh." Kubu nodded. "It's Cinderella. Can you beat that? How can parents do things like that to their children? Have you ever heard of *anyone* called that before?" Kubu shook his head keeping a straight face. Cindy watched him for a moment. "You're pretty good," she said. "You didn't even check your watch to see how close it was to midnight." This time Kubu did laugh. Had circumstances been different, he would have enjoyed her company a great deal. Smart and attractive with a good sense of humor. The thought made him worry guiltily if it was too late to call Joy. Now he did check his watch.

"I need to call my wife. We have a baby, and it's been a bit of a battle recently. And I am tired after the drive. Will you excuse me?" He climbed to his feet.

Cindy stood with him and touched his arm. "I hope they're okay. Thanks for having dinner with me. I hope we can do it again while we're here. I think you're quite a special man,

Kubu. Good night." And it was she who turned away and headed for her room leaving Kubu to look after her.

Khumanego didn't go straight back to his small room. Instead, he walked down the road that led to the border post at Mc-Carthy's Rest. After several hundred yards he turned into the barren land that lay beside it. There was just enough light from the quarter moon to pick his way between the scattered thorn-bushes, past a few stone *kraals,* until he was far enough from town that he wouldn't be disturbed.

He gazed up. The sky was filled with the gods and his ancestors. Watching him, bright-eyed. They were so close, he could hear them whisper. He flung his arms upward to embrace them and started to dance, slowly at first, then picking up speed. Feet stamping, body spinning. Dancing faster and faster. Eyes closed. Spinning. Spinning. His ancestors clapped in time to the music, urging him on. Around and around he went. Around and around. Until he fell onto the red sand, exhausted. And his mind left his body and joined the spirit world.

When it returned, he was lying on the ground, shaking. Eventually he stood and dusted the sand from his clothes. Then he headed back toward the lights of the town.

Six

"The Bushmen see things very differently from other peoples."

Khumanego was sitting in the backseat of the police Land Rover. Lerako was driving, furious that he had to make the long trip yet again, and Kubu was in the passenger seat. Lerako had said it would take about two hours of hard driving to get to where the Bushmen had found the body. He commented that the road had improved a great deal in the past year. Before that it would have taken all day, if they got there at all. Kubu was thankful that the murder had happened this year—the Land Rover was unbearably hot, and the bumping and fishtailing down the sandy road made him very uncomfortable.

"Your people see themselves as separate from everything," Khumanego continued. "We see ourselves as part of everything. We are part of the sky and of the earth. And the sky is part of the earth, and the earth part of the sky. Just as the day is part of the night. And night part of day. And you and me are part of each other. When you dream, you change my world, just as my dreams change yours."

"That's nonsense!" Lerako growled. "Rubbish!"

Khumanego ignored him.

"When a kudu dies after we have hunted it, we feel its pain, and at the same time, it knows it is providing for us. We have a shared purpose. We never hunt for more than we can eat, because if we did, we would be robbing the animal we had killed. Stealing its destiny. The world would get out of balance. Bad things would happen.

"When we stop in the desert, we never eat all the food that is available. Or drink all the water. We always leave some for those who come after. We would rather take hunger and thirst with us than leave it behind.

"We are all part of the same world. All connected. That is why the men you have arrested did not kill the man who died. Bushmen don't kill other men. If they did, they would be killing themselves."

Lerako shook his head, but said nothing.

The Land Rover continued to bump and slide, and Kubu and Lerako continued to sweat. The heat didn't seem to affect Khumanego. They drove in silence.

They trudged to the edge of the *donga* where Monzo had been found. Lerako pointed down. "That's where the body was. And the rock used to kill him was further up the *donga*. Up there." He waved toward the spot where he had found the calcrete.

"Let's take a look," Kubu said, spotting a less precipitous way into the *donga*. That was probably the way they'd used to carry Monzo back to the vehicles. He clambered down and stopped where Monzo had been found. Monzo could have fallen, Kubu thought, or been pushed.

There were footprints everywhere, mostly from heavy boots, but occasionally of small bare feet. Kubu wondered if the Bushmen's feet had adapted over the years so that as little flesh as possible touched the scorching sand. They had extraordinarily small hands as well, he thought. Where did that come from?

He walked with Lerako to where the murder weapon had been found. No footprints continued up the riverbed.

"There were no footprints here before I walked up," Lerako said, reading Kubu's mind.

Kubu could see why Lerako suspected the Bushmen. There was no evidence to implicate anyone else. But what was their motive? It didn't make sense. He looked around for Khumanego, but he was still standing at the top of the *donga* watching Kubu and Lerako.

"Okay," Kubu said to Lerako. "Let's go and talk to your suspects' friends."

"How did you find them?" Kubu gasped as the Land Rover slid down a sandy slope into a dry riverbed. Lerako gunned the engine to maintain forward momentum. To stop would mean sinking into the sand, and even though a winch was mounted on the front, there were no trees to which a cable could be attached. We shouldn't be here alone, Kubu thought. We should have a second vehicle. That's basic survival procedure. On the other hand, Lerako must have made it before, judging by the tire tracks they were following.

"We have a Bushman tracker working for us," Lerako said when he had a moment.

Although they were moving slowly, avoiding rocks and holes, the engine raced with the gears in low range. Kubu glanced at the temperature gauge. The needle was moving toward the red. Even with all the windows open, the heat from the engine was beginning to overpower even the stifling heat from outside. Sweat poured off the two black men. Khumanego wasn't sweating, but even he looked uncomfortable.

"For us, the desert is like a city is to you," Khumanego said suddenly. "I can tell a friend where to meet me in the middle of this wilderness, and he'll know how to get there. We have a name for every feature that you see. This riverbed has a name. That bend in the river has a name. That unusual rock on the bank has a name. They are all addresses to us."

The Land Rover suddenly rocked violently from side to side. The right front wheel had climbed a small boulder.

"Shit!" Lerako wrestled with the steering as the wheels jerked to the right. Then there was a loud bang as the wheel descended, dropping the chassis onto the rock.

"Go, you bitch!" He swung to the left hoping he had enough speed to get off the rock. Another screeching sound as the Land Rover slid off and veered left. In the passenger seat, Kubu was clinging for dear life to whatever was handy. My God, he thought. No wonder the Bushmen walk through the desert.

The tracks turned toward what appeared to be a sheer wall of sand. Lerako wrestled the wheel and shifted into the lowest gear. Miraculously the Land Rover climbed the steep slope and popped back onto a flat area again.

A few minutes later, Lerako stopped the vehicle on a piece of hard ground near the trees. Lerako and Kubu opened their doors and staggered out, exhausted from the trip. Khumanego seemed unfazed. They walked to the edge of the trees. Kubu looked around. Surely this was the wrong place? There was nothing here. No huts, no signs of life, no people.

"You still can't see, can you, David?" Khumanego exclaimed. "I thought you'd learned all those years ago when I taught you about the desert." He shook his head. "You think nobody is here. That we're in the wrong place, don't you?"

Kubu nodded.

"Open your eyes, black man! See that clump of grass over there? Look carefully. See the *scherm*, the little grass hut? And there's another one a bit to the left." Kubu stared and eventually saw what Khumanego was pointing at. It wasn't a hut in any traditional sense. A few reeds were bent to form an arch. Below them the sand had been shaped to form a small depression. "That's where they sleep."

"What's that?" Lerako pointed toward a tree where two sticks were stuck in the ground on either side of another small depression.

"One of the group has marked his area. That's where he sleeps. The others will respect that space and not walk over it."

"Where are they?" Kubu asked.

Khumanego shouted—a series of clicks and other sounds foreign to Kubu's ears. Their language is so difficult, he thought. I've forgotten everything he taught me. As if by magic, seven figures emerged from the reeds and huddled together thirty or forty yards away. Two men, one very old, three women, and two children.

"Where are the rest?" Kubu asked.

"This is everyone except for the three in Tsabong," Khumanego said. "The desert can't sustain big groups." He walked over to the group and squatted on his haunches. The others did likewise. They talked for about ten minutes, sometimes all the adults at once. Eventually Khumanego returned.

"They are very upset. They don't know what has happened to the men. Don't know if they are dead, or if they have been stolen to watch cattle on a farm." He glared at Lerako. "It's been very difficult for them to find enough food with only one hunter."

He walked to the Land Rover and pulled out a plastic bag he'd brought from Tsabong. He opened it and pulled out dried fruit, *biltong*, and a large plastic bottle of water.

"They are very hungry. The men you have in Tsabong are the main hunters. These people haven't eaten meat since you arrested them."

Khumanego handed them the provisions. The younger man carefully divided the fruit and meat into portions of different sizes and handed them out, keeping the largest for himself. The smallest portion went to the old man. Kubu wondered how the division worked, but everyone seemed satisfied with their share. The man opened the bottle, took a long drink and passed it to the old man, who sipped sparingly. Then the women took the bottle, and finally the children. Kubu noticed that more than half of the water was left after all had drunk. The future was always in mind.

"Please ask them if they have had any problems with the rangers from the park."

After a brief consultation, Khumanego reported Monzo often came and shouted at them. He would point to the north and tell them to leave. They couldn't hunt in this area, so they should go elsewhere. But he had never harmed any of them.

"The last time that happened was when the sun last chased the moon away. That's new moon to you. About three weeks ago. That's about two weeks before he died." He paused and turned to Kubu. "They want to ask you a question." Kubu nodded. "They want to know why you are holding their brothers and not looking for the man with big feet."

"The man with big feet? Who's that?" Kubu was perplexed.

"The man who left his mark near where Monzo was found."

"They've found some footprints? Why didn't they tell us?"

"They found them yesterday. And how would they tell you?"

Kubu turned to a frowning Lerako.

"Did you check the whole area around where Monzo was found?"

"We looked at the top of the *donga* and up and down the riverbed for about one hundred yards. If someone other than the Bushmen was close to Monzo, he would have had to be flying," Lerako said defensively.

"Where are these footprints, Khumanego?"

"I am not sure. I've not seen them. They say they are on the ridge above the riverbed."

"Please ask if one of them will show us where they are."

Khumanego took the younger man aside, and a long exchange followed with gestures and discussion. Lerako fumed, and Kubu wondered why his simple request was taking so long to resolve. At last Khumanego returned.

"They will describe to me exactly where to go. But they want you to release their brothers."

Kubu turned to Lerako. "I don't think the men you are holding murdered Monzo. Do you still think they did it?"

Lerako nodded. "Yes. I do. There's no indication that anyone else was nearby. My intuition tells me they're guilty, and I'm usually right. Let's go and see these so-called footprints."

"If the prints are real, will you release them when you return?"

"Maybe." Kubu heard the reluctance in his voice. "But I doubt some footprints by themselves will change my mind. There'll have to be something else."

Kubu put his hand on Khumanego's shoulder. "I'm sure we'll release the men as soon as we get back to Tsabong. We'll drop them off as close to here as possible."

Lerako glared at him but said nothing.

"Thank you," Khumanego murmured. "Before we leave, the old man wants to pay his respects."

Lerako shook his head. "I'm not going to waste any more time." But Kubu was intrigued.

"What's his name?"

"He is Gobiwasi. He remembers you. You were two weeks walk from here, three years ago, looking for a big bird. He means an airplane. What was that about?"

Kubu recalled meeting Gobiwasi and his group in the desert near Maboane.

"He helped me solve a difficult case. Provided some very useful information. Please apologize that I don't have a gift for him."

Khumanego translated and then turned to Kubu.

"He trusts you. He wonders why you think his sons would kill a man."

"Tell him that we saw no other footprints near the body, so we wondered who else could be responsible. Tell him also that we now don't think they killed anybody."

Gobiwasi spoke at length at Kubu, ending his speech with burst of laughter and a wide smile of toothless gums.

Kubu looked at Khumanego quizzically.

"He says he respects you. He says you have always been fair to his people. He also says you have the mind of a Bushman, but not the body!"

Kubu laughed and turned to Gobiwasi, one hand over his heart.

"I will think of myself as an honorary Bushman."

Gobiwasi struggled to his feet and held out his hand to Kubu. He spoke again, quietly.

"He says you will not meet again. He is old and getting ready to move on—to meet his ancestors."

Kubu bowed his head. "Tell him that he looks well, not sick, and should live for many more years."

Khumanego passed on the message.

"He says he is now a burden on his family because he cannot hunt. He is an extra mouth they cannot afford to feed. It is time to leave." He walked over to Gobiwasi and gently took him by the elbow. "Please give me a few minutes alone with him." Without waiting, he led the old man away.

Kubu shook his head and wondered whether he would ever understand these little people. Lerako looked as if he were about to explode.

Khumanego and the old man squatted under a tree with few leaves. Khumanego addressed him respectfully in the IGwi language.

"Gobiwasi, old man. You are wise. You have seen many things. I fear for the future. For our people."

Gobiwasi nodded sadly. "It may be so."

"I can talk for only a short time. So I must be direct. I wish to talk of The Place."

Gobiwasi looked at him at length with rheumy eyes. "What is this place?"

"Please, old man. I need to talk about The Place. I am sure that you know about it. I have questions that I must ask."

Gobiwasi rocked back and forward and closed his eyes.

"It was soon after I killed for the first time," he whispered. Khumanego had to lean forward to hear. "I shot a springbok and ran after it for many hours, waiting for the poison to work. My father followed me. I remember that the animal smiled as I pushed my spear into its heart. My father watched and said I had become a man."

Gobiwasi paused for a long while, dragging memories from deep within.

"We skinned the animal and cut it into pieces. When we had finished, my father took hold of my right hand. He told me he had a great honor to give me. I didn't know what he was talking about. He told me of a place near where the sun sets; a hill where the spirits live. The spirits who guide our lives, who look after our people, who provide food and water for us. He said they are the spirits who rule the world, who control our destiny. It is they who judge each of our lives, whether we have lived well or not. He said that this place is known only to a few."

Another long pause.

"I did not know what to think. I wondered if The Place was more sacred than Tsodilo, the birthplace of mankind, which I thought was the most sacred of all places. To be revered and respected. That is where the first spirit knelt down near the top of the Male Hill and blessed the earth after he had created it. I have been to Tsodilo and seen with my own eyes the marks in the rock where the spirit prayed. I have seen the Female Hill, where most of the spirits live, where they rule the world. Could this place be as great even as Tsodilo?"

"Did you find out?"

Gobiwasi continued to rock, but said nothing, his eyes still closed.

"Were you successful?"

"What is success?"

"Old man, I need your help. I need the benefit of your wisdom. I have many questions." There was urgency in his voice.

Gobiwasi opened his eyes and stared at Khumanego. "I have said too much. I swore not to talk of these things." He took a deep breath. "I see you are eager, but you must be careful and let the spirits guide you. If you do not, the ancestors will be angry."

He struggled to his feet. Khumanego followed suit, many questions unanswered. Together they walked slowly back to the waiting group.

Khumanego said a few words to the Bushmen, then walked to the Land Rover. Kubu and Lerako followed. Kubu didn't know whether he should wave to the group, so he turned and touched his forehead. There was no response.

They tumbled into the Land Rover, Lerako hesitating only to mark the spot on his GPS. "Shit! We're only about half a mile from where the body was found. It seemed much further than that."

Kubu strapped himself into his seat and prepared for another bout of torture. For the next twenty minutes, they followed Khumanego's directions, Lerako's mood deteriorating with each passing moment as he wrestled with the steering wheel. Eventually Khumanego told them to stop. They climbed from the vehicle and carefully made their way to a calcrete ridge. Khumanego searched around, but the ridge appeared solid and unmarked.

Lerako was hot and irritated, and he lost his temper. "This is all a complete waste of time! There's nothing up here. They just wanted to get rid of us! Let's get out of here." But meanwhile, Khumanego had walked some distance up the ridge and shouted for them to join him. He was pointing at the ground.

There, between two ridges of hard calcrete was a small island of sand. In it were two prints, clearly of a hiking boot or something similar. They were pointed away from where Monzo had been found—about two hundred yards to the east.

"Could they be Monzo's?" Kubu asked.

Lerako shook his head regretfully. "The print of the sole is different. Monzo's boots had a distinct pattern. This one is smooth."

"So there *was* someone else here," Kubu said, pulling a camera from his pocket.

"You know prints can stay in the desert for a long time," Lerako growled. "We've no idea whether they are linked to the murder."

"True," Kubu said.

"And why weren't any of these prints close to the body? My tracker didn't find prints like this anywhere."

Kubu shook his head. "If you look carefully, you can see there are long ridges of calcrete on either side of the prints. Someone could walk all the way to the edge of the *donga* where the body was found, without leaving a trace. We're lucky there was this patch of sand."

Lerako clenched his teeth. He knelt on the edge of the sand and examined the prints carefully. After a couple of minutes, he stood and shook his head, but said nothing.

He walked back to the Land Rover and settled behind the steering wheel. Kubu climbed in, not looking forward to the upcoming journey. Khumanego followed.

"You'll let the Bushmen go now?" Kubu asked Lerako as they pulled off. Eventually Lerako gave a curt nod. "What do two footprints by themselves mean? I still believe they did it. But I don't have the hard evidence to hold them."

Kubu turned to Khumanego. "Your brothers will be freed tomorrow. Detective Sergeant Lerako will arrange for them to be dropped back near here."

Back at the ranger station, they splashed their faces and rapidly downed several tepid cold drinks. Then Kubu prowled around looking for something to eat. It was well after lunchtime, and he was getting desperate. Eventually his hunger overcame his judgment, and he poured pula into a vending machine, ending up with a pile of junk food.

Not what I'd call lunch, he thought. And I'd better not tell Joy.

He found an empty desk and settled down to appease his hunger. Lerako was not a happy man and paced while Kubu methodically worked his way through the rustle of wrappers. Khumanego sat silently, shaking his head at offers of the junk food. When Kubu had finally consumed everything, he and Lerako went to talk to the head ranger, Vusi, and office manager, Ndoli, leaving Khumanego staring out at the desert.

Despite Kubu's thorough probing, Vusi added nothing to what they already knew. However, it was obvious that Vusi wasn't greatly upset that Monzo was dead.

"Monzo could be difficult," he said when pushed. "Did whatever he liked, when he liked. Problem was he was good at what he did. Otherwise I'd have fired him."

Kubu wondered whether that was the only reason Vusi didn't like him. He turned to Ndoli.

"How did you find Monzo? He was quite far from the road."

"I saw his *bakkie* and stopped to take a look. He wasn't

there, but I found his footprints. I followed them to the top of the *donga*. Then I saw him with three Bushmen."

"Was the engine of Monzo's *bakkie* running?"

Ndoli frowned. "I don't think so. Why?"

"Well, if it was running, he didn't expect to be away for long."

"So he thought he would be away for a while?"

"Looks like it. How did the Bushmen react when you appeared?"

"No reaction. One was squatting next to Monzo, trying to get him to drink. The others were watching."

"That doesn't sound as though they were trying to kill him."

Lerako interrupted, his frustration showing. "But he wasn't giving him water when you arrived at the top of the *donga*, right? When they saw you, they probably decided they needed to look friendly. Water was the only thing they could do." He glared at Ndoli.

"They weren't hostile at all." But now there was a shade of uncertainty in Ndoli's voice.

Kubu asked Ndoli a few more questions, but learned nothing new. He turned to Vusi.

"Rra Vusi, before we head back to Tsabong, can you take us to Monzo's wife? I'd like to talk to her."

Even though the house was several hundred yards away, Kubu thought it preferable to walk rather than spend more time in the Land Rover.

"That's Monzo's house," Vusi said pointing ahead. "Her name is Marta."

"How long had Monzo been here?"

"Two years in May, I think."

"How long had he been married? Did he have kids?"

Vusi hesitated. "They weren't married, but they had two

kids. Apparently his real wife is in South Africa somewhere." Kubu wondered why Vusi looked so uncomfortable.

A handsome woman, traditionally dressed, answered the door. She smiled warmly at Vusi, but her faced closed when she caught sight of Kubu and Lerako.

Vusi introduced them. "Marta, this is Assistant Superintendent Bengu. He wants to ask you some more questions. Is that all right?"

Marta nodded, but looked unsettled. Nevertheless she answered Kubu's questions confidently and nothing unexpected emerged. She confirmed everything that Lerako had told him. Kubu noticed that from time to time she would look to Vusi for confirmation or support. It seemed there was some connection between them. Leaving, Kubu wondered about that. Was Vusi just being opportunistic after Monzo had died? Taking advantage of the presence of a now single woman? Or did they have a relationship before Monzo died?

That was worth pursuing.

Seven

The next morning Kubu and Khumanego went to the police station to check on the release of the three Bushmen. All three were already out of the holding cells, waiting for their lift back to their group. They greeted Kubu respectfully, and there was much enthusiastic discussion with Khumanego in their own language. Kubu stood back, allowing himself to enjoy the feeling of righting injustice. There was no sign of Lerako; his office door was closed.

Eventually the three climbed into the back of a police Land Rover. The driver was a uniformed constable, and a man, another Bushman, sat next to him in the passenger seat. Perhaps an interpreter? Kubu wondered. Was Lerako coming around? It seemed a sympathetic gesture.

At last they were ready to go and the vehicle pulled away. Khumanego was still talking to them, laughing and waving as they left. He came inside looking happy for the first time on the trip.

"Look, David. See what I have here." He opened the palm of his hand revealing a large desert-brown praying mantis sitting there. It seemed content and quiet in the darkness of his hand.

"Where did you find it?"

"No, I didn't find it. It flew to me and settled on my hand. It is a great sign, a wonderful thing!" Khumanego's face glowed. "The Mantis created the world and all its people. But we don't think of him as a god. He is sort of a good friend to the Bushmen. He's always playing practical jokes. He makes us laugh.

"He created us first," Khumanego continued. "That is why we call ourselves the First People. We were here before the Hottentots, before the Batswana, before the whites. Before everybody." Suddenly his face fell, and bitterness was in his voice again. "Now it seems we will be the first people to disappear."

Kubu could see why the Bushmen had chosen the mantis over the lion or elephant as their creator. It was small, like the Bushmen, and its little triangular face resembled a Bushman face. Even the light brown color was similar.

"It's wonderful he came to you himself," he said, trying to help Khumanego recover his earlier joy.

Khumanego shook his head. "She. Too big for a male." He hesitated. "David, you have done a wonderful thing for our people here. I thank you, and my people give you their thanks. You are our friend, indeed." He held out his hand, and Kubu took it.

"I just did my job."

Khumanego nodded. "But many don't. Some just go with their prejudices. Like him." He nodded toward Lerako's closed door. Kubu said nothing.

"Well, David, I must go too. There is a truck taking water to the settlements in the Kalahari leaving today. I'd like to visit the people there, hear what they know, see if they are all right. I need to be ready soon."

This was a surprise to Kubu. He had assumed that his friend would return with him to Gaborone. He had looked forward to the company now that things were resolved.

"How will you get back to Gaborone?" he asked.

"Oh, there are minibus taxis, but I'll probably get a lift with one of the aid workers or someone else. There's a lot of traffic." Kubu hadn't noticed that, but it seemed Khumanego's mind was made up. He gave him a playful shove which nearly knocked the Bushman over. "Go well, my friend," he said. Khumanego nodded and was gone as suddenly as a ghost.

Kubu turned and headed for Lerako's office. With the Bushmen out of the picture, the case would need to be solved from scratch. Kubu felt a prickle of excitement.

Lerako was nowhere to be seen, so Kubu took advantage of the privacy of his vacant office to call Joy. He didn't expect her to be happy that he was staying on in Tsabong, and he was right.

"Kubu, I really need you home. It's hard enough to cope when you're here! Now I have to do everything myself. I can't manage. I can't." She sounded close to tears.

"Darling, I'll be home as soon as I can. Soon, I promise."

"But *when* will you be back?"

There it was again. How could he possibly be expected to answer that? "Why don't you take some leave? Stay at home with Tumi. Get some rest."

"I used up all my leave after she was born. There's nothing left."

Kubu grasped for a straw. "Well, when I'm back I'll take some leave. Stay at home with Tumi. Then you can get out with your friends in the afternoon. See Pleasant."

"You should save your leave for when we . . ." But Joy seemed to lose that thought. "I'd still have to cook for us as soon as I get home anyway."

Kubu had an inspiration. "That's what I'll do with the leave! I'll take up cooking. You know how interested I am in food. I can choose a cuisine. Maybe Chinese. I'll enjoy it, and you will have free time."

Joy thought about it, seeing a glimmer of hope. "Would you really enjoy cooking?" she asked hesitantly. Cooking wasn't traditional male behavior among the Batswana.

Kubu had never thought about it before and had no idea if he would enjoy it. "Absolutely! It's something I've always wanted to do, but there's never been time. And you cook so well I thought you might be offended if I even suggested it."

"Oh, Kubu, I don't know. But if I had some time. Not to see friends, but perhaps to visit Pleasant. And rest a bit. I would be so grateful."

"I'm sure I'll manage. I'll cook the very day I come home." He felt he was laying it on a bit, but his enthusiasm was building up. He loved Chinese food. How hard could it be? Everyone in China cooked it, and there were billions of people there. And, after all, Mabaku couldn't refuse Kubu some leave. Compassionate leave. For Joy.

"So when will you be home?"

"I'm sure it will only be a few days. What about getting Pleasant to stay over till then? She can help. She loves Tumi."

For the first time Joy sounded enthusiastic. "Oh, Kubu, I'm

sure she would. Just for a couple of days till you come back. I'll ask her. I think she'll come. She knows I'm struggling."

"Then, when I've cooked a delicious Chinese meal—the whole thing—sweet-and-sour pork with pineapple and rice with all the trimmings, washed down with a Riesling perhaps, and I've cleaned everything up while you put Tumi to sleep, we can go to bed. And you'll be fresh and enthusiastic. I've heard Chinese food contains things that increase desire. We'll have a wonderful time!" Kubu's mouth was watering. He wasn't sure if it was the thought of Joy—always tired lately—in his arms, or the sweet-and-sour pork. Joy too sounded enthusiastic, and the conversation finished on a happy note. Kubu sighed with relief. He was a little tentative about his promises, though. The Riesling was fine, and so was the lovemaking—more than fine, he thought rather smugly—but he had undertaken to cook a full meal and clean up. More or less the day he got back. And perhaps for several days thereafter. And get leave from Mabaku, who was not in a particularly good mood at the moment. Well, I should have paternity leave, Kubu thought, feeling a most liberated man.

When he returned to the Mokha Lodge, Kubu found Cindy waiting for him. She wanted to say good-bye. "There's nothing more to follow up here, Kubu. I'm happy that you saved the Bushmen. I'll put it in the story."

"Detective Sergeant Lerako will love that!"

"I want to thank you. For helping them. And for spending time with me." She leaned forward seemingly to peck him on the cheek but, turning her head, kissed him on the lips. It was a sisterly kiss, but Kubu was surprised, yet not displeased. She wiped his lips with her fingers. "Lipstick," she said.

Kubu smiled. "Do you know anything about cooking Chinese food?"

She laughed. Her laugh always seemed ready. "You're going to cook for your family?" Kubu nodded. How did she guess? Was she related to Mabaku?

"Well, no, not actually," she continued. "I'm not into Chinese. But all you need is a cookbook. And the ingredients. I'm sure you can get those. Otherwise you'll have to improvise."

A cookbook! Of course. "Thank you very much. A cookbook. That's the answer."

Cindy gave him her card, on which she'd written a local cell phone number. "Will you call me when you get back to Gaborone? Please. I'd like to see you again, Kubu."

Kubu promised to do that, and held out his hand. She shook it with a slight smile. Then she let him go.

Eight

Joy was delighted that her sister could accompany her to see Kubu's parents. It wasn't that they'd grown apart, but for the past three months she'd been so tired attending to Tumi that they didn't get together as frequently as before.

Pleasant had jumped at the chance to visit Wilmon and Amantle, Kubu's charmingly old-fashioned parents, and insisted that Joy drive so she could hold and pamper the baby.

After Joy had negotiated the maelstrom of traffic, people, and animals that populated Gaborone's streets, she relaxed a little and felt able to give some of her attention to Pleasant.

"So how are you and Bongani getting on?" she asked, twisting to look at Pleasant, who was sitting behind her. Kubu insisted that Tumi should always be in the backseat, which disrupted years of habit for Ilia, who had to learn to sleep on the passenger seat. Ilia still was unsettled by the change and occasionally sought reassurance from Joy by jumping up and licking her on the ear. "I hope you're prepared for Amantle's cross-examination! You know how she feels about women your age being single!"

Pleasant laughed at the memory of previous visits. "I always think I'm ready, but when I get there she finds all the chinks in my armor. How about you? How are you doing?"

"Other than being exhausted all the time, I'm well. I just wish Tumi would sleep through the night sometimes, but I suppose it's too much to expect after only three months. But even once a week would be good. I need the sleep."

"Is Kubu still not helping?"

"I really don't know what to do. He says he wants to help, but he never hears Tumi crying, and he's almost impossible to wake. I just don't have the energy to get him up. It's seems easier to deal with Tumi myself. It's beginning to affect our relationship."

"Too tired even for sex?" Pleasant's eyes twinkled.

"Yes, and I miss it. But more important, we don't have the same relaxed time together in the evenings. If I'm not dealing with Tumi, I'm too tired to listen to him like I used to. I'm not sure what he's up to anymore. And I don't tell him much about what's going on at the school." Joy took a deep breath, feeling tears welling up. "And I feel resentful when he has to go away. I know it's not true, but I feel sometimes that he's happy to go away to get some peace for himself."

"Kubu wouldn't do that! He's the most devoted husband I've ever met."

"What if he meets someone on one of his trips? It seems like ages since we had sex."

"Kubu never looks at anyone else. You've got to trust him."

Joy didn't respond, but focused on the road ahead, trying to banish the tears and the doubt.

Pleasant loved the stalls that populated Botswana's roads, with their creative names. As they drove down Kgafela Drive in Mochudi, only a mile or two from the Bengus' house, they passed the More and More Tuck Shop, the Taliban Haircut and Car Wash, and the dubious Jailbird Security Company. She laughed out loud, startling Ilia, who uncurled, stood up, and looked out of the window. Suddenly her stumpy tail wagged furiously. She knows where she is, Pleasant thought. She knows she's about to be spoiled.

They drove into a poorer part of the town and pulled up in front of a small house. Ilia bounded out of the car, up the steps to the Bengus' home, and into the lap of Wilmon, who was seated on the veranda as usual awaiting his visitors. Amantle stood at the top of the stairs beaming. She loved Joy as her own daughter and frequently chided her son for taking so long to marry her. You are very lucky she waited, she often said.

Amantle hugged Joy, then Pleasant. She had long ago adopted the more informal Western form of greeting. Wilmon struggled to his feet, tipping a disgruntled Ilia to the floor, and was likewise hugged by both women. Joy knew this caused turmoil in the old man. His upbringing demanded a more formal greeting—a handshake at most—but he couldn't refuse the intimacy of a hug.

"*Dumela*, Joy. *Dumela*, Pleasant. You are welcome at my house," he said. "How are you both? And how is Tumi?"

"We are all well, thank you. You too are looking well."

"I am fine, even though I am feeling old these days. Please sit down."

"I know Amantle wants to spoil Tumi, so I'll put out lunch. I didn't have time to cook, so I bought cold meat and salads. Not as fresh as your vegetables, my father, but they look tasty."

Wilmon was proud of his herb and vegetable garden at the back of the house, which he tended with loving care. The previous year's crop had been spectacular, but he was concerned for this year's, due to the prolonged drought.

Joy handed Tumi to Amantle, who sat down and immediately started gently rocking the sleeping baby. Joy smiled and walked into the small interior of the house. "I'll call you when I'm ready."

"Where is my son?" Wilmon said, looking around.

"Wilmon, I told you he was away on business." Amantle's voice had a hint of irritation. "You must get your ears checked again. He is somewhere in the south." She rocked Tumi a little more vigorously which, fortunately, didn't wake her.

Wilmon didn't respond.

"He is with his old friend, Khumanego. Do you remember him?"

"Of course I do," Wilmon replied. "He and David used to play together around our house when they were children. He was one of those Bushmen. From the desert. I never understood why he was at school. He and David looked strange together—one big and one small."

Wilmon seemed taken aback by the length of his speech, particularly in front of only women, and sat down, patting his lap for Ilia, who needed little encouragement.

For the next few minutes, Amantle and Pleasant admired Tumi's features. Amantle exclaimed how much Tumi looked like Joy.

"But she looks like you," Pleasant said, pointing to the baby's nose and mouth. "Her face is just like yours."

Pleasant could see that Amantle was pleased.

"Lunch is ready!" Joy shouted.

Ilia's hopes for having a prolonged tummy scratch were dashed as Wilmon stood up again.

Lunch was delicious and enjoyed by all. Ilia gave Wilmon another chance to spoil her and sat panting next to his chair. This time she wasn't disappointed. A steady trickle of morsels fell from the table, which she immediately gobbled up.

The conversation was largely gossip: Amantle telling the visitors what was going on in Mochudi, Pleasant talking about new shops in Gaborone, and Joy describing how quickly Tumi was growing. Meals were not the time for anything contentious.

While they were clearing up, Kubu called and Joy chatted to him for a few minutes, smiling and happy. It seemed things were going well in Tsabong, and Kubu was pleased the family visit was going smoothly. He sent his love to his mother and respectful greetings to his father, and then said he needed to hurry to lunch. Joy laughed and warned him to watch his diet. Then she served tea on the veranda, and they all caught up on Kubu's news.

But between nods and exclamations, Amantle was eyeing Pleasant, who knew that her time was coming. And come it did, after the tea things had been cleared away.

"My dear," Amantle said pulling her chair closer to Pleasant. "My heart grieves, and I spend sleepless nights worrying about what your dear mother would be thinking if she were still alive. I am sure her time in heaven is disturbed because you are still single."

Joy slid her chair back to enjoy the bout. Wilmon's eyes were closed, as were Ilia's, who snored gently on his lap, occasionally twitching as she dreamed of catching snacks dropping from the table.

"You are so kind to me," Pleasant said, putting her hand out to touch Amantle. "You are truly now my mother."

Amantle shrugged the flattery aside. "Then it is my duty to warn you that soon you will no longer be attractive to the right men. You will be too old. They will think of you as a raisin, not a grape. Men today want young women, who do not work. And you are no longer young. And you do work!" She glared at Pleasant, daring her to contradict. "What happened to the man you told me about—the stupid man, who was too clever to appreciate your beauty, your broad hips?"

"Bongani!" Pleasant replied. "I still see him. We still go out . . ."

"Still go out?" Amantle burst out. "How much longer will it take him to make up his mind? You should tell him to marry you or leave you. He is wasting your time."

"We are getting closer."

"Getting closer? You have been doing that for how long? Three years? Even snails are faster than that."

Pleasant capitulated. "I will tell Bongani what you have said. You are right as always, my mother." Joy managed to turn a snort of laughter into a sneeze, then stood up and said it was time for them to leave.

"Pleasant has a date with Bongani this evening. She has to make herself even more beautiful than she is. He won't be able to resist her this time."

Now it was Amantle's turn to snort. "Call me on the telephone tomorrow. I will expect good news." She too stood up, nudging her husband to do likewise. "I hope my son is being a good father? He is providing enough for you?"

"He is. But he finds it difficult to feed Tumi at night. He never wakes up when she cries."

"Tumi is perfect. She has slept the whole time you were here. And it is for the mother to feed a baby, not a father. And I hope you will give up your job. Mothers should not work for five years. That is what I did with David, and look how well he turned out."

Joy knew not to contradict Amantle in this mood. Wilmon had at last managed to get to his feet, so Joy turned and hugged him. A glimmer of a smile lit up his face, as pleasure momentarily overcame reserve. Pleasant did likewise.

Amantle walked down to the car with them, handing Tumi to Joy at the last possible minute. "Look after my beautiful granddaughter and give my love to David. Tell him he shouldn't work on Sundays. God does not approve."

Joy and Pleasant climbed into the car, Pleasant the driver this time. They waved at the elderly couple as they drove away. Ilia gave a single bark and lay down to sleep.

"They are so special," Pleasant said. "You are so lucky to have them."

"Yes, but they always take Kubu's side. He does nothing except sleep when Tumi cries at night, and they think that's just fine. It's the woman's job, no matter what."

"You're not going to change them. Just be thankful they love you so much."

"I suppose you also think I should do all the work! Just wait until you have kids—if you ever get around to it!"

"All I said was that Kubu's parents belong to a different generation. You can't change them."

"Half the time, Kubu thinks he's a liberated, New Age man—drinks wine, loves opera. But when it comes to domestic things, like work around the house and looking after Tumi, he's as traditional as you can get. It's the woman's responsibility. Very convenient."

"I think you're being too hard on him, he—"

But Joy interrupted. "He won't learn how to do up the nappies properly. It's as if he does it wrongly on purpose, so I'll have to do it all over again. Basically he's just lazy when it suits him!"

Pleasant decided that the chaotic traffic of Gaborone deserved her attention, so they drove in silence until they reached her apartment.

"It was a lovely day. Thanks for inviting me," Pleasant said, getting out of the car and walking around to the sidewalk.

Joy climbed out of the passenger side, clutching Tumi, who had slept the whole trip. She walked over to Pleasant, hugged her, and started to cry.

"I'm sorry! I didn't mean to snap at you. You know I love you. It all just gets me down sometimes."

Pleasant held the embrace, patting Joy comfortingly on the back.

"Don't worry. Everything will be okay. You'll see."

The sisters kissed good-bye.

Pleasant watched as Joy drove away. It's true, she mused. Kubu can be lazy. I'm lucky. Bongani may be quiet, but he gets things done.

They'll work it out, she thought. I've never seen two people so much in love.

But for the first time, she felt a twinge of concern.

Nine

For Kubu, Sunday was a relaxing day. He rose quite early as usual, dressed in a colorful shirt and shorts, and enjoyed a leisurely breakfast involving porridge with butter and sugar, followed by eggs, bacon, fried tomato, and toast with marmalade. While he kept an eye on his diet, he felt he had some slack available on a tiring trip. Then while it was still reasonably cool, he relaxed on the veranda of the hotel with a glass of iced water and thought about the case. It seemed that he was imprisoned in Tsabong until the murder—if indeed it was murder—of Monzo was resolved. So he closed his eyes and mentally reviewed the case.

What were the facts? There was the calcrete chunk that had apparently been used to bash in Monzo's skull. How had that happened? Could it have been thrown? Almost certainly not. The force might have knocked Monzo out and injured him, but it was very unlikely to have enough energy to break his skull. Did someone creep up behind him? Possible. But it would need to be a tall and powerful man to do such damage with such a clumsy weapon. Certainly not a Bushman. Perhaps Monzo had been attacked in some other way first? Knocked out and then dealt a heavy blow from the rock once he was on the ground. That seemed more likely. He would need to ask the pathologist if there was anything in the autopsy that either supported or negated that idea. Why had the murderer thrown the stone away? It was too far away to be the result of Monzo's fall from the cliff. And why not remove it completely?

It must be homicide, Kubu decided regretfully. But perhaps not premeditated, since the disposal of the murder weapon seemed poorly planned. And how could the killer know that Monzo would go to that particular area that particular morning?

The waiter topped up Kubu's water quietly, suspecting that Kubu was dozing.

"Thank you," said Kubu, startling the man.

Then there were the footprints. Plenty of Bushman footprints, but just the two large boot prints. It appeared that someone had walked along the calcrete ridge presumably until he was out of the area where the murder had been committed. Perhaps after covering his other tracks? But where had the man come from? How had he left the area? On foot in the heat of the desert day? Kubu shook his head firmly. There was more to find around the scene of the crime. There must be. He would have to get Lerako to help. They had only two footprints, but they could lead to the murderer.

And what of motive? None of his co-workers seemed to have much time for Monzo. He had been difficult and unpopular. And he appeared to have an ambivalent relationship with both his boss and his wife. But there's nothing obvious right now. Nothing that would lead to a murder. So there must be darker undercurrents. Someone with reason to hate Monzo, or with something to gain from his death. That's where I'll need to start, Kubu thought.

He sighed. He had a plan for the next day, but it meant more travel, more heat, more dust, and more Lerako. He would have been happier to have none of them. Still, the decision relaxed him, and he drifted into sleep.

He woke to the tinkle of ice cubes entering his water glass and a smile from the waiter. It was getting hot again, and Kubu decided that a swim was in order. He was not by nature a lover of cold water, but he felt the exercise would prepare him for lunch. So he changed into swimming trunks and wallowed in the pool for half an hour, even managing a few lazy lengths. Joy is right, he thought. This exercise is good for me. I have worked up an appetite for the chicken curry and *sambals* that make up the hotel's Sunday lunch.

Back in his room he showered and got back into his shirt and shorts. He called Joy and was delighted that she was having a good time with his parents and everyone was fussing over Tumi. It seemed that everything was working out after all. He worked his way through several arias from *Don Giovanni*, striking appropriate poses in the dresser mirror. When he had completed those to his satisfaction, he headed back to the dining room.

Since he was restricting himself to just one helping, Kubu piled his plate with rice and curry, balancing the sliced banana, desiccated coconut, and sweet chutney on the top. In the absence of steelworks, he ordered a light beer to wash it down. And after that I will be ready for a serious nap, he thought.

So it was disappointing that a day that had started so well was to end so badly. For just as he was settling to his nap, his cell phone rang. He was surprised to hear Lerako's voice.

"Bengu? It's Lerako here. I have some news for you."

Kubu grunted.

"Well, I sent my Bushman tracker out with those three suspects yesterday morning. The three you were so sure were innocent. I thought he could follow the trail from those two footprints, see where they led."

He paused, and Kubu commented that he had been thinking along the same lines.

"They don't lead anywhere," Lerako stated.

"What do you mean?"

"The tracker followed them back to the *donga*, and he did find signs that someone had been walking along the calcrete. Not footprints as such, just smudges and slip marks. Also he thinks something big was dragged to the *donga* edge and probably pushed over."

"So there was someone else there!"

Lerako ignored him. "But when he followed the boot prints in the direction away from the murder scene, he found nothing. No smudges, no slip marks, nothing."

"Maybe he missed them, or the man was moving more carefully."

"Actually there was no point in being careful. About five hundred yards further on, that ridge peters out into the dunes. And there are no footprints in the sand there. So where did he go after that?"

There was a suggestive pause, and Kubu feared that there was worse to come.

"The tracker is a good chap. Shows you can make something of a Bushman if you get him out of the bush and train him. He went back to the footprints the Bushmen found so conveniently for a more careful look. He thinks they're fakes. The weight isn't distributed the way you would expect if a man—a big man with big feet—was walking along the ridge. And they are too close together for the stride of a big man. He thinks the prints were deliberately set, maybe the boots were just pushed into the sand by hand."

Kubu's heart sank. Mabaku was not going to be pleased with this development. Had he allowed himself to be fooled into believing the Bushmen were innocent because that was how he wanted it to be? On the other hand, why would a murderer leave a few isolated boot prints? If they were fakes, could it be misdirection?

But Lerako wasn't finished.

"He headed back here yesterday afternoon and reported all this to me this morning. So I got onto Vusi at the ranger station and told him to send someone out to keep an eye on the Bushmen until we could interrogate them again. He was irritated but eventually sent someone out there."

Kubu bit his lip. He guessed how this was going to end.

"They're gone, Bengu. They probably left as soon as the three were dropped off. There aren't clear tracks either; obviously they don't want to be followed. We won't catch them now. Monzo's killers have vanished into the Kalahari."

Part II

*Itən /ne kaŋ ≠ĩ:, ts³a de xa a:, !kwi á: a, ha
/kʉ ⁻o: se /ku :kən ã:*

*We wonder why this person is about to
die*

Ten

The group had traveled far in the day and a half since the three had been released by the police. But they had gone carefully, avoiding any unnecessary trace of their progress. Now they huddled around a small pile of barely glowing ashes. Unlike most nights, when the men told stories of great hunts or tales of the gods, this night was without entertainment. Unlike most nights, usually filled with jokes and laughter, this night was somber.

It was a night to end an era, to mark a passing, to begin a future.

"My people," Gobiwasi said quietly. "Many times I have watched the sun chase the moon from the skies. And have seen the moon sneak back and grow bolder, until it thinks it can challenge the sun. Only to be chased away again. I have seen summers when I thought we would all die, and times when Rain jumped on the ground and made the sand green.

The ancestors have smiled on me while I have been here. I have enjoyed a good life and have a fine family." He peered at the figures around the fire, not able to distinguish one from the other. All were quiet.

"But now I am old. I cannot hunt and cannot run, and I walk too slowly. Today I could hardly keep up. I cannot provide for you. I cannot provide for myself. I am a burden."

Everyone stared into the embers, even the children knowing where this was going.

"You will have many challenges ahead." Gobiwasi cleared the phlegm from his throat and spat into the fire. "The world is changing too fast for our people. We cannot keep up, and when I talk to the ancestors, they do not tell me what to do."

The children huddled against their mothers.

"Our people believe the earth is for all, for humans, for animals, and snakes, and insects, and plants. But those who came after us believe the earth is for them. That it is there to be owned. That they should not share the land with others. And so it is that our people are treated like thieves and robbers. Because we hunt to survive. And sometimes what we hunt no longer belongs to the earth, to all, but to one man who has thunder in his head and fire in his hand. And he hunts us, as we hunt the eland. Or he ties us with rope and drags us to look after his animals, which he treats better than he treats us."

No one saw the tears leaking from Gobiwasi's eyes.

The group sat in silence, waiting.

Eventually Gobiwasi spoke again.

"It is easy to be angry. To want to fight. But that is not the way of the Mantis. The Mantis tells me that we must remain who we are. We must become invisible to the men who want to change our ways just as we become invisible to the animals we hunt. Standing up and fighting will not work. We have survived from the beginning of time because we understand the world around us. We must do the same now even though what we see is not what we know. If we are to remain true to the First People, we must be clever and disappear even further into the place of the great thirst."

"Grandpa!" One of the children could contain himself no more. "Where will you be in the sky? Tell me, so I can look at you every night."

Gobiwasi smiled. "Only the ancestors know that. They will tell me soon."

He stood up and gazed at the upturned faces.

"The Mantis will look after you!"

He turned, collected his few belongings and walked into the night.

Eleven

As Kubu drove the slow trip from Tsabong to the Wildlife offices at Mabuasehube, he decided that his view of the Monzo case hadn't changed. He still couldn't believe that a group of peaceful Bushmen had set upon and killed the ranger. He remained convinced that the missing clues were at the ranger station, with the people who had known, but mostly not loved, the prickly man.

He started with Marta. She seemed surprised to see him again, but was pleasant and offered him coffee and a slice of bread and jam, which he accepted. While he ate, they spoke of her plans. The older boy would be going to school next year, so she would look for work in Tsabong. She had a relative there and would be able to stay until she had some money and found something of her own. Kubu made a few suggestions about work prospects. He was in no hurry, and wanted to see how the conversation would develop. At last, after he had finished his bread and had drained the coffee, he looked at Marta and asked, "Do you know if Monzo had any enemies? Not people he rubbed up the wrong way, but real enemies? People who might want to do him harm?"

She shook her head. "A lot of people didn't like him much, but there's no one who would want to kill him."

Well, Kubu thought, someone did.

"Was Monzo good to you?"

"What do you mean?"

"I mean did he provide for you and the children, was he a good father? Did he love you?"

"Yes, I suppose so."

Kubu shifted in his seat. "I'm sorry to ask you these questions, but I'm trying to find his murderer. It's not curiosity."

She nodded, but said nothing.

"I understand that you were not formally married. Why was that?"

Her face hardened. "Yes. It's true. He was already married. To a woman somewhere in South Africa."

"Did he have other women in Botswana also?"

She shrugged.

"Do you know of any other women?"

"No."

"But you suspected?"

"He went away on trips for days, even weeks. It was possible. He liked women."

"These trips. Were they for the National Park?"

"So he said."

"But?"

She hesitated. "Once I looked. When he was packing for a

trip. He took two tents, a double and a single. I asked him why he was taking two tents. He said another man was going with him. And that I should mind my own business."

"And did someone go with him?"

She shook her head. "No one from here. He left on his own. He was away for nearly two weeks. I asked Ndoli where he had gone. He just shrugged. Said Monzo had told him he was doing a survey along the northern border. But no one had authorized it."

Kubu thought that over. So Monzo helped himself to weeks of government time to do what? Maybe he just liked to be in the bush. But who had been with him? And what had they been doing? If it was something illegal, then the murder investigation would have a different perspective. Perhaps Monzo demanded more money, maybe he knew too much. Kubu sensed the fuzzy outline of a motive. He would need to check Monzo's bank account.

"When he went on these trips, did he take fuel, food, and water? As though he was going deep into the bush?"

"Sometimes. I didn't watch what he was doing all the time."

Kubu paused, then changed tack. "What relationship do you have with Rra Vusi?"

She bristled. "What do you mean 'relationship'?"

Kubu just waited.

"He's kind to me. To us. He likes the children. He has supper with us sometimes."

"I need a definite answer to the next question, and I warn you that if you lie I will find out. Everyone knows what's going on in a little community like this. Was there anything between you and Vusi before Monzo's death?"

"No!"

Kubu believed her, but of course, he'd check.

◁▷ ◁▷ ◁▷

Kubu found the office manager at his desk. Ndoli looked busy, but not averse to being interrupted. He offered Kubu tea, and Kubu accepted to be sociable, but there were no biscuits to go with it. They took their cups to a small anteroom, which was more private than the general open-plan office where the staff worked.

"Now, Superintendent," said Ndoli once they had settled, "how can I help?" He obviously expected more questions about the discovery of the critically injured Monzo, but Kubu surprised him.

"I gather Monzo was in the habit of making bush trips. More or less when he chose. Is that right?"

Ndoli looked away. "Yes. I was against it. But he persuaded Vusi these so-called survey trips of his were important."

"How did he do that?"

"Actually he just went on and on until Vusi said he'd think about it. After that he did what he liked."

Kubu's mouth twitched as he imagined someone trying that technique on Mabaku. But he said nothing, waiting for Ndoli to go on.

"Vusi's not a very strong manager, you see. Very nice guy. Really cares about the job and the staff. But he doesn't make a lot of decisions."

"Did Monzo tell you where he was going on these trips? Surely you had to know where he was?"

"Yes, but I don't know if he stuck to what he told me. He took one of our satellite phones with him in case of emergency, but he never used it."

So Monzo had been a free agent with a perfect cover as a ranger for whatever he might want to do in the Kalahari area. Kubu felt a motive for the killing coming more into focus.

He tried another line of questioning.

"Do you know why Monzo decided to go after the Bushmen that morning?"

"He didn't 'go after' them. He had a report that they were poaching in the reserve. He went out to check up."

"One of the other rangers told him?"

Monzo looked puzzled. "No, we knew they were around the border, but no one suggested they'd been hunting. We would all have heard about that."

"So it's possible that Monzo made the whole thing up?"

Ndoli shook his head. "He was cross. He said he was going to sort them out." He hesitated. "Maybe some tourist tipped him off as he was driving around."

"Wouldn't he have investigated right away in that case?"

Ndoli frowned. "Maybe someone reported it at the main gate. Or maybe called in. I really don't know. Does it matter?"

Kubu dropped it, but he felt it might be important. He had learned to trust his intuition. It usually kicked in when someone else couldn't see why some niggling issue mattered.

Instead he explored some operational issues with Ndoli, and slipped in the question about Marta and Vusi. But Ndoli was clear that he kept out of other people's business, especially if one of them was his boss.

Vusi wasn't in his office, so, while he waited, Kubu helped himself to another cup of tea from the urn. The office cleaner was washing up the cups. Kubu greeted her politely.

"You shouldn't drink so much tea," she told him by way of response. "It's not good for you." Apparently she had noticed the first cup. Kubu realized that by luck he had come upon the office busybody. He introduced himself.

"What are you doing here then? From what I hear, Gaborone isn't safe to walk around anymore. Why don't you do something about that, eh?"

Now Kubu wasn't so sure about the encounter being fortunate, but explained that he was investigating what was now believed to be the murder of Rra Monzo. If he thought this would impress the lady, he was mistaken.

"Monzo! Serves him right. Always sneaking off after a woman or heaven knows what. You know he had a regular in Tshane? Someone else's wife? Always making a reason to go up there for a couple of days. And Marta's a real lady. She gave him two good boys too."

Kubu wondered if simple jealousy could be the motive after all. He decided to push harder. "Well, she has Rra Vusi for comfort."

She gave him a dirty look. "And why not? Monzo's dead. Vusi's alone here. No harm done."

"What about before Monzo's death?"

"She never looked at another man. You can take my word for that." Kubu thought he probably could.

"I see you keep your eyes open, Mma. You probably know what Monzo was doing on these special trips of his too. His private missions into the bush?"

She shrugged. "Probably up to no good. With a woman, I bet." She wagged a finger at him. "Now I have work to do. And no more tea for you!" With a disapproving sniff she was off.

Kubu smiled. Another item to add to the growing list of things someone thought he shouldn't eat or drink.

Vusi sat behind the security of his desk. He looked nervous and in a hurry and claimed he had told the police everything already. Kubu said he wouldn't take long, but made it clear that he wasn't going to be rushed.

"Do you know how Monzo came to believe that the Bushmen were poaching?"

"No idea. Ask Ndoli, he's the office manager. Or Kweto. He does reception. Takes messages and answers the phone and so on. Maybe he'd know."

Kubu nodded.

"I understand that Monzo did a lot of work in the bush. Surveys and so on. Is that correct?"

"Yes. It was part of his job. He had to keep tabs on what's happening in the whole area. This is a huge area to manage, Superintendent. Ten thousand square miles! People don't appreciate that."

Kubu nodded. "What did he do on these trips?"

"He'd check an area, see what was going on, count game, things like that."

"Were these trips on some sort of schedule?"

Vusi found a pencil to play with while he talked. "Yes and no. They were done when we could fit them in."

"Did Monzo always discuss the trips with you? Or did he sometimes use his own initiative?"

"Well, we discussed what was needed in general, and then he went ahead. What's all this about, Superintendent? Why the sudden interest in park management?"

"I have the impression that Monzo pretty well scheduled these trips as he saw fit, and it wasn't always clear what they were for. Is that right?"

"Certainly not! I'm in charge here, and Monzo reported to me. I was satisfied with his work."

"Wasn't it a problem that he was away so often?"

Vusi put down the pencil. "Actually, the others got more work done when he was off on a trip."

Yes, Kubu thought. Everyone including Vusi was happy to let Monzo go his own way.

After that he explored the manager's feelings toward Marta. Vusi admitted that he visited Marta occasionally to cheer her up and was helping her with financial issues until the government gave her a settlement. There was nothing more to it. Kubu decided that Vusi's relationship with Marta, whatever that was, had started after the murder and wasn't relevant to the case. So he left it at that.

Vusi pointed out Kweto and said good-bye, clearly glad that the interview was over.

Kubu asked the receptionist about the report of the poaching, but Kweto had no idea. However, as Kubu turned to go, he said, "Monzo did get a call late on the afternoon before he died. I remember because the man wanted to speak specifically to him, no one else, and he wouldn't give his name. Said it was personal. He had to wait while I found Monzo for him."

Kubu thanked him. He'd check up on the phone call later, but it was a pretty long shot. Right now it was time to get back to Tsabong and talk to Lerako.

Kubu was hot and tired by the time he got back to Tsabong, but he went straight to the police station. He wanted to start things moving on the new leads. Lerako heard him out, but then lived up to his name. "You've added nothing new, Kubu. Nothing. So Monzo took some unauthorized trips, which, incidentally, Vusi denies were unauthorized. So what?"

"Don't you see? He could have been involved in something illegal—animal smuggling or something. Once you step over the line, if you turn up dead it's no big surprise. Maybe that's what the personal phone call was about. Someone setting up a secret meeting at the *donga*." He paused. "And the girl in Tshane? Her husband may have decided that he'd had enough of Monzo. We need to follow this up."

"What do you suggest? I'm trying to track down the Bushman group. Or is that a waste of time in your opinion?"

"We have people in Tshane. They can make door-to-door inquiries. Everyone knows everything that goes on in these small places. I'm sure we'll find connections. Anyway, these new possibilities make more sense than the nonsense that the Bushmen did it."

Kubu had gone too far. Lerako leaned forward across his desk, angry.

"You won't believe the Bushmen could do it, will you? They're all just good gentle folk who want to be left alone to get on with their lives. Well, let me tell you something, Assistant Superintendent. Some of them are. But many just hang around in rags looking for handouts, refusing to work. They beg or commit petty theft, usually for booze rather than food. I work with these people. I know them. You just have your educated friend. Good for him. But that's not how they all are!"

"Monzo still had his money and watch. What's supposed to have been their motive?" Kubu asked mildly.

"Who knows what they took? Maybe they were after something else."

Kubu felt himself getting angry too. "I'm here to make sure these men aren't railroaded like Maauwe and Motswetla. They were Bushmen too. That was a travesty of justice!"

Lerako's voice rose. "Travesty, you say? I agree with you. But you know what people forget when they're bleating about how badly they were treated? That they stole someone else's ox and killed it. Nobody disputes that."

"They killed it for food."

"The man who owned it wasn't rich. He also had a family to feed. They stole his ox and killed it; he went to find it and got murdered for his trouble. Who looks after his family now, hey? Who protects them from the droughts? Yes, it was a travesty. And we carry the blame either way. Either those men were guilty, and the police and prosecutors did such a bad job that they weren't nailed down and hanged, as they should have been, or they were *not* guilty, in which case a murderer is free out there. And no one went looking for that murderer!" He thumped his fist on the desk and got to his feet. "I'm going to get some coffee." He stalked out of the cramped, baking office, leaving the door wide open.

Kubu sat and fumed, and then cooled. Was it possible that Khumanego's representations had blinded him to the obvious? Was he unable to see that the Bushmen—like everyone else—could have their rotten apples, their renegades, their *murderers*?

At that moment of introspection, his cell phone rang. Kubu had a premonition, and he was right. It was Director Mabaku.

"Bengu! I spoke to Lerako a bit earlier. It seems that the footprints you so conveniently discovered are fakes. And now the suspects have disappeared!"

Kubu gave a detailed report on what he had discovered at the ranger station. But Mabaku didn't seem impressed.

"Well, I'm sure this will all be wrapped up quickly," Mabaku commented at the conclusion. "Now that we have our star detective on the case." Kubu knew better than to imagine that this was a compliment. Mabaku continued. "Perhaps you will need to explain the case on TV. Point out how you have to guide your bumbling colleagues through their investigations."

Kubu's heart sank as he realized what had happened. "Cindy Robinson wrote about me?"

"Yes, indeed, and she was most impressed. I'm so glad we have *one honest, intelligent policeman in Botswana,* as she generously put it."

"Well, these reporters always have to make a big story out of routine police work." It was the wrong thing to say. The volume escalated so suddenly that Kubu had to move the phone away from his ear very quickly.

"I told you *not* to talk to that woman. Instead, you seem to have become friends! I'm not impressed. The commissioner is not impressed." Suddenly the volume dropped dangerously. "Bengu, you'd better start following orders. Orders are not suggestions. They are instructions you *have to* follow. That's why they are called orders!

"Now I want you back here. I'm sick of paying expensive hotel rates so that you can mess around in other detectives' cases. Lerako can manage this one on his own. Drive back tomorrow."

Without waiting for a response, the director rang off. Kubu breathed a sigh of relief. The blast had been because he talked to the reporter, not about what he had said. Cindy must have dealt the police a reasonable hand. But it had been a close thing. He mopped his forehead with a handkerchief. It was stifling in the office. It was hardly surprising that he and Lerako had lost their tempers. As if on cue, the detective sergeant returned with a cup of foul-looking coffee. He seemed to have cooled down too.

"There's no harm in making enquiries about what Monzo was up to," he said. "Might turn something up. We can check the phone records for the ranger station, if you like. And it should be easy enough to find the girlfriend too. Do you want to go out to Tshane?"

Kubu shook his head. "Director Mabaku wants me back in Gaborone. Anyway, it's your case, and it should be coordinated here. But I'd like to stay involved. I feel we're starting to make progress."

They shook hands formally, and Kubu left to fetch his stuff from the Mokha Lodge.

He hated leaving just as the case was warming up. But the good part was that he was going home—home to his family.

Twelve

Gobiwasi stood up, steadying himself against the stunted tree that had been his shelter for the past six hours. The last two days had tested him to the limit. Physically, his seventy-year old body was nearly depleted. Mentally, he was determined, but the pain and the relentless heat were wearing away his resolve. One more day, and he would be there—at The Place—where he would appease the spirits and sleep his last sleep. He wondered whether he could stay alive long enough to reach it and die in peace.

He slung his leather hunting bag over his shoulder. It was his oldest friend, and its contents knew his entire history, had shared his whole life. From a time before he could remember, it had been with him—a gift from his grandfather. It had been with him when he had met his wife. It was on his back when he had made his pilgrimage to the sacred hills of Tsodilo, several weeks' walk to the north, where man was first born on this earth. It had seen every springbok and eland that he had hunted, run every mile in pursuit of the slowly dying prey. It had danced the dance of the ancestors, and been with him whenever he visited their world.

He picked up his spear. It had saved him on one of his first hunts, when a desperate hyena, a front paw lost in a skirmish over carrion, attacked him as he slept in the heat of the day. He had been lucky that he could pull the spear from his bag as he was being dragged away and plunge it into the shriveled stomach of the once proud animal. It had let him go and, rather than retaliating with traditional ferocity, had sat down, looked at him, and died with resignation and relief.

And this was his bow, used so many times to help feed his people. How many times had he hunted? He was too tired even to guess. And the arrows, so lovingly crafted into missiles of death, which enabled the Bushmen to survive in the harshest of environments. Their poison eventually downing the strongest of animals, whose deaths completed the circle of life.

He lifted the ostrich egg, dribbled the last drops of water onto his tongue, then placed it gently on the ground. For how many miles had it been his companion? How many times had it been his link to life?

He turned toward the hill in the distance, put emotion aside, and set off across the shimmering sand, walking, no longer able to run, clutching a large tuber that would provide his liquid for the day.

Gobiwasi rested in the shadow of a small blackthorn bush. The sun was low now, turning the dusty air into swirls of reds and purples. A few thin clouds shined gold before darkening to indigo.

He had been walking for three hours over the hot sand and was exhausted. Again, fear ran through him that he wouldn't reach The Place, which still looked far away, silhouetted against the sky. He gnawed on the tuber, relishing the moisture oozing onto his tongue. He didn't swallow it right away, but let it sit there as he anticipated it sliding into his body. He swirled it around in his mouth, then swallowed. He imagined it to be a long drink of water rather than merely a few drops of tuber sap. That made him feel better.

Finally he opened his hunting bag and unwrapped some *Hoodia* flesh and chewed it. From before anyone could remember, his people had used this plant to prepare for the hunt. It took away hunger and provided energy. Hunger was no longer important, but he needed the energy for the next few miles. Not long now before he could start his final journey.

He stood up, focusing on the distance still ahead, feeling the exhaustion. He admitted to himself that he needed help. Would his ancestors help him still? He put his hand into his hunting bag and pulled out a small animal horn, closed at one end with a cap of leather. Carefully he took the cap off and poured a small heap of the white powder onto his left hand. He licked his palm until all the powder was gone.

As he set off once more toward the hill on the horizon, Gobiwasi's mind wandered back to his first hunt. How old had he been? Twelve? Thirteen? His father had been teaching him how to stalk prey and hunt with bow and arrow and spear; had told him about poisons and about the importance of taking only what was needed, never more. Always leave something for whoever follows, his father had admonished. The desert is hard, and we must support each other.

As the drug crept into his brain, Gobiwasi's mind began

to spin and slowly left his body. Now he was crawling in the sand toward an eland, huge with horns that spiraled tightly to the sky. As he slithered closer, the eland grew even bigger and turned its head toward him. Its eyes, dark brown and sad, grew larger and larger and slowly sucked him in.

Now he was in the eland's mind, tumbling, rolling as a tree in a rare flood.

"What brings you here?" the eland asked.

"You bring life to our people," Gobiwasi whispered. "I have to know your thoughts."

"I have no thoughts. I am born; I survive; I protect my family."

"And if you do not survive?"

"Then I bring life to your people, or to the lions, or to the hyenas. And they survive."

"Are you not sad to die?"

"I do not feel. I am, or I am not. That is how it is."

Gobiwasi understood. His people were nearly the same. They lived to survive, and they survived to provide for themselves and each other. The one was insignificant against the whole. The one would always die to save the others.

Now Gobiwasi flew from the majestic beast back to the scorching sand. He stood up, and the eland turned and ran, dust trailing, into the mirages of the Kalahari. Gobiwasi raised his hand. We are brothers, he thought. And then there were a hundred eland running into the desert. And then a thousand. Then he too was running, running. Was he a man or an antelope? The pace got faster. He couldn't keep up.

Suddenly he fell.

Reality returned to Gobiwasi. He had stumbled over a small calcrete ridge. His heart was pounding. Looking back, he saw his tracks in the sand, not the stumbling tread of an old man, but the lope of a runner. He had been a runner once, and now he had run again. How long had he been dreaming? The hill was close now. Less than an hour to go. He put his head down and walked.

The light was nearly gone, and it was only the dark red of the western sky that allowed the aging Gobiwasi to see The Place. There would be no moon tonight. But in just a few minutes, he would be there.

He wondered about his own final journey. Would his ancestors welcome him? Or would they spurn him for what he had done? It had been his most difficult decision, torn between his people's age-old commitment to the sanctity of human life and his reverence for the spirits. Twelve years earlier, Gobiwasi had watched at The Place, moving from bush to bush, always invisible. Watched as a white man went in and out of the caves, disturbing the ancestors, chipping at the walls with the paintings. For two days he had waited his chance, following the man until he was far from The Place. Then Gobiwasi had done the unthinkable.

In the desert, he had taken a human life.

When he arrived at the base of the *koppies* that were The Place, Gobiwasi was exhausted, but relieved. Even in the dark, and after all the years, he soon found the cave with the spring and drank deeply. Then he found a sheltered place, arranged his blanket, and sat down. He gazed upward at his thousand ancestors, all looking at him. How often had they comforted him and guided him to safety? Tomorrow he would be one of them.

He finished what was left of the tuber and chewed his last piece of *Hoodia*. He would need energy for tomorrow. A good sleep was important. He was tempted to have more of the white powder, but decided against it. He would need what he had left for his last journey.

He lay down, pulled the blanket over his wizened body, and slept.

Gobiwasi was awake before the sun eased its way into the sky. Although exhausted from the walk, he had not slept well. There was too much to think about: long-past deeds, his family, and where today's journey would end. Dying did not worry him. It came to everyone. It was what happened thereafter that was of concern. How would his ancestors judge his life and his actions? Would they accept him even though he had killed another human? Would they understand why he had done it?

He wasn't used to resting when awake. Normally he would rise at once and be active around the camp. Today, however, he decided to lie where he was for a little longer. He needed to prepare for when he met his ancestors and justified his life. He wanted to be strong but humble, proud of his life but modest about his accomplishments.

He thought back to when the black men found their camp but a few days ago. And a Bushman, Khumanego was his name, had sought him out. The wrinkles on Gobiwasi's forehead deepened. The man seemed to be asking for help, for guidance. Who was this man? Had he been sent by the ancestors to talk to him? Perhaps he should have let him speak more, should have answered his questions. Gobiwasi shook his head slowly, his spirit weeping. Everything was changing. And he doubted it was for the better. He feared for his people. They might not survive.

◀▶ ◀▶ ◀▶

When the whole cliff face was covered in orange light, he rose and carefully folded his blanket. He had a long trip ahead today. He gazed one last time at the rising sun, to where his people and family were, dealing with his departure. Already the trees quivered and floated above the sand in huge pools of water. And animals sought shelter although it was still early.

He went to the cave with the spring and sipped only two scoops of water—enough for the trip. He walked toward one end of the hill. He had seen a scrawny shrub clinging to the cliff about halfway up. If there is a bush there, he thought, there will be a small cave behind that has nourished it over the years. Drips of water for the thirsty. Gobiwasi liked the idea of leaving from a place of plenty.

He scrambled up, pushed the branches aside and peered into the darkness, initially seeing only black. As the black eased into gray, he saw that it was as he had thought. Small, but big enough to lie down. Hidden from view, unlikely to be seen. And high enough to protect him from predators. Perfect, he thought. A good sign, he hoped. Perhaps the ancestors would forgive him.

He unfolded his blanket and spread it on the rocky floor. Then he slowly removed all the contents of his hunting bag and arranged them in a circle around the blanket. He placed two small leather-capped horns on the blanket, and gently put an arrow tip next to them. He thought back to the similar arrangement of the hunting bag and its contents that he had seen so many years before.

Finally, he picked up one of the small horns, poured the remaining white powder into his hand, and swallowed all of it. I am now ready to meet the ancestors, he thought. I am ready indeed. Then, he wrapped several strands of cocoons around his neck for his final dance. He looked around, pleased.

◀▶ ◀▶ ◀▶

The climb down from the cave was straightforward. He hoped that the final climb up would be as easy. That would depend on the conversation he was about to have. What if they are not pleased? He quickly banished the thought. I am proud of what I have done, of the man I have been.

He walked slowly to the middle of the hill and stopped on a flat, hard area directly in front of the cave of the spirits. How many others like me have stopped here too? he wondered. He turned toward the hill, his back to the sun, which was already fiery hot. The hill was now white; gone was the orange of earlier. Gobiwasi gazed up at the cave and began a slow dance, his cocoon necklaces rattling to his rhythm. For twenty minutes he shuffled backward and forward, side to side. He sang the songs of the gods, the songs of the ancestors.

When he stopped, he lowered his hands and waited. He did not know what to expect. Would the ancestors cast judgment now? Would he learn now what they thought of his life, where he was headed? Or would his future remain hidden until he left this earth and started his journey?

He stood and waited.

And the sun was cruel, even on his leathery skin.

He felt drained.

I must soon go to the cave, he thought. I cannot stand here much longer. I will have to trust.

He stood and waited some more. Weaker. Having difficulty standing.

"It is time!" he croaked. "I must leave."

He walked slowly to the far end of the hill where his journey would begin. He turned to the east and raised his hand, a final farewell to his family, to his people. He climbed carefully up to the cave, resting twice on the way. He pushed the bush aside, let his eyes adjust, and sat on the blanket, facing the entrance. A glimmer of light fell on his head. My ancestors must be able to see my face, he thought.

He took the top off the second horn and dipped his finger into the paste it contained. Thanking the plant from which the poison had come, he sucked the paste off his finger and repeated the process. Then he placed the horn back in the circle of his possessions.

He closed his eyes. The journey had started.

He smiled, lay back, crossed his hands on his chest, and waited to join his ancestors.

Part III

Ha ka /ku ⁻/arro i, au i k''auki ≠enna

It will strike us without our knowing it

Thirteen

Wolfgang Haake pulled his Toyota Land Cruiser into the Tshane police station, leaving the engine on to run the air conditioner, and sat for a few moments composing himself. He yanked off his floppy hat and used a handkerchief to wipe the sweat off his face, neck, and shaved head. He ran his tongue around his dry lips, feeling the prickle of his moustache and tasting the sweat-salt. Glancing into the rear of the vehicle, he saw shards of glass from the shattered back window all over the seat. He shrugged. He needed to clean it up and replace the window, but that would have to wait until he was back in Windhoek. He wanted to get out of Botswana as soon as he could.

At last he turned off the engine, climbed out of the vehicle, and made his way into the police station. "I'm Haake," he told the duty officer. "I'm the one who called in about being shot at. And about finding the murdered man."

◆ ◆ ◆

Detective Tau kept his vehicle on the two wheel ruts through the thick sand. Scorching air blew through the open windows. As he drove, he glanced at his passenger. The man wasn't big, but was wiry, strong, and darkly tanned. What had he been doing alone in the Kalahari? He said he liked to explore, to find places no one knew about except the Bushmen, and to follow the trails of the German explorers through the area using old maps. It sounded suspicious, but Tau expected foreigners to do strange things.

A Namibian of German descent—from Luderitz, according to his statement—Haake had entered Botswana four days ago at Mamuno to the northwest on the main Windhoek road. His passport confirmed that.

"What did you want to find out there?" Tau asked, nodding his head toward the driver's window and the Kalahari beyond.

"Solitude."

Tau glanced at Haake with a puzzled look. He didn't recognize the English word.

"I wasn't looking for anything. I wanted to be alone in the bush. By myself."

Tau thought about it. He had grown up in the village of Hukuntsi, about ten miles from Tshane. There was plenty of bush there. He wanted promotion to somewhere like Gaborone or Lobatse. It seemed only people from cities were attracted to the bush.

"Alone in the bush? That can be dangerous."

"Only if someone is shooting at you."

They were heading into the remotest part of the whole area. Yet it seemed there had been three people out there. Haake himself, and a white man who was now dead with his head bashed in, and a murderer. Not exactly the sort of solitude Haake had in mind, Tau thought.

Tau wasn't taking any chances. Haake's vehicle had been hit by two bullets—one through the back mudguard and one through the back window—so he'd brought along two armed constables. They were now speculating about Haake's single gold earring, assuming that because he was white and foreign he wouldn't understand Setswana. Tau, not so sure, told them to shut up.

"If you were off the road, how did you find the dead man? Was it just luck?"

"I was following my own tracks back to the road. It's easier and stops you getting to a dead end—bush too thick to push through, or a *donga*. So I was surprised to see another *bakkie* there, pretty much on the route I'd taken. And a tent. Of course I stopped to check who it was."

"And you found the body. Did you recognize him?"

Haake shook his head. "He was lying face down, and I didn't touch him. He was obviously dead. Back of his head smashed in. Blood all over the place. I didn't recognize his *bakkie* either." He gave Tau a grim look. "I started fiddling with my satellite phone. I was going to call you people from there. That's when I heard the first shot."

"You didn't see the shooter?"

"No! I got out of there as fast as I could. I'm not armed! I'm damn lucky. I could've been killed. Or the tires could've been hit. I didn't stop until I was back on the main road and made fucking sure no one was following me. That's when I called you."

Tau nodded. He'd asked Haake to wait on the main road, but the Namibian had insisted on driving to the safety of the police station. Still, he looked calm enough now. The two young constables in the back were giggling and chatting again—this time about their girls. Tau sighed, hoping it didn't come to a shootout.

"Slow down. I turned left off the road up ahead where that dry riverbed comes across the road."

Sure enough, when they got there they could see Haake's tracks turning off the dirt road into the sand river. A good way to travel if you know what you're doing. Haake apparently does, Tau thought with grudging respect. He stopped the vehicle and looked at the tracks in the sand. The easiest way to follow them was to drive with his wheels in them. He guessed that's what Haake had done on the way back also.

He shouted to the constables to get out, walk on either side, and be on their guard. The two young men shut up immediately and did as they were told without enthusiasm, their rifles cradled. It had dawned on them that they did not have the safest of assignments. Tau put the Land Rover into low range and slowly started following the tracks.

After half an hour the tracks turned right off the riverbed into the bush.

"Where were you going? You must've been heading somewhere."

Haake hesitated. "There's a hill about five miles away. You can't see it from here, but I thought it would have a good view of the surrounding area. Maybe interesting historical stuff. I was heading for that using my GPS."

"Did you find anything there?"

"No. The going was too hard. It was farther than I thought. So I found a nice ridge above the riverbed and explored there instead. I camped there for two nights and headed back to the road this morning."

Now they had to follow the tracks through the bush. It

required care, but wasn't difficult. Eventually they climbed a ridge and paused for a moment on the hard calcrete cap. From here they could see the group of hills that had interested Haake still some way off in the distance. On the far side of the ridge was a lake of fine Kalahari sand; Tau stayed in the grooves from Haake's vehicle to avoid getting stuck.

Ten minutes later, Haake turned to the detective. "His camp is just ahead. Maybe you should warn the constables."

Suddenly Tau stopped. A new set of tire tracks came in from the right and converged with Haake's. Did they have something to do with the murder? he wondered. Ahead, through the trees, he spotted a parked truck. He edged toward it, stopped fifty yards away, and looked around.

"Okay. You stay here, Rra Haake. Therapo will stay with you. Lato, you and I will take a look around."

Tau got out into the sweltering sun, pulled his gun from its holster, and told Lato to keep his eyes open for an ambush. Gingerly they walked toward the one-man tent. Lying on the sand in front of it was the body of a man, bloated after the hours in the sun and crawling with flies and other insects. They gave it a disgusting illusion of movement. There were marks of sharp teeth and tears at one of the arms. The scavengers had begun their work.

Suddenly there was a movement in the bush, and Lato jerked up his gun, hands unsteady. But it was only a jackal scurrying away into the bush.

Tau turned back to the body, trying not to gag from the awful stench. The back of the man's head was a mass of congealed blood. From the dent in the cranium, it looked as though he had been hit from behind and fallen face down into the sand.

A camp stool lay on its side; perhaps the man was sitting on it when he was attacked. A half-empty bottle of beer stood upright in the soft sand, and a cooler box lay on its side with torn food wrappers spread about. Some animal—probably the jackal or perhaps a baboon—had been investigating the provisions. The area around the body had been scuffed, probably to hide any footprints. Tau sighed. It was all pretty much as Haake had described it. They would need a senior CID person from Tsabong, forensics people, and maybe the pathologist from Gaborone. He would have to stay until they arrived. Once he was sure no one was about, and they had unpacked the gear from the Land Rover, Lato could drive Haake back to Tshane. He couldn't see any reason to keep the Namibian in the middle of the scorching desert.

They spent an hour carefully searching the area, photographing tire tracks and footprints, and looking for cartridge cases, which they didn't find. One of the constables stayed on guard all the time, but the only activity was the arrival of two hooded vultures, which took up hopeful residence in one of the nearby thorn trees.

Tau was intrigued by the number plate of the dead man's truck. A Namibian registration. He made careful notes, intent on doing a good job. This was a chance to be noticed, a chance to make a name for himself as a detective, maybe a chance to move to the city.

Fourteen

Late that afternoon, Kubu was preparing to leave his office. When he'd walked in the day before, after a relaxed weekend, he'd found an oppressive amount of work awaiting him. The week away in Tsabong, and the three days' leave afterward that he'd wrung out of Mabaku to be with Joy, had taken their toll. Reports, e-mails, meetings. The work I really enjoy, he thought sourly. It had taken him both days back in the office to catch up.

He'd called Lerako on Monday, first thing. Monzo's girlfriend in Tshane had been traced with little trouble, but it was a dead end. Her husband was a contract worker at the Orapa diamond mine, and a call confirmed that he had been there when Monzo was killed. And she was adamant that he didn't know about her affair and begged them to keep it that way lest they have another murder on their hands.

As for the issue of Monzo's bush trips, Kubu got the impression this was not high on Lerako's agenda.

And Kubu had decided not to call Khumanego to tell him that the footprints appeared to be fakes; he guessed that if he did so his next call would be from Cindy.

He checked his watch and started packing his briefcase. He'd managed to put off—at least for the moment—the full meal he'd promised to cook, and had weathered some acerbic comments from Joy. As a compromise, rather than sitting on the veranda while Joy cooked, he now joined her in the kitchen helping with small jobs and entertaining Tumi. Tonight she was doing a curry; he didn't want to be late.

His thoughts were interrupted by a knock on the door followed by the entry of the pathologist, Ian MacGregor. Ian was a Scotsman with slender, sensitive hands that were equally at home painting watercolors as they were exposing secrets at an autopsy. He and Kubu had been friends for many years.

"Ian! What brings you to my side of town?"

"I had to brief Edison for the inquest hearing on those two poisoned students. Two young lives thrown away. Tragic. Anyway I thought I'd pop in and see how you were getting on." Ian settled himself into Kubu's guest chair. "I've got the report on the Monzo business for you too. There's no doubt that the calcrete rock found in the gully was the murder weapon. It had traces of hair and tissue that matched those of the body, and so did the dried blood. And calcrete particles were recovered from Monzo's skull fracture."

Kubu nodded; this was no surprise.

"There's another issue I wanted to ask you about, Ian. Can you say anything about the angle of the blow? I'm interested in the physique of the murderer. Could it have been a Bushman?"

Ian took out his pipe, filled it with tobacco from a small tartan pouch and carefully pushed it down in the bowl with his thumb. Then he sucked on it contentedly while he thought. It was many years since he'd actually lit the tobacco.

"The wound is on the back of the head on the right. That indicates the assailant was probably right-handed. It's likely the blow came from behind, but not from a Bushman. Monzo was too tall. But, of course, there's another possibility. He could have been knocked out first with something like a crowbar, or a tire iron, or a *knobkierie*, and then battered with the rock in the same spot. That's possible. Otherwise it would've had to be a very powerful assailant."

They were interrupted by the telephone. It was the director's assistant, Miriam.

"Kubu, the director wants to see you at once. You better come right away." She sounded nervous. That was not good. She normally negotiated the choppy waters of the director's office as if they were pond calm.

"Thanks, Ian. I've got to see the boss. But this has been helpful."

Ian nodded, returned his pipe to his pocket, shook Kubu's hand, and left for home. Kubu headed to Mabaku's office.

The director was standing at the window watching the shadows lengthen on Kgale Hill. He returned to his desk and waved Kubu to a chair. Not a good sign either, Kubu thought.

When Mabaku spoke, his voice was taut, and there was no hint of the usual sarcasm.

"Kubu, you and I have a serious problem. There's been another murder out near Tshane. Seems like the same MO. But this time it's a foreign tourist, a white man from Namibia, they think. Another tourist spotted the body and was shot at."

"What happened?" Kubu was shocked. At least Mabaku had lumped the two of them together as the owners of the problem.

"That's all that Lerako told me. He had a call from the police in Tshane—Detective Tau. He's going up to the scene tomorrow. I told him to wait in Tshane until you join him at noon. I can't say he was delighted."

"You're sending me to Tshane?"

"Kubu, you're not thinking!" The temper Mabaku had been fighting to keep under control erupted. "You and that damned reporter talked me into letting you mess around with Lerako's case—mess up Lerako's case, it turned out. To make sure the Bushman suspects were fairly dealt with, you said. But you fell for the fake footprints that appeared so conveniently, and we released the men Lerako wanted to hold." Mabaku took a deep breath. "Then they disappear, and now two weeks later someone else is killed nearby in a similar way. What's the implication of that for you and me?"

Mabaku was right. Kubu hadn't thought it through. "But the cases may not be connected. . . ." Kubu petered out. Of course they were connected. Neither of them believed in coincidences. Kubu pulled himself together. "If I'm right, and Monzo was involved in some shady dealings out in the Kalahari, then the crimes could be related, but have nothing to do with the Bushmen."

"You better hope that's true! And more than that, you'd better be able to prove it. Because if this turns into a tourism disaster, and the Bushmen turn out to be the murderers, I'll be running a private security company, and you'll be demoted to constable—whatever your contacts in the media!"

Kubu tried to think of something reassuring to tell his boss, but Mabaku wasn't waiting.

"Be at Tshane police station at noon tomorrow. Lerako will take you to the murder scene. Work with him this time. And keep me informed of every development. Is that clear?"

Kubu went back to his office, the sun gone from his day. He should never have let Khumanego drag him into a political matter. But it was too late now. The Bushmen *had* to be innocent. He *had* to be right about that.

And the evening still lay ahead. He wasn't looking forward to telling Joy he was going away again. But I'll tell her it's just till the weekend, he decided.

He hoped that would be true. The case needed to be solved quickly. There was a murderer in the Kalahari and now he'd struck again.

Fifteen

When Kubu left at 6:00 a.m. the next morning, Joy and Tumi were fast asleep together. Joy must have got up during the night to feed the baby and brought her back to bed, but Kubu had no recollection of that. He wanted to say good-bye, but didn't want to wake them, so he brushed Joy's cheek with his lips. She didn't stir, but he thought she smiled slightly.

It was already broad daylight and the city was beginning to go about its business, but the traffic was light and he was soon out on the main road to Jwaneng. There he filled up the car and topped up on the breakfast of toast and jam that he'd had before he left home. Surprisingly, the fast-food place attached to the gas station actually served decent coffee, and he swallowed two cups before getting back on the road.

Kubu enjoyed long trips because it gave him a chance to play the CDs of his favorite operas and sing the baritone parts.

The miles flew past as he sang lustily. Strange, he thought, I'm off to investigate what seems to be another brutal murder in the middle of nowhere, but I'm happy. Well, it *is* my job. Still, he felt a twinge of guilt.

Four and a half hours later he reached Kang and filled up again. After his experience in Tsabong, he wasn't going to rely on the fuel supply in small towns in the Kalahari. Then he headed southwest toward the three towns of Tshane, Hukuntsi, and Lehututu, which formed a triangle around the pans of the Kgalagadi. Although it was a good road, he was struck by how few vehicles he encountered. It was exactly noon when he arrived at the small police station in Tshane. He recognized Lerako's Land Rover parked outside in the sun and sighed.

It was a hot, dusty drive, but Lerako was cheerful. "No doubt about this one, Kubu. Tau says the victim was hit from behind, hard enough to smash the skull. He's found the murder weapon too. Good man, Tau. Another chunk of calcrete. What do you make of that?" His good humor faded. "Still no sign of the Bushman suspects, however. They're lying low—once you gave them the chance to get away."

Kubu ignored the bait and just grunted. He'd hoped for lunch before they left, but Lerako had said they must go at once to have enough time at the murder scene before nightfall.

"Who is the victim?"

"We don't know yet. I told Tau not to disturb anything until Forensics got there."

Kubu nodded. He would've preferred a bit of a head start with that information, but couldn't really fault Lerako for wanting to prevent contamination of the scene.

When they arrived, it was well into the afternoon. Even so,

when they opened the car doors, heat engulfed them. Kubu took a few moments to drag himself from the vehicle and introduced himself to Tau. Then he stood bending his back for a few minutes to remove the cricks. Only then did he move toward the body, keeping his distance. Dead human bodies repelled him, especially ones that had been in the blazing sun for two days, even if covered by a tarpaulin.

With a grimace he asked Tau to expose the remains. He slipped a mask over his face and, breathing only through his mouth, he went in for a closer look. He nearly gagged as the stench reached him.

There was a severe dent in the skull, the result of a very heavy blow and that was almost certainly the cause of death. Once he and Lerako had viewed the corpse, they gave the forensics team the go-ahead to search the body.

Tau had found the calcrete lump some distance from the body. He'd left it in place carefully protected. Kubu took a good look. It was a large rock, hard to wield with the sort of force required to smash in someone's head. It would take a large hand to hold it, certainly not a Bushman's. It had a brown-red stain, very probably the dead man's blood, but Kubu was suspicious. He wouldn't use such an object to attack someone. But he said nothing to Lerako and Tau. Let Ian and the forensics people come to their own conclusions. He merely agreed that the rock could be collected and sealed in an evidence bag. Then they completed a careful tour of the area while the forensics people hunted for footprints and cartridge cases.

"We set up the tents over there," said Tau pointing a considerable distance away from the murder scene. Kubu noted with approval that one of Lerako's men had started a fire, and was preparing a three-legged pot of *pap* to go with meat. Hopefully there were also drinks that were merely warm rather than disgustingly hot.

"Have you found out who the victim is?" Kubu asked Tau.

"No. But probably he has identification on his body."

"Tell us about the man who discovered the body."

Tau fidgeted, realizing that this was a crucial point in the interview with the senior officers. He filled them in on what he'd learned from Haake.

"Why didn't you keep him here?" Lerako interjected.

"Did he say why he came to exactly this spot?" Kubu wanted to know.

Tau looked from the one to the other. At last he answered Lerako first. "He volunteered all the information, but wanted to get on home. And I didn't think we should hold him here at the scene where he'd been attacked. He made a full statement at the police station in Tshane."

"And why was he here?" Kubu repeated before Lerako could respond.

"He said he wasn't looking for anything in particular. I asked him about that very carefully, but he said he was just following an old map."

"Did you see the map?" Lerako again.

"No, I . . . I didn't ask to see it."

"Where did he get the map?" Kubu asked. Tau shook his head vaguely, but Kubu's thoughts had already moved on. "What exactly did he say about being shot at?"

Tau consulted his notes. "He went back to his vehicle to call for help—he has a satellite phone. Then he heard a shot, and it hit his vehicle. He took off as fast as he could, following his own tracks back through the bush. He called from the main road. I told him to wait, but he insisted on coming in to Tshane. He said he wasn't waiting out here alone with a murderer."

"Did he have any idea where the shots came from?"

"It was from behind the vehicle."

"How many shots did he hear?"

"He thinks he heard three, but he was concentrating on driving, and there was a lot of noise. Two hit the vehicle. One went through the body over the rear wheel, and the other smashed the back window."

"Did you find the bullets?"

"Just the one inside. I gave it to the forensics guys. The other one must've bounced off the chassis. It'll be in the sand somewhere." He hesitated. "One of our men looked through Haake's vehicle while he was taking us to the body, but found nothing else. So after Lato got Haake back to Tshane, we let him leave. He was in a hurry to get home to Windhoek, and it's a long way."

By this time the sun was setting, producing bands of golds and reds in the wispy, sterile clouds. The leader of the forensics group walked over and handed Kubu a travel wallet.

"From the dead man. His name is Joseph Krige. There's a passport and a Namibian driving license in it. We've taken prints off all three. We also found a portable Garmin GPS in one of his pockets."

Kubu looked through the wallet. Driving license, passport, some Namibian dollars and Botswana pula—several hundred of each—and a page of notes giving what looked like GPS coordinates against each of which was a short description of terrain, presumably at that location. What made them special? Why had Krige stopped at each and described it? Presumably the last referred to where they were now.

"We should check the GPS," Kubu said to the forensics man. "With luck it will tell us exactly where he's been on this trip. Better search the *bakkie* again in the morning; it's getting too dark now." He flipped through the passport. Krige had crossed the border at Mamuno three days before.

"When did Haake cross from Namibia?" he asked Tau.

"Four days ago."

Kubu passed the wallet to Lerako, who made a show of going through it much more thoroughly, studying every page of the passport.

"Anything else?" Kubu asked the forensics people.

"We've identified the tracks from Krige's vehicle and where Haake drove out and came back. And the police vehicles, of course. But no other set of vehicle tracks. Of course they could be anywhere out there if the murderer stopped some distance away."

"What about footprints?"

"Well, there are some from the shoes that Krige was wearing—quite distinctive. There are also some others that must be from this Haake person. There are plenty around where he parked his vehicle, but there are a few behind the tent that look similar. Smooth sole, about size ten. Most have been smudged over. Deliberately I'd say."

Immediately Kubu was excited. "Let's take a look."

The man from Forensics led them carefully into the scene and pointed out several boot prints. As he had said, most were scuffed but one or two were quite clear. Kubu whistled.

"What do you think, Lerako?"

Lerako looked down without expression. "They're similar to the ones we think are Haake's. They're also similar to the ones near where Monzo was killed. More misdirection, I'm sure. It's those Bushmen all right!"

Kubu sighed. Turning back to the forensics man, he said, "Can you see where these prints go?"

The man shook his head. "These are the only ones we found away from the vehicle. The rest must've been smudged out."

Kubu nodded and stood staring down at the prints.

At last the forensics man interrupted his thoughts. "What do we do with the body?"

Kubu turned to Lerako. "We can't leave the body in the sun for another day, and it won't be fun guarding it from predators all night. I think they should bag it, and get it down to Gaborone tomorrow. Then we can see what our pathologist can discover in his laboratory." Lerako nodded, and the forensics team headed off to take care of that unpleasant business.

Kubu turned back to Tau, trying to integrate the clues. "There's no direct evidence of a third person here. Tau, what did your people make of the bullet and the bullet holes?"

Tau shrugged. They didn't have anyone at Tshane trained in forensics. He thought about the size of the hole in the vehicle, and held his thumb and forefinger close together to indicate the size. "Maybe a thirty-eight or a nine millimeter."

"Apart from looking for the bullets, did you search Haake's vehicle carefully?"

"We went through it," Tau replied uncomfortably.

Kubu grunted. "Let's eat. I'm ravenous. We skipped lunch." This wasn't quite true since Lerako had supplied sandwiches, but Kubu regarded those as a snack at best. Nevertheless, as the others headed toward the campfire, Kubu hung back and called Tau over to him so that they could talk privately as they walked.

"Our friend Detective Sergeant Lerako believes that the most likely culprit is the person you find at the scene of the crime, Detective Tau. Did that occur to you?"

Tau looked at Kubu, a little puzzled. "You mean Haake? But he was shot at. There's no doubt that was a bullet hole in his vehicle . . ."

"He could have done that himself. He murders Krige, then shoots at his own vehicle, and pretends that there was some third party involved. We haven't found any traces of anyone else."

"But Haake told me he was unarmed, and we didn't find a gun in his vehicle."

Kubu shook his head in frustration. "Don't you think he could've got rid of it before talking to you? And what about the license plate?"

"I wrote it down," Tau stammered. "It was also from Namibia."

"Didn't that seem strange to you? He's from the same place as Haake?"

Tau bit his lip, waiting, but Kubu said no more. At last he said it himself. "I should've kept him in Botswana, Rra. At least until you and Detective Sergeant Lerako arrived."

"I'm not saying he is the murderer, just that he's a possible suspect. So, yes, you should have kept him in Botswana. Tomorrow we'll scour the scene again for bullets, more evidence, whatever. But we're going to need a much more detailed interview with Rra Haake as soon as we can arrange it."

Then they caught up with the others, queuing for plates of *pappa le nama*.

Sixteen

"What do you want?" The clerk was surly. It was nearly closing time, and he wanted to cash up. It was drinking time in Windhoek. But the stocky man with the single gold earring, the only remaining customer in the vehicle registration office, took his time.

"I am selling my *bakkie*," Wolfgang Haake told him. "But I have lost the registration papers. I need another copy."

"You will need the proper form completed and signed, a receipt for payment, and have your identification. It's late now. You'd better do it tomorrow."

"I have all that." The man was carrying no papers, but he took out his wallet. He laid a one hundred Namibian dollar note on the counter. "As you see, here is the completed form." He matched it with another note. "Here I have the receipt you require." A third hundred joined the others. "And my ID, of course."

The clerk glanced around, but no one else was in sight. "It seems to be in order," he said, quickly gathering the money. "What is the *bakkie*'s registration number?"

Haake gave him a scrap of paper with a string of letters and digits written on it. The clerk nodded and searched for that number. After a few moments the printer started to hum. The clerk glanced at the truck owner's name on the printout and handed it over.

"Here you are, Mr. Krige."

Haake checked it, nodded, and left.

Haake took a bottle of whisky. It was Ilse's favorite, and he didn't mind it himself. People thought that because of his German upbringing he'd like schnapps, but actually he couldn't stand its motor-spirit harshness. He preferred something that slid comfortably down his throat. Something like a good whisky.

He let himself into the apartment. He had his own key. Ilse wouldn't be expecting him, but he didn't care. And if she was otherwise engaged, Haake wanted to know about it.

She was sitting on a threadbare sofa watching television in her nightdress. She still had a good figure, firm breasts, and adventurous hips. She watched her weight and walked everywhere for exercise. The door opening startled her, and she jumped to her feet.

"Oh, Wolfie, you scared me," she said in German. "I didn't expect you till next week. You said . . ."

"Yes, I know. But I came back early. Aren't you glad to see me?"

"Of course I am," she said, and kissed him. She felt the bottle through its paper bag and smiled. "Did you bring me a present? I have cold water and ice."

Quickly she cleared away the remains of a cheap take-out

supper and turned off the television. Haake liked the way Ilse's attention focused on him when he was around. He got good value for the rent he paid. And when they weren't together, they did whatever they liked. It was an arrangement that suited them both.

"Are you hungry?" she asked. "I have some wurst and some cheese and bread. Or I can cook something."

"The bread and stuff will be fine. I'll pour the Scotch."

He made her a tall drink with ice and water and poured himself a whisky on the rocks. She busied herself cutting bread, slicing the sausage and cheese. Moving up behind her, he pressed his body against her back and held her with his hands on her breasts, squeezing gently. She wriggled against him, dropped the knife and turned to kiss him.

"Shall we eat later, Wolfie? Afterwards?"

He laughed, liking her eagerness and the feel of her body rubbing against the hardness in his shorts. "No, I'm hungry, and we need to relax and have our drinks." She laughed too, and kissed him again hard, exploring his mouth and tongue. She pushed her breasts against his chest. Satisfied that he was completely aroused, she let him go and picked up her glass. "Right, eat and drink first," she said. She grinned and moved away from him.

Haake watched her appreciatively. She would tease him now, but when they made love she would be very accommodating.

Ilse flopped on the sofa with her whisky. "Bring the snacks over, Wolfie."

He brought his whisky and the plate to the sofa. Then he told her the news that he'd been keeping to himself ever since the trip to Botswana.

"I'm close, Ilse. I know I'm close. But I ran into some trouble. Had to get out of there in a hurry."

"What trouble?" she asked, nervous.

Wolfgang hesitated. "Someone has been following me. When I was in the bush, and I stopped to explore, on two occasions I heard another vehicle. It must have been following me. I was in the middle of nowhere. No one else would be out there. I think they know what I'm after, and they know I'm close. I'll be damned if I let them get one cent. I had the guts to stick with this, and no one's going to take it away from me."

"But who was it?"

"I know who was following me now. And I've got a pretty damn good idea who's behind it, and I'll find out for sure. But don't worry. It's sorted out."

"What happened?"

Wolfgang gave her a hard look. "I said it's sorted out. I don't think I'll have any more trouble. But I'll be ready for them if they try anything."

Ilse sipped her drink. Wolfgang had a short fuse and a nasty temper on occasion. She knew when he didn't want to be pushed. She said nothing, but he quickly regained momentum.

"Anyway, it's all looking good. I know I'm close. Damn close."

Ilse tried to look enthusiastic. She'd heard it all before, from this man and from others. The huge schools of fish to be caught at Walvis Bay, the massive uranium deposits hiding under the Namib Desert, the diamonds lying almost exposed on the beaches. The pot of gold at the end of the rainbow. Why couldn't they just be happy with what they had?

"You don't believe me. But now I've put it all together. Those idiots at the company couldn't see the forest for the trees." He laughed. "Hell, they couldn't even see the trees." He looked pleased and helped himself to another chunk of sausage. "And the samples I took! I tell you, it's there. I can almost touch it."

Ilse smiled. He's such a boy, she thought. They're all the same. Boys chasing their dreams. And if he does find his dream? Then what will become of me?

"I'm glad, Wolfie," she said, meaning it. He smiled back and offered her a slice of bread he'd lathered with butter and heaped with cheese. She shook her head and sipped her drink. She'd eaten enough. Her body was *her* pot of gold. She had to be careful as time went by. She'd put away some of the money he gave her too. Just in case. But Ilse was happy. Happiness comes from things being the same, she thought. Not from hoping things will get better, but from knowing that they won't get worse.

When she finished her drink she sat on his lap, licking whisky from his lips and moustache.

"Do you have to leave early?" she asked. Haake shook his head. She pulled her nightdress over her shoulders, tossed it to the floor. Then she unbuttoned his shirt and ran her hands over his chest, playing with the medal that always hung around his neck. He said it was a present from his paternal grandfather, who had earned it in the Great War, but she knew he'd never met the grandfather. So it must have been given to him by his father, but she'd never asked. No one dared ask him about his father, who had deserted his squat, thickening wife and his son and disappeared with a black woman.

"I'm glad you can stay," she said. Then she loosened his belt and started playing in his shorts with clever fingers.

Ilse woke at about 2:00 a.m. Haake was having a bad dream, talking aloud. He muttered something about a map, then about being followed, and a theft, something about death.

Suddenly he sat up. "You can't have it," he said clearly. "It belongs to me!"

"Wolfie, wake up. It's just a dream. A bad dream. Everything's all right. Nothing has been stolen."

Haake looked at her, but didn't seem to register her presence. After a moment, he dropped back on the bed and rolled over. A few minutes later he started to snore.

Ilse tried to get back to sleep too, but she was shaken by the strange event. Nothing like this had happened before with Wolfgang. Something was wrong. She tried to piece together what he'd said. Something about being followed. A map. Death. Someone trying to steal a map? He had never mentioned a map to her.

It doesn't concern you, Ilse, she told herself.

Eventually she abandoned her attempts to get back to sleep. She got up quietly, went to the living area, pulled on her nightdress, and put the kettle on the electric hot plate. Perhaps a cup of tea would help. While the water heated, she cleared up and picked up the rest of the discarded clothes from the floor. She felt the comforting bulk of Haake's wallet in the back pocket of his shorts. Almost without thinking, she took it out and opened it. Namibian and Botswana banknotes and change. She explored the side pockets. A picture of her! It was cut from a picture someone had taken of them together at a party. A credit card. A picture of his mother. And a folded piece of paper. It looked old, well used. She unfolded it to reveal a map, hand drawn in pencil, with a sketch of what appeared to be three *koppies*. Small circles dotted the faces of the hills, and one, near the bottom, had an arrow pointing to it with the letter *W* written next to it. Nearby there was what appeared to be a crack in the *koppie* face. It had an arrow with an *E*. On the back of the paper was another sketch, with regions filled in with different shadings and different patterns. Written in heavy letters at the bottom was *"Ich habe es hier gefunden!* HS." Who was HS and what had he found?

"What are you doing?"

Ilse swung round to see Haake standing naked in the bedroom doorway watching her, frowning, fists clenched. She could see he was furious, and she was very scared.

"You were talking in your sleep about a map. That someone was stealing it! I came to check that it was all right." Her voice was unsteady. "I didn't touch the money."

Frowning, Haake walked up to her and took the map. "This is priceless. Do you understand? No one is to know I have it. Do you understand? Tell no one about it."

"Yes, of course, Wolfie. I won't tell anyone. Ever. I'm sorry. I'm really sorry." She took his hand and held it to her breast, moving it so that he could feel the nipple through the silky fabric. He was still frowning, but seemed less angry. She rubbed against his crotch with her hip.

"Look," she said pointing. "He wants to play again. Me too. Come, let's go back to bed."

Haake folded the map and returned it to his wallet, which he took with him. He placed his free hand on Ilse's buttocks and steered her back to the bedroom. Minutes later she rushed out naked, laughing at Haake's amused protests, to still the whistling kettle.

Seventeen

I may never have to go on another diet if this keeps up, Kubu thought as Lerako stopped the Land Rover in front of the Tshane police station just after 4:00 p.m. *Pap* and an appalling watery stew for dinner last night, if one could call it dinner. And nothing to wash it down except warm water or instant coffee with powdered milk. Even a bad red wine would have been better. And if dinner was awful, yesterday's stale sandwiches for breakfast this morning were even worse. Even the diabolical instant coffee tasted good in comparison. And the final disappointment was that no one had brought anything for lunch.

"Lerako, I need some decent food! Lots of it and quickly!"

"Can't take roughing it in the bush?" Lerako grinned. "You wouldn't last long out here. I suppose that's why you have a cushy job in Gaborone. Big desk, paved roads, and lots of restaurants."

"You're right. This would be hell on earth for me. So where's the nearest restaurant?"

"It's where we're going to stay—the guest house in Hukuntsi. It's about ten miles away. Nowhere else worth eating at around here. I'll take you there. We can clean up and then eat. Can't have you telling the director that the detectives in the Kgalagadi district are inhospitable."

The morning had been fruitless. They had spent much of it scouring the area as far as several hundred yards from where Krige's body had been found. But nothing turned up. The killer had left no trace, not even footprints.

Kubu and Lerako could conceive of only two possible scenarios for this to happen. First, the killer could have covered his tracks so well that they didn't find them. Lerako favored this alternative, arguing that only Bushmen had the skills to deal with the desert and disappear without a trace. The second possibility was that Haake himself was the killer, but this seemed unlikely since he had reported the murder and now the police knew who he was. Why hadn't he simply disappeared back to Namibia?

Throughout the morning, Tau had worked hard, trying to regain favor. Now back at his office, he contacted the Namibian police in Windhoek, reporting Krige's death, giving them all the personal information he had. He asked them to locate Haake because Kubu wanted to question him. Tau then turned his attention to preparing a detailed report of the murder and crime scene.

The Endabeni Guest House was on the outskirts of Hukuntsi. Guests were welcomed by a concrete and plaster *gemsbok* mounted in a patch of sand. But it had no legs—perhaps they'd broken, or the sculptor had lost interest at that point—so it appeared to have been sucked in by quicksand.

The rooms were small and the furniture rudimentary. After washing his hands and face, Kubu went to eat. The restaurant was clean and boasted half a dozen Formica tables with stainless steel legs. A reed mat decorated with a small Botswana flag hung between the doors marked Gents and Ladies, and a couple of wooden carvings were scattered around the room. A glance at the other tables reassured Kubu that the portions were generous. Kubu ordered a rump steak—rare—and, in the absence of wine on the menu, two cans of Coke Zero. Lerako ordered goat stew and a glass of water.

"Tau has probably already been in touch with Windhoek," Lerako said. "He says they're pretty good. He's dealt with them before."

Kubu grunted, looking hopefully toward the kitchen door.

Lerako continued. "You have to admit now that letting the Bushmen go was a mistake."

"And you have to admit," Kubu retorted, "that you didn't have enough hard evidence to convict them! What was the motive? Everything was circumstantial. A murder weapon with no prints. No signs of a struggle. And what about the boot prints? Is it really likely that a group of nomadic Bushmen would carry a pair of heavy walking boots around the desert in case they wanted to commit a murder or two? Come on, Lerako."

He again turned to look at the kitchen door. *If it takes much longer, I'm going to have to go in and get the food myself.* "Look, Lerako, I would arrest them in a minute if I thought they'd done it."

Now it was Lerako's turn to grunt.

At that point Kubu's cell phone rang. It was his friend Ian MacGregor, the pathologist, calling from Gaborone.

"Kubu, good you're back in one piece. I got your message

about the murder down there. Sounds intriguing, but I'm glad you didn't need me to come out. I love the peace and quiet of the Kalahari, but I prefer to paint my watercolors in winter, not February."

Kubu didn't need to be reminded of the heat. "The body is probably in Gaborone already. They drove it there this morning. We think the man was hit from behind and collapsed forward—we took pictures, which we've sent you too—and the murder weapon was conveniently nearby. A big chunk of calcrete."

Kubu paused, waiting for Ian's off-the-cuff reaction.

"Calcrete. Wasn't that what was used in the other case? The game ranger?"

"So it seems."

"I suppose it's easy to find in the Kalahari. All those ridges."

"When will you have a chance to look at the body?"

"Not too busy at the moment. I'll call you as soon as I've examined it."

"Thanks. I must warn you that the body was in the sun for two days. It stinks!"

"I'm used to it. I've worked with worse than that. Anyway, I'll soak my mask in Scotch before I start!"

Kubu laughed and, after a few more pleasantries, hung up and turned his attention back to Lerako. Fortunately, at that moment, the waitress brought two large plates piled high with food, and the two men turned their attention to eating.

Eighteen

The next morning, after a good night's sleep and a decent breakfast, Kubu felt much better. And the large coffee in his hand was palatable.

"So where do we go from here?" he asked Lerako as he settled on one of the uncomfortable chairs in Tau's office. "You're in charge."

Lerako turned to Tau, who was sitting behind his desk, a little in awe of the other two, and still eager to please.

"Have you heard anything from Windhoek yet?"

"Yes, but not much." Tau pulled out his notebook. "Krige lived in Windhoek. The police have an address for him. The vehicle he was driving was his own."

"Anything else?"

"He's not married. He's divorced, but no children. The policeman I spoke to—a Detective Sergeant Helu—suggests we send someone to Windhoek and go through Krige's place with them. They're not sure what to look for."

Kubu interjected. "I can't believe that it's a coincidence he was found by Haake."

"What do you mean?" Tau asked, puzzled.

Kubu helped him. "Doesn't it seem a bit strange that one Namibian finds the body of another Namibian, far from anywhere, in the middle of Botswana?"

"I suppose so. That's why I should have asked Rra Haake to stay here until you arrived, right?"

Kubu nodded. "What do you think the next steps should be?"

"Umm. We should find Haake and question him?"

"Right. And before that?" Kubu glanced at Lerako, who was showing signs of impatience, and motioned him to relax.

Tau was quiet for several moments. "Maybe someone in Tshane or Hukuntsi saw Rra Krige before he headed to the desert?"

"Good. And?"

Another silence. Kubu was pleased that Lerako didn't interrupt.

"Maybe someone saw Rra Haake?"

"Good. And?"

Tau smiled. "And maybe someone saw them together!"

"Well done. You see detective work is not very difficult. You just have to think logically. Now, let's take it a step further. There are too many people in this area to ask everyone. So where would you start?"

Tau scratched his head. "Well, if you've driven a long way, and you're going south into the desert, you probably would spend the night. So I'd check all the accommodation and the campgrounds."

Kubu nodded.

Tau started to feel more confident. "And everyone stops for gas at the filling station in Hukuntsi. So I'd go there too."

"He's learning fast, isn't he, Lerako?" Kubu asked and was pleasantly surprised to see Lerako nodding.

"Okay," Lerako said sitting up straight in his chair. "Let's get organized. Tau, after this meeting, you go and see whether anyone has seen Krige or Haake. Report back to me this evening. I should be back in Tsabong by supper.

"Kubu, could you follow up with Forensics about Krige's GPS? Then let me know if there is anything of interest there." Kubu nodded in agreement.

"Then I think you should go to Windhoek. See if you can speak to Haake and work with the Namibian police. You've got more experience than me sifting through files and papers. Most of the cases in Kgalagadi are fairly straightforward. One man steals another's cow. Or wife. Or girlfriend. Has too much to drink—if he can afford it these days—and revenge seems sweet. One ends up dead or in hospital."

Kubu was surprised that Lerako would hand over the case so easily. He was soon set straight.

"While you're in Windhoek enjoying fine German beer and sausages, I'm going to find those Bushmen."

Before he could retort, Kubu's cell phone rang. It was Ian MacGregor.

"Ian! Don't tell me you've done the autopsy already! It's only ten thirty."

"I was awake early so I thought I'd get it over with. Anyway, I've some interesting news for you. Krige wasn't killed with the stone you found. The indentation in the skull wasn't consistent with its shape. It was more like a crater. More consistent with a blow from a *knobkierie*. You know the ones I mean—hard wood with a long handle and a round knob at the end. If you hit someone hard enough, it can crush the skull. The person who did it must have rubbed the rock in the wound or perhaps even hit the skull with it after Krige was unconscious, but the blow wasn't hard enough to change the shape of the fracture."

"Ian, think back to Monzo's death. You were sure that he was hit with the rock then, weren't you?"

"Yes. I double-checked because I knew you'd ask. Monzo's injury looks different. Doesn't have the same shape. But it's possible that the murderer knocked Monzo out and then bashed his head with the stone, changing the shape of the original wound. Anyway, it certainly looks like the murderer tried to make this killing look like the first. Who knew about Monzo's wounds?"

"The police, the park rangers, the Bushmen. We didn't try to keep it a secret. A comment or two over a beer, and anyone could've known." Kubu thought for a moment. "Was there any indication of a struggle?"

"No. There were no scratches or contusions anywhere. Nothing under his fingernails. I think he was hit from behind while sitting or standing. More likely sitting, from the location of the wound. It was just off center at the top of the skull—to the right. That may indicate a right-handed person hit him. Same as with Monzo. I also don't think he died immediately because there was a lot of blood around the wound and on his face. More likely he died shortly afterwards. But I suspect he never regained consciousness."

"If the assailant rubbed the rock in the wound, could he have left any fingerprints in the blood, or something we could get DNA from?"

"Hmm. I didn't see any fingerprints, but then I wasn't really looking for them. And the only likely source of DNA would be a hair, and I didn't see any that were different from Krige's. No black curly ones, for example, if you're thinking of the Bushmen."

"Time of death?"

"Pretty hard to say with any accuracy. Probably the night before the body was discovered, but it could have been a bit earlier even."

Kubu could see that Lerako was getting impatient, so he thanked Ian and asked him to fax a copy of the report to the Tshane police station.

"That was Dr. MacGregor, the pathologist." Kubu brought Lerako and Tau up to date with what Ian had told him. "So it seems the rock was misdirection as I suspected all along. Krige was probably killed with something like a *knobkierie.*"

"The sort of thing a Bushman would use," Lerako said, nodding.

Kubu lifted himself with some difficulty out of the uncomfortable chair.

"Well, I'll have to persuade the director that a trip to Windhoek is necessary. And he'll have to send someone up here with my passport. And then I'll have to placate my wife!"

Tau was pleased to have such an important role. He enlarged the photocopies he had made of Haake's passport. The pictures were grainy, but recognizable. And he made similar copies of Krige's passport and driver's license.

His first stop was the only accommodation in the immediate area—the Endabeni Guest House, where Kubu and Lerako had been staying. The Guest House was very small, and Tau was confident that the manager would remember all the guests who had recently stayed in its six rooms. If he learned nothing there, he'd have to make a trip to Kang, on the Trans-Kalahari Highway, where there were several places travelers could stay.

After the important introductory pleasantries, in which the two men shared information about mutual acquaintances, Tau showed the manager the photocopies.

"Rra, have either of these men stayed here in the past few weeks?"

The manager scrutinized the photos and pointed to the one of Haake.

"Yes, he was here about five or six days ago. He's stayed here several times before. I'll get the details for you. But I've not seen the other man. Why do you want to know?"

Tau gave an abbreviated account of what had happened, while the manager dug out the information.

"Here it is! Wolfgang Haake from Namibia. Didn't put any address other than that. And he didn't put down his license plate number either. I'll have to speak to the staff. Tell them to always make sure the forms are filled out properly."

"And you're sure that you haven't seen the other man?"

The manager nodded. "I remember all my guests."

Next Tau went to the gas station in Hukuntsi. It was the only place to refuel between Kang and Tsabong. Everyone filled up there before going into the desert.

As soon as he pulled in, an attendant with the slight build of a Bushman ran up, eager to be of service, eager for a tip. Tau recognized him.

"Fill up? Diesel? Clean windscreen?"

Tau shook his head. "Take a look at these, Willie. Have you seen either of these men?"

The attendant glanced at the policeman, and then looked at the pictures carefully. "This one," he said pointing to Haake, "is Rra Haake. He's from Namibia." He nodded to emphasize that. "The other one I haven't seen." He passed the pictures back to Tau.

"When did you see Haake?" Tau was excited.

Willie hesitated. "Maybe a week ago? He comes through here sometimes. That's why I know him. I don't know the other man." He shook his head firmly.

Tau thanked him and then asked each of the other attendants the same question. No one else recognized either Haake or Krige. Finally Tau went to the cashier inside. "Have you seen either of these men, Mma?" he asked. Again he was unsuccessful.

Tau felt deflated. After his success at the guest house, he'd been optimistic that his job would be over quickly. But then he had another thought.

"Mma," he asked, "how many cashiers are there?"

"Four or five," she answered. "We are open every day for sixteen hours."

"Do you have a list of when they will be here?"

She handed him a roster from behind the counter. "Do you have a copier?" he asked. She shook her head, so Tau copied the list into his notebook. He thanked her and left. He was going to have to come back several times over the next few days.

He drove back to the police station to call Lerako, who was on his way back to Tsabong. Tau knew he'd have to wait several hours, but wait he would. He wanted Lerako to notice how well he was doing.

Nineteen

Kubu decided to split the trip to Windhoek over two days. He only received his passport at midday on Saturday, and he wasn't keen to drive at night. Cattle and game often wandered onto the road and became transfixed by oncoming headlights, resulting in serious accidents and even deaths—of drivers as well as animals. So he would spend the night in Ghanzi and drive to Windhoek the next day.

The sun was dropping through a purple haze as Kubu pulled into the Kalahari Arms Hotel in Ghanzi. He quickly checked in, asking for a chalet as far from the raucous swimming pool as possible. He dropped off his luggage in the room and returned for food and drink. He settled himself on the terrace under the cloudless sky and ordered a beer, instead of his normal chilled white wine. A beer seemed the remedy to wash the dust from his mouth; the wine would come afterward.

An hour and a half later, Kubu felt better. The steak had been very tasty and cooked as he'd requested—rare, of course. The vegetables were not overcooked, and he was delighted to find that the merlot he'd ordered had been slightly chilled to ward off the desert heat. He was impressed.

After ten minutes in a cool shower, Kubu went to bed and didn't wake until sunlight pushed its way through the thin curtains.

It was mid-afternoon by the time Kubu reached the Namibian police headquarters in Windhoek. When he arrived at the building, he was escorted to the office of Detective Sergeant Helu, one of the detectives in the Namibian Crime Investigation Department. Helu shook Kubu's hand and welcomed him to Namibia.

"Coffee, Assistant Superintendent?"

"Please. Thank you for meeting me on a Sunday when you should be with your family."

For several minutes Kubu described in detail all he knew about the deaths of Monzo and Krige. Helu listened carefully, taking detailed notes, and let Kubu finish before asking questions.

"Now, the man who found Krige's body—Haake—is also from Namibia?"

Kubu nodded.

"And you don't suspect him?"

"Well, there's nothing else linking the two of them at the moment. The only thing that worries me is the coincidence of one Namibian finding another Namibian dead in the middle of the Kalahari Desert. Coincidences always worry me." Now it was Helu's turn to nod. "Anyway, I want to talk to him while I'm in Namibia if I can."

"I've already set it up. Your man Tau gave me his cell phone number. He's coming in tomorrow morning at nine."

"I thought he lived in Luderitz?"

"I asked him about that—he owns a house there and has rented part of it out ever since he moved to Windhoek three years ago. Never bothered to change his address."

"Thanks for arranging that. I don't expect to learn much, but you can never tell."

"No problem." Helu shrugged. "Your detective sergeant in, uh—what is the name of the town?"

"Tsabong."

"So, it looks as though he may be right about the Bushmen?"

Kubu shook his head. "My intuition tells me they aren't involved. There's almost no evidence they did it. But, I have to admit, there is no evidence at all that there was anyone else at the scene of Monzo's murder. It's a real puzzle."

The two men sat in silence for a few moments.

"Thank you for your quick response to our query about Krige," Kubu continued. "What else have you found out? I really need your help to dig into his affairs. Maybe something will pop out that will help us."

"We traced his mother. His father is dead apparently. Anyway, we called her and gave her the bad news. She was very upset, of course. I said we'd call her back after we got more information. She wants to know what's happened to her son's body. She wants to bury him here in Windhoek."

"I'll contact the pathologist," Kubu responded. "I'll let you know when he's likely to be finished with the body."

"We asked her about her son. All she said was that he had his own business. Wasn't sure what it was. Anyway, his apartment isn't far. Why don't I drive you over there and we can take a look?"

After picking up the keys from the caretaker, Helu opened the security gate and then the door to Krige's apartment. "We have some petty crime in this area," he commented.

The apartment had two small bedrooms, one of which was used as an office. The dining room and lounge were in a single area, bounded on one side by a tiny kitchen and on the other by sliding glass doors opening onto a small balcony. Kubu looked at the contents of a glass-fronted cabinet—family photographs, pewter tankards, decorative saucers, a large tankard with the letters HB in blue, and some medals with ribbons. On one wall hung a faded print of a castle in a forest and two tatty photographs of *gemsbok* in the desert. Not an art lover, thought Kubu. And not married, given the very masculine flavor of the living area.

"You go through his desk, and I'll take a look at his filing cabinet." Kubu pulled a chair in front of a green four-drawer cabinet. Although it had a lock, the drawers slid open easily; none of them were labeled even though they had label holders. Helu rifled through the drawers of the large wooden desk.

Kubu started at the top and began flipping through the files. After a few minutes, he turned to Helu and said, "Krige was a private investigator. Look here."

He passed Helu a sheet of paper from the first file. "See, he had to locate this person. This is the letter telling the client where to find him. The second is the same thing. The third is different. Take a look at these!"

He handed Helu a sheaf of photos of a balding man with a young blond girl. The Namibian detective flipped through them and whistled.

"I'd say he's screwing around behind his wife's back," he said, handing the photos back.

"You're right," Kubu said, reading a letter from the file. "Mrs. Vorback wants all the dirt, and quickly. She wants to take him to the cleaners, it looks like." He extracted another letter. "And here's his report." He paused as he scanned the letter. "Vorback's been very naughty. There wasn't only one, it seems. I'm sure this divorce got very messy."

"So how can we find who Krige was working for in Botswana? If he was working for someone."

Kubu sighed. "We may have to go through all of these files one by one. And then we still may not know any more. What have you found?"

"Nothing much in the drawers. The usual: pens and pencils and stuff. He has a desk diary on top though—almost like a blotter—with names and times on it."

"What's there for last week?"

"A line starting on the twenty-sixth of February for a week with the name Muller."

Kubu flipped through the files. "Nothing under that name. Give me a couple of other names from the diary."

"Okay. On the seventh, there's the entry 'Dorfmann.'"

Kubu found the Dorfmann file and opened it. "Looks like a bad loan. Trying to find the guy who owes Dorfmann twenty-five thousand Namibian dollars. Here's the final letter, dated the seventh, and there's an invoice attached for one thousand Namibian. He found the guy."

Together Helu and Kubu went through several of the names in the diary. In all cases, there was a folder with a final letter and an invoice.

"I've got an idea," Kubu said. "A trip to Botswana is a big

job. If I were Krige, I'd get an advance. Can you get his bank records?"

"That should be no problem. Should I get his phone records too?"

"Good idea. Then we can fit a few of these pieces together. Can you have one of your guys come in here and make a list of all the names on the files and the date the final letter was sent, as well as the invoice amount? Shouldn't take too long. You can ignore ones that are over a year old. It looks as though there are only about sixty or seventy files total."

"I'll get someone in here early tomorrow. If we're lucky, we could have all that information tomorrow by lunch."

Kubu looked at his watch. It was already nearly 6:00 p.m.

"Well, if there's nothing else we can do now, we may as well go and have a drink. Care to join me?"

Helu nodded. "Let's go and have a beer, and I can tell you what the best eating places are."

The two drove in Helu's car to Joe's Beerhouse—a Windhoek fixture, according to Helu. "Even locals come here," he said. Kubu smiled, looking forward to the evening.

Kubu didn't sleep well. He kept waking up thinking of Joy or Krige or Haake. At about 7:00 a.m. he decided to take a walk around the city center to find an appropriate place to eat.

After a decent breakfast with steak, tomato, fried potato, and eggs, not to mention the toast and jam, Kubu walked over to the police station at about 8:30 a.m. He was looking forward to meeting Wolfgang Haake.

When Kubu arrived at the police station, Helu met him and handed him a piece of paper.

"Here's the list from the files. And I'm getting the necessary authority to get the phone and bank records. One of my guys is working on that right now. Anyway, come along. Haake's waiting for you in one of the conference rooms."

"Will you join us?"

"No thanks." Helu shook his head. "It's your case, and I've a lot to do."

Kubu walked into the room, introduced himself, and shook hands with Haake. There was a tea tray on the table, and Haake had already helped himself. Kubu poured himself a cup and sat down, indicating to Haake to do the same.

"It must have been a shock to find a body in the desert, Mr. Haake," Kubu began.

"It certainly was. And more of a shock when I was shot at. I was really scared."

"I believe that. I read your statement, but please go through exactly what happened once again."

For the next few minutes Haake recounted what had happened in the desert, and Kubu noted that it matched the statement closely. There was a pause after Haake finished.

"I find it an amazing coincidence that you stumbled across the body in the middle of nowhere. How could that happen?"

"I've no idea. I went as far as I could, then turned round and followed my tracks back to the road. And when I came over that small rise, there he was."

"And you'd never seen him before?"

Haake shook his head. "I couldn't tell at the time. Krige was lying facedown in the sand. I didn't recognize his vehicle."

Kubu caught his breath. How did Haake know the dead man's name? He stood up and poured himself another cup of tea. He needed to proceed carefully.

He sat down again and passed Haake a copy of Krige's passport photo, watching Haake's face. "That's a photo of Krige. He's also from Windhoek. It's not such a big city, Mr. Haake. Are you sure you didn't know him?"

"I'm sure! Never seen him in my life."

Kubu took the photo back. "How did you know his name was Krige? I didn't mention his name."

Haake frowned. "I suppose I read it in the newspaper. Or maybe heard it on the radio. A Namibian getting murdered in Botswana is big news."

"Think carefully. Can you remember exactly how you learned his name?"

"No. I don't remember things like that." Haake hesitated. "I think it was on the radio." He shrugged. "Do you know why he was in Botswana?"

Kubu had to decide whether to keep pushing on the name issue or to check it later. He chose the latter route. He knows something that he's not telling me, Kubu thought.

He shook his head. "We are still checking him out. We expect to have more details in the near future." Kubu turned the page of his notebook. "When you saw the dead man, did you go up to the body?"

"I took a look and then went straight back to my vehicle. To call your people."

"Were you ever behind Krige's tent?"

"No, I walked towards the body and then ran back."

"In that case, how do you explain the fact that we found footprints that matched yours on the far side of the body?"

For a moment Haake looked nonplussed. Then he burst out, "Well that was probably the man who shot at me! Lots of boot prints would look the same. It's obvious!"

Kubu nodded, and said nothing for a few moments. Then he changed tack.

"What do you do for a living, Mr. Haake?"

"I'm a geologist and have worked for a number of companies in Namibia. At the moment I'm between jobs. Enjoying my freedom."

"What were you doing in Botswana?"

"I love the desert and love going where there's nobody around. Solitude—that's what I look for."

"Why not in Namibia? There's plenty of space for solitude here."

"True. But I like to follow the trails of old explorers, especially the Germans. And Botswana appeals to me for some reason."

Kubu decided to push him. "What were you looking for, Mr. Haake?"

Haake frowned. "I told you—solitude. I was exploring."

"Mr. Haake. I don't believe you. You told Detective Tau that you were following a map. What were you really looking for?"

Haake shifted in his seat. "Detective Tau's got it wrong. I said I often follow old maps. I've told you already. I follow the trails of old explorers." He stood up and poured another cup of tea. Kubu could see he was agitated.

"Tell me more about these maps."

"They're just old maps. Nothing specific. I get some from the library. Some from old books by explorers. It's interesting to follow where they went, imagining their difficulties and bravery."

"Did you have one with you on this trip?"

Haake shook his head. "No, I was just wandering around."

"Let's return to Krige. Is it possible that he was looking for you?"

"Why would he do that?"

"He was a private investigator."

Haake gave him a strange look. "He was? I can't imagine why he'd be looking for me. Much more likely he was tracking the person who killed him. Maybe he found him, and the killer didn't want to be found."

Kubu nodded. That possibility had occurred to him also.

"Where do you live, Mr. Haake?"

Haake hesitated before answering. "I have a house in Luderitz."

"How about last night? I'm sure you didn't fly up from Luderitz just to see me. And tonight? Where will you stay tonight?"

Another hesitation. "I stay with a friend here in Windhoek."

"And the address, Mr. Haake?"

"My friend's got nothing to do with this."

"That may be true. I just want the address, please. And I wouldn't play games if I were you."

Haake jumped to his feet. "What the fuck is going on here?" he shouted. "You're treating me like a fucking criminal. I could've left the body in the desert, and no one would've known any better."

"I'm not treating you like a criminal, Mr. Haake. You're behaving like one. What are you hiding?"

"I don't have to answer your questions!"

"That's true, Mr. Haake. But if I suggest to the Namibian police that you're a suspect in a murder, you *will* have to answer questions. All I want is the address where you're staying. That's not difficult, is it?"

Haake glared at Kubu. He spat out the address. "Now can I go?"

"Yes, Mr. Haake. Thank you for your time." Kubu heaved himself out of his chair and offered his hand. After a moment's hesitation, Haake shook it.

"How often do you go to Botswana?" Kubu asked as they walked to the door.

"Once every month or two."

"Always to the same place?"

Haake shook his head. "I go to a lot of different places. Botswana's got plenty of interesting areas."

"Do you ever run into Bushmen?"

"No. They're all in settlements now, aren't they? None roam around anymore like they used to, do they?"

Kubu didn't answer that. "I hope you find your solitude, Mr. Haake," he said.

Kubu sat thinking about Haake. He's got a quick temper, he thought. Still, he said nothing that made me suspicious, except that he volunteered Krige's name. And I didn't feel he was really surprised about Krige being a private investigator. But maybe it *was* just a coincidence that both he and Krige were from Namibia. He shook his head. Sometimes there are coincidences.

At that moment Helu walked in.

Kubu sighed. "I didn't make any progress. I think Haake's clean. But do me a favor, please. Can you check whether there've been any radio, TV, or newspaper reports of Krige's death? Haake knew Krige's name even though I never mentioned it." Helu's face expressed surprise, and he promised to find out. "Also can you find out who lives at this address?

Haake says he stays with a friend there. He didn't want to give me the address. I'd like to know why not." He scribbled the address Haake had given him onto a slip of paper.

"Finally, is there an office I can use?" he asked, wanting some time alone.

Helu showed Kubu to a vacant office and told him to use the phone as much as he wanted. Kubu shut the door, took his shoes off, put his feet on the desk, and closed his eyes. Not to sleep, of course, but to let his subconscious massage the few known facts in the case.

After lunch Helu walked into Kubu's office.

"The address Haake gave you—it's an apartment, which he rents but, according to the manager, a young woman lives there. He's not sure whether she's Haake's girlfriend—he stays there quite often—but she has occasional visitors when he's away on business. Her name is Ilse Burger, and she's a part-time receptionist. No record. And we did release Krige's name to the press after we'd spoken to his mother, but now we'll have to check to see whether they used it and when."

Helu tossed a piece of paper onto the desk, and Kubu glanced at it. It confirmed the address Haake had given him, as well as the details Helu had told him. There was also a phone number, which Kubu assumed was for the apartment.

With nothing left to do, Kubu wandered around the city center before returning to his hotel. He called Joy and told her he would be back on Thursday evening. He hoped he was right and that he wouldn't have to disappoint her again.

On Tuesday morning there was indeed progress. Helu met Kubu shortly after 9:00 a.m. with a big smile. "I've got the bank statements and phone records. And amazingly quickly. Normally they'd take a week to get to me."

He sat down next to Kubu and they compared the most recent bank statement with the list of payments recorded in Krige's files. All the large deposits checked out except the last one, an amount of N$10,000.

"What's the date of the deposit?" asked Kubu.

Helu checked it. "Friday, twenty-fifth of February."

"That's just a few days before he left for Botswana. Who paid it to him?"

It took Helu some time to get that information, while Kubu waited impatiently wishing he was doing the job himself. At last Helu hung up the phone and turned to him.

"It's an operation called the Namib Mining Company. Never heard of them. And I'm sure that Krige didn't have a recent case file for them. But we'll check again."

Kubu was already exploring the telephone directory. "They're here in Windhoek. Let's give them a call."

Finding the right person and persuading her to give the information they wanted over the phone didn't take long. Kubu hung up and turned to Helu with a disappointed grunt.

"The person who authorized that payment is a Mr. Muller—Henk Muller. The same name as on the diary. He's their managing director. But he's in South Africa until tonight and not reachable there. And we *still* don't know why Krige was hired, if he was hired at all. Muller's secretary told me Muller would be in at about nine tomorrow morning, so I made an appointment with her." He flipped through the file of papers. "Let's look at those phone records." Sure enough, they found several calls from Krige to the mining company in the two weeks before his trip.

"I'm sure this is why Krige went to Botswana, Helu. Would you check your database for Muller and this company? See if there is anything on them?"

He climbed to his feet and started to pace. How was he going to wait until the next morning to find out?

Twenty

Tau had returned to the gas station several times since his first visit. To no avail. None of the cashiers or attendants remembered either of the men in the pictures he showed them.

Now it was Wednesday morning, and Tau hoped the last of the cashiers was going to be on duty. He'd discovered that the roster he'd so carefully copied was only a guideline of who would be on duty when. The reality was quite different.

"Hello, Mma," Tau said politely to the cashier. "Have you seen either of these two men recently?" He handed her the two photographs.

"Hmm. They look familiar. I think they were here about a week ago. Maybe two weeks." Tau's heart jumped—she knew them!

"Were they together?"

"No. I don't think so. One came in around lunch. This one

came in later in the afternoon." She pointed at the picture of Krige.

"Did he say anything to you?"

"No. Bought some gas and bottled water, then left."

"How do you remember that? You must have hundreds of customers."

"We don't get too many white customers. This one, he wanted sparkling water, but we were out of it. But he made me go into the back and check. Wasn't happy that we had none. What have they done?"

Tau pointed to the picture of Haake. "We just need to ask this one some questions. If he stops in again, please call me." Tau wrote his name and phone number on the copy of Haake's passport photo and left it on the counter.

Just as Tau was getting into his car, the cashier came running after him. "Rra Tau. Rra Tau. I just remembered. The man who came later did ask me something. He asked me if I'd seen this one." She waved Haake's photo in the air. "He also showed me a photo. On his camera. I'm sure it was the same man."

Tau jumped out of the car in excitement. The other detectives would be very pleased with him. He pulled out his notebook and laboriously took down all the details, ignoring the shouts of several customers wanting to pay for their gas. He checked that the attendant was sure which of the two men had asked about the other. It was definitely Krige who had asked about Haake. When he was finished, he thanked the woman, and she scuttled back inside to deal with a restless line of drivers.

Tau was ecstatic. He couldn't wait to get back to the station and call Lerako.

"They knew each other," he would say importantly. "Krige was looking for Haake."

Helu picked up Kubu punctually at quarter to nine and drove to the offices of the Namib Mining Company, which were situated close to Eros Airport. As far as he had been able to determine, Muller and the company were clean.

They were sipping coffee when Henk Muller walked in.

"Mr. Muller," the secretary said the moment he stepped in, "these gentlemen are from the police. They want to talk to you."

Muller frowned. "Come into my office." He held the door open. "Please sit down. What can I do for you?" He walked behind his desk, sat down and leaned back, arms folded.

"I'm Detective Sergeant Philemon Helu, and this is Assistant Superintendent David Bengu of the Botswana police." He turned to Kubu. "Why don't you explain why you are here?"

"Mr. Muller. Do you know a man by the name of Joseph Krige?"

Muller didn't answer immediately, but looked from one detective to the other.

"Yes. As a matter of fact, I do."

"How do you know him?"

"I recently hired him to do a small job for me."

"What sort of job?" Helu asked.

"Sonya," Muller shouted, "please bring me some coffee and get some more for the detectives. And get some cake as well."

He ran his fingers through his hair and put his elbows on the table.

"About three weeks ago, I discovered that some valuable

data was missing from one of our filing cabinets. Secret stuff. I suspected that it had been stolen by an employee we fired about six weeks ago. I hired Krige to see whether he could confirm that."

"Just what was actually taken?" Kubu asked.

"It was a folder containing several DVDs of data, as well as printouts of that information overlaid on maps."

"Why didn't you come to the police?" Helu snapped.

"As you know, we are in the mining business. We have a lot of highly confidential information about prospects, and I felt that . . ." Muller hesitated, "that I'd rather handle it myself. I felt I couldn't make accusations until I had hard evidence. I was planning to come to you when I had that evidence."

"Who was the employee you got rid of?" Kubu asked.

"It was a geologist who'd been with us for several years. Very good, but had no discipline. Often disappeared for days without telling anyone or filing for leave. Always said he was on company business. It's hard to check when people are in the field. His name is Wolfgang Haake."

Helu whistled in surprise, and Kubu sat upright in his chair.

"You know him?" Muller asked, puzzled at the reaction he had provoked. "How do you know him?"

Kubu took a deep breath and marshaled his thoughts.

"So let me be sure I understand what's going on. One: you had a geologist on staff—named Wolfgang Haake?"

Muller nodded, frowning.

"Two: you fired him because you thought he was abusing the leave policy?"

"Well, that. But mainly he wouldn't follow orders. He always had his own views on everything, so ignored what head office wanted him to do. Just went off and did his own thing."

"Okay. Then, three, a few weeks after he left, you noticed an important folder of information missing?"

Muller nodded again.

Kubu lifted his hand with four fingers extended. "Four, you suspected Haake and hired Krige to find out whether Haake had indeed stolen this data?"

"Yes!" Muller's frown deepened.

Kubu gathered his thoughts.

"What did Krige report back to you?"

"A couple of days after I hired him, he called and said he'd found Haake and was going to follow him. But I haven't heard from him since." He leaned forward, staring at Kubu. "Do you mind telling me what's going on?"

At that moment Sonya arrived with a tray of cups and three slices of chocolate cake. This is much better than mixed biscuits, Kubu thought. She handed each man a cup of coffee, offered them milk and sugar, and then passed the cake around. A silence descended for a few minutes, punctuated occasionally by the rattle of a cup against its saucer.

Helu got the meeting back on track. "What's going on here, Mr. Muller, is that Krige is dead, and the Botswana police think he was murdered."

"Krige dead? Murdered?" Muller leaned back, a shocked expression on his face. "And you think Haake did it?"

"We don't know who did it, Mr. Muller," Kubu replied. "We are trying to find out. Do you think Haake is the sort of person who would kill someone who was prying into his business?"

Muller didn't answer at first. "I don't think so. He has a short fuse, but I never thought of him as violent." He thought for a moment. "Mind you, he had some secret project of his own. He seemed obsessed by it. Some sort of huge mineral discovery, I think. But he would never talk about what it was. I think that was where the stolen company time went too. Maybe that's why he wanted the data." He shrugged. "You know, detectives, there are lots of people like him all over the world—looking for the pot of gold at the end of the rainbow. The trouble is that almost always it doesn't exist."

"And what was the information you had that he wanted?"

"It was a set of gravity data for a section of southwest Botswana."

"What's gravity data?" Helu asked.

"You fly an airplane low over the ground and measure the change in the earth's gravitational field. The changes are caused by different rock structures under the ground. You process it, and you can get an image of the gravity field over the area. By analyzing that you can often learn what is under the surface. All the big mining houses do it. It's very important in an area like the Kalahari because there's little outcrop. Everything's covered by sand." Kubu glanced at Helu, who shrugged—this was obviously way beyond him.

"When was Krige killed?" Muller asked.

"About a week ago, in a very remote part of Botswana. It looks as though he was following Haake. Maybe Haake spotted him and they got into a fight. Krige's skull was crushed."

"This is terrible," Muller said. "I feel as though I'm responsible. For hiring Krige to dig around Haake. If I hadn't done that he wouldn't be dead."

"You aren't responsible for what happened, Mr. Muller."

"There's something else I should mention. Haake called me on Friday, sounding angry. Told me he had nothing to do with this company anymore, and I should get off his back. I got angry too, and told him to return my data, and we'd call it quits. He was furious. Shouted at me. Told me to watch my back. I told him he could talk to me when he was willing to be polite. I thought nothing of it at the time. I told you he has a hot temper. But this changes all that."

Kubu leaned forward. "Did he mention Krige? Either by name or in terms of being followed?"

"He just said he knew I had someone watching him. That we were trying to steal his discoveries. That's all nonsense, of course. He doesn't have any discoveries to steal anyway."

Kubu nodded. "So Haake knew he was being followed, and knew—or guessed—that Krige worked for you."

"How did you know I hired Krige?"

"We found the deposit your company made into Krige's bank last week. It was a lot of money."

"It was important to find our confidential material, and that's what Krige asked for. I didn't think it was out of line."

After a few more questions, Kubu heaved himself to his feet. "Thank you for your time, Mr. Muller. Here's my card. If you hear from Haake again, please call me or Detective Sergeant Helu immediately. I think he could be dangerous. Don't meet with him alone." They shook hands and the two detectives left.

"Well, what do you think?" Helu asked as they stood in the sun outside the office building.

"Well, if Haake was the thief, he may've had a strong motive for murdering Krige. And apparently he knew Krige was following him. We need to interview him again at once. This time it won't be so friendly."

Helu nodded. "What about Muller himself?"

"I don't think he's involved. Do you?"

Helu shook his head.

As they were driving back to the police station, Kubu thought about Haake's call to Muller.

"Do me a favor. Take a picture of Haake and show it to the caretaker at Krige's apartment. It's a long shot, but maybe she'll recognize him." Kubu was interrupted by the ringing of his phone. He glanced at the caller ID.

"Lerako, I was just going to call you."

"Kubu, I have some important news. Tau found out that Krige knew Haake. Krige asked about him at the gas station in Hukuntsi a few days before he was murdered. You need to check this out with Haake. Have you interviewed him yet?"

"Yes, I interviewed him yesterday morning. I pushed quite hard, but felt that he didn't know Krige before finding him dead. However, he did know his name without me telling him. He said he got it from the radio. We're checking that, of course."

"Yes, but now we know Krige knew Haake."

"Knew *of* Haake is a better way to put it. Lerako, please tell Tau I'm pleased with his work in uncovering the Krige connection. But I have news for you too. Helu and I have just left the offices of a mining company that Haake used to work for. They think he stole some information from them before they fired him. So the company hired Krige to find out whether it was, in fact, Haake who stole the material and to try and get it back. *That*'s why Krige followed Haake into Botswana. And, after the murder, Haake called the head of the company and threatened him. I'm sure he guessed Krige was working for Muller."

There was a pause on the line. Kubu glanced at his phone's display to see whether he had lost the signal. He still had five bars. Obviously Lerako was taken aback by this development.

"Where's Haake now?" Lerako finally asked.

"We're just about to set up another interview with him. He has a lot more to answer to this time."

"Please call me as soon as you have more information." Lerako sounded despondent. He thinks that my discovery has blown his Bushman theory out of the water, Kubu thought.

"This may be a copycat murder, Lerako. Haake could've heard about Monzo from someone in Hukuntsi. We haven't tried to keep it secret, have we?"

"Okay. Let me know what you find out from Haake."

"I'll call you as soon as I've finished with him."

Kubu hung up. He had a premonition that finding Haake wasn't going to be easy.

Twenty-one

Haake was indeed difficult to find. There was no answer when Kubu rang his cell phone or the number where he said he'd been staying. There was no reply to several voicemail messages left at both numbers. And the Luderitz police reported that Haake hadn't returned to his home there.

Kubu persuaded Helu to check with Immigration at all the border posts between Namibia and both Botswana and South Africa. They also alerted Immigration at Windhoek's international airport.

Just before 5:00 p.m., Helu received a call from the woman staying in Haake's apartment.

"I'm Ilse Burger. You left a message to call you. Has something happened? What's going on?" She sounded scared. Helu switched the call to the speakerphone and motioned for Kubu to come closer.

"Ms. Burger, you are now on speakerphone. Assistant Superintendent Bengu from the Botswana police is also here. We're trying to find Wolfgang Haake. He was in here on Monday, and we have some more questions to ask him."

"He's not here. He left yesterday. Why do you want to see him?"

"Ms. Burger, we would like to speak to you face to face. We can be there in twenty minutes. Will you be there?"

"I suppose so. Is everything all right?"

"Thank you. We'll be there shortly." He pressed the button on the speakerphone and disconnected the call. "Come on, Kubu. Let's see if we can learn more about your Mr. Haake."

Ilse Burger opened the door immediately when Kubu and Helu arrived. She's very anxious, thought Kubu, as they shook hands. Must've been peering through the window waiting for our arrival.

"Come in, please. I've made some coffee. Would you like some?" She sounded tense.

Both detectives took her up on her offer. Helu settled himself on the sofa, and Kubu pulled out a dining-room chair, thinking it would be easier to get up from it. Ilse returned with mugs of black coffee and offered milk. Helu declined, and Kubu accepted. Kubu noticed that Ilse didn't pour herself a mug.

"How can I help you?" she asked, her eyes flitting from one man to the other.

Helu answered, pointing at Kubu. "Ms. Burger, Assistant Superintendent Bengu is from the Botswana police. He's investigating a case in Botswana and needs to talk to your friend, Wolfgang Haake."

Ilse didn't respond.

"Mr. Haake came to the police station on Monday so we could ask him about his last trip to Botswana. But it was only afterwards that we got some new information, and now we have follow-up questions. But we can't find him. He doesn't answer his phone, and hasn't returned our voicemail messages. Do you know where he is?"

"No. He left yesterday morning and said he'd be away for a week or two."

"Did he tell you where he was going?" Kubu asked.

"No. He just said he had business to take care of."

"What sort of business?"

"He's a geologist."

"He just got back from Botswana. Do you know what he was doing there?"

"Not really. He doesn't tell me about his work."

"How long have you known Mr. Haake, Ms. Burger?" Helu interjected.

"About four years."

"What's your relationship with him?"

"Well, it's his apartment, but I live here." She paused and frowned. "And he stays here when he's in town."

"Is he your boyfriend?"

Ilse hesitated. "I suppose so. But he probably has girlfriends in other places too."

"Why do you say that?"

"Well, he doesn't tell me much about what he does. He's quite secretive. I've always assumed that's because I'm not the only woman in his life."

"And you're okay with that?"

"He's very nice to me. I stay here for free, and we enjoy each other's company. He makes me laugh."

Kubu glanced around the room. The place was clean and tidy, and there was nothing extravagant. She's careful with money, he thought. He turned back to her.

"You're sure he hasn't said anything about what he's doing? Hasn't told you where he's going?"

"All I know is he goes to Botswana quite a lot. I think he's searching for something because he sometimes says he's nearly there. But I don't know where that is or what it means."

"And you don't know what it is he's looking for?"

"Well, he's a geologist, so I suppose it's gold or diamonds or something."

"And he's never talked to you about it? Never shown you anything? Samples, or something like that?"

Kubu noticed her body tense. She looked challengingly at Kubu. "No, nothing like that."

There is something, he thought. He decided to take a different approach.

"I appreciate your trying to help. But if there is anything you know that you haven't told us, please tell us. Even if it seems insignificant. Mr. Haake's life may be in danger. There've been several murders recently in Botswana around the area he was last seen. It's really important that we find him."

"Someone may kill him?"

"Ms. Burger, as I said there have been several murders, including someone from Namibia." He paused for effect. "And if Mr. Haake dies, what will happen to this apartment? To you?"

Ilse looked down. The detectives let the silence work on her.

Eventually, she looked up, wet-eyed, frightened.

"He's got a map."

"What sort of map?"

"I don't know. It's old and drawn by hand. It had something written in German. Something like 'I found it here.' With some initials. HS, I think. But I've no idea what the map is about."

"Can you describe it?"

"On one side, it looks like some of the geology maps he has. Contours and things. I don't understand them at all. On the other side, there was a drawing that looked like hills."

"When did you see it last?"

"About a week ago. I saw it in his wallet and took it out to see what it was. He saw me with it in my hand. He was very angry. Told me to tell no one. Please don't tell him I told you about it. He could throw me out of here. Please."

She'd be lucky if the only thing he did was evict her, Kubu thought.

"Thank you. Perhaps don't tell him that you mentioned it to us. We'll also be discreet." Kubu paged back in his notebook to see if he had missed anything. "Does he have any other friends?"

"Not that I know about. Just me."

"And enemies?"

"Not enemies, really. He has a few people he doesn't like—mainly people who disagree with him."

"What sort of people?"

"Well, he sometimes has very strong opinions on things. When people tell him he's crazy, he stops being their friend, or he gets angry with them. He's got a quick temper."

"Would he hurt someone who disagreed with him?"

"Oh, he might try to punch them or something, but nothing more."

"Are you sure about that?"

She nodded.

"Did he tell you anything at all about his last trip, Ms. Burger?"

"Not really. He told me he was close to finding whatever it is he's looking for. I don't think it's even real. Big dreams—that's all it is. Like all the other dreams people have. Winning the lottery, marrying someone handsome and rich. You know what I mean?"

"Did he tell you that he found a body?"

Ilse gasped. "A body? Whose body?"

"It was the body of someone who was following him."

"Oh no! And you think he killed him?"

"We didn't say that, Ms. Burger," Helu replied. "We just want to ask him some questions. You're sure you don't know where he is? He's not answering our calls."

"You'll have to wait until he comes back. I'll tell him to call you as soon as he can."

"Did he tell you he'd been fired from his last job?" Kubu asked.

"He wasn't fired. He left because his boss wouldn't listen to him. Wolfie said that he could have made both of them rich, and the company. But they just laughed at him. He didn't like that."

"Do you think he took the map from the company?"

"I don't know. He didn't even want me to see it. But it didn't look like the sort of map a company would have. It was in pencil on a piece of paper." She looked up at Kubu. "You're after the wrong man, Mr. Policeman. Wolfie would never kill anyone—even for diamonds or gold."

For a woman in a precarious position, Kubu thought, she's got a lot of grit.

Helu and Kubu asked a few more questions, but learned nothing more.

"Thank you for your help, Ms. Burger. If you think of anything else or if Mr. Haake contacts you, please call Detective Sergeant Helu immediately."

"What do you think?" Helu asked Kubu as they drove back to the police station.

"I'd like to get hold of that map. It might give us more information about where he's been in Botswana. Maybe Muller could check whether it's got anything to do with the data Haake stole. That would be a strong motivation."

"And the woman?"

"I'm sure she knows nothing important. She's a convenience for Haake. But if he's close to a big find in Botswana, he may not want anyone else to know about it. That could be a strong motive to get rid of someone who got too close."

"Or gets too close! We'd better find him quickly."

At about 6:30 p.m., Helu received a call from the Mamuno border post. Haake had driven through into Botswana at about 2:00 p.m. on the previous day.

"Perhaps he's back looking for the diamonds or whatever," Helu said to Kubu. "And he's not trying to hide his trail."

Kubu wondered about that. Obsessive people lose track of reality, he thought. Perhaps Haake is so focused on his discovery that he doesn't realize we'll find the connection with Namib Mining and come after him.

He turned to Helu. "This has changed from enquiry to manhunt. I'm going back to Gaborone tomorrow." He grabbed the phone and reached Lerako in Tsabong. He was to alert all police stations to be on the lookout for Haake and to treat him as dangerous. Lerako could use the photo from Haake's passport to make Wanted signs, which should be distributed throughout the southern Kalahari and to the border posts. It was very important to question Haake as soon as possible.

And, thought Kubu, it was important not to have any more bodies piling up.

Twenty-two

Lerako had tried everything he could think of, but he had nothing to show for it. He looked down his checklist. He'd contacted the Central Kalahari Game Reserve and asked them to look out for Bushmen they didn't know. He had contacted the resettlement villages outside the park and asked the officials there to show the villagers pictures of the three Bushman suspects. No one had recognized them. No one had been any help. But they wouldn't be, would they? he thought bitterly. They'll all stick together. He had alerted all the police stations. He had asked the charter pilots who regularly flew over the desert taking tourists to their comfortable camps to be on the lookout. Nothing.

The last item on the list was heavily underlined: <u>Helicopter search?</u> Mabaku had vetoed that until Lerako at least had direct evidence to link the Bushmen to one of the killings. So what else could he do? Explore on horseback? Or ride one of the camels that had served the Kalahari police so well in the old days? He thumped his fist on the desk in frustration.

But he had to admit to himself that part of his frustration was generated by Kubu's success in Namibia. While Kubu hadn't been able to corner Haake, he had discovered enough about Haake's motivation and movements—and his connection with Krige—to make the man a serious suspect. And there *was* something suspicious about Monzo's activities. Lerako rummaged on his desk and found Monzo's bank-account details. There was a variety of cash deposits scattered between his salary payments with no obvious pattern. They weren't large, but they were significant. And, of course, neither Vusi nor Marta knew anything about them. Lerako drummed his fingers on the desk.

Could Kubu be right? The assistant superintendent might be fat and sedentary, but he wasn't stupid. He'd allowed himself to be led by the nose by his activist Bushman friend from Lobatse and had fallen for the fake footprints, but his analysis of the cases made sense.

Coming to a decision, Lerako picked up the phone and called Tau in Tshane. Tau had found a crucial link between Haake and Krige. Maybe he could use his local contacts to come up with something else useful.

"Tau. It's Lerako. I want you to see if you can find out anything about what Monzo did on those bush trips. There is extra money in his account. Paid in cash. Just as the assistant superintendent thought. Ask around. See if anyone knows anything." Tau asked what he should do, but Lerako wanted him to use his initiative. "Do what you did last time. Think about who might know something and go and chat to them." He paused. "Just be careful. If Kubu is right, and Monzo was up to no good, this could be dangerous. And we don't want to scare anyone off." Lerako didn't really believe that was likely. He listened to Tau's enthusiastic suggestions for a moment, but then interrupted. "Yes, good, do that." He paused. "Nothing on the Bushman suspects, I suppose?" But there, Tau couldn't help.

Tau started at the scene of his first success, the Endabeni Guest House in Hukuntsi. Once more the manager was affable. He carefully examined the photographs of Monzo that Tau offered him.

"Yes, he used to come in sometimes and spend the night. Usually had a few people with him. Not hunters, but people who wanted to visit the desert." He shrugged. "Fine by me. Good money."

Tau could hardly believe his luck. "What was Monzo's connection with these people, Rra?"

"He was showing them around."

"What for?"

"Sometimes the tourists went with him on his field trips. Sometimes he took them someplace else they wanted to go. I don't want to say bad things about the dead, but everyone likes a little extra money, don't they? I suppose the government could spare him for a week or so."

"But how do you know all this, Rra?"

The man shrugged. "It wasn't a secret. I'd hear them talking in here, or planning what food to buy for the trip."

Tau made careful notes, partly to make sure he didn't miss anything and partly to give himself time to think of more questions. But he already had the answer he wanted. He knew what it was that Monzo did with his extra time in the bush, and where those mysterious cash deposits came from.

◁▷ ◁▷ ◁▷

Before he heard from Tau, Lerako had a visitor. He had met the man before—Tsabong was not a big place—but didn't much like him.

Craig de Wet was in charge of the mining prospect to the west of the town. Its owner trumpeted it as the world's largest kimberlite field, covering the remarkably large area of five thousand square miles. Lerako would have been more impressed if the prospect had generated a working mine and jobs, rather than simply PR. But De Wet was a straight talker, even if he talked too much. Lerako greeted him and offered him a seat.

"What can I do for you, Mr. de Wet?" he asked.

"Well, it's really the other way around." De Wet shoved a flyer across the desk. "My security people picked this up."

Lerako recognized it at once. It was the Wanted poster for Haake.

"Wolfgang Haake. You know the man?"

De Wet nodded. "Bloody nuisance. He was snooping around our mine. Taking samples on our lease! Can you beat that? And when we caught him, he had the cheek to tell us we were wasting our time, that this wasn't an important kimberlite! I was tempted to call your people and have him arrested for trespassing and prospecting without a license, but in the end I got a couple of our larger guys to throw him out." He paused. "They may have been a bit rough with him," he finished with satisfaction. "He took a punch at one of them. Couldn't expect them not to defend themselves, could you?"

Lerako sat back and digested this news.

"When did all this happen?"

De Wet thought about it. "About six or seven weeks ago."

So it wasn't part of the trip to Tshane. In that case, what had Haake been up to on the mine property?

"Do you know any more about what he was doing out here?"

De Wet shrugged. "We didn't exactly have a social chat. I think he was staying out at Berrybush. You could ask Jill."

Lerako nodded. "I think I'll do that," he said.

De Wet got up to go. "Remember, Detective, you owe me a beer."

Lerako headed northeast out of town. He could've just phoned Jill Thomas, owner of Berrybush Farm, but he liked her, and she would give him coffee. And his time was not in heavy demand right at the moment.

While he drove, he thought about the phone call from Tau. So Monzo had been moonlighting, showing tourists the desert instead of concentrating on his national park work. He might be fired, but it was hardly likely to get him killed. Unless, of course, he was guiding people who were not tourists at all, but criminals. Was it possible that he'd found out too much? Become a liability to someone dangerous?

He reached the clearly signed turnoff to Berrybush Farm. It was simply a dirt track heading into the arid landscape. Berrybush Farm attracted its share of tourists and business people, who preferred the guest farm setting and personal attention to the hotels in the town. Many of the guests became Jill's friends. Many had liked and respected her husband, who had been very well known in the area.

When he came to the border of her property, he had to stop. A herd of camels was crossing the track. Jill supplied them with the little water they needed, and let them wander through her piece of the desert. They were the remnant of the herds that had once been the police transport of the Kalahari.

When the herd had crossed, he drove past Jill's modest house with its one luxury—a small swimming pool shared with guests—and pulled up outside the main buildings. He got out of the car and wandered into the wide lounge that opened onto a covered veranda overlooking the desert scattered with the wild raisin shrubs that gave the farm its name. He found Jill watching a program on an elderly television set whose life support was an inverter attached to two car batteries.

Jill rose to greet him. "Detective Sergeant Lerako! What brings you to Berrybush? Want your camels back?" It was a standard joke between them.

Lerako laughed. "Not yet! You can keep them a while longer, Mma Jill. I just wanted to chat."

She nodded, knowing there was more to it than that. She settled him in a comfortable chair and went to make coffee. He watched her. She was past middle age, slim, and comfortable with herself. When he'd first met her, he thought it odd to find a single white woman living alone in the Kalahari. But as he got to know her, his opinion changed. She was of the desert, loved it, knew its peoples and its plants. It was impossible to imagine her anywhere else.

She brought the coffee and for a while they chatted. She told him she was pleased with the water reticulation from the town, which had recently replaced her well's supply. And the springbok herd was doing well; it had been a good lambing season. At last when the coffee was drained, she asked, "So who are you looking for this time, Detective? More smugglers or rustlers?"

Lerako shook his head. "I wanted to ask you about a Namibian. Evidently he was a guest here. A man called Haake. Wolfgang Haake."

She nodded. "Yes, he stayed here for two weeks. About two months ago, I think."

"What was he doing? Did he tell you?"

She met his eyes and held them. "He was quite secretive in a way, but he was very interested in the history of the area. Asked me all sorts of questions. He went out to the diamond mine. I told him he wouldn't be welcome out there, but he went anyway. Came back with a black eye and several bruises, and his wrist was swollen. I thought it might be broken, but it was just a sprain. I made him a sling, and he was all right after a few days. He had a temper, though. I wouldn't be surprised if he started it. He wouldn't hear of reporting it to the police. Or seeing a doctor. He insisted he would be fine."

"So he didn't tell you what he was doing here?"

She hesitated for a moment. "He didn't tell me, but I knew. When he'd been here for a while, he showed me a hand-drawn map . . ."

"A map?" Lerako exclaimed. Could it be the same one Kubu had mentioned? he wondered.

"Yes. But he wouldn't tell me what it was supposed to be, or where he'd got it. On one side it looked like a drawing of a few *koppies*, with some arrows and letters, and the other had what could have been a geology sketch. He wanted to know if I could help him find the area the map was supposed to represent. But I don't know about geology." She shrugged. "Anyway, it's all under the sand, isn't it?" Jill's gaze wandered past the *braai* area and out into the desert. "There's supposed to be a city buried out there too."

Lerako snorted. He didn't believe in old legends of lost cities and vanished cultures. He did believe in murderers, though. But Jill hadn't finished.

"I was sure I'd seen that map before, Detective. That's how I guessed what Haake was after."

Lerako was interested in that. "Where had you seen it?"

Jill sighed and thought for a moment. "Do you know the story of Hans Schwabe? He was a German prospector, also from Namibia—South West Africa it was then. It was more than fifty years ago. He was also after the diamonds. He was caught prospecting around the Kalahari where he wasn't allowed to be. That map was supposed to have been drawn by him.

"About twelve years ago a man named Herman Koch came out here. He wasn't secretive like Haake. He was trying to discover where all the alluvial diamonds of the Namibian coast come from. Nobody's ever found out. He actually thought it might be the big field of diamonds down the road here—the one that de Wet is trying to develop now—but it's not nearly rich enough. Anyway, I remember he showed us a map and told me it was drawn by this Schwabe. He knew Schwabe's family in Germany, and they had given it to him. The police here must have sent Schwabe's belongings to them after he died. My husband and I had just settled here, and neither of us could make anything of it. Seeing the map again jogged my memory, and I remembered the arrows pointing at the hills. I'm pretty sure it was the same map that Haake had." She shook her head. "I know you'll laugh at me, Detective, but I think that map is unlucky."

"Why do you say it's unlucky?" Lerako was intrigued.

"Well, Schwabe was supposed to have drawn the map, and he died in the desert. The rangers from the Kalahari Gemsbok Park in South Africa followed his car tracks and found it abandoned. Not long after that they found Schwabe himself dead of exposure out in the desert. They buried him there; you can still see his grave."

She waited a moment while Lerako digested that story. Then she continued: "Herman died too. That's why I remember the incident so well. It was shortly after he was here. He went up towards Mabuasehube. Some tourists found him at his camp. He was in a coma. They got him to hospital, but he never regained consciousness. So they could never ask him how it happened. The autopsy indicated he had died from some plant poison or other. There was some talk that the Bushmen killed him. But why would they do such a thing? Probably he ate something he shouldn't have.

"I don't know how Haake got the map after that. Maybe there was an auction of Herman's belongings—he told me he didn't have any family. Anyway, it seems to find its way to these prospectors with a fixation on fields of diamonds."

"Did you warn him?"

"Haake? I told him to be careful. That the areas he was exploring are remote, the most isolated parts of the Kalahari. It could be dangerous."

"And how did he react?"

"He was polite, but basically told me to mind my own business and that he knew what he was doing."

"Do you think he would kill someone who tried to stop this search of his, or to keep it secret?"

Jill thought about that for a while. At last she said, "I don't think he's a bad man, Detective, but I think it's possible. He has a filthy temper if you cross him."

They talked a little more, but Lerako learned nothing further. Haake had stayed for two weeks. He would sleep on a mattress on the concrete walkway that ran in front of the small block of rental units, finding it too hot inside the rooms. He liked the communal *braai* dinners, but kept to himself if there were guests he didn't know. And he disappeared off on day trips, but Jill didn't know where he had gone except for the day he went to the mine site.

Lerako readied himself to leave, but on a sudden impulse he asked, "Mma Jill, did you know Tawana Monzo from Mabuase-hube?"

She nodded. "Of course. It was awful about his accident."

Lerako sat back. "How come you knew him?"

"Well, sometimes he met people who spent a few days here. Took them on the next section of their trip. I suppose it was an arrangement with the game reserve."

"Was this often?"

"Well, from time to time. Over a few years."

Lerako rubbed his chin. So, he had confirmation of Tau's discovery. "We think it might not have been an accident," he said mildly.

Jill nodded. "I heard a rumor. Of a fight or something. Well, Monzo had a nasty temper too, as bad as Haake. Funny that they seemed to get on together."

Lerako had to ask her to repeat the last sentence. Then he said, "You mean they knew each other?"

"Monzo joined Haake the day he left. I think they were going off to explore some area together. Obviously Monzo had a much better knowledge of the Kalahari than I have."

"Please tell me exactly what happened. It could be important."

"Well, the day Haake left, Monzo joined us at breakfast time. He had driven from the game camp and hadn't had much to eat, so I gave him toast and marmalade while Haake had his omelet. They talked about an area they meant to go to. Monzo said they could get there in a couple of days, and Haake seemed quite excited. They had second cups of coffee, then Haake paid, thanked me very nicely for my help and trouble, and they left. That's all there was to it, I'm afraid."

Lerako leaned forward. "Did they look like old friends, or as though they'd just met?"

"I think they'd met before. Haake recognized Monzo as soon as he arrived. But they shook hands formally, not as though they were good friends or anything."

"Did you see either man again after that?"

She shook her head.

Lerako got to his feet. "Mma Jill, you've been a great help. And the coffee was excellent as always."

"You're welcome, Detective. Just don't steal any of my camels on your way out." She laughed.

Lerako drove slowly back to the main road, his mind testing out the new development of the link between Haake and Monzo. Two men with hot tempers and things to hide.

He didn't even notice a camel watching him superciliously from the side of the road.

Twenty-three

After the previous day's grueling drive back to Gaborone from Windhoek, Kubu came into the office late on Friday. It was only that afternoon that he heard what Lerako and Tau had discovered. Not only did the new information linking Monzo and Haake support his view of the murders, but he noticed a change in Lerako's attitude also. Lerako was coming around. The stone wall was crumbling.

And there was interesting news from Windhoek too.

He felt he had enough to take to Director Mabaku, and he wanted to share the story. Perhaps Mabaku could enjoy a pleasant weekend, also.

The director was dealing with e-mail and paperwork. How does he stand it? Kubu wondered. He must have three times the amount of administrative stuff that comes across my desk.

Mabaku swung round and gave Kubu a dubious look. "I hope you have something good to report for a change, Kubu."

Kubu settled himself into a chair without invitation and nodded. "I think we know what happened," he said. "Not all the details. But the outline. We can see the picture now."

"Who's 'we'?"

"Lerako and me."

"Lerako's in agreement with this?"

"Ninety percent, I'd say." He hesitated and shrugged. "Eighty at least."

Mabaku leaned back, looking more relaxed. "Let's hear it."

"It's Haake. We believe he's on a treasure hunt for the source of the Namibian coastal diamonds. It seems to have become a passion, perhaps an obsession. And he's afraid of anyone stealing his ideas. So when he discovered he was being followed on one of his exploring trips, he took action."

Kubu filled Mabaku in on Muller's story of the theft of the data, his hiring of the private investigator, Krige, and his recent phone call from Haake. "Krige would've needed to keep quite close to Haake, and we think that at some point Haake noticed him. That night—if Ian's right about the time of death—he doubled back, crept up on Krige, and killed him. He spent the night there and in the morning set up the fake shooting attack. The forensics people found ammunition in Krige's car, so we think he had a handgun with him, which we never found. Probably Haake did find it and used it to make it look as though another person shot at him. But his story falls down because there was no trace of a third person there. There are no footprints that we can't link to either Haake or Krige, and no sign of a third vehicle. The two of them must have been alone out there. Once we discovered the connection between them and understood what Haake was doing, we could see a motive. It was all pretty obvious."

Kubu paused and frowned. "The thing is, when I spoke to Haake, he was quite convincing. His story hung together and was pretty much what he told Tau. And, of course, he denied any knowledge of Krige. I knew he was hiding something, perhaps that his visits to Botswana had a more serious purpose than hobby trips. But nothing set off an alarm in my head. There was one thing, though. He used Krige's name before I mentioned it. When I asked him how he knew the name, he said he'd heard it on the radio. But he couldn't tell me where or when. The Namibian police have established that Krige's name did appear in the Windhoek newspaper on the Monday, but there'd been no report on the radio. What's more, when they showed Haake's picture to the caretaker at Krige's apartment building, she recognized him. On Thursday he came to the apartment building and asked her if she knew when Mr. Krige would be back. She told him Krige was away on one of his cases. She knew Krige was a PI, so Haake found that out and probably linked it to Muller. I'm sure that led to the threatening call to Muller."

Mabaku wanted to know more about Haake's motivation, and Kubu went over what they'd learned about his project from Muller, Ilse, and Jill. At last the director appeared satisfied.

"It seems to make sense," he said. "Certainly enough to grill him and see what you can get." He hesitated. "But what about Monzo?"

Kubu described the deposits in Monzo's bank account and the information from the Endabeni Guest House and Berry-bush Farm.

"He was obviously moonlighting. But the most significant thing Lerako discovered was that Haake and Monzo met up at Berrybush Farm and went on a trip together. Monzo seems to have been a greedy type. I'd guess he tried to muscle in on Haake's plans—or even his discovery if he's actually discovered something—and that Haake decided to put a quick stop to that. So he came back on another trip, kept out of sight, and killed Monzo with the rock, hoping it would be taken as an accident."

Mabaku thought this through. "How would he know where Monzo was going to be that day?"

"Probably he set up a meeting. Lerako found exactly one phone call to the ranger station the afternoon before the murder that couldn't be traced. It was about the time Monzo took a call, and it came from a public phone in Hukuntsi near the gas station there. So Monzo made up the story of sorting out the Bushmen and met Haake in the desert. That's when Haake made his move."

"And what about the fake footprints?"

Kubu shrugged. "I don't think they were fakes. Probably Haake checked out the area before Monzo came."

Mabaku shook his head. "It's very thin, Kubu. All guesswork. All you know is that the two of them went on a field trip together. There's no evidence they had a fight or indeed *any* contact after that. Maybe Haake has an alibi. Maybe he wasn't even in Botswana on that day. You'd better check with Immigration."

Kubu had thought of this too. "Director, you're absolutely right. But you agree we have a strong case against Haake for the Krige murder. How likely is it that there are two murderers running around in the middle of the Kalahari at the same time? I'm pretty sure that once we have Haake in custody, we'll get to the bottom of all this. He'll be forced to admit to the Krige killing, and then he'll come clean on Monzo too."

Mabaku nodded. He could accept that strategy, but there was one flaw. "And where *is* Haake right now?"

Kubu wriggled uncomfortably in his chair. "It's strange. We know he crossed into Botswana on Tuesday. We should have him by now. He had no reason to believe we were after him, nothing that would make him run for it. But there's no answer on his cell phone. My guess is that he's on one of his trips, probably deep in the Kalahari again and so out of contact."

Mabaku looked doubtful. "I hope this isn't another of your vanishing suspects, Kubu. I wouldn't start celebrating until Haake is safely behind bars, if I were you."

But Kubu was confident. "We've alerted the South African police, Interpol, the lot. There's nowhere for him to go, and I don't think he even knows we're looking for him. In a day or so he's going to drive into a town or approach a border post. And then we'll have him!"

Twenty-four

Kubu spent Saturday morning at the office catching up on paperwork that had accumulated during his visit to Namibia. But his spirits were good, and he hummed a Mozart tune as he plowed through the stack of papers. The week had been successful. He was confident that his prime suspect for the Krige murder would be apprehended in the near future and Monzo's death would then be explained.

He was looking forward to the evening. Pleasant had invited them to dinner, and Joy had arranged a babysitter for the first time. Kubu felt a pang of guilt as he eagerly anticipated being with Joy for a whole evening without Tumi. As much as he loved the two of them, when they were together, he felt he was getting too little of Joy's attention.

Appreciating the evening off, Joy smiled the whole way to Pleasant's apartment. They knocked at her door, both expecting a frazzled Pleasant to greet them. Joy's sister was not an accomplished cook—probably because she was single and often invited out—and was invariably running late. To their surprise, Pleasant looked completely composed, and greeted them with a wide smile and hugs all around.

Kubu was immediately suspicious. Something's up, he thought.

The next surprise came only seconds later as they walked into the small living room. Standing there was Bongani Sibisi, lecturer in ecology at the University of Botswana, and Pleasant's on-and-off boyfriend.

"Bongani! How nice to see you," Joy said enthusiastically, shaking his hand.

"Where've you been hiding?" asked Kubu, giving him a thump on the shoulder.

The handsome young man with John Lennon glasses smiled shyly. "I'm well. And very happy to see both of you. It's been a long time—my fault. I've been busy on a new project."

"I've a surprise for you," Pleasant said with a big smile.

I knew it, Kubu thought. Here it comes.

"We're going *out* to dinner. Bongani's treat. He wants to celebrate—he's just been promoted to associate professor. We'll have a drink here, and I've made some snacks. Then we're going out to Rodizio at Riverwalk."

"Congratulations, Bongani. That's wonderful!" Joy gave Bongani a big hug, to his mild embarrassment.

"Well done," said Kubu giving Bongani another thump. "Very well deserved too, if a little late. The university doesn't realize just how good you are."

◁▷ ◁▷ ◁▷

Rodizio was a newish restaurant and none of them had been there before. They spent a few minutes perusing the menu. Both men ordered Meat Rodizio, described as an unending supply of different types of meat—chicken, fillet, pork ribs, veal, chorizo sausage, and others. Kubu was delighted. All-you-can-eat meat! He sighed contentedly. The women both ordered vegetarian dishes, as though they could offset the amount of meat about to be consumed. Finally, Bongani ordered a bottle of South African sparkling wine for the occasion. Kubu would have preferred a decent red, but made no comment.

After they'd all had a chance to tuck into their food, Kubu lifted his glass. "I have a few toasts I'd like to make. First, to you, Bongani. Congratulations on your promotion. It is well deserved, and we are proud to know someone who knows so much!"

The four clinked their glasses.

"The second toast is also to Bongani—thank you for this lovely dinner. You shouldn't have spoiled us like this—but we love it. I hope your promotion to full professor comes soon. I have a suggestion of where to eat that evening!"

More leaning across the table to ensure all glasses were touched.

"And my third toast is to my dear sister-in-law, Pleasant. Thank you for not cooking!"

After the laughter had died down, the four resumed eating. Kubu was particularly impressed with how frequently waiters appeared at his side holding swords skewering the different meats. I've gone to heaven, he thought.

Finally, Bongani raised his glass and said quietly. "I also have a toast." He paused for effect. "To my fiancée, Pleasant."

The whole restaurant turned to see what the shrieking was

all about. Joy was uncontrollable. She jumped up, tears welling in her eyes, and hugged Pleasant. Then she hugged Bongani. Then Pleasant again. Bongani and Kubu were a little embarrassed by the commotion, but did nothing to stop it. They couldn't have even had they tried.

Pleasant rummaged in her bag and pulled out a small box. She opened it and lifted a ring with a small diamond in a contemporary setting. She slipped it onto her ring finger and flaunted it with a huge smile. Joy and Kubu admired it and exclaimed how beautiful it was.

Kubu lifted his glass and drained it with a flourish. "You must come back to our place and have another drink. This is a wonderful evening. We must enjoy it to the full."

Eventually they ended up back at Pleasant's apartment, having made a detour via Kubu's liquor cupboard for the best of his stock. They had realized that continuing the party with Tumi in hearing distance could ruin the evening. The babysitter was promised double payment for a few more hours.

The celebration continued until midnight, when they left; Kubu prayed that there would be no roadblocks on the way home. It wouldn't look good for an assistant superintendent to be caught driving under the influence.

If Tumi cried that night, neither Joy nor Kubu heard her. They both slept as though drugged. Before his eyes closed, Kubu had a momentary fantasy that he and Joy would make love. They'd had a wonderful evening with nothing to spoil the enjoyment. But although the spirit was willing, the flesh was weak, and it was only seconds before Kubu's snores reverberated through the house. Fortunately Joy was equally inebriated and heard nothing. In fact, although Kubu didn't know it, she made nearly as much noise as he did.

◁▷ ◁▷ ◁▷

Kubu awoke on Sunday morning with a fierce headache, made worse by Tumi's incessant crying. Both he and Joy had overslept by more than an hour, and Tumi was letting them know, in no uncertain terms, that such neglect was unacceptable. To make things worse, Ilia howled every time Tumi hit a certain note.

The weekly trip to Mochudi to enjoy Sunday lunch with Kubu's parents was further delayed because Pleasant and Bongani were late in arriving, no doubt victims of the same malaise.

When they eventually set off, the hour's drive was uneventful. Pleasant sat in the back seat with Joy, who was trying to console Tumi. Bongani was even quieter than usual, and Ilia had been relegated to the back of the Land Rover, where she was frustrated by being so close to the cold meat and salads Joy had brought for lunch.

As soon as the car door was open, Ilia raced along the fence, skidded around the corner at the gate, and jumped up at the elder Bengu, who smiled broadly and lifted the dog affectionately.

Kubu walked up to his parents and greeted them, "*Dumela*, Rra. *Dumela*, Mma." He then extended his right arm to his father, touching it with his left hand as a mark of respect.

Wilmon responded solemnly: "*Dumela*, my son."

"I have arrived," Kubu said formally. "And I apologize for being late."

"You are welcome in my house. How are you, my son?"

"I am well, Father. How are you and Mother?"

"We are also fine, my son." Wilmon's voice was strong, but quiet. Joy and Pleasant gave Wilmon and Amantle hugs, and Amantle took Tumi from Joy, kissing her on the forehead and rocking her in her arms. As if by magic, the baby stopped crying. Then Kubu introduced Bongani. "Father, Mother, this is Pleasant's friend we have told you about. Dr. Bongani Sibisi. He's a professor at the university."

As Bongani shook hands with his parents, Kubu watched his mother with amusement as she thoroughly scrutinized the newcomer.

"So, you are the man who has been giving Pleasant such a difficult time."

Bongani had been warned of Amantle's directness, but this was not the greeting he'd expected.

"Um," he spluttered. "I don't try to be difficult . . ."

"It is important to be nice!" Amantle interrupted. "Pleasant tells me that you spend too much time working and not enough time paying attention to her."

"But, Mma, . . ."

"No 'buts,' Bongani! Pleasant deserves your attention all the time. Not just when it is convenient to you. That is very selfish!"

"My mother," Pleasant broke into the exchange. "Don't be too hard on him, because I have good news for you. He has asked me to marry him!"

Amantle hesitated for only a fraction of a second. "I hope you have accepted?"

Pleasant nodded. Only then did Amantle's wrinkled face break into a huge smile.

"Hallelujah! I am so happy for you." She handed Tumi back to Joy and enveloped Pleasant in her arms. The two swayed back and forth, locked in shared joy. Then Amantle broke free and shook her finger at Bongani. "It is about time! I was very worried that Pleasant would end up unmarried and without child." For her that was the ultimate horror. Bongani smiled weakly.

Then Wilmon smiled and extended his hand. Pleasant pushed the hand aside and gave him a huge hug. As usual he wasn't certain whether to be shocked or delighted. Delight won, and he patted her cautiously on the back. "I am very happy for you. I wish you both a very happy life together—like Amantle's and mine."

Then he turned to Bongani. "Bongani, I do not know you, but if Pleasant loves you, you will always be welcome at our home."

"Thank you, Rra. Pleasant always has such kind words to say about you and your wife. It will be my privilege to get to know you."

"Congratulations, Bongani." Amantle extended her hand. "If Pleasant loves you, so do I. But make sure you respect her and treat her well."

"I will, Mma. I promise."

Joy and Kubu watched the felicitations with approval. Ilia, on the other hand, was less enthusiastic. She wasn't receiving the attention she'd come to expect.

After Kubu had hauled the cooler boxes into the kitchen, he retrieved a folding chair from the Land Rover—his parents only had five chairs, four of their own and one already loaned by Kubu. The six then sat down and chatted for a while, mainly about plans for the wedding. When the women went inside to prepare lunch, Wilmon beckoned Bongani to sit next to him. "I regret to say I have already forgotten your name."

Kubu glanced sharply at his father. This was unlike him. He was a man with a good memory, especially for people's names.

"Bongani Sibisi, Rra."

"Ah, yes." Wilmon nodded. "Tell me about your family." Kubu smiled. He knew that Wilmon would want to know all about Bongani's heritage.

For the next ten minutes or so, Bongani related how his father was dead, but his mother was alive and in good health. He told Wilmon about his grandparents, where they had come from, what they did, and how fortunate he'd been that they had lived in health to an old age.

"My grandparents, especially my grandfathers, were very important in my life, Rra. When I grew up, my father spent most of the year in Lobatse. That is the only place he could find work. So when he was away, I spent many hours listening to my grandfathers' stories. I was very lucky, because they had been to school and could read. It was they who helped me love to learn."

Wilmon listened carefully, nodding in appreciation for Bongani's respect for his elders. When he had exhausted his questions, he slowly stood up. He turned to Bongani. "You will excuse us, please." He beckoned to Kubu. "My son, please walk with me."

Kubu struggled out of his low chair, shrugged at Bongani, and helped his father down the stairs to the street. Bongani would have a chance to enjoy a few moments of peace, which Kubu was sure he needed.

"My son, we need to talk about *lobola* for Pleasant. Her father and mother are both dead, and your mother and I are now like parents to her. We must negotiate a fine *lobola*. Her family will get many fine cows." Kubu understood now why his father had summoned him away from the veranda. It would be improper to talk about *lobola* in front of the future groom.

They turned the corner into another dusty street. Wilmon nodded his head at several neighbors who shouted greetings.

"Father, you are right, as usual. But it isn't for us to initiate the discussion, like you did with Joy's family. Bongani's family will decide who will negotiate for them. Then Pleasant will tell Bongani that you will be her father in the matter. They will then approach you for her hand." He put his hand on his father's shoulder—a rare touch of affection between the two. "Pleasant is blessed to have you take her father's place. You will have the respect of Bongani and his family."

They walked in silence for a few more minutes, and Kubu could see that his father was very proud.

Lunch was a happy affair. Kubu noted with approval how Pleasant and Bongani paid a great deal of attention to each other, with frequent and affectionate touches. Joy and Amantle had already made progress in planning the wedding, which they had been told was to be in the spring—early October, in fact, so that the heat would be tolerable. Wilmon sat quietly, sometimes dozing, with Ilia content on his lap. Even Tumi behaved, sleeping quietly just inside the front door.

That evening, after Pleasant and Bongani had made their way home, Kubu relaxed in a comfortable chair with a ten-year-old KWV brandy. Joy had finally got Tumi to sleep, and settled herself on Kubu's lap with his arm around her shoulders. She took a sip of his brandy and wrinkled her nose as she always did.

"I think they'll be happy," she said. "He's a good man. She loves him for his mind and his character. That's a good basis."

Kubu grunted. He knew that it was best not to get involved.

"Pleasant told me that professors have what they call sabbaticals," Joy continued. "Apparently they are paid holidays to places overseas. And Pleasant loves to travel."

"I think they actually work at other universities. It's to continue their research. It isn't really a holiday."

"Oh, I see," said Joy, sounding unconvinced. "If you had a sabbatical, you would carry out research in the South African wine country."

Kubu laughed. "Yes, I probably would." He turned his head and kissed her.

"Hmm," she said. "The brandy tastes better that way."

Kubu finished it, set the glass aside, and kissed her again.

"Definitely better that way," said Joy. She looked at him in her special way.

"Let's go to bed," said Kubu.

This time the flesh was willing too.

Part IV

Ha ka /ku ¯/arro i, au !khweitən a: -hóäka

It will strike us in the dark

Twenty-five

Kubu arrived early at his office on Monday with a bounce to his step. He greeted Edison with a wave and offered smiles all around. He helped himself to tea and settled in his office, half expecting the day to be made at once by news of Haake. But when his e-mail and office mail arrived, they offered only the usual tedium. Even that couldn't spoil his mood, and he doggedly worked his way through it.

By mid-morning it was done. Feeling hopeful, he called Lerako, but he had nothing to report. Somehow Haake still remained undetected after another two days. Kubu wondered if someone had tipped him off that the police were after him. Perhaps Ilse had managed to reach him on his cell phone. Was it possible that he was now on the run? Someone with his experience of the Kalahari could easily find places to slip through the border into South Africa.

What he needed was someone who knew the Kalahari as well as Haake himself. Suddenly Kubu realized he knew someone exactly like that. He scrabbled in a drawer and found the piece of paper he'd used to jot down Khumanego's numbers. He owes me a favor, he thought. Let's see if I can collect. He tried the landline first, and it rang only a few times before Khumanego answered.

"Hello?"

"Khumanego? Hello, it's Kubu."

"David! How are you? Good to hear from you. Did you catch Monzo's killer?"

"Well, the good news is that we believe we know who it is, and it's not one of your friends. Did you read about the Namibian found dead near Hukuntsi?"

Khumanego said he'd followed the case quite carefully, half expecting that murder to be pinned on Bushmen as well. Kubu didn't tell him how close he was to being right.

"We now think that the man who discovered Krige's body actually killed him. And what's more, he'd had some shady contacts with Monzo. We're pretty sure he's our man."

"David, that's great news! I knew I was right to come to you for help. I'm sorry if it was embarrassing for you, but it's worked out really well, don't you think? Do you have this man in custody?"

This was exactly the opening Kubu wanted. "Well, that's the bad news. He seems to have gone to ground somewhere in the Kalahari. He may not even know that we're after him yet. My guess is that he's gone back to his exploring in the Hukuntsi area where he found Krige. But he may be hiding. What I was hoping was that you might be able to get the Bushmen in the area to help find him."

Khumanego hesitated. "Bushmen aren't enthusiastic about helping the police."

"That's understandable, but this is very much in their interests. If we get these murders sorted out, then people will leave them alone."

Khumanego sighed. "I wish that was true, David. But I'll see what I can do. Leave it with me. I do have a few contacts out there."

"Thanks, my friend. But be very careful. No one must try to stop him if they see him. If we're right, he's violent, and he's committed two murders already. I'll fax you one of the Wanted flyers for him."

They chatted for a few more minutes, and then Kubu rang off. After that he talked to the Interpol liaison officer. They decided to alert the Zimbabwe border posts as well.

Kubu felt a tinge of frustration. How could someone disappear for a week with the whole of Botswana looking for him? But he knew the answer already. Botswana has a lot of empty space.

Twenty-six

When he saw Haake's Land Cruiser pulling into the Kgalagadi Filling Station, Willie ran to be first there. He always tried to serve Haake because he tipped well. And surprisingly, the Namibian seemed to have taken a shine to the diminutive Bushman, laughing whenever Willie agilely used the front wheel as a leg up to reach the middle of the windshield. They'd spend a few minutes chatting before Haake took off again. Willie liked to hear about Windhoek, a place he could hardly imagine. And sometimes he would ask Haake what he was looking for in the Kalahari. He was interested and, of course, he'd been told to ask. But Haake would laugh and tell him he'd find out if he was patient. He said he'd give Willie a hundred-pula tip on the day he found what he sought. That hadn't happened yet. It was a standard joke between them. "No hundred pula today," Haake would say, and Willie would laugh.

But this day was different. Willie was nervous. He knew the police were looking for Haake; he'd seen the picture that Constable Tau had brought around. He didn't know what to do. But he smiled and waved, pretending everything was as usual, and Haake smiled back.

"Fill it up, Willie," he said.

"Jerry cans too, Mr. Haake?" Willie indicated the fuel cans on the roof rack.

Haake shook his head. "No, thanks. I'm heading back home tomorrow."

He didn't seem in the mood to talk, so Willie went about the business of putting diesel into the thirsty tank. He carefully cleaned the windshield, making sure no marks were left when the water dried. He would have cleaned the back window too, but was puzzled to find a cardboard sheet in its place.

"Broke the window, Mr. Haake?"

"Had an accident and didn't have time to get the glass replaced. Hardly matters. Doesn't look like rain out here!" They both laughed.

Haake got out and checked the Cash and Carry shop next door, but found it closed, hardly surprising as it was after 7:00 p.m. Willie hoped the other attendant didn't recognize the Namibian, but it was quiet at the gas station this late, and the other man was sitting some distance away.

"You want stuff at the Tuck Shop, Mr. Haake?" The Tuck Shop was attached to the gas station and sold snacks and cold drinks. But Haake shook his head. "I'll try to get a hot sandwich at the Endabeni place rather than junk food."

Willie finished fueling and told Haake the amount owed.

"You fine, Willie? All well here? You look a bit upset today."

"Fine, Mr. Haake." He hesitated but knew he had to ask. "You find what you looking for out there?" Willie waved his hand to indicate the Kalahari. Haake just smiled and handed him money to cover the diesel. Willie came back hopeful with the change, but Haake took all of it from him. Then he opened his wallet, took out a hundred-pula note, and handed it to the Bushman.

For a moment Willie looked at it openmouthed, his anxiety forgotten. "You found it, Mr. Haake? Really? After this long time? Really? Where? What is it?"

Haake laughed at the torrent of curiosity. "You'll find out one day, Willie. No hurry. Now I need to get something to eat. Don't spend all that money at once, hey!" He climbed back into the vehicle and headed up the tarred road through Hukuntsi.

Willie watched him go, rubbing the hundred-pula note between his thumb and fingers as if to prove it was really there. For a moment he hesitated—Haake had been nice to him—but then he picked up the phone and rang the man who called himself Piscoaghu, who had been waiting for several days.

"Did he give you the money? The hundred pula?" The voice was tense.

"Yes, Piscoaghu. He gave me the money."

"So he found it. Did he tell you about it?"

"No, I must wait to find out. He said nothing else."

"But you're sure he found what he was looking for?"

"He gave me the money," Willie repeated.

There was silence. Willie squirmed. "Look, Piscoaghu, the police want him. I've seen the poster! Must I tell them he was here? Maybe I'll get in trouble."

"Tell them nothing. Don't talk to anyone about this. No one. Did he say where he was going?"

"He wanted food. From Endabeni. He's going home to-morrow."

"All right. Good. Now I have things I must do quickly."

Without a word of thanks or farewell, the man hung up.

Wolfgang Haake pulled up outside the Endabeni Guest House and sat for a few moments thinking. Why had he given Willie the hundred pula? Was he really that sure? "I have found it," he told himself. "The *koppies* match the sketch. And the *W* on the map must mean *wasser*, because there's a spring at the back of the cave the arrow points to. And now I know what the *E* stands for too—*Edelstein*—'gemstone.' There are amethysts in that cave—but not the diamonds I'd hoped for." He rubbed his forehead. "But they *must* be there."

However, there were still issues to address. If the diamonds were there, the kimberlite would have to be skulking below the surface hidden from view. How was he going to check that? I'll work it out when I'm back in Windhoek, he thought, trying to drive the doubt from his mind.

He went inside to the reception counter, which divided the dining room from the kitchen. A young woman he didn't recognize greeted him, but explained that dinner was over. The staff left at eight, but he managed to persuade her to make him a sandwich with Russian sausages and heat it in the micro-wave. It would only take a few minutes, and there would be a few pula for her.

After about five minutes, another woman—one he thought he knew this time—came out and looked at him, but didn't return his greeting. Thinking he might stay the night, he asked her if she had a room. She shook her head vehemently and went back. He heard agitated voices in the kitchen. What a fuss over a sandwich! He was getting tired of waiting. At last the first woman produced the sandwich on a plate and suggested that there might be a room after all, but Haake had had enough. The food was scalding hot—too long in the microwave—and he wanted to get going. I'll have it in peace with a beer when I find somewhere to camp, he decided. "Wrap it for me, please. I will take it with me." She nodded, slid the sandwich onto a piece of newspaper, closed it gingerly because of the heat, and offered it to him apologetically. He paid, gave her the tip he had promised, and went out to his car.

At first he noticed nothing wrong, but when he started to reverse he realized that the cardboard covering the back window was now loose. That was odd, it had held well until now. He stopped the car and examined the adhesive duct tape. It had come away from the metal and was loose on three sides. It was as though someone had pulled it open like a door and then tried crudely to reattach it. Suspicious now, he turned on the car's interior light and looked around. Almost immediately he realized that the GPS was gone. Cursing, he wondered if this was a petty theft, opportunistic with the vehicle essentially open, or if it was something more sinister. Was it possible that someone wanted the record of his trip to the prospect? Or that someone wanted him not to have a record? But it wasn't a disaster. He knew the coordinates off by heart.

Briefly he considered contacting the police, but they'd never bother with a petty theft, and that is what they'd think it was. The best thing, he decided, was to get moving. Find a safe, private place to camp, not visible from the road, and head back to Windhoek as soon as possible using the shorter dirt road through Kule. Then he could decide what to do next. He had friends at home. Maybe they would help when he showed them the samples he'd collected, including the amethysts he'd picked up off the ground.

He pulled back onto the road and headed west out of Hukuntsi. He'd find a good camping spot not far out of town.

Fifteen minutes later Constable Tau and three other policemen, all armed, arrived at the Endabeni Guest House. There was much excitement from the ladies running the establishment, including criticism about how long it had taken the police to get there from neighboring Tshane. But no one had any idea where Wolfgang Haake had gone.

Haake found a spot off the road under a group of trees where he couldn't be seen by passing cars, although he expected none to use this track at night. He switched off his engine but oddly the sound seemed to continue for a few moments as though the motor had run on. He sat and listened for several minutes, but there was no other sound. It must be my imagination, he thought. This is getting to me. I've got to keep calm.

He would use the roof tent to sleep, but he set up a table and chair and enjoyed a chilled beer from his camping fridge, while he ate the now cold sandwich. He began to relax. His mind mulled over the loss of the GPS. Was someone trying to steal his discovery? Or were these the people who already knew about it and simply wanted to stop him interfering? He'd spent years looking for the source of Namibia's diamonds. No one was going to take it away from him, whoever they were. He downed another beer. After a while he needed to relieve himself. He'd once been told that you never own beer, you just borrow it.

He stood up, and in doing so, he moved into the pool of light from the rechargeable camping lantern on the table. He heard the sound of a vibrating string, and the next instant he screamed at the sudden pain in his right thigh. A thin shaft about twenty inches long protruded from his leg.

Haake knocked over the light and scrambled back into his vehicle, gasping in agony when the door caught the arrow shaft. Gritting his teeth, he tried to yank it loose, but the pain was too much. With a yell, he started the vehicle, accelerated back to the track, and drove toward Hukuntsi as fast as he could go.

Twenty-seven

"Where's a doctor? Where's a doctor?"

The night nurse was startled out of her doze by the frantic shouts from the entrance to the Hukuntsi Primary Hospital. She shook her head and rushed toward the door.

"I need a doctor!" There was panic in the voice.

"Rra, Rra, what's wrong?" the nurse called as she pushed through the door from the clinic to the entrance. A white man was bent over, clutching his thigh. He looked up, face drained of blood by the pain.

"Are you a doctor? Can you get this arrow out?" he said, grimacing, pointing at the shaft that protruded from his blood-stained shorts.

"No, Rra. I'm a nurse. I'll call the doctor right away. Come with me."

She took Haake's arm and helped him into the clinic. He

limped along squeezing the top of his thigh, trying to stop the pain.

"Fucking Bushmen!"

She led him into a small consulting room. "Rra, lie down here." She pointed at a bed. "Try not to move."

Haake sat on the edge of the bed, bent over.

"What if it's poisoned?" he gasped. "It'll kill me."

"Please lie down, Rra."

Haake shook his head. Sitting was less painful.

"I'll be back right away." The nurse darted out of the room to phone one of the doctors on call.

A few minutes later she returned with a glass of water and two tablets.

"Please take these. Painkillers. The doctor will be here in fifteen minutes."

While they waited, the nurse took down all of Haake's particulars. The same form all over the world, he thought as he answered the litany of questions about his health and history. Eventually the nurse was finished, and he closed his eyes to await the doctor's arrival.

"How did this happen?" The doctor had cut Haake's shorts to get to the wound. Haake winced as the doctor probed around the shaft.

"Must be a fucking Bushman! They're the only ones around here who use bows and arrows."

"Where were you?" The doctor swabbed away the congealing blood. "What were you doing?"

"Camping just out of town. Minding my own business. Arrow came from nowhere. I didn't hear or see anyone."

The doctor looked closely at the wound. "I'll have to cut it out."

"I tried pulling it out, but it was too painful."

"You'd have done a lot of damage if you'd succeeded."

"What if there's poison on it? They use poison that can kill an eland! What if they've put that stuff on this arrow?" Haake was beginning to panic.

"Just lie still, and I'll get a local anesthetic for you. I'll take the arrow out, then we can deal with the poison, if there is any."

Haake closed his eyes. The painkillers were beginning to take effect.

Soon the doctor returned. "I'm going to inject you around the wound. It'll take about ten minutes to take full effect. Then I'll make incisions next to the shaft and take the arrow out."

Haake nodded his assent, keeping his eyes closed. He didn't like injections. Moments later he felt a series of pinpricks in his thigh. That wasn't bad, he thought.

He lay there mulling over what had happened. First his GPS had been stolen. Now he had been shot. Obviously by a Bushman. Someone was definitely trying to keep him from getting back to his discovery. But who was it? He shook his head. He knew his thinking was becoming increasingly confused.

"Okay, let me know if you feel any pain." In his musings, Haake had almost forgotten his wound—the pain had disappeared.

"I promise I'll scream." His voice was now tired and a little slow.

"Here goes!"

◁▷ ◁▷ ◁▷

The operation didn't take long, and Haake felt no pain, just an occasional tug on his leg. The doctor stitched up the wound and wrapped a bandage around the thigh. He held the arrow for Haake to see.

"Take a look. This is a very dangerous weapon. If it hit you in the wrong place, it would kill you. You were lucky it hit you where it did. Should heal quickly and easily, and I doubt you'll even have a limp."

He handed the arrow to Haake. It was about twenty-five inches long with a small metal head. Some sort of resin held the tip onto the shaft. But he was surprised when he looked at the other end. There were no feathers. He remembered the bows and arrows of his childhood—they all had feathers to stabilize the arrow in flight. But in this arrow, there was only a small notch in the end of the shaft for the bowstring. He rubbed his thumb over the edge of the tip. It was very sharp indeed. Then he noticed that there was some paste just below the head.

"Look here! That paste. I'm sure that's poison! Why else would it be there?"

The doctor took the arrow from Haake and scrutinized the paste.

"I don't know what it is. It could be anything, but to be safe, I'll send it to Gaborone tomorrow for testing, but I don't think you've got anything to worry about. However, if you feel bad during the night—not from the wound, but from something else—let the nurse know, and she'll give me a call."

"Can you give me something so I can sleep? I don't want to be awake all night with the pain."

"I'll give you a sedative as soon as you've spoken to the police."

"The police? Why are they here?"

"We have to inform them whenever there's an assault. And in your case, they wanted to see you right away."

Before Haake could respond, the door opened, and two policemen walked in. Haake recognized Detective Tau from the Tshane police station. Tau walked over to the bed; the other policeman stayed at the door.

"Mr. Haake, we've been looking for you."

"Looking for me? What for?"

"I have to inform you that you are under arrest for the murder of Joseph Krige."

"I'm under arrest?" Haake sat up abruptly causing him discomfort even though the anesthetic hadn't worn off. "For murder?" His brow creased into a frown.

Tau didn't answer, but read Haake his rights.

"Are you fucking mad?" The color was coming back into Haake's face. "I *found* Krige. I didn't kill him. Are you on some sort of quota system? Three whites arrested for murder each year? You're crazy."

Tau pulled a chair over to the bed.

"First, I would like to ask you some questions about what happened tonight." He took out his notebook and pen. "Where were you when you were shot with the arrow?"

"Well, I didn't shoot myself! You can write that down!"

"Mr. Haake, please. We want to find out what happened tonight and find who was responsible."

"It was the bloody Bushmen. Can't you see? There's the arrow!" He pointed to the bedside table. Tau nodded and asked the other constable to put it in a large plastic bag.

"You can't do that!" The doctor intervened. "I need to send it to Gaborone tomorrow for testing. In case there's poison on it."

"Then, we'll need to photograph it first. Before you send it. When will it go?"

"If you get it back by eight, that'll be fine."

Tau nodded and turned back to Haake. "Where were you when you were attacked?"

"It doesn't matter where I was. What's this shit about a murder charge?"

"Mr. Haake. Please answer the questions. If you want to know who shot you, we have to get the information now so we can start looking. Where were you when you were hit?"

"This is bullshit." His face was now flushed. "I was camping just outside town on the road to Kule. Eating my supper and having a beer. Got up to pee, and the arrow hit my thigh. I remember hearing the sound of a bowstring just before."

"Do you know anyone who would want to kill you? Somebody you've fought with?"

Haake hesitated and decided not to tell Tau about what he had seen at the *koppies* in the desert.

"I tell you it's the fucking Bushmen. But I've no idea why they'd want to kill me. Maybe they were after someone else."

"Are you sure there's no one else who would want to kill you?"

"I'm sure!"

He lay back, beginning to feel nauseous. From the anesthetic, I suppose, he thought. And he had a headache coming on.

"I'm not feeling well. I want to sleep. Can't you come back in the morning?"

Tau pondered what to do. Eventually he decided it was better to leave Haake to recover.

"I'll come back in the morning, Mr. Haake. But don't try to

escape. There are bars on the windows, and Constable Mopati here will be on guard outside the door. And he's armed."

Mopati patted the holster on his belt.

"I'll be back at seven."

Tau asked the nurse where he could make some phone calls, and she showed him into another consulting room. He shut the door and dialed Lerako in Tsabong.

"Yes?" The voice was sleepy. "Who is it?"

"It is Detective Tau from Tshane. We've got Haake."

The voice came alive. "You've got Haake? Is he handcuffed? Is he in a cell?"

"He's in hospital. He was shot with an arrow and came to the hospital to have someone take it out."

"Shot with an arrow?" There was a pause. "It's those bloody Bushmen again! How is he?"

"He's in pain. I asked him some questions, then he was too tired and sick to go on. The windows are barred, and I've put Constable Mopati outside the door to make sure he doesn't try to escape. He wasn't looking very well."

"What did he tell you?"

"Not much." Tau pulled out his notebook and told Lerako what Haake had said.

"I didn't have a chance to ask him about Krige. I thought it was better to find out what happened tonight. Tomorrow I can ask about the murder."

"I'll come up early in the morning. Should get there around lunch."

Now wide awake, Lerako decided he'd better call Kubu. Fortunately he'd added both Kubu's numbers to his cell phone. He called Kubu's home. I hope I wake him up too, he thought with a touch of malice.

"Assistant Superintendent Bengu." Kubu had indeed been asleep.

"Kubu, it's Lerako. They've caught Haake."

Kubu's voice perked up immediately. "Where is he?"

"He's in the Hukuntsi Hospital. Apparently someone shot him with an arrow, and he went there to have it taken out."

"Shot with an arrow?"

"I told you it was those Bushmen!"

Kubu suddenly felt cold. "If it really was a Bushman arrow, it could have been poisoned. I'd better call the hospital right away."

"I told you we should have kept those suspects in Tsabong. Krige would have been alive, if we had, and Haake in good health."

"Come on, Lerako. Don't be so stubborn. Haake knew Monzo, and Krige knew Haake. There's something else going on here. It can't all be a coincidence!"

There was no reaction from Lerako. Then he said, "I'm going up to Hukuntsi in the morning. What are you going to do?"

"I'll meet you there around lunch. We can interrogate him together. And bring him back to Gaborone if he's well enough." Then Kubu thought about how sloppy Detective Tau had been when dealing with Haake in the Krige affair. "Is Tau in charge up there?"

"Yes. He's got an armed guard outside Haake's door. And the windows are barred. Should be okay."

"All right. Get some sleep, and I'll see you tomorrow."

Wide awake now, Kubu called the Hukuntsi Hospital and

spoke to the night nurse. She sounded tired, but knew all about Haake and the arrow wound.

"Please tell the doctor that the arrow may have a deadly Bushman poison on it. The arrow should be handled very carefully and bagged. The doctor should also keep a close eye on the patient."

"I'll call the doctor again, if I think it's necessary," the nurse promised before she hung up.

Kubu lay back and sighed. After two days with no progress, he thought, I have to be woken in the middle of the night.

Haake couldn't sleep. His headache had worsened, he felt increasingly nauseous, he'd thrown up once, and his wound had started to throb. Bloody hell, he thought. This is worse than I expected. He poured the rest of the water from the jug next to his bed into a glass and drained it. He had heard once that anesthetics made you thirsty. He'd have to go and pee soon.

Sure enough, fifteen minutes later he called for Mopati.

"I have to go and pee," he said.

Mopati wasn't sure what to do. He'd been told to make sure Haake didn't leave the room. But a man had to pee. He pulled out his automatic and pointed it at Haake. "If you try to run, I'll shoot you," he said. "Get out of bed. Put your hands above your head."

Haake swung his feet off the bed and onto the floor. As he stood up, he staggered and had to use the bed to steady himself.

"Wait a moment," he said weakly. "I got up too quickly. I'm a little dizzy."

When he indicated he was feeling better, Mopati backed slowly out of the door, indicating to Haake to follow.

"Nurse! Nurse!" Mopati didn't take his eyes off Haake.

Again the nurse was startled from her snooze.

"Where's the toilet?"

The nurse indicated that they should follow her. She walked down the corridor and pointed to the men's. "There you are."

The two men went in, and Mopati backed into a corner so that Haake wouldn't be too close. "Do it!" he said waving the automatic towards the urinal.

Haake shuffled over and lifted his gown.

"Shit! There's blood in my pee!"

When he'd finished, and they were going back to the room, Haake told the nurse about the blood.

"Anything else that feels bad?"

"Well, I've thrown up a few times and have a splitting headache."

The nurse frowned. "Go and lie down. I'll call the doctor and let him know."

The doctor was alarmed when the nurse told him about Haake's symptoms. The operation had been simple and straightforward. And it was highly unlikely that Haake was allergic to the anesthetic.

"Oh, shit!" he said to himself. "Maybe the arrow *was* poisoned as the detective from Gaborone had suggested." He didn't know anything about Bushman poisons and, of course, there were all sorts—from bushes, from snakes, and from beetles. All different. All fatal.

He dressed again and rushed to the hospital. On the way he called the emergency room at the Princess Marina hospital in Gaborone for help. They took his number and said a doctor would call back.

He hurried to Haake's bedside and unbandaged the wound. It looked healthy. But Haake told him the headache was intensifying, as was the nausea. And his muscles felt listless. Just as the doctor was about to take Haake's pulse and blood pressure, his phone rang. He walked outside the door and described to the doctor in Gaborone what had happened.

"You'd better get him here as quickly as possible," was the response. "Can you get an ambulance at this time of night?"

Mopati was now in over his head. His responsibility was simple enough—don't let Haake leave the room. He'd already used his initiative to let him go to the toilet. Now the doctor wanted to take him to Gaborone and had sent the nurse to arrange an ambulance. Mopati had no idea how to react. Quickly he called Tau. Tau was horrified and decided he needed direction from Tsabong, so he called Lerako again.

"Yes?" Lerako was obviously fast asleep when the phone rang.

"Detective Sergeant Lerako, this is Tau. They want to take Haake to Gaborone. They think the arrow was poisoned."

"Who wants to?"

"The doctor. He called Princess Marina and that's what they told him to do. I'm not sure what to do."

Lerako thought for a moment. "How are they taking him? In an ambulance?"

"I think so."

"Well, send Mopati with the ambulance. Just make sure Haake can't escape. He may have a plan."

"Okay. What do they do when they get to Princess Marina?"

"I'll arrange to have someone there."

◁▷ ◁▷ ◁▷

After he hung up, Lerako called Kubu again, who was not pleased. But after Lerako explained what had happened, Kubu was wide awake.

"So the doctor thinks the arrow could be poisoned. That's what I was afraid of. When will they get here?"

"Don't know. Depends when they can get the ambulance organized. But it won't be before eight or nine in the morning."

"I'll interview him as soon as I can. Thanks for letting me know. I would have headed for Hukuntsi early and passed Haake going in the opposite direction. I'll call you as soon as I've spoken to him."

It was just after 3:00 a.m. when the ambulance eventually left Hukuntsi Hospital. It had taken some time to locate the driver. Eventually he'd been found and awakened at a girlfriend's house. Then he still had to go home and find the keys to the ambulance. Constable Mopati was seated very uncomfortably next to Haake in the back, and Haake, now even more heavily sedated, lay on the gurney breathing roughly.

Even to Mopati's untrained eye, Haake looked very ill. Mopati wondered whether he would be alive when they arrived.

Twenty-eight

The ambulance driver managed to stay on the road the whole way from Hukuntsi, missing all the animals that wandered into his way—quite a large number, in fact. About the only benefit he derived by having the siren on was that an occasional cow would turn and look at the noise coming down the road. This allowed him to see the headlights reflected in its eyes.

The road had always puzzled him. He had originally been very impressed by the fences that ran down each side of the Trans-Kalahari Highway. That will keep animals off the road, he had thought. This night, as he drove down the Highway for the umpteenth time since it had been paved, he decided that the fences were to keep the animals *on* the road so they couldn't stray too far. They liked it there anyway, because the runoff of what little rain the area received collected next to the road, causing the grass to be green and lush.

While the animals liked the new fences, drivers didn't, and there were frequent confrontations between vehicles and animals. The number of carcasses on the side of the road was a testimony to how often accidents happened.

Kubu was not in a good mood. He'd been waiting at the emergency center at Princess Marina Hospital since 8:00 a.m. He'd discovered which doctor had advised the Hukuntsi hospital and had managed to talk to him for a few minutes. But the conversation had been discouraging.

"We don't really have much useful information about Bushman poisons," the doctor told him. "The best we can do is to find out what type of poison it is—neurotoxin, hemotoxin, or cytotoxin. The Bushmen use all three. Once we know that, we can do our best to get the victim through this."

"Is it likely he'll die?" Kubu asked.

The doctor frowned. "Impossible to say at this point. We'll get help from a toxicologist at the university. But you must understand it takes time. I'm not at all optimistic that she'll be able to provide feedback in time to be of real help."

"What about antidotes or antivenoms?"

The doctor shrugged. "We don't know what the poison is. Anyway, many of the known toxins have no antidote. It really depends on the man's natural defenses and on how much has got into his system. Given what they've told us about his reactions so far, my guess is that the poison used is hemotoxic." The doctor noticed Kubu's frown. "That means it attacks the blood in a variety of different ways; sometimes it impairs its oxygen-carrying capability resulting in hypoxia—oxygen starvation—or sometimes it acts as an anticoagulant, causing bleeding. More often than not, it does both."

Kubu had other questions, but a nurse interrupted to tell them that the patient had arrived. The doctor nodded to Kubu and hurried off with her.

Tau had sent the arrow with Constable Mopati in the ambulance, so Kubu was able to examine it before it was sent to the laboratory. He extracted it carefully from its evidence bag and photographed it, including several close-ups of the tip and the paste around it. He thought it looked a little different from the ones Khumanego had shown him many years ago, but the small head, slender shaft, and lack of fletching were typical. It's amazing, he thought, how the Bushmen had been able to isolate such lethal poisons and use them so effectively—poisons that killed animals, yet did not cause problems for those who ate the meat.

About half an hour later, the doctor came to where Kubu was sitting impatiently.

"He's not doing well. In addition to the headaches, nausea, and small traces of blood in his urine, he's now having some difficulty breathing. It's almost certainly a hemotoxin that's been used. They act slower than most neurotoxins, which go after the nervous system."

"Can I talk to him?"

"Yes, but not for long. He needs rest, and we're considering some blood transfusions. My colleague has contacted the Poison Information Centre in Cape Town for help."

Kubu accompanied the doctor to Haake's ward, where a policeman sat inside the door. Haake was sitting up with a glass of water. He's turning yellow, thought Kubu, surprised at the man's color.

"Mr. Haake, we meet again," he said, not offering to shake hands.

Haake nodded and said in no more than a whisper, "Why did your man in Hukuntsi arrest me? I've done nothing wrong. He said I'd murdered that Krige guy I found in the desert. What's going on?"

Kubu frowned. He'd not expected Haake to raise the issue of Krige's death. Rather, he thought, Haake would avoid it.

"Mr. Haake, we spoke to your previous employer, Mr. Muller of the Namib Mining Company. He said you stole some documents or data from the company, and he'd hired Mr. Krige to follow you. You phoned him when you got back to Windhoek and indicated that you knew about Krige."

Haake hesitated. "I found out Krige was a private investigator and guessed Muller hired him to follow me. I wanted Muller off my back. He had no right to pry into what I was doing. No right!"

"It's an unlikely coincidence that you just happened to find a man dead in the desert—someone who was specifically following you. Especially as there was no evidence whatsoever that anyone else had been anywhere near."

"I didn't kill him! There *was* someone else there. He shot at me!"

"You had motive and opportunity. And we can't find anyone else who would want to get rid of Krige."

"I'm telling you, I didn't kill him." Haake's voice was no more than a croak.

Kubu sat down and pulled out his notebook. "I need some information from you, Mr. Haake. First, what do you do every time you come into Botswana? It seems you go into the same area of the Kalahari each time."

"I'm going to die, aren't I? Those fucking Bushmen have poisoned me."

"The doctors are trying to find out what's happened to you. It's going to take a few hours."

"Even if they do, I'll die. Nobody survives those poisons." He leaned forward and grabbed a blanket from the bottom of the bed. He wrapped it around his shoulders. "I'm so fucking cold!"

"What have you been doing in Botswana, Mr. Haake?" Kubu repeated sharply.

"I've been prospecting."

"For what?"

"This and that. Anything I could find."

"And what did you find?"

"Nothing much. A few gemstones—amethysts, mainly."

Kubu pulled his chair closer—Haake was becoming difficult to hear.

"Are you sure that's all?"

"I took some samples here and there. Wanted to have them looked at in Windhoek."

"Where are they?"

"In my four by four. I expect you know that already. Been through it while I was in hospital, I suppose."

"No, we haven't been through it. But we'd like to. Do we have your permission?"

"Why not? There's nothing there but a few rocks."

"Mr. Haake, I need your help if we are to find the person who shot you. I need more information about what you've been doing and where you've been."

"I've just been looking around." He was breathing rapidly, as though there wasn't enough air in the room.

"You've been following a map. Where is it? I'd like to see it."

Haake frowned.

"Assistant Superintendent! Please." The doctor stepped forward. "He needs rest. You'll have to come back later."

"I've just one more question. Have you received any threats or warnings?

Haake frowned. "No," he gasped.

"Come on, Detective. That's all." The doctor took Kubu by the arm and led him into the passage outside.

"Doctor, you don't understand. We have several murders we think he is responsible for. I need to talk to him."

"You can do that later. He needs all the rest he can get if he wants a chance to pull through this. Come back at two this afternoon, and we'll see how he's doing."

Having no option, Kubu left the ward, and then called Tau in Tshane.

"Tau! This is Kubu. Get your forensics person and go through Haake's vehicle very carefully. Get his GPS—make sure you don't turn it on. Check for anything unusual—rocks, papers, anything like that. Also see if you can find a hand-drawn map. Check for fingerprints on all the door handles."

"Okay. I'll have to drive it up to Kang first."

"No, no. Get the forensics person to come down. I don't want anything disturbed any more than it has been already."

"Okay. It looks as though he never got the glass at the back of the vehicle fixed. It's covered by a piece of cardboard taped to the car. Half of it has come loose, as though it was pulled away. He used duct tape, so it shouldn't have come loose by itself."

"Make sure they dust around that too then. I'm not sure what we're looking for, but I've a hunch there will be something there. Some sort of clue as to where he's been or what he's been up to."

After ending the call, Kubu went back to the CID offices at Millenium Park to call Lerako and debrief Mabaku.

Kubu was frustrated. He had a man suspected of being a murderer, but couldn't interrogate him properly. And, to make things worse, there was a chance the man would die before he could get the information he needed. Back at his office, he paced and paced, accomplishing nothing. The solutions to one and perhaps two murders lay tantalizingly close, but were just out of reach.

At 12:30 p.m. Kubu couldn't stand it any longer. He drove to the Wimpy at Game City. Normally he would prefer to go to the Mugg and Bean upstairs, but he was impatient and didn't want leisurely service. He wanted food right away. Steak and eggs!

When he finished he headed back to the Princess Marina Hospital and arrived there at 1:45 p.m. He went in at once hoping that he could talk to Haake earlier than the doctor had indicated.

He was in luck. When he stuck his head around the door, the doctor waved him in.

"He's feeling a little better. The rest did him good. Probably didn't sleep at all last night, what with that siren going all the time. I'll be back in twenty minutes."

Kubu sat down and pulled out his notebook.

"Mr. Haake, I'm pleased you're feeling a little better. That's a good sign, I'm sure."

Haake hauled himself to a sitting position and adjusted his pillows for more comfort. "What do you want to know?"

"I've been asking around about you and it seems you've been looking for the source of the Namibian diamonds. Is that what you've been doing?"

Haake shook his head weakly. "No. I was just looking around. No diamonds."

"And what *did* you find?"

Haake didn't respond for a few moments. He breathed heavily.

"Found some *koppies*. Not marked on my maps. Found some amethysts there. But . . ." Haake stopped talking and shut his eyes.

"But what?"

There was no response, and Kubu could see Haake was struggling to breathe.

"But what, Mr. Haake?"

Haake opened his eyes. "Nothing. There is nothing worthwhile there."

"Where are your maps?" Kubu asked. "We'd like to see them."

"No maps. Had them on previous trips."

"Come on, Mr. Haake. I don't believe you. Where are your maps?"

Haake should his head. "No maps."

Kubu was becoming exasperated. "Mr. Haake, I'd like to look through your belongings here at the hospital. Do I have your permission to do that?"

Haake shook his head.

"Dammit, Mr. Haake. You've got to help me! A few minutes ago you mentioned *koppies*. Was that where you were going when Krige was following you? Is that why you killed him? Because you didn't want him to report back to Muller where you'd been? Didn't want him to know where the diamonds were?"

"There are no diamonds at the *koppies*! I only found them

on this last trip anyway. And I wasn't near there when I found Krige."

"But if Krige was still alive, he would have followed you there too. You didn't want that, did you? It was easier to murder him and make it look like someone else did it."

Haake shook his head. "You've got it wrong. I didn't kill him." He took several deep breaths. "Why do you think it was me? What evidence have you got?"

"Mr. Haake. You stole information from the place you last worked. When they sent someone to follow you, you had an obvious motive to kill him. And you had the opportunity. There isn't a scrap of evidence that anyone else was in the vicinity. You'll have a difficult time convincing anyone of your innocence."

Haake shook his head again. "Why don't you fuck off, Detective. I'm tired. I don't need this shit."

As if on cue, the doctor walked in. "Time to leave, Assistant Superintendent." He opened the door for Kubu.

"I've got lots more to ask him. When can I come back?"

The doctor followed Kubu into the corridor. "Come back at five. I'll see how he's doing. Maybe you can speak to him again."

"Have you heard anything about the poison?"

"Not yet. We gave him some blood plasma, and he seems to have stabilized a little. At least he hasn't deteriorated much since he got here. I'm hoping that's a good sign."

"When will you know what his prognosis is?"

The doctor shrugged. "We'll have to watch him carefully and see how it goes."

Kubu shook his head in frustration and stalked out.

◁▷ ◁▷ ◁▷

Just before five, Kubu walked back into the hospital, only to be stopped by the receptionist.

"Superintendent Bengu?"

Kubu nodded.

"The doctor says you must wait here for him, please."

"Has Haake deteriorated? Will I be able to speak to him?"

"You'll have to speak to the doctor. Please sit down over there."

It was nearly half an hour before the doctor appeared. Kubu stood up as he approached.

"Can I see him now?"

"Yes, but only for a few minutes. He's getting weaker. I think there's some internal bleeding—his urine has more blood in it." The doctor shook his head unhappily as he walked with Kubu to Haake's room.

Kubu opened the door and nodded to the policeman sitting inside. He was shocked by what he saw. Haake was now attached to what appeared to be a heart monitor and several drips, and had an oxygen mask over his mouth and nose. How am I going to hear what he says? Kubu wondered. I could hardly hear him before. He sat down next to the bed.

"Mr. Haake?"

No reply, but the monitor showed life and Haake's chest rose and fell ever so slightly.

"Mr. Haake?"

Haake's head nodded almost imperceptibly.

"Mr. Haake. I need to ask you some more questions."

Again a slight nod. Haake battled to sit up a little and removed his mask.

"I'm dying, aren't I?"

Kubu wasn't sure how to respond. "You'll have to speak to

the doctor. I haven't heard anything. I want to find who tried to kill you. Do you understand?"

A slight nod.

"It would help me if I knew where you went. We searched your car and couldn't find your GPS. Where is it?"

"Gone."

"What do you mean 'gone'?" Kubu voice was beginning to rise in frustration.

"Gone." Haake paused. "Stolen in Hukuntsi. Someone broke into my four by four. Must be the people from the *koppies*."

"People from the *koppies*? Who are they?"

Haake shook his head. "Never saw them. But they got there before me."

"Why would they want to attack you?"

"Don't know. Maybe they thought I would steal whatever's there."

"What do you think that could be?" Kubu was getting confused.

"Don't know."

"How did you know someone got there before you?"

Haake shook his head. "Didn't see anyone."

"What did you see?"

"Very strange. Motorbike tracks in the desert. Around the *koppies*." He took a deep breath. "But nobody there."

At that moment the doctor interrupted. "Detective, you must leave. You're exhausting my patient. He needs to rest. And I need to get him back on oxygen. As you can see, he's struggling to breathe."

"Just one more thing! Mr. Haake, this is very important. Give me the map. If we know where the *koppies are*, we can see who's there. It's possible someone saw you and didn't want you coming back."

"Don't know."

"What do you mean, you don't know!" Kubu's voice rose in exasperation. "Where are the *koppies*, Mr. Haake?"

"It was on my GPS." He gasped, struggling for air. The doctor put his hand on Kubu's arm. "Come along, Assistant Superintendent. He needs to rest."

Kubu brushed the hand aside. This was a crucial moment. "Can't you remember the coordinates? Or how to get there? Please give me something I can work with." Kubu thought he saw a glimmer of a smile flitter over Haake's face.

"You've got to leave now." The doctor grabbed Kubu's arm and pulled him toward the door. "If you don't let him rest, you'll never get anything more out of him."

Twenty-nine

Kubu came into the CID later than usual on Friday morning, having spent much of the previous night waiting fruitlessly at the hospital. He went straight to the director's office, gave the door a perfunctory knock, and walked in. Miriam glanced at him with surprise and gave a small shake of her head, but Kubu ignored her. He had news Mabaku would want to hear.

He found the director at his desk looking through a collection of newspapers. He was reading the *Daily News*.

"They've gone mad!" Mabaku exclaimed. "This one is talking about tourists being in danger in the Kalahari! Look at the other headlines." He held up the front pages so that Kubu could read them. TOURIST NEAR DEATH. BUSHMAN KILLER STILL FREE—POLICE HELPLESS. POISON ARROW ATTACK.

Kubu nodded. The Botswana press tended to be calm and measured. Minor events made the headlines, and political speeches were covered respectfully. Even Krige's murder, which had been reported with gusto, was presented calmly. But the attack on Haake had turned that upside down. A poisoned arrow striking from the dark. People are scared, Kubu thought. They think of Bushmen as small and harmless, if they think of them at all. Suddenly they seem dangerous. He sighed.

"Haake's dead," he said. "He died early this morning."

Mabaku dumped the newspapers and leaned back. "Well, it's murder now. But they'd already decided that." He nodded at the spread of paper on his desk. "I've called a press conference to nip this thing in the bud. Tell them it's all under control. An arrest is imminent and so on. I'm going to get our three helicopters out to Hukuntsi. We'll find these Bushmen if it means looking under every grain of sand. That should get the press on our side and calm them down. You'd better come. It's at two."

"I'll come, but there's quite a bit I need to tell you, and it may change how we handle the search and the reporters too. This isn't as straightforward as it seems."

Mabaku glared at him. "Only Lerako thought it was straightforward. And it seems he was right."

Kubu wondered where to start. "I spoke to Ian MacGregor last night. You know that he's a big lover of the Kalahari—he paints it and just enjoys the area a lot." Mabaku gave a grunt that seemed to say there was no accounting for taste. "He knows quite a bit about Bushmen and their culture too." Kubu didn't add that he did also, because of Khumanego. He doubted that Mabaku would want to be reminded of where the case had started. "Anyway, he's consulting a toxicologist at the university, who examined the gummy material on the arrow that shot Haake. He's pretty sure it's one of the Bushman poisons. It's going to take a while to be certain, though—most of these poisons aren't recorded."

"We already guessed it was a poison."

"Yes, but Ian's comment on the arrow was interesting. And I'd noticed it too. It's not a real Bushman arrow. He mentioned it at once."

"Not a real arrow?"

"The arrow's real enough, but it isn't the way the Bushmen normally make them. They attach the head to the shaft with a short connecting piece so that the shaft falls off almost at once. That way the arrowhead and the poison stay in the animal. Otherwise the shaft might catch on something as the animal runs, and the arrow might be pulled out before the poison gets into the bloodstream. This arrow isn't like that. The head is solidly attached to the shaft. In fact Haake tried to pull it out by the shaft. A real Bushman arrow would have come apart at once."

Mabaku thought that over. "So what? They don't hunt like that anymore anyway. Probably whoever set out to murder Haake decided to make a simpler arrow. He wasn't going to get it back anyway."

"Yes, but why make a special arrow? Why not just use one he had? If he was a Bushman."

"*If*? Is this another one of your wild theories, like Haake killing Monzo?"

Kubu ignored that and continued. "I got a report from Detective Tau. Yesterday they went out to the spot where Haake was shot with the arrow. It wasn't hard to find. He'd left some camping stuff there, and they could see where he pulled off the road. They searched carefully for footprints, and they found something."

"And they weren't Bushman footprints," Mabaku guessed.

Kubu shook his head. "No. An ordinary boot print. Something like size ten, much too large for a Bushman. The same size as the prints we found at the Krige murder scene and the supposed fakes near where Monzo was killed. And something else. They found what looked like the tracks of a motorbike that had pulled off the road. Whoever it was tried to scuff out the tracks, but it was pretty dark by then—new moon—and he didn't do a complete job."

"So Haake could've been followed from Hukuntsi by someone on the bike. Wouldn't he hear it?"

"Only if it was close and he turned off his engine. But as soon as he stopped, the murderer would have cut his engine too."

"Was there a bike track on the road?"

"No, but if he drove in one of the ruts made by car wheels, it would be wiped out by the next vehicle. Haake driving to the hospital, for example. Or Tau driving out to the spot to investigate."

"You think it's a setup? Made to look like a Bushman? Riding on the Monzo and Krige business?"

Kubu nodded. "It's quite possible."

"What does Lerako think?"

"He's not committing himself. The bike could've been there at a different time. He's convinced all the boot prints are fakes."

"But if that's the case, where are the Bushman footprints? This whole thing's giving me a headache!"

"There's something else. Haake told me that when he found the *koppies* where he took the rock samples, there were off-road motorbike tracks there too. It would have been easy to follow Haake's tracks through the desert. Maybe he was hunted all the way from the *koppies* until he was caught outside Hu-kuntsi."

"Can we find this place? Send a helicopter to take a look?"

Kubu shook his head. "I'm sure Haake knew where it was, but wouldn't tell me. And he claimed his GPS was stolen from his vehicle, so we can't use that. We did find Haake's map after he died. It was in his wallet in a side compartment. Not really hidden. It doesn't seem to help much, though."

He carefully unfolded a sheet of paper, and spread it on Mabaku's desk. At first sight it wasn't impressive. The folds had worn and started to tear, and a stain disfigured one edge. On one side, there was a hand-drawn sketch of three *koppies*, with two arrows pointing to them, labeled *W* and *E*. The other side had a patchwork of areas with different styles of shadings. But there were no coordinates or any other markings that could help determine the location, just a single inscription, annotated with the initials HS.

"It says 'I have found it' in German," Kubu said. "I think the shadings may have something to do with geology."

Mabaku grunted. "People were killed for this? It seems un-likely. I drew better treasure maps when I was a child. And we used to singe the corners in the cooking fire to make them look older and give them character."

Kubu chuckled.

"Well, get someone who knows about geology to look at it. Maybe we're missing something, but I doubt it." Mabaku shook his head in frustration.

Kubu had one further piece of confusion. "We searched Haake's vehicle. They found some interesting gemstones as well as rock samples in the glove compartment. Haake told me they were amethysts, but we'll check that. But they found something much more interesting that he didn't tell me about. A revolver. We checked the serial number with Detective Sergeant Helu in Windhoek. It belonged to Krige."

Mabaku rested his elbow on the desk and held his chin in his hand. He was obviously digesting this new fact, but he said nothing.

"It's a Smith and Wesson thirty-eight Special. Would fit with the damage to Haake's vehicle. And there are three live bullets in the cylinder and three fired."

"So that would fit with your theory that Haake murdered Krige, stole his gun, and shot at his vehicle himself. And also explain why there were no cartridge cases at the scene. But where was the revolver when Tau's men looked through Haake's vehicle after he reported the murder?"

Kubu shrugged. "They weren't looking for a gun; they were looking for spent bullets. For that matter, Haake might have hidden it somewhere outside Tshane and picked it up on his way back to Namibia." He hesitated. "Of course there's another possibility. If Haake's telling the truth about the GPS, then the gun could've been planted in his vehicle when the GPS was stolen."

"But what would be the point?"

"Maybe just to confuse us. Misdirection."

Mabaku snorted again. He was quite confused enough as it was.

"Any fingerprints? Where was the gun hidden?"

"There were a variety of prints on the vehicle and one partial on the cylinder. Obviously Haake's are all over the vehicle, but there are also a few we can't identify. And the partial on the gun matches one of those. There are also partials on the back casings of the cartridges. Those belong to Krige. So it looks like no one reloaded the revolver. It was shoved in the springs under the backseat. Obvious if you looked. But they never do at the border posts."

"And not easy to get at if you're attacked. That's odd."

"He wasn't expecting to be attacked. He was probably worrying about someone following him from Namibia again."

"But he saw motorbike tracks at the *koppies*!"

Kubu shrugged. "He didn't know who made those tracks, and he didn't know he was being followed by a motorbike. It was all a very big, very unpleasant surprise."

Mabaku nodded, but said nothing. Kubu waited, wanting to give the director a chance to arrange all the new pieces of the puzzle.

"We'll try a little subterfuge, Kubu," he said at last. "Maybe we can turn this to our advantage. We'll pretend we're completely taken in by the whole Bushman story. Say nothing to the press about the arrow or the footprints. Let the murderer think we've fallen for his ploy. We'll tell them about the gun, though. That should shake them up a bit."

Kubu nodded but he realized that Mabaku had an ulterior motive. If the murderer turned out to be one of the Bushmen after all, then face would be saved by not mentioning the red herrings to the press. He was making a bet each way.

"Director, I think we should get the Namibian police to follow up with Muller of the Namib Mining Company again. He may know more than he's letting on. Perhaps they know about the *koppies* and are keeping it to themselves. If Haake was right about it, it could be worth a huge fortune."

Mabaku nodded. "Good idea."

"And you're not going to find anyone from the air. Forget about the Bushmen. You could walk right past them and not see them if they wanted it that way. And the others—whoever they are—are going to be keeping their heads down at the moment. We're going to have to go out there ourselves and look."

Mabaku frowned. "That could just be a wild goose chase. How many men would we need? And we don't know where to start!"

"We know it's a group of *koppies*. The Kalahari is pretty big, but it's pretty flat. And we know where Haake went before, so that should give us the general area. I'll try and narrow it down."

Mabaku looked dubious. "Do that. See if anything turns up." He looked at his watch. "Press conference at two p.m. And don't forget our strategy—nothing about the arrow or the footprints."

Clearly the discussion was at an end for the time being.

Kubu returned to his office deep in thought. Mabaku wasn't the only one confused by what was going on. Haake had had a motive to kill Krige, and the mining company might have had a motive to kill Haake. Haake knew Monzo, but they hadn't established any motive why he would want to kill him. And, as far as they knew, no one else had a motive to kill Monzo. Yet he was sure the murders were all related somehow. He flopped into his office chair and pulled a survey map of the Hukuntsi area toward him. It showed no hills. In fact it showed very little other than a few dirt roads and gradual elevation changes. Three murders, he thought. Was it all about Haake's dream of treasure? Had that dream finally led to his death?

His musings were interrupted by a gentle knock on his door and when he looked up, Cindy Robinson was there.

"Cindy!" he said enthusiastically. "What brings you . . ." He let the sentence trail off. He knew what had brought her to his office.

"Hello, Kubu. I'm coming to the press conference later on. I thought you might want lunch. I can see you've lost weight. Been starving yourself?"

Kubu laughed. "Hardly. But I'm afraid I'm tied up for lunch." He thought of the salad and tasteless low-fat cheese in his briefcase. But this wasn't the moment for a relaxed lunch with a reporter, let alone an attractive female one. "Some other time, perhaps."

By this time Cindy had settled herself in a chair. She looked at him intently. "Were we wrong, Kubu? Were the Bushmen the killers after all? I feel so guilty. I pushed your boss, and he pushed you, and now I'm wondering about that poor man dying horribly from a poisoned arrow."

Kubu shrugged. "We don't know whether we were wrong or not. The point is that Lerako didn't have enough evidence. He'd have been forced to release them eventually in any case. Anyway, if it is a Bushman, it could be a different one."

"You still think it may not be a Bushman?"

"Well, the poisoned arrow is pretty convincing," said Kubu a little too quickly.

At that moment Edison came in, interrupting them.

"Sorry, I didn't see you were busy," he said. "I just wanted to tell you I took a call for you while you were with Mabaku. From an Ilse Burger in Windhoek. It's about Haake. She said it was urgent. Here's the number."

"Thanks. I'll call her now." He turned to Cindy. "I'm sorry. Will you excuse me? It's pretty hectic here at the moment." He was relieved when she just nodded, said good-bye, and left. Edison watched her with appreciation.

"Who's she?"

"A reporter from the U.S. after a story," Kubu replied curtly. "I'd better make that call." Edison got the message and left him alone.

What is she actually after? Kubu wondered. She always left him feeling uncomfortable.

He picked up the handset and hesitated, collecting his thoughts. One of the doctors had spoken to Ilse late the previous night after Haake died. Why did she want to talk to him? He sighed and dialed the number.

"Yes, hello?"

"Ms. Burger? It's Assistant Superintendent Bengu from the Botswana CID. I'm very sorry about your friend Mr. Haake. I wouldn't have disturbed you today, but I understand you wanted to talk to me."

There was a brief silence. When Ilse spoke, Kubu could hear the strain in her voice. "Thank you. I wanted to ask you something. When you spoke to me you said that Wolfie might be in danger. That's why I tried to help. So do you know what happened? Who was responsible for this?"

Kubu hesitated. "There had been two murders in the area, and Mr. Haake was heading there alone. I think that's what I meant."

There was another pause. "I thought you meant someone might attack him. He was worried about the Namib Mining Company. I think they were after him. Is it possible they were behind this?"

Kubu turned it around. "But why would they kill the private investigator they sent to follow Mr. Haake? What sense would that make?"

Ilse hesitated. "When I saw Wolfie after the trip, he knew

he'd been followed. He said it was sorted out. I didn't know what he meant. But now I wonder about it."

Yes, indeed, Kubu thought. "Well, what would they gain by killing him?"

"Maybe they wanted the map. That could be it. Did you find it?"

"Yes, but it doesn't say anything about the location. As you told us, it only has drawings of some *koppies* and geological structures. It's useless for finding anything."

There was a silence on the line.

"Ms. Burger, we will get to the bottom of this, whoever did it. I promise."

"What will happen to his things?"

"At the moment everything here is evidence. Eventually it will go into his estate. Do you know if he had a will? Who his next of kin is?"

"No. It doesn't matter to me. I just want a few keepsakes. Nothing else."

Kubu found he had nothing more to say. It seemed that Ilse didn't either, and soon the conversation was over.

Kubu thought about Ilse's new information. It seemed to strengthen the theory that Haake had discovered that he was being followed by Krige and had murdered him. Had that led to the Namib Mining Company deciding to hit Haake—using the elaborate Bushman ruse as cover? Or was there another group involved?

Kubu wished he could get Henk Muller into an interrogation room. He would need to have a discussion with Detective Sergeant Helu in Windhoek very soon.

Kubu pulled the topographic map toward him again. Spotting Edison walking past, Kubu gave a shout and signaled him into the office.

"Take a look at this map, Edison. The murders seem to cluster in this area." Kubu had carefully plotted the locations of the three murders; they made a small triangle in the southern desert between Mabuasehube and Hukuntsi. "Maybe there's a group of bandits operating in the area. But maybe the murders are taking place because of something *in* the area—maybe Haake's *koppies* full of diamonds." He stabbed the triangle with his finger. "The first murder—Monzo's—was made to look like an accident. Once the murderers realized we'd seen through that, they tried other misdirection. Krige's murder was made to look like a copycat killing, and Haake's like a Bushman killing. But suppose the murders aren't related to each other, but rather to the location? Do you see?"

Edison nodded firmly. A sure sign that he didn't see at all.

Kubu drew a big circle on the map roughly centered on the place Monzo had died. "What I want you to do is to check this general area for deaths—supposedly natural deaths that could be something different. Say, over the last five years."

"You think there may have been earlier murders? Ones that were made to look like accidents?" This Edison could understand.

Kubu nodded. He had another thought. "The lady at the Berrybush B and B outside Tsabong told Lerako about another prospector who died—a German called Koch. I think that was more than ten years ago. But maybe it's related somehow. See if you can find out more about that. And where he died."

Now it was time for lunch. With a sigh he lifted his briefcase onto his desk and opened it to reveal a Tupperware container of salad. It seemed very cruel to be forced to face the press on an essentially empty stomach.

Thirty

On Sunday morning Cindy was relaxing after a run, a cool shower, and a breakfast of fruit. She preferred to jog early in the morning when it was cool, although she didn't mind the dry heat of Gaborone. She disliked the humid summers of her home in the Southern United States, which left her drenched and sticky after a run. She poured herself a cup of strong coffee and walked out onto the small veranda.

Her piece was written and e-mailed to the news agency, but she wasn't entirely happy with it. It combined the nastiness of the murder with reactions from different individuals. What came through very strongly was the ambivalence with which people regarded the Bushmen. Interesting people living in difficult circumstances, she'd been told repeatedly. But there was always the sense that they were regarded as inferior and uncivilized. She wondered if she'd overdone that angle.

She also wondered if she'd overdone things with respect to Kubu and the press conference. She'd included several quotes from him, but none from Director Mabaku. She liked Kubu. He was so huggable. And she enjoyed his sense of humor. She smiled, thinking of his reaction to her full name.

"Stop it," she said aloud. "You've been alone so long that every man looks attractive." Traveling around the world as a freelance reporter was fun and exciting, but it didn't lend itself to lasting relationships. Not that she usually had trouble finding male companions. "Now I have a crush on an overweight, married policeman!" She laughed at herself.

As she refilled her cup, her cell phone rang in the bedroom. She had to rush to reach it, but grabbed it just in time.

"Yes, hello?"

"Cindy? It's Khumanego."

"Khumanego! How are you?" She hadn't spoken to him since their surprise meeting in Tsabong.

"I'm okay. Look, have you seen what the newspapers are doing? They're whipping up public opinion against the Bushmen again! Something really nasty could happen. It's outrageous!"

Cindy was caught off guard. Khumanego always saw things so starkly, no shades of gray. "They're just excited about this latest murder. Don't worry, it'll all die down after a while."

"After a while? Can you imagine what might happen in the meantime? Do you know what this could do to relations between the Bushmen and the other population groups? It could take years to fix."

"I think you may be overreacting, Khumanego."

"That nasty piece of work Lerako is behind this. I'm sure of it. They don't even know it *was* a Bushman!"

"But Haake was shot with a poisoned arrow," Cindy said mildly.

"But was it a Bushman arrow? There are lots of different types of arrows. And do they know what sort of poison it was?" Khumanego paused, and when he went on he sounded calmer. "It would be so easy to frame a Bushman for the murder. Get hold of some black mamba venom, or something like that, take a bow and arrow and shoot this Haake. And the police might well fall for it! Especially because that bastard Lerako can't be bothered to look beyond the obvious. Perhaps he doesn't even *want* to look beyond the obvious."

Cindy hadn't thought of this possibility, and she recalled Kubu's remark suggesting he wasn't entirely sure about the murderer being a Bushman either. On the other hand, how would one lay one's hands on mamba venom? She shuddered.

"Why don't you tell Kubu all this?"

There was silence from Khumanego. "Maybe I am overreacting," he said at last. "David's been fair to me. But I don't trust the police."

"What do you want me to do?" Cindy asked.

"Write a story. Point out that the Bushmen are being framed again. Just like before. Force the police to look below the surface."

"I'll think about it, Khumanego. Maybe I'll interview Kubu. See if the police are covering all the angles." She hesitated. "I think Kubu is doing his best," she finished weakly.

"Sorry, Cindy. I shouldn't keep coming to you. I'm just very upset and angry. I'm expecting something bad to happen. Really bad. Anyway, think about what you can do."

Cindy promised she would, and said good-bye with relief. She finished pouring her coffee and returned to the veranda.

She felt disturbed. Khumanego had been so intense, so angry. She rummaged in her handbag until she found the card that Kubu had given her in Tsabong.

Joy answered the phone and passed it to Kubu. He wasn't pleased to hear from Cindy on a Sunday; he'd had enough questions at the Friday press conference. Initially he was quite short with her, but as she described the call from Khumanego, he became intrigued. He hadn't considered the possibility of a backlash against the Bushmen when he'd agreed to Mabaku's ruse of keeping their suspicions about Haake's murderer to themselves. Now Khumanego was getting worked up because he thought that the police were again taking the easy option rather than looking for other possibilities. At the end of the call he thanked her and promised to look into the issue.

"Who was that?" Joy asked, rocking the baby.

"Just a reporter after a scoop," he said. Somehow his dismissive description rang oddly false.

Joy gave him a strange look. "Do you know her?"

"Yes, she was at Tsabong after a story when I was there with Khumanego."

"Oh," said Joy. "You never told me about her."

"Didn't I?"

Joy shook her head. "Tumi's asleep. I'll put her in her crib." She walked through to their tiny second bedroom, now proudly referred to as the Nursery.

Cindy *is* just after a story, Kubu thought. Why do I feel guilty that there's a tiny part of me that's sorry about that?

"Would you like some coffee, my darling?" he called out. After all, it was too early for wine.

Thirty-one

A pensive Kubu arrived at the CID on Monday morning. He was still digesting the conversation with Cindy. And now he was faced with how to find Haake's mysterious *koppies*. Bongani had offered to help, but the best he could do quickly was print out a satellite image of the area from Google Earth. But nothing stood out clearly. Much of the area was semi-desert, but some parts were covered by scrubby trees that might disguise the topography. Bongani suggested that there might be small hills there, camouflaged from the satellite by the vegetation. Without more information they'd be forced to fly over the area or explore it on the ground and compare any *koppies* they found with the drawing on Haake's map. Kubu wasn't sure he could get Mabaku's support for either option at the moment.

"You've got a visitor," the officer at reception told Kubu

in reply to his greeting. "A Bushman. I put him in the waiting room upstairs."

Kubu climbed the stairs to his office and then looked into the waiting room. Khumanego was sitting stiffly, an untouched polystyrene cup of tea next to him.

"Khumanego! Let me grab a cup of tea. Bring yours into my office." The Bushman nodded without smiling and picked up his cup. Kubu helped himself from the urn, and they went to his office together. Khumanego closed the door.

"Have you seen the newspapers, David? They're building up a frenzy against the Bushmen. There's going to be trouble. Some people are just looking for an excuse to get nasty. This could be it. Why are you doing this to us?"

Kubu nodded and sipped his tea. "Cindy told me you were upset."

"She called you?"

"Yes. She was also concerned by the newspaper reaction. What do you mean by 'doing this'?"

"The police! You're deliberately letting the blame fall on the Bushmen again. Even encouraging it!"

"That's not true."

"Have you investigated the crime scene? Looked into matters? Yourself, not that Lerako."

Kubu opened a file and extracted three glossy prints of the pictures he'd taken of the arrow at Princess Marina. He tossed them across the desk to Khumanego, who picked them up and looked at each one in turn. Kubu watched his reaction.

"Is this the arrow that shot Haake?"

Kubu nodded.

"It's ridiculous! No Bushman would've made a thing like

this. It's clumsy. And the head should detach. You know what a Bushman arrow is like!"

Kubu decided to play devil's advocate. "Yes, we noticed that too. But maybe the Bushman didn't have the time or the patience to make the arrow properly. He knew it would be easy to get close. Why bother with the niceties?"

"Why bother? It would be a matter of pride!"

"There's not much pride in preying on lone visitors."

Khumanego started to retort but Kubu cut him off. "We're looking at all possibilities, Khumanego. All possibilities."

Khumanego's expression changed. "What other possibilities?"

"Well, it's tentative at the moment. Let me show you some prints that Pleasant's fiancé made for me over the weekend—he works with this sort of thing at the university." He dug out the Google Earth images from his briefcase. "We think there's a group of *koppies* in here somewhere that someone wants kept secret badly enough to kill for it."

"Why do you think that?"

"Haake told me about it before he died. He saw some strange things there."

"Did he tell you where they were?"

"No. I think he knew, but he wouldn't say. Now it's too late. And we can't follow his GPS because it's gone. He said it was stolen."

Khumanego shrugged. "It's almost impossible to find a small hill in the middle of the Kalahari unless you know where to start looking. You'll have to wait for something else to happen."

"I want to try. I think there are other ways we might find it. And after all, the Kalahari doesn't have too many hills. I think we could find it using this information"—he tapped the images on his desk—"and Haake's map. Haake said there were other tracks there too. Maybe we'll come across them. Someone is out there and up to no good, and I'm going to stop it."

Khumanego thought about it for several seconds, then reverted to his concern about the press. "You should tell the newspapers about the arrow. Otherwise something really bad could happen."

Kubu ignored that. "I need a guide. Someone who knows that area of the desert. Who could help follow tracks and so on. Do you know any Bushman who would help?"

Khumanego shook his head. "No one will head out there. It's an area with a bad reputation. A place of spirits. Unlucky. It's avoided."

That, thought Kubu, might explain why whoever was there was able to come and go unnoticed. "The only other option will be low-level flights over the area looking for the tracks. Bike tracks apparently. Might spot them from the air. But I don't think my boss will go for that in a hurry."

"Maybe Haake made the whole thing up. Maybe he was after something else in a different part of the Kalahari, and just used this *koppie* story to confuse you."

Kubu shook his head. "It's possible, of course. But he was dying and knew it. I don't think he would make the whole thing up. Why should he? He had nothing to gain. I'm committed to this, Khumanego. Maybe Lerako's tracker can help me."

"The one who thought the footprints near Monzo were faked? What use is he? You'd trust your life to someone like that?"

"I'm still going to go." Kubu held Khumanego's gaze.

"Very well," said Khumanego, not blinking. "I grew up in

that area, remember? I know it as well as anyone, and I'm not superstitious. I'll help you. The two of us can go. Not a police invasion. That area is important to my people. It has religious significance."

"Why are you willing to do this? It could be dangerous."

"You helped me before. It's my turn now. I pay my debts."

Kubu thought about it for a while, then he nodded. "All right. We'll leave the day after tomorrow. Can you do that?"

Khumanego nodded. "You'll talk to the press?"

"I'll discuss it with my boss. Maybe Cindy gets her scoop after all."

Kubu was pensive after Khumanego left. He carefully returned the arrow pictures to his file, then tidied his desk. He picked up the forensics report on the bullet found in Haake's vehicle. It seemed likely that it came from Krige's gun, but they couldn't be sure. Nothing surprising or helpful there. He tossed the report aside.

Ideas were floating in his head. Puzzle pieces turning around, but still not fitting. Not in the right places anyway. Opportunity, he thought. Suppose Haake was innocent. Then who'd had the opportunity to commit all three murders? In each case there was no trace of the murderer, so how had he reached the victims and then disappeared? And suddenly the answer was obvious. They'd worked out how the murderer had reached Haake without leaving any tracks; the same method could be used for the murders of Krige and Monzo. Driving on a Kalahari road, cars gouged paths for themselves in the soft sand. If a skilled off-road motorbike rider stayed carefully in one of those ruts, there would be no trace—certainly not after the next vehicle went through.

But he wasn't ready to take it to Mabaku. He needed something more. He needed someone who could tell him about diamonds. He picked up the phone and called Africa Ndlovu at the diamond branch of the CID. He needed to speak to the Walrus.

The Walrus was Dr. Waskowski, a senior scientist at De Beers, who had helped Kubu before with another case. His bushy beard, handlebar moustache, and bouncing eyebrows made Kubu think of a surprised walrus. So the Walrus he had become.

Africa listened to Kubu's story. "Yes, call him," he said tersely. "He'll help you if he can." He gave Kubu the number.

Kubu was put through immediately when he said who he was. De Beers liked to cultivate a very close relationship with the Botswana police.

"Bengu? This is Waskowski. What can I do for you?"

"Dr. Waskowski, thank you for your time. I have a very strange case. A man—a prospector from Namibia—was killed in the Kalahari recently. I'm trying to understand what he was doing there."

"That chap Haake? Who was shot with a Bushman arrow?" Apparently Waskowski took an interest in the news.

"Exactly. Although he didn't admit it, we think he was looking for diamonds. Specifically, the source of the Namibian diamonds."

"The Namibian alluvials? The mother lode? That old story."

"It's not a new idea?"

"Hardly. Obviously it's been a source of great interest in the diamond community for many years. A flood of diamonds washed to the coast. Millions of years ago. There were so many, you could pick them off the beach at one stage, so the area had to be closed. It was called the *Sperrgebiet*—the forbidden area."

"Do scientists know the source?"

"No. There are lots of theories and speculation. Possibly some huge field of kimberlite pipes—maybe in Botswana— eroded away over millennia. Gone now. Or maybe they moved across the continent from the Drakensberg mountains over an even longer time period. Diamonds are very old, Assistant Superintendent. They have lots of time to move once they are separated from their mother rock."

"Is it possible that the mother rock *is* still out there? Full of diamonds and hidden under the sand? That Haake knew what he was doing?"

"Anything's possible. I'd be very surprised though. It's just another wild goose chase."

Kubu grunted. "Haake had an old map. We think it might go back to a man called Hans Schwabe."

"Schwabe? Another treasure hunter? With a treasure map? Grow up, Mr. Bengu."

"Well, it has what appears to be a geological map on one side. Could I fax it to you and get your opinion?"

"A geology map? Well, that might be of more interest. Sure, fax it to me."

Kubu's thoughts turned to the Namib Mining Company. He asked Dr. Waskowski if he knew of it.

"Yes, I believe so. A junior exploration company. It's look- ing for uranium in the Kaokoveld, I think. Appears legitimate. I wouldn't put my money there though. Uranium's past its peak."

"They wouldn't have an interest in diamonds? Do you think if they came across a rich find they might try to keep it secret? Mine it on the sly?"

Waskowski laughed. "Hardly! You don't understand junior

mining companies, Assistant Superintendent. Their bread and butter is mining the stock exchange, not the earth. An announcement of a big discovery is their bonanza. Shares shoot up, they're able to raise lots of cash, dish out bonuses. Their idea of keeping something under wraps is to invite only ten mining analysts to the briefing!" Waskowski laughed again, enjoying his little joke. "And what would they do with the diamonds anyway? You've heard of the Kimberley Process? Every legitimate diamond is tracked from where it's mined until it ends up in a piece of jewelry. It's like a pedigree. They'd have no way to sell their diamonds outside that process. Complete waste of time."

Kubu sighed. So much for his idea of the Namib Mining Company being behind all this.

But Waskowski wasn't finished. "Now if you had a gang of smugglers or the like, and the diamonds were close to surface, that would be a different story. For a few individuals, there could be real money in it. The Kalahari has kimberlites all right. No reason why someone couldn't stumble on a small, rich lode somewhere in the middle of nowhere. "

"But wouldn't they also come up against the Kimberley Process?"

"Of course. But if you get something for nothing, anything you sell it for is a good profit."

Kubu realized that the Walrus might have given him what he needed to convince Mabaku. His heart beat a little faster.

"Dr. Waskowski, you've been a big help. Thank you very much."

"Always happy to help the police." The line went dead.

Kubu hung up, his mind in high gear. Pieces of the puzzle were clicking into place now, but something still worried him.

It was as if the pieces fitted perfectly, but the picture they made wasn't really the same as the one on the front of the box. Yet he couldn't find the flaw. He shrugged off his doubts. Let's try it on Mabaku, he decided.

"Diamond smugglers!" Mabaku actually jumped out of his chair. Kubu enjoyed that. He had always wondered just how it would look. "That changes the whole case."

Kubu nodded. "It could be a gang, exploiting the Bushman issue to cover up the murders of anyone who stumbles across what they're doing. And the area is supposed to be unlucky, so the Bushmen keep away."

Mabaku snorted. "But three murders?"

Kubu shook his head. "Edison has been following up any unusual deaths in the area. There is at least one more, probably three. And one long ago. But that doesn't fit with this, of course." Mabaku looked puzzled, so Kubu continued. He spread his topographic map on Mabaku's desk, pushing the director's paperwork out of the way. The map had two new crosses marked on it and a dotted line and a solid line running through part of the region.

"This spot"—Kubu pointed to one of the crosses—"is where a prospector by the name of Herman Koch died twelve years ago. Also looking for diamonds, it seems. Not close to where Monzo or Haake died, but not that far from Krige. Is that a coincidence? Maybe. But maybe not, because he was the previous owner of Haake's map."

"How do you know that?"

Kubu related Lerako's conversation with the proprietor of Berrybush Farm outside Tsabong.

"And here"—Kubu pointed to a cross near Kang to the

north—"is where a Bushman was killed about two years ago—stabbed multiple times and left to die. The police were unable to find any suspects or a motive. But the victim apparently lived to the south, around where Krige died." Kubu's finger moved back to where the other murders had taken place. "Now this line is an interesting possibility. And I must give Edison full credit for this. Nice lateral thinking. He knew I was looking for suspicious deaths *in* the area but he extended that to suspicious deaths *connected* with the area.

"Do you recall the case of the two botany students? They were found dead after ingesting some Bushman poison bulb? We thought it might be a suicide pact, but they had no history of homosexuality, and the coroner eventually settled for death by misadventure. Perhaps they weren't experimenting with a hallucinogen. Perhaps someone slipped it into their food."

Mabaku caught on at once. "So one line is where they went through this area collecting plants? You got the route from their GPS?"

Kubu nodded. "Yes. We kept that data when we closed the case. Perhaps it needs to be reopened. They drove from Gaborone to Mabuasehube and then on to Hukuntsi. Mabuasehube was a detour. They must have gone there for a purpose."

For a moment Mabaku was lost, then light dawned. "You think Monzo was on one of his fly-by-night guide jobs? With the students?"

Kubu shrugged. "We'll have to follow up with Monzo's boss. But I'll bet they didn't go into the area alone."

"And what's this line?" Mabaku pointed to the dotted line on the map.

"That's from Krige's GPS. We assume he followed Haake, so it's Haake's route as well. For the most part it is to the south and west of Hukuntsi. There is just this one branch further east. Where it stops is where Krige died. Maybe he was killed just because he was following Haake and unwittingly went into this area. An accidental target, so to speak. The students were to the south and east of Hukuntsi or, more accurately, north and east of Mabuasehube. Then they headed to Sekoma."

"Where they died!"

Kubu nodded. "Where they died."

The director thought for a moment, shook his head, and then counted off on his fingers. "Forget about the prospector. Too long ago. A Bushman is murdered. Could be by another Bushman. Then two students are murdered—if you are right about that—using a poisonous hallucinogen known to the Bushmen. Then three Bushmen are found with a dying man, but they are saved by some footprints that later appear to be fakes. Next a man is murdered with a *knobkierie*—often used by Bushmen. Finally a man is killed by a poisoned arrow. Do you see a common thread here?"

Kubu nodded. "But maybe someone went to a great deal of trouble to make it look that way. And Khumanego's worried that our strategy of hiding our doubts about the poisoned arrow from the press could backfire. That there might be some sort of racially motivated attack on groups of Bushmen. He could be right. We *have* to act quickly."

"What happened to your theory that Haake was behind it all?"

Kubu shrugged. "It became much less likely after he was murdered. It may still be that Haake killed Krige, but I'm convinced there's more to it than that."

Kubu had played his cards. It was time to call the hand. "I want to go out there and take a look." Mabaku started to react, but Kubu stopped him. "Hear me out. Khumanego has agreed to guide me. He knows the area well. I couldn't do better. I'll ask Detective Sergeant Lerako to come too. We have the GPS tracks from the students and Krige. We can follow those and scout around—particularly south and east of Hukuntsi, where Krige died. If they saw something that got them killed, it must be close to where they went. We have my friend Dr. Sibisi's satellite data about the possible position of the *koppies*—the student track goes near that area. Krige's is a bit farther away. So I know where I need to go now. I know where to start."

"And what will you do when you get there, and it turns out there's an armed gang there or a group of Bushmen with poisoned arrows? Get Khumanego to protect you? Run?"

"Obviously I can't go alone. I thought we could take two vehicles and two or three armed constables." Kubu was keeping his fingers crossed that Khumanego wouldn't consider that an invasion.

Mabaku was starting to shake his head, but Kubu plowed on. "Director, we have to stop these people before someone else dies."

The director cast around for some way out. The idea of searching the Kalahari on the ground for a nest of vicious bandits struck him as madness. And yet what choice did he have? "Damn it, Kubu. This plan is too dangerous. We'll fly over the area. Find them that way."

Kubu shook his head. "That could take too long. And you won't be able to arrest whoever it is from the air. And once warned, they'll be gone. Until it's safe to come back and start again."

"I don't like it. Why must you go yourself?"

"We'll never find anything without a good guide, even with

the GPS tracks. Khumanego is doing this as a favor to me; he won't go with anyone else."

Mabaku hesitated, torn. "Okay. Two vehicles, three constables. Take a satellite phone and report in, morning and night. You better start organizing this junket. And talk to Lerako. When will you leave?"

"Day after tomorrow."

"April Fool's Day. Very appropriate, I'd say. Keep me informed."

Kubu nodded, and left before Mabaku could change his mind.

Thirty-two

That evening Kubu broke the news to Joy. He was sitting in the kitchen playing with Tumi while Joy saw to the curry. The days of relaxed sundowners on the veranda were behind them. They tried to do things together, and that meant being where the things had to be done. In the early evening, it was the kitchen.

Kubu was holding Tumi's pacifier and using it to tease her nose, popping it into her mouth, rubbing her cheek. She gurgled and waved her arms and smiled. Joy smiled too, looking at them over her shoulder, as she fried the garlic.

"I'm going to have to be away for a few days this week, my darling," he said casually. "Do you think Pleasant could stay for a day or so? The two of you could work on arrangements for the engagement party, and Pleasant could help with Tumi." The baby opened her mouth as if to cry, so Kubu popped the pacifier into it and out again. She chortled at him.

"Where are you going?" Joy sounded wary.

"We're going to do an excursion around Hukuntsi. Try to pick up where the Namibian geologist who was killed discovered the *koppies* he spoke about. We'll check it out and see whether there's anything valuable there."

"Who's 'we'?"

"Khumanego is going to guide us through the area. I'll take along three armed constables in two vehicles. We don't expect to find anyone, but rather be absolutely safe."

"How long will you be away?"

"Three, perhaps four, days. We're leaving on Wednesday."

Joy took the garlic off the hot plate and turned to face him. "You're lying to me, Kubu. You're not exploring. You're looking for the murderer."

Kubu sighed. Joy always saw through him. "We think there's something at those *koppies*, and Haake mentioned tracks. Tracks can be followed. We'll just see what turns up."

"Why do *you* have to go? It's not your area. You have to drive halfway across the country before you even start to look for this lions' den. Let that other detective do it. The one in Tsabong."

"Lerako? He's not really convinced this is the right thing to do, and he's not interested in other possibilities. He's still focused on the Bushmen in the area."

Joy turned back to her cooking. She started grating fresh ginger, knowing that Kubu liked plenty of it. "Maybe he's right. From what you've told me, all the murders are connected to Bushmen in some way."

"It can't be Bushmen. It's just not their culture. Khumanego says . . ."

But Joy interrupted him, banging down the grater and turning to face him again. "Khumanego! I hear so much about him. But he only cares about one thing, Kubu. His precious Bushmen! He doesn't care about you or the case. As soon as his friends were released at Tsabong, he lost interest and left you there on your own. And don't tell me no Bushman could be a murderer! They're not that different from us. Their culture's not that perfect. There are going to be criminals amongst them. They've come from Adam and Eve too, you know."

Kubu was surprised by Joy's outburst and had forgotten Tumi, who couldn't reach her pacifier and didn't like her mother's raised voice. She started to cry.

"Oh, give her to me," Joy said, scooping the infant from Kubu's arms. "Just watch that nothing burns. I'll feed her." She carried the baby into the bedroom and closed the door, cutting off Tumi's wail.

Kubu pretended to busy himself with the curry until Joy reappeared fifteen minutes later. She seemed calmer and took over the cooking again. "I put her down for a sleep. She'll be fine now. She was just hungry." She worked on the food in silence for a few minutes. Then she said, "I'm scared, Kubu. You're going out there in the middle of nowhere looking for people who are part of the desert. People who kill with poisons that have no antidotes." She swallowed, close to tears. "And Khumanego's a Bushman! If it turns out the murderers *are* Bushmen, whose side will he take, do you think?"

Kubu tried to reassure her, but she brushed it aside. "You're not taking that reporter-woman with you, are you?"

Kubu's jaw dropped. "Cindy Robinson? Of course not! It's a police matter, and it could be dangerous." Kubu stopped, realizing he had said too much, but Joy just nodded.

"She was with you in Tsabong. Oh forget it. There's no

point in arguing. You won't listen anyway." She put the lid on the pot, and put it on the stove at low heat. "The curry has to cook now. Let's have a drink. I feel like some wine. Get something nice from the fridge."

So Kubu did as he was told and poured a fruity sauvignon blanc that would stand up to the curry. Assuming there's any left by then, Kubu thought as Joy swallowed a large gulp. Why did he feel guilty? He was only doing his job. Joy was forgetting that.

Kubu took a mouthful of the wine, but found a sudden sourness to it.

Thirty-three

Tuesday was a frustrating day for Kubu. He had difficulty requisitioning the vehicles. One was easy, but the second was a problem. The license had expired on one of the satellite phones and had to be reinstated. No one could spare three constables for four days so he had to settle for one constable and a sergeant. Food needed to be organized. And they would need camping gear. Kubu rejected the cots out of hand. It would be impossible for him to stay on one of those, let alone sleep. He would use a blow-up mattress on the ground. He decided to take a box of wine with him for consolation.

Mabaku appeared from time to time, offered advice, and left. He issued a further statement to the press indicating that the police were on top of the situation and following up all possibilities. He hinted that the culprit might not even be a Bushman, but gave no details as to why that might be the case.

The statement read like what it was: an attempt to calm things down without giving any extra information. No one took any notice of it.

Khumanego was furious about the second vehicle and what he called the "army" of constables, and threatened not to come. It took Kubu half an hour to calm him down; he seemed completely unwilling to accept the potential danger of the situation.

Dr. Waskowski called. He'd had a good look at the map and seemed to find the geological structures quite interesting.

"Seems to show some igneous intrusions into the country rock. That could produce the sort of rocky hills shown in the sketch. Main problem is that there's no key. Nothing to indicate what the different styles of shading actually stand for. Maybe whoever drew the map had all that in his head."

However, there was nothing that really helped in terms of what they might be looking for out in the Kalahari.

By lunchtime Kubu was in a foul mood. He took his Tupperware of salad and cottage cheese and emptied it into a garbage bin. Then he headed out to find a large pizza with all the trimmings and as many steelworks as he could drink.

When he returned to the office, he received a call from Detective Sergeant Helu in Windhoek. He'd had another interview with Muller at the Namib Mining Company office, but had basically discovered nothing more. The man had clearly been shocked by Haake's death, but he had not followed the details in the press. But he had stuck to his story about Haake and Krige and obviously regarded the suggestion of other involvement by his company as ludicrous. It all seemed consistent with what Dr. Waskowski had said. Kubu thanked the Namibian policeman for his efforts, promised to keep him informed, and hung up.

Edison was waiting for him to finish the call. He had a tid-bit for Kubu. "I spoke to Tau today. He talked to Monzo's boss, Vusi, and he remembers the two students. Monzo said he'd take them on a game count. Vusi isn't sure where they went or how long Monzo was away, but they definitely left together."

Kubu gave Edison an enthusiastic thump on the shoulder, causing his colleague—no small man himself—to stagger. "You did a great job there, my friend. Really good detective work. I thought the connection was between Haake and Monzo, but that wasn't it at all. The connection was between Monzo and the two students, and, more importantly, with where they went. All the murders seem to link with a specific area now. And I bet that's the mysterious *koppies* in the southern Kalahari."

Edison nodded and stuck out his hand. "Look after yourself, Kubu." Kubu gave it a firm shake.

When Edison left, Mabaku came in and collapsed in Kubu's guest chair.

"I think we should call this off, Kubu. I'm really unhappy about it. If something happens to you, Joy will never forgive me, and what's worse I'll never forgive myself. And there's this Bushman civilian involved. How will we explain it if he's injured or killed? The whole thing reeks of a disaster waiting to happen."

Kubu was tempted to agree. He could go home to Joy, tell her all was well, and get a warm welcome from her, Tumi, and Ilia. And sleep in a proper bed.

Until the next murder.

He shook his head. "I want to clear this up, Jacob. We can't have any more murders. And we need to get the press off our backs. It's like going to the dentist. Get it over with. Don't wait until you lose the tooth."

Mabaku grimaced. He had no love for dentists. "I hope it's no worse than a visit to the dentist. You'd better be damned careful out there, Kubu."

"I know what I'm doing, Director," he replied, hoping that was true.

Mabaku nodded and started to leave. But at the door he turned around.

"Make sure you come back, Kubu," he said.

Part V

Au ha /khi: tʃweŋ, ha-ka !khweja ˉkʼ ʼao

When he kills things, his wind is cold

Thirty-four

When Kubu arrived at his office at 8:00 a.m. on Wednesday morning, the sight of two police Land Rover Defenders baking in the sun jolted his anxiety into high gear. Was he making a mistake in undertaking this mission? Would he find those responsible for the murders or was it, in fact, a wild goose chase?

He walked over to inspect the vehicles. They were identical, except that one had an off-road trailer attached. Both had roof racks with four jerry cans of extra fuel, two spare wheels, a gas cylinder, a spade, and a high-lift jack. Both vehicles were equipped with winches at the front in case they became stuck in the Kalahari sand. Inside each was a low-voltage fridge strapped to the floor, stocked with meat and other perishables. Next to the fridge were three plastic barrels of water—the most important supply of all. In a box on the backseat were two high-intensity handheld spotlights. He was pleased to see that both vehicles had two-way radios and satellite phones nestling in their cradles.

Kubu walked over to the trailer and peered in. There were tents and cots and a large inflatable mattress for him. There were several duffle bags containing sleeping bags, pillows, and extra blankets to ward off the cold of the desert nights. Also two more gas cylinders, a variety of pots and pans, and boxes of canned vegetables and soups. He made a mental note to check that someone had packed a couple of can openers and plenty of matches. He was pleased to see plenty of toilet paper, a toolbox, and several pints of engine oil. Whoever had prepared the vehicles knew what they were doing.

Kubu fetched his suitcase containing a few changes of clothes, his toiletries, and his boxed wine, and put it behind the driver's seat of what would be the lead Land Rover. He didn't want the wine to get too hot. Finally, he checked that he had his copy of Haake's map in his pocket.

Two uniformed policemen walked over, one a sergeant and one a constable. Each had a holster on his belt and carried a rifle. They introduced themselves as Sergeant Pikati and Constable Moeng. Kubu chatted to them for a few minutes to make sure they understood the nature of the trip and the dangers associated with it, but it was clear that they'd been fully briefed.

"I have bulletproof vests for everyone, Rra," Pikati said. "But I'm not sure . . ." He hesitated. "I'm not sure you'll fit into our biggest, and the smallest may be too big for your guide, if he's a Bushman."

"Bring them along anyway. I just hope we don't need them."

They eventually left Gaborone about 10:00 a.m.—an hour later than Kubu had hoped. Khumanego was late because of bad traffic on the road from Lobatse. He arrived with a small hold-all and his Bushman hunting kit.

"What's the hunting bag for?" Kubu wanted to know.

Khumanego frowned. "We're going into the Kalahari. No Bushman goes into the desert without this. Ever."

Kubu shrugged. He told Sergeant Pikati to drive the Land Rover with the trailer, and he would lead in the other.

Neither Kubu nor Khumanego spoke much, but when Khumanego did speak, he tried to persuade Kubu to give up on the mission.

"You're wasting your time, David. You think you can drive into the desert with a convoy of Land Rovers and sneak up on these so-called bandits?"

"There are only two Land Rovers. Hardly a convoy."

"They'll see you, and you won't see them. If they're out there, they know the desert, where to hide, where to watch. If they want to, they'll pick us off one by one. What are you try-ing to prove?"

"I'm not trying to prove anything, Khumanego. People are being murdered. There must be a reason. If I can find that, I'll find the people responsible. I've got to look, and the area around Tshane seems the most promising."

"Just because I'm a Bushman, I can't guarantee your safety, you know. I'm just a guide, not a guard."

Kubu didn't reply. Khumanego was right. The trip was dan-gerous. But they had no choice.

All the while the sun rose higher in the sky. Mirages ap-peared and disappeared, and the three policemen were soaked in sweat. Khumanego appeared unaffected by the heat.

Kubu was relieved to reach the Tshane police station. He sent Moeng for take-out sandwiches and cold drinks, while he conferred with the station commander and Tau, who was going to join them. Kubu had asked Lerako first, but Lerako had suggested Tau, who knew the area around Tshane much better. Obviously Lerako didn't expect much to come out of the adventure.

Given how late it was, they decided to postpone their departure until early the following morning. Although he was frustrated by the delay, Kubu had to agree that leaving that evening made no sense. Of course, the silver lining was he could call Joy and then enjoy a decent meal at the Endabeni Guest House.

The four policemen were at the Tshane police station by 8:00 a.m., but Khumanego was late. The previous afternoon he'd said he would stay with friends, but no one knew who they were or where they lived. Kubu fretted and fumed.

Khumanego eventually arrived, without excuse or apology, and it was nearly 9:00 a.m. before they set off into the Kalahari proper.

They initially headed southwest out of Tshane toward Mabuasehube. Kubu and Khumanego were in the lead Land Rover, the other three in the one pulling the trailer, keeping a good distance behind to avoid being overwhelmed by dust. Fortunately the road was sandy but firm, so the going was good.

Kubu talked about his parents and about Joy and Tumi. In broad terms, he tried to describe the changes at home since Tumi had been born and how he found the demands of child rearing sometimes difficult to mesh with his professional duties. Khumanego listened but said little, staring out of the open window. Suddenly he changed the subject.

"This isn't your world, David. This isn't Gaborone. It's very dangerous here—people get stuck and die of exposure and thirst in a matter of days. Even the Bushmen avoid it. Why don't we just drive for a day or two, look around, and head back. Your boss will be satisfied, and you'll have done your job."

"I'm not doing this for show! I'm serious about finding these bastards." Kubu was beginning to lose his temper. "If you don't want to help me, why did you come?"

Khumanego returned his attention to the red sand and scrubby shrubs that lined the road for miles and miles.

They had driven for just over two hours at a reasonable speed when Kubu pulled off the road and stopped. Everyone got out of the vehicles and took the opportunity to drink some water and stretch.

"We've reached the first waypoint. This is where we turn off," Kubu said, looking carefully at his handheld GPS. He pointed to an X on the large map of southern Botswana that he had unfolded on the hood of the Land Rover. "We'll drive for another hour and stop for lunch. Then we'll push on for about three or four hours, so we can set up camp in daylight. It's always useful to practice these things when you can see. Then when we set off tomorrow morning, we'll start looking for any small *koppies*. The problem is that they may only be thirty or forty feet high, so they'll be hard to see."

The rest of the day passed uneventfully. Progress was quite slow due to the soft sand, and all the men, except Khumanego, suffered in the heat. When they eventually stopped for the day, the policemen showed that they were experienced in setting up camp. The three tents went up quickly without a problem. Two cots were set in place in two of them. The large mattress, inflated using a little pump that was plugged into a cigarette lighter socket, was put in the third. Khumanego declined a cot and said he'd be more comfortable sleeping on the sand a little away from the camp.

"Isn't that dangerous?" Constable Moeng asked. "Aren't there wild animals that could attack you? Like hyenas or lions? Aren't there snakes or scorpions?"

Khumanego shook his head. "Bushmen know how to live *with* the animals and plants. We don't fight them like other people. We respect them, and they respect us. There's nothing to be afraid of."

"Aai. I'd never sleep out there. No matter what you say, I'd be scared. The tent is going to be bad enough. If a hyena can eat bones, it can also eat through the canvas. I'll be lucky to get any sleep at all."

While the camp was being prepared, Kubu took the satellite phone and walked a short distance away to make his check-in call to Edison. He gave their coordinates, and said he'd call again around eight the next morning.

Kubu turned the satellite phone off and walked back to camp. Before joining the others, he replaced the phone in its charger in the Land Rover.

Kubu was impressed with the food. His steaks arrived medium rare as he had requested, and he found the peas and baked beans quite tasty. Sitting under the brilliant stars, he even enjoyed the box wine. It's incredible, he thought as he gazed upward, how many stars you can see when there are no lights around. There was the Milky Way; and the Southern Cross and its pointers; and Orion with his belt and sword; and there was the brightest star of all—Sirius, the eye of Orion's hunting dog, Canis Major. Billions and billions of stars. It wasn't surprising that people looked upward in awe and wondered about the universe and how it began and what was going to happen to it. It was easy to see how so many people saw gods when they looked at the night sky.

Khumanego spoke little during the meal, but when he saw Kubu looking upward, he told the group stories about how the Bushmen viewed the skies.

"You think of those three stars as Orion's belt," he said, pointing. "We have a different story. For us they are zebras, a male in the middle with a female on each side. A god was standing on one of the star clouds and shot an arrow at the three zebras. You can see the arrow close to the zebras—it is those three stars close by. But the arrow fell short. So the zebras lived and, as the night wears on, the zebras will sink towards the earth. Then, one by one, they will step onto the earth and soon they will no longer be left in the sky. But the arrow will remain."

Nobody said anything for several minutes as they gazed upward.

"The moon was once a man who made Sun angry. Sun stabbed the man with his knife. And a bit fell off the man. Sun stabbed again and again until the man was nearly gone, had nearly disappeared. 'Spare me,' the man cried. 'Spare my children.' And Sun relented, and the man grew again. But when he was whole again, Sun grew angry once more and started to stab him again."

The men sat in the dark, lost in thought.

"If you listen carefully," Khumanego eventually continued, "you can hear the stars whispering. They are your ancestors talking to you, watching you, watching over you. They see what you do, how you live, and decide whether you will join them."

He turned to Kubu. "I'm sure Gobiwasi is now holding hands with his ancestors, watching us, remembering old times."

Kubu thought back on the wizened old man he'd seen not long ago. A man of dignity and grace, he thought.

After a while, Kubu stood up. "Time for coffee. Then to bed."

"Moeng will stand guard until one. Then I'll take over until dawn," Pikati told Kubu.

"Good idea," Kubu responded.

The rest stood up and went to try to get some sleep.

The group woke early and had finished a light breakfast and several cups of coffee by 6:00 a.m. They wanted to leave in the relative cool of the morning. They knew that the terrain was going to be much more difficult than the previous day because they'd be driving off road on soft sand through a part of the Kalahari that was covered with scrub. They'd have to maintain speed to prevent the vehicles from sinking into the sand, but that would be difficult because they'd constantly be avoiding bushes and small trees. Kubu had decided that he didn't want to drive under such conditions and brought Tau into the lead vehicle to take over.

It was only about five minutes after Kubu's Land Rover set off that they received a radio call from the second vehicle.

"Come in, KUBU ONE. Come in, please."

Sergeant Pikati told them that the second Land Rover's engine had spluttered to a stop moments after they had started. He asked them to return.

When they reached the vehicle, Kubu saw that Pikati was already at work, head under the hood, and Moeng was near the back wheel looking carefully at the fuel filter.

"It has to be something with the fuel," Pikati said as he stood up. "As far as I can see, all the electrics are okay."

"The filter is pretty clean," Moeng said, handing it to Kubu. Although Kubu knew little about the workings of a vehicle, he could see that the filter wasn't clogged.

"Try it again. Maybe it's like my computer. When something happens I just turn it off and then on again. It usually works."

Moeng replaced the filter, and Pikati slid behind the steering wheel and tried to start the engine. It cranked over and over, but did not start.

"Maybe it's the spark plugs," Kubu offered.

"I don't think so. The engine spluttered to a stop just after we got going. That wouldn't have happened if the plugs weren't working. It would've cut out right away. Anyway I checked them before you got here, just in case."

"I don't know much about cars," Kubu said, "but let's think this through."

Pikati nodded.

"One. Is there fuel in the tank?"

"Yes. The fuel gauge shows full—we topped the tanks this morning. And there have been no leaks. We'd have noticed that."

"Two. Is the fuel pump working?"

"We can hear it."

"But you don't know for sure?"

"No. But it is easy to check. Moeng, unclip the fuel line from the filter housing. I'll turn on the ignition."

Moeng went back to the rear wheel, felt inside the wheel well and unclipped the fuel line to the filter.

"Okay. Start her."

Pikati turned the ignition and fuel sprayed out of the line.

"Stop!" Moeng shouted.

Pikati turned the key off.

"And you're sure the spark plugs are okay?"

"Yes."

Kubu shook his head. "I've no idea what else to ask."

The three men gathered around and tried to brainstorm what else could be the problem, but to no avail. Nothing else made sense.

Kubu called to Tau and Khumanego, who had found a little shade and were watching the proceedings with interest.

"Come over here! We need to decide what to do."

Kubu waited until 8:00 a.m. to call Edison. This time it took a couple of attempts to get through.

"Good morning, Kubu. How are things in the desert?" Edison was obviously in a good mood.

"We've got a problem, and I need you to do something for me. We haven't moved since last night."

"What's the problem?" Edison asked.

"It's one of the Land Rovers. We can't figure out what's wrong with it. The engine turns over, but doesn't catch. It seems the fuel system is working, and so are the spark plugs. We've run out of ideas."

"What do you want me to do?'

"Find a couple of Land Rovers and send them out. I'd like them to reach us tomorrow evening at latest. Also, talk to a mechanic and see if he's got any ideas."

Edison whistled. "That'll be difficult. It's the weekend tomorrow. I may have to get them to Tshane from Gaborone. They'd have to leave by tomorrow morning to get to you in time. I'm not sure I can get everything organized by then."

"If they left at dawn, they'd be here by evening. I need them here as soon as possible. We've got to push on, otherwise the murderer may strike again. I can't afford to wait here forever."

"I'll have to clear this with the director first. Call me in a few hours, say at noon, and I'll let you know."

Kubu knew there was nothing he could do but wait—not his favorite pastime.

Thirty-five

Kubu thought it was one of the worst days he had ever spent. Worse even than those dark days when he had been taunted and bullied at school. They waited hour after scorching hour, passing the time with nothing to do. Kubu fretted, wondering where the murderers were, and what they planned. He felt sure that the wasted time was critical, that something bad was ahead.

The three policemen spent the morning uncomplaining under the vehicles—the best shade available. Kubu envied them as he looked from the broken shade of a nearby tree at the three sets of boots sticking out from under the Land Rovers. His morning was spent shifting from one uncomfortable position on his camp chair to another, following the shade, mopping his forehead and toweling off his soaking upper body.

Khumanego was nowhere to be seen. He had left camp,

saying he'd return later. Where was he? Kubu wondered. What could he be doing in this heat? He was probably happily trotting through the Kalahari feeling quite at home! Or was he meeting with his Bushman friends who roamed the desert?

Every hour or so, each man would drink several large glasses of water. Nobody ate anything after breakfast—it was just too hot.

Kubu was very thankful when it was noon. He walked slowly to his Land Rover and took out the satellite phone. He needed to share his misery. When Edison answered he asked for Mabaku, and the director came on the line almost immediately. He must have been listening over Edison's shoulder, Kubu thought.

"Kubu, it's Mabaku here. Look, this whole venture is getting out of hand. We won't be able to get the Landies to you before the day after tomorrow. Around lunchtime, we think."

"But, Director! We need them tomorrow at the latest."

"I'm sending more men. And they have to get provisions and so on. These things take time. They'll only be able to leave Tshane around lunch tomorrow."

"Then they should reach us late that night."

"They're not going to travel at night. I don't want them to get lost, let alone attacked."

"I can't sit in the desert twiddling my thumbs when people are being murdered left, right, and center!"

Mabaku's voice rose. "Don't do anything stupid, Kubu. If you don't follow orders this time, I'll transfer you to the Camel Corps or something worse!"

Kubu didn't laugh.

"Look, why don't you go back to Tshane and wait in comfort?"

There was some merit in that suggestion, Kubu thought. But it meant another two days of sitting in the Land Rover, bouncing up and down. That might be worse than sitting in the sun doing nothing.

"No. I'll wait here," he decided. "I'll be careful. I promise."

"What's gone wrong now?"

Kubu gave a start and turned. He hadn't seen or heard Khumanego come back, but now he was there, standing quite close.

· "It's going to take them two days to get here. There's nothing we can do but sit and wait. It's infuriating!"

Khumanego walked closer and spoke softly. "David, it's time to give this up. Be patient. Wait until these people make some mistake and give themselves away. Let's go back to Tshane. Perhaps we can work something out from there."

Kubu shook his head. "I'm not giving up. That's final."

Khumanego said nothing for several seconds. "Where's the sensible David I used to know? At school you always did the right thing. I was the one who'd take risks and get us into trouble."

For a while the two men stood next to each other in silence. At last Khumanego sighed, and said, "Look, I really do want to help. It all just seems so pointless. But maybe we *can* do something while we wait for the other vehicles. Actually, I think there *is* a group of small hills not too far from here. We could take a look from a safe distance. Then come back and report to your boss. If we don't see anything . . ." He shrugged.

Kubu hesitated, thinking about Khumanego's change of mind. "How far away are they?"

"Perhaps two or three hours."

"Are they on the GPS track we're following?"

"More or less. I don't use a GPS. I just know."

Kubu knew Mabaku wouldn't approve of this adventure, but he couldn't sit around for another two days doing nothing. He'd die of frustration and boredom. And if they found something, perhaps Mabaku could lay his hands on a helicopter or two.

"Tau!"

Tau walked back over.

"Tau, we're going to scout around the area for a while. See if we can see anything. You come with us. We'll drive for a couple of hours, then come back for the night."

Tau did not look happy. "Assistant Superintendent, are you sure? Shouldn't we wait for the others? You know how easy it is for a Landie to get stuck in the sand. You should never travel in the desert with one vehicle."

"We can't just sit here roasting in the sun, doing nothing. We're not going far, and we have radios and the satellite phone. Khumanego thinks there are some hills not too far away."

"Why don't we wait until tomorrow? We can leave at sunrise. At least it will be cool." Tau's voice betrayed his anxiety.

Kubu shook his head. "No. We'll do a short trip this afternoon. If it takes longer than expected, we can try again tomorrow."

"But . . ."

"We're going!" Kubu snapped. "We'll drive for a couple of hours, then come back." He stalked off to the Land Rover. Khumanego was already there, waiting.

After half an hour they stopped to give Tau a break. Wrestling with the wheel was hard work, and Tau was dripping, as was Kubu. Tau took advantage of the stop to stand on top of the vehicle and scour the landscape with his binoculars to see whether he could see any *koppies*, small or large. Kubu, of course, refused to scramble onto the roof for fear of damaging government property. Khumanego just shook his head. "It's still too far," he said, but wouldn't elaborate when they asked how far it was. He seemed to be getting increasingly withdrawn and said little.

After another half an hour, Khumanego asked Tau to stop at the top of a small rise. "Your map says we should go in that direction," Khumanego said, pointing to the southeast. "There is nothing there. I know it well. We should go further east, in that direction. We'll have a better chance there, I think."

"But what about the GPS track? Of the students who died? They were further south."

"But you don't know if they were murdered, do you? You're just speculating again. Another death by a poison used by Bushmen. Therefore it must have been a Bushman. Right? That's how you are thinking. You've become one of them, David. You're no longer a friend of the Bushmen."

Kubu lost his temper. "Damn it, Khumanego! I'm not one of *them*, whoever *they* are. And I'm not one of *you* either. I'm a police detective, and I'm trying to catch a vicious murderer— maybe a gang. I'm interested in facts. I don't make them up. And I don't believe them unless I have double-checked them, if that's possible."

"If you trust me, you'll go in that direction. If you don't, why did we come on this trip in the first place? We might as well have relaxed at the camp. Going east is where we'll find the hills I remember."

Kubu was in a quandary. Khumanego was asking him to deviate from the planned route. But of all of them, only the Bushman knew this area. Not from maps, but by having spent time here, by being here. He didn't need maps, indeed didn't really see the point of them. To him the desert was a map unto itself.

Eventually Kubu decided he had to trust Khumanego's knowledge. They would follow his directions.

About an hour later, Khumanego asked Tau to stop. He walked a couple of hundred yards up a slight slope and waved for the other two to follow. When they arrived, he pointed to the horizon.

"See those black lines?" he asked. "Those are a small range of hills. That's where I'm taking you."

"What's there?" Kubu asked, out of breath.

"I don't know. I've not been there. My people regard them as sacred. We are not allowed to go there."

"Have you heard anything about them? Could there be precious stones there?"

"I've heard nothing, so I can't answer you. Wait a minute, I'll go and get your binoculars. Then we can take a better look."

Khumanego loped off toward the vehicle.

"What do you think?" Kubu asked Tau.

"I think we should go back to the others. It's getting late. When the new vehicles reach us, we can come back here and investigate." He hesitated. "About Khumanego, I don't know what to think. I don't know whether to believe anything he says. Sometimes he's easy to read. Sometimes I can't tell whether he is lying or telling the truth."

"We were close friends when we were young," Kubu said. "We were both bullied and teased a lot. Me for my size. Him for his race. It was a bad time for both of us. His friendship means a lot to me."

As Kubu turned to see where Khumanego was, he heard the Land Rover start. Kubu was stunned, but Tau realized what was happening at once and sprinted toward the vehicle, shouting. "Stop, you bastard! Stop!"

He was still a hundred yards from the Land Rover when it started moving and roared away. He pulled his gun from its holster and fired at the vehicle, but he knew it would be in vain. The distance was too great.

"Bastard! He's leaving us to die." Tau was drenched from his short run in the scorching sun.

"He'll be back," Kubu said doubtfully. "Maybe he's just taking a look around."

"Bengu!" shouted Tau. "Wake up! You're a fool! Khumanego has led us by the nose. The deviation from the proper route. The broken-down vehicle. It's all been planned. And you fell for it! You're the reason we're going to die! Believing a Bushman? You must be mad! You can't trust anything they say."

Kubu swallowed. His stomach ached, and he could feel a headache coming on. Think! he said to himself. Think! Keep your head, and you'll get out of here. Panic, and you're dead.

"We're going to die, Bengu. All because you believed a Bushman!" Tau grabbed Kubu's shoulder and shook it repeatedly. "It's your fault. It's your fault."

Kubu came to life. He brushed Tau's arm aside.

"Calm down, Tau," he hissed. "If we panic, we *will* die."

"He's taken all the water. You can't live without water. The radios too. And they don't know where we are! They won't be able to find us."

"Listen to me. We can get out of this. I know how to survive in the desert. They'll find us in a day or two at most. Just believe me, and we'll be okay." Kubu didn't feel as confident as he sounded, but he needed to get Tau under control.

"Come on, Tau. Come with me." Kubu grabbed Tau's arm and pulled him in the direction of where the Land Rover had been. "First thing is we have to get out of the sun. Otherwise we'll go mad. We'll sit there in the shade for half an hour, then we'll be calm, and we can work out what to do. Come on!"

Kubu dragged Tau to the small trees that offered a little shade.

"Half an hour, Tau. In half an hour we'll figure out how to get out of here." He collapsed on the ground, head and stomach aching. "We'll get out of this. Just keep calm."

Kubu sat on the sand and let his head drop into his hands. It was time to put his mind to work.

Thirty-six

When Kubu lifted his head, he understood his predicament and knew what they must do.

The situation was dire. Nobody knew where they were. It's Friday afternoon now, he thought. When he didn't report that evening, Edison would check with the other Land Rover and when they told him he hadn't returned, he'd report to Mabaku that they'd lost contact. He wondered what Mabaku would do. Probably nothing until tomorrow morning, because it was so difficult to arrange anything after hours.

And the relief Land Rovers couldn't reach them before Sunday night even if they knew where to go, which they didn't. So it was unlikely that they could be rescued before Monday at the earliest.

Kubu thought back to his survival course. "A human can survive three to five days without water depending on the conditions," the instructor—a humorless ex-Special Forces sergeant major from the British armed forces—had told them. "You can live for weeks without food, but only days without water. Don't forget that. Be prepared."

Monday evening was three days away.

Tuesday evening was four.

And if they weren't found by Wednesday evening, it would be too late.

And they were not prepared. They had no water, no food, no tools, no shelter, no blankets. Nothing! So even Tuesday evening might be too late.

Khumanego had certainly planned this well, Kubu thought. He'd been blinded by his affection and friendship for the Bushman. Why hadn't he questioned Khumanego's motivation—the sudden change of heart volunteering to lead them to the *koppies*? He'd let his emotions override his brain. Suddenly he remembered the boot prints in the desert near where Monzo had died. Supposedly the Bushman group had discovered them, but the exchange between Khumanego and the other Bushmen had all been in their own language, and it was Khumanego who had led the detectives to the prints. His heart sank. It *was* his fault. Tau had a right to scream at him.

But screaming was not going to save them. Thinking was.

"Tau!" Kubu said loudly. "Tau, listen to me!"

Tau was lying on his side in the sand, like a baby, clutching his knees to his chest.

"Tau! Sit up. We need to talk."

Slowly Tau stirred and sat up. Kubu could see the stress in his face and the hostility in his eyes.

"Tau. It *is* my fault we're here. I'm sorry for that. But now we've got to get out and capture Khumanego. If he isn't the murderer, he knows who is."

Tau nodded without saying a word.

"Our best chance is to stay here. The tire tracks lead here. They are what the others will look for and follow. Our greatest danger is dehydration. We must do everything we can to conserve water."

"We don't have any water!" Tau growled.

"In our bodies, I mean. We must minimize our sweating. Move as little as possible during the hot hours and try and find some better shade than this." Kubu looked at the meager foliage of the surrounding trees.

"Just wait to die, you mean!"

"No, no. Doing nothing is a positive step. It's not giving up. It gives us the best chance to get out of here. I took a survival course from an ex-British Special Forces instructor—best in the business. Stay put is what he told us. As soon as you start wandering off, you make it harder for the rescuers. He also said that you should build a nest—make yourself as comfortable as possible. It helps you mentally as well as physically."

Kubu pointed at the sun, which was sinking rapidly toward the horizon. "It's going to be dark soon. Before the light goes, we should build a better canopy in this tree. That'll help with the sun tomorrow."

He walked to some scraggly bushes nearby and started breaking off branches with leaves, sometimes standing on them where they joined the trunk if he couldn't break them off by hand.

"Come on Tau," he shouted. "Don't just sit there. We've got to protect ourselves from the sun. Come and help."

Tau shrugged his shoulders, but didn't move.

Kubu tried a couple more times to motivate his colleague, to no avail. Exasperated, he turned away and concentrated on what he was doing. After fifteen minutes he had gathered quite a pile, which he carried back to the small trees where Tau was still sitting. He then wove them into the branches. When he finished it was almost dark, and he was satisfied they would have better shade the next day.

He turned to Tau. "It's going to get cold tonight, Tau, probably down to fifty degrees, maybe colder. We should sleep next to each other to use each other's warmth."

Tau shook his head. "I'll sleep over there," he said, pointing at another clump of trees about fifty yards away.

"Don't be stupid. It's important that we stay right together. Not only for body heat, but in case something attacks us at night—a hyena or lion. We've got handguns. We may need them, but it won't be much use if we're far apart and possibly shooting at each other in the dark. We should also try to shoot an animal or large bird, if we can. We can eat the meat and drink the blood. That'll help. Tomorrow we'll try to find some *tsama* melons and tubers. I know how to do that."

Kubu could see the fear in Tau's eyes. He may have been brought up in the Kalahari, Kubu thought, but he's clearly afraid of it. "Don't panic, Tau. We've got to keep calm, even if we're terrified. Panicking will only create more problems."

When Edison didn't receive the call from Kubu at 6:00 p.m., he decided to wait half an hour before doing anything. When he hadn't heard by 6:30 p.m., he called the other satellite phone. Sergeant Pikati answered almost immediately.

"Kubu?"

"No, it's Edison. Where's Kubu?"

Pikati recounted what Kubu had done. When he hadn't

returned by dusk, they'd tried reaching him by both radio and satellite phone, but hadn't been successful. They wanted to know what to do.

Edison said he'd speak to Mabaku and call them back.

"I should fire him," Mabaku exploded when Edison told him about Kubu's trip into the desert. "I told him not to do anything stupid, and now he's gone off with only one vehicle. Idiot!"

"I need to call the others back and let them know what to do."

Mabaku leaned back and pondered his options. "Tell them to monitor their satellite phone all night and check in first thing in the morning. They should continue to try and contact Kubu, and if they hear from him, they're to contact you immediately. If you hear anything, call me, no matter what the time. In the meantime, get hold of the backup group and tell them to be ready to leave as soon as possible."

"What do you think's happened?"

"We've already had one breakdown, so it's possible that Kubu's vehicle did the same. But then to have his phone not work as well is highly unlikely. I don't like the smell of this, but there's not a lot we can do until morning."

Neither Kubu nor Tau slept much that night. Both were miserable, tossing and turning as they tried to find a comfortable position in the sand; and both were scared—scared of what animals might be wandering close to them; scared of their predicament. To make things worse, as the night wore on, the desert cold took a deeper and deeper hold on their bodies, causing them to shiver, sometimes uncontrollably.

The half moon provided only a little light and no comfort.

Their eyes kept playing tricks in the dim light as they thought they saw things lurking nearby.

As the sky lightened, both men stood up, thankful the night was over, slapping themselves and stamping their feet to increase circulation. God, Kubu thought, I've got at least two more nights of this torture. Maybe three. But if it's four, I won't have to worry anymore.

"How are you doing, Tau?" he asked.

"Terrible. I was scared all night. I didn't sleep at all."

"I didn't either. Well, let's get to work. First thing we have to do is make something that can be seen from the air." Kubu hesitated as he thought what their physical state might be by Tuesday or Wednesday. "And from the ground. In a few days we may not be able to signal for help ourselves."

Kubu started to unbutton his shirt. "Take off your underwear, Tau. We can make a white cross on the ground. A signal that'll be easy to see from the air. We can put them back on at night for warmth."

"Assistant Superintendent, your plan is crap. We can't just stay here and wait. What if they don't come? We'll just die. I'm going for help."

"Tau! Listen to me. Leaving is the wrong decision. If we're to survive, we have to conserve energy and, more important, water. If you walk, you'll sweat ten times as much as if you lie here in the shade. You can't survive without water. You'll die before you get back."

"Bullshit! If I leave now, it'll be cool for another couple of hours. Then I'll only be a few hours away. We drove two sides of a triangle. If I cut the corner, it'll be much shorter. Maybe only twenty miles. I can walk that in six or seven hours, even in sand."

Kubu grabbed Tau's arm. "Don't be stupid! If you don't keep to the tracks, you'll get lost. There is nothing to navigate by. No hills. Nothing. It's impossible to walk in a straight line even on good ground. In the desert you'll end up going in circles."

"I don't have to walk exactly in a straight line. I'll intersect the vehicle tracks somewhere before we turned off. I'm going, no matter what you say. I know you can't walk far, but that doesn't mean you have to force me to stay."

"Staying has nothing to do with my size, Tau. It's basic survival to stay here. I know you want to do something. But believe me, staying is the right decision. You'll never make it if you try to walk back."

"You'll thank me when I arrive with help. You got me into this, Assistant Superintendent. I'm going to get myself out of it. Why would I trust your judgment now?"

"Tau, as your superior, I order you to stay!"

Tau laughed at him. "You're ordering me to stay? Ha! I'm going. Hope to see you soon!" With that, Tau stripped off his shirt and put it over his head. He turned and, ignoring the vehicle tracks, walked resolutely into the desert.

"Tau! Tau!" Kubu shouted. "Don't take off your shirt! You'll sweat more. Lose more water. Put it back on!"

Tau walked on without looking back.

Kubu shook his head. Tau was making every mistake. He shouldn't have left, and he shouldn't have taken off his shirt. And he should have followed the tracks. He'll get lost, Kubu thought with anguish. His chances of getting through are close to zero.

Kubu spent the next fifteen minutes dragging dead branches into the center of the tracks. If I'm unconscious, they'll know I'm near, he thought. Then he put his white undershirt and underpants on top of the pile, spread out as much as possible. Not very big, he mused, but at least it's a different color from the surroundings.

He looked up into the sky. "Please, God, let them find me! And help Tau. He needs it."

Mabaku was at the office at 6:00 a.m. Edison was there to meet him. He was looking tense and hadn't slept much.

"There's been no word from Kubu," he said.

"What's the status of the backup Land Rovers?"

"They'll be ready to leave just after lunch."

"Get them to leave as soon as they can. Make sure they both have satellite phones with them. If they haven't got everything they need, get the police at Tshane or Kang to take care of it and have it waiting when they arrive. I want them to push on tonight and get as close to the others as possible."

"Can we get a helicopter to search?"

The director pressed the button on his intercom: "Miriam, where are the helicopters? I need to know now!"

Only a few minutes passed before Miriam stuck her head in. "One is having its annual service, and the other two are in Kasane working with Immigration on the illegal alien stuff."

"Damn! Call the Molepolole Air Base and see if any of their choppers are available. Tell them it's an emergency." Miriam's head disappeared.

Mabaku waited impatiently until Miriam returned. "You can have a Defence Force helicopter when it returns tomorrow night. But you'll have to find a pilot, if you want to use it before Monday morning."

"See if one of the police pilots can get to Molepolole tomorrow. Let me know as soon as possible."

Mabaku turned again to Edison. "You'll report to me every hour on the hour as to what is going on. I don't want any surprises. If something important happens between the hours, I want to know about it. Immediately! Understand?"

"Yes, Director. Every hour on the hour."

Mabaku stood up and walked to the window. He gazed out at Kgale Hill. He had a dilemma. Should he call Kubu's wife and tell her that they'd lost contact with him or should he wait until the following day? Phoning her would send her into a fit of anxiety, perhaps greater than usual because of the baby. But not phoning her was unfair. She deserved to be in the loop.

He paced up and down, unsure of what to do. Eventually he decided to call. He knew he couldn't face her if something happened to Kubu and he'd kept quiet.

The phone rang just as Joy was giving Tumi a bath. She put her down on a folded towel and answered. A chill ran through her as she recognized Mabaku's voice.

"Is there anything wrong? Has something happened to Kubu?"

"Joy, relax. I am just calling to say we've lost radio contact with Kubu. We don't expect anything to be wrong. His satellite phone is probably not working. But I thought you should know. We've dispatched two additional vehicles, because one of Kubu's broke down, and I've a helicopter standing by at Molepolole Air Base just in case. I'm sure there's nothing to worry about."

"Are you sure he's okay?"

"He was fine when we spoke to him yesterday morning. It's probably nothing, but I'm not going to take any chances. Why don't you have your sister spend the day with you? I'll call you this evening and let you know what's happening."

Joy put down the phone with tears in her eyes. What if Kubu was dead? What would she do?

As the relief Land Rovers were moving along the Trans-Kalahari Highway to Kang, Kubu was lying on his back in the little shade afforded by the rough canopy he'd built. He'd hollowed out a depression in the sand in which he could lie. His arms were folded across his chest, and a handkerchief covered his face. He tried not to move at all, but that was difficult, especially when little insects started to explore his body.

Not only was he very hot, but he was ravenous. He hadn't eaten a thing since lunchtime the previous day. He'd poked around in the sand, hoping to find a tuber the way Khumanego had shown him so many years earlier. A couple of times he saw the telltale vines that led to the edible roots, but even after digging down a few feet with his bare hands, he'd found nothing. And he was parched. He could almost feel the heat sucking the water from his body.

Part of the time he tried to blank out his mind, to meditate, to detach his physical discomfort from his consciousness. The rest of the time he thought about the murders, and in particular about Khumanego. And when he thought about Khumanego, his emotions swung rapidly between anger, disappointment, and self-recrimination. How could his old friend have become so greedy that he would leave Kubu in the desert to die? And for what? Some gemstones? After all they had gone through together? How could Khumanego have used him the way he had—on the flimsy pretext of looking after Bushman interests? And how could he have been so gullible as to believe Khumanego?

Kubu tried to build a murder case against Khumanego in his mind. But he found it hard to pull all the pieces together. Was that because the evidence just wasn't there? Or was it because it was becoming harder to focus his attention?

It was all so confusing that he closed his eyes and tried to empty his mind.

The relief Land Rovers reached Tshane by mid-afternoon. The Saturday roads had been relatively quiet, and they'd made good time. The four policemen were drenched in sweat by the time they arrived and were pleased to have a break to stretch and pour cold water over their heads, while the vehicles were refueled and provisioned. The next part of the trip would be far less comfortable and, most probably, dangerous.

Kubu couldn't bear it anymore. He'd been lying on the sand for nearly eight hours. He had to stand up and move about. Despite his lack of activity, his shirt was wet through and although his face was covered, his brow was dripping wet. My God, he thought, if I'm sweating like this, what about Tau? He was mad to leave. In this heat he may only last two days. I hope he doesn't get lost. But maybe he can shoot something to eat. Perhaps there's a chance he'll get through.

Kubu was getting desperate to urinate, but was trying not to in the hope that would slow dehydration. I've no idea whether it helps, he thought. But why take the chance? Now if I had a couple of big plastic bottles, I could use the sun to turn my pee into water easily enough.

As that thought ran through his head, so did a childhood rhyme:

"If 'ifs' and 'ands' were pots and pans,

There'd be no need for tinkers' hands."

He grinned. "I'm losing it," he said out loud. He glanced at his watch. "Four o'clock. The Land Rovers may not even have left Tshane yet."

That's not the way to think, he admonished himself. Be positive.

He thought about Joy and Tumi. They were reason enough to get through this. He pictured Tumi's little fingers curled around his own. And Joy in bed with him, caressing each other. Softly. Gently.

"The Land Rovers will drive through the night until they meet up with Pikati and Moeng. And then they'll find me a few hours later. That would be tomorrow morning." He liked the sound of his own voice. He felt he had company in this barren place.

Mabaku called Joy at 6:00 p.m.

"They haven't reached the place where the Land Rover broke down. It may get too dark to drive off road. They'll be there early tomorrow morning. I'm sure there's nothing to worry about. I'll call as soon as they get there."

Joy poured herself a large glass of wine. Pleasant had gone home at Joy's insistence because she had a date with Bongani.

"I'm sure Kubu's fine," Joy muttered to herself. "I'll have an early night, and Mabaku will call in the morning."

In fact, she did not sleep well. A combination of a little too much wine and her fear of losing Kubu kept her awake. She spent most of the night admonishing herself for being so hard on Kubu for not pulling his weight around the house. He works so hard, she told herself. He needs a break when he gets home. I'll try to be more understanding in future.

That decision made her feel slightly better.

◁▷ ◁▷ ◁▷

The Land Rovers did indeed drive through the darkness, keeping a close watch on their GPS. They found the tracks at the first waypoint, where Kubu and his group had left the road, and set off to follow them. But after an hour, they decided to stop for the night—they'd been driving for over ten hours, the last part in very difficult conditions, and they were afraid of losing the tracks. In the morning, it wouldn't take long to reach the disabled Land Rover.

They reported to Edison, who was resigned to living at CID headquarters for the weekend, and asked him to tell Pikati and Moeng that they'd be there early in the morning

The second night was much worse than the first. Kubu had no company and a body that ached for food and water. His physical discomfort made it much more difficult to lie still. He was too cold to sleep and tossed and turned, uncomfortable in the extreme.

To make things worse, there were jackals close by. He could hear them howling, as though inviting others to a banquet. And he thought he heard the eerie call of a hyena in the distance. That was the animal he was most afraid of. Fearless, a hunter as well as a scavenger, with the strongest jaws of any animal, a hyena ate everything, including the bones, of their prey.

When he woke up, Kubu spent half an hour scouring the area for melons and tubers, but found none. Despondent, he lay down in the shallow depression—his nest in the desert. He tried not to move, and lay there, eyes shut, willing his rescuers to find him.

Thirty-seven

The relief team set off as the sun rose. Although they didn't know any of the original team personally, they had heard of the fat detective and his ability to bring criminals to justice. Police always looked after their own, so they were eager to find out what was happening.

They came upon the disabled Land Rover about 7:30 a.m. Pikati and Moeng had crawled from under the vehicle at the sound of their approach and were delighted to see the newcomers.

After a short conference, they decided to take the two vehicles to follow Kubu's tracks. They'd leave a note explaining what they were doing in case he returned.

Sergeant Mogale, the leader of the relief team, phoned Edison, who was waiting with great anxiety for news. He briefly explained what the situation was and what they were planning.

"The director wants you to report every thirty minutes from now on," Edison said. "No exceptions! I think he'll personally wring your necks if you don't. I've never seen him so worked up."

"Joy, this is Mabaku. The relief vehicles have reached where Kubu last reported from. But they still haven't heard from him."

Joy was so distraught, she couldn't say anything.

"Joy, I know how you must be feeling, but there is nothing to suggest something bad has happened. The vehicles have plenty of food and water. Try to keep calm and don't think about it. Kubu is a very resourceful man."

When Joy put down the phone, she slumped into a chair. She was exhausted. Not only was she sick with worry, but Tumi was crying incessantly, no doubt affected by her mother's anxiety.

I need help, Joy thought. She picked up the phone to ask Pleasant to come over again.

As the day wore on, so the temperatures rose. Even partially shielded from the sun by the makeshift canopy, Kubu was intensely uncomfortable.

"You have to keep your mind occupied, Kubu," he said aloud, trying to mimic the survival instructor's British accent. "If you don't, you'll go mad!"

Kubu decided to hum all the arias he knew—he would have preferred to sing them, but feared it would take too much energy—a commodity in short supply. So for the next hour or so, the insects of the Kalahari were treated to a collection of operatic favorites.

"Am I going to make it?" Kubu wondered after his second

encore. He wasn't feeling nearly as optimistic as on the previous day. That morning he'd tried to imagine what Khumanego would have done after driving away to make rescue unlikely.

If it were me, Kubu thought, I'd circle back on my tracks until I reached where we left the planned route. Then I'd hide the tracks where we turned off and continue on as originally planned. After several hours, I'd hide the Land Rover and disappear.

This speculation depressed Kubu. It would be very difficult for anyone to find him. They'll drive right past where we turned, he thought.

Perhaps I *should* walk out, he thought. If I walk at night, it'll be cool enough, and I should be able to see the tracks in the moonlight. And if I sleep in the day, I won't lose too much water. And I'll be closer when they come for me.

If they come, a little voice said.

"When they come," he said out loud. "When they come! I'm going to make it. I know how to survive."

Even in his tired state, Kubu was worried by the little sliver of negativity that had insinuated itself into his brain. He realized that dehydration was beginning to affect his thinking and attitude.

He closed his eyes and tried to will his discomfort away.

The searchers made their first call back to Edison where Kubu, Tau, and Khumanego had made their first stop. It was easy to see the footprints around the track.

They made their second call where Khumanego had persuaded them to deviate from the planned route. No footprints left the area of the vehicle. Still, they felt they were getting closer.

On the third call, they had nothing to report. The tracks seemed to stretch out endlessly ahead of them. The fourth and fifth calls were again the same. Nothing to be seen, except the tracks leading them on.

On the sixth call, however, Director Mabaku was on the phone. "Mogale, you need to pick up the pace. We've got to find them. It's been more than two days since they left the others."

"Director, we're going as fast as we can. It's not easy out here. They're probably still with the vehicle, so they've got water and food."

"Try to go faster. I'm worried about them."

The group took a short break, eating stale sandwiches, and drinking a lot of water. Then they set off again.

Almost exactly half an hour later, they saw Kubu's Land Rover. They stopped several hundred yards away and approached cautiously, weapons at the ready.

"Kubu! Tau!" Pikati shouted. "Are you there?"

No response.

"Kubu! Tau. Are you there?"

They spread out and moved ahead carefully. When they got to the Land Rover, they saw there was nobody inside. Mogale immediately called Edison, gave him their coordinates, and told him what they'd found.

"But no Kubu? None of them?"

"Not that we can see. But we're going to look for footprints now. I should be able to tell you, when we talk next."

They spent the next thirty minutes scouring the area for clues to what had happened. All they found, leading away from the Land Rover into the desert, was a single trail of barefoot prints. Very small.

"It has to be a Bushman," Pikati said. "Maybe it's Khumanego."

"But he had shoes! And where are the others then?"

No one had an answer.

Mogale picked up the satellite phone. "I need to speak to Director Mabaku," he told Edison.

"He's right here!"

It took a few minutes to explain the situation. "What should we do now, Director? Should we follow the footprints? Should we go back?"

Mabaku thought for a few seconds. "If you're sure the footprints aren't Kubu's or Tau's, don't worry about them right now. Drive back to the disabled Land Rover and keep a close lookout for footprints next to the track. They must've left the vehicle somewhere along the way. You found some already, but maybe you missed some too. If you don't find any others, spend some time where you did find them. Search all around the area. There has to be an easy explanation. If none of that works, I'll have a helicopter go to your camp first thing in the morning. Maybe it'll see something you can't."

When Mabaku told Joy that they had found Kubu's Land Rover, but he wasn't with it, she dropped the phone and burst into tears. Pleasant put her arm around her sister and picked up the phone to speak to the director.

"Director Mabaku. This is Joy's sister, Pleasant. I'll stay with Joy until you find Kubu. She's not taking it very well."

"Thank you, Pleasant. If you need any help, please say so. Any shopping, a police psychologist, anything. All you have to do is ask. But please try to reassure Joy. There's nothing to indicate that anything has happened to Kubu."

The temperature was over a hundred degrees under the little tree where Kubu lay on his back, but he wasn't sweating nearly as much as he had the previous day. He felt very lethargic and didn't want to get up and walk around. I'll wait till it's cooler, he thought.

He knew he was losing water fast. When he'd urinated that morning, the liquid was a dark orange brown—a sure sign of dehydration. He resigned himself to the fact he wouldn't find anything to eat or drink, and hoped his body knew it could feed off his fat for nourishment. Maybe my extra pounds can be put to good use after all, he thought.

It took the two Land Rovers over four hours to get back to the camp. They hadn't seen any additional footprints on the way. And they had found nothing useful at the two spots where they'd previously seen footprints. To all intents and purposes, Kubu and Tau had disappeared into thin air. And maybe Khumanego had too.

It was a very worried Mogale who made the final report to Mabaku for the day. "We need the helicopter," he said. "We've done everything we can. There's no sign of them."

Mabaku promised to send the BDF helicopter as early as possible the next morning to where they were camped. They should stay there until it arrived.

Mabaku stopped in at Kubu's house on his way home on Sunday evening.

"You shouldn't have let him go!" Joy cried. "You knew it was dangerous. You should've told him to stay here. You know we've a new baby. Someone else could've gone."

Mabaku nodded guiltily. "You're probably right, Joy. But we weighed all the factors, and thought it was worth doing. Still, we don't know what's happened. We've got a helicopter going there first thing in the morning. It can cover a much bigger area much more quickly. I'm confident that it will answer all our questions and find Kubu."

Joy was not consoled.

On Monday morning, Kubu had lost track of how many nights he had spent in the desert. Was it three or four? He didn't really care. He didn't stand up when the sky started lightening in the east. It took too much effort.

He decided just to lie where he was all day. Conserve energy. But then he wondered if he should walk back along the tracks and get help. It couldn't be too far. After all, they had driven there in only a couple of hours. But it was too much trouble, and he drifted back to sleep. He dreamed he could glide, if only he could work up enough speed to get airborne. There had to be thermals in the desert.

The helicopter arrived at about 1:00 p.m. with two additional policemen. There had been a delay due to a technical problem, which had infuriated Mabaku, who had again come in to work at 6:00 a.m. Mabaku instructed Mogale, Pikati, and Moeng to go with the chopper directly to Kubu's Land Rover and to search the area once more for clues. The others were to retrace their tracks on the ground and look again for signs that people had left the vehicle.

It took about forty-five minutes for the helicopter to get to the Land Rover. The pilot found a place to land and for the next two hours they painstakingly searched the area once again. They found nothing of interest. They photographed the Bushman footprints, although they knew they couldn't use footprints for identification. But doing it made them feel more useful.

Eventually, Mabaku ordered them to fly back directly over the tracks to look for anything unusual. He was beginning to feel despondent. He should never have allowed Kubu to go, he kept telling himself. If something had happened to them, it would be his fault.

The pilot told Mabaku he was going to Tsabong to refuel and would follow the tracks first thing in the morning. Despite Mabaku's angry spluttering that people's lives were at stake, the pilot insisted, saying that the director didn't want more people missing in the Kalahari.

Even Mabaku realized the good sense in that.

Kubu was fading. It was now more than three days without food or water. His body was crying out for sustenance, and his mind was slowly slipping into a state of not caring. Every now and again he would rally and try to do something to keep his focus on survival. As he was lying there, handkerchief over his face, a childhood song crept into his mind.

Good King Wenslus last looked out
On the feast of Stephen.
Snowball hit him on the snout;
Made it all uneven.
Brightly shone his nose that night,
And the pain was cruel,
Then the doctor came in sight,
Riding on a mule.

Kubu giggled. He even remembered the boy at the Maru a Pula school who had taught him the song. He recalled being shocked at first, thinking it sacrilegious.

Another song that he'd treasured as a young boy floated into his head. He'd thought it so rude that he'd protected it like a valuable jewel, sharing it only with a few.

Hey diddle diddle,
The dog did a piddle,
Right in the middle
Of the floor.
The little cat laughed
To see such sport,
And the dog did a little drop more.

Kubu snorted, remembering how he had pulled his friends into the toilet and sung them the song in a whisper, petrified that one of the teachers would hear him.

Then, from even deeper in his mind, came a familiar nursery rhyme.

Humpty Dumpty sat on a wall.
Humpty Dumpty had a great fall.
All the king's horses
And all the king's men
Couldn't put Humpty together again.

A shiver went down Kubu's spine. As the song spun through his head, he pictured Humpty falling off a wall. And he was Humpty.

It was a haggard Mabaku who arrived at Joy's door on Monday evening. "Joy. The helicopter spent the day around Kubu's Land Rover, but found nothing. There were some Bushman footprints, but nothing else. So it seems that Kubu and Tau left the vehicle somewhere else. We don't know whether the footprints were Khumanego's or some other Bushman in the area. The men couldn't tell how long they had been there."

Joy turned away and put her head in her hands. Mabaku could see her shoulders shaking as she sobbed. In an uncharacteristic move, he put his arm around her shoulders and patted her.

"The helicopter is going to retrace the tracks again. There has to be some sign of what happened. We'll find them even if it means my men walk the entire way. I'm sure we'll have news soon."

On Tuesday morning, the helicopter started flying along the vehicle tracks at first light. It flew about a hundred feet above the ground—low enough to make out detail, but high enough to see a reasonable distance on either side. It was tedious work— staring at the ground, looking for anything that may provide a clue to the disappearance of the two policemen.

Suddenly Moeng shouted from the backseat. "Hold it. I think I've seen something."

He directed the pilot back about fifty yards and pointed away from tracks.

"Go over there. I thought I saw some tire tracks."

The helicopter slid above the bushes to where the man was pointing.

"There they are! They are tracks! Let's follow them."

The pilot noted the GPS coordinates.

Kubu was talking to his grandfather—a wise old man who had told him many things about their family and culture. Then his grandfather was suddenly dead. And Kubu was talking to his mother, who was crying, and holding him close to her bosom. Now he was in school and big boys were pointing at him and laughing. Where was Khumanego? He couldn't find Khumanego. He needed to find him! Then he was lying in the sun watching cricket, and the rich white boy, Angus, came and called him Kubu. And he was embarrassed to be called "hippopotamus," but the white boy wasn't teasing. He said "Kubu" in friendship, and they became friends. Now he was talking to an important man in the police—the director of the Criminal Investigation Department. Kubu wanted to help his country. The director said he should go to university and become a detective.

"The tracks fork up ahead!" The pilot pointed.

"Take the right fork. We can come back and follow the other if we don't find anything."

The four men eagerly searched for signs on the ground.

"There's a signal of some sort! Looks like clothing on a bush."

"And there are footprints going off to the right! About a hundred yards. And coming back!"

"Land and let's take a look."

The helicopter landed in a clearing not far from where the footprints went up a small hill. Mogale restrained the others from running up the hill and called Edison to tell him where they were and what their intentions were. Only then did the policemen follow the footprints.

"Three people," Pikati observed. "Up and back." But when they got to the hill, there was nothing else to see. Whoever had walked up the hill had turned and come back.

"We'd better take a good look around here," Mogale ordered, directing the others in different directions.

◁▷ ◁▷ ◁▷

Kubu was sitting in the front row at university listening intently. There was so much to learn. And this teacher was friendly, drinking a glass of wine, teaching Kubu to smell and taste. And now he was being given his police badge. His parents were so proud. He was so proud. His first case—he had to go to the airport so a BDF helicopter could take him to the scene of the murder. He'd never been in a helicopter before. Never flown before. He heard the noise of the engines, getting louder, and louder, and louder. Suddenly the noise stopped, and Kubu startled to consciousness. There was still a noise, of rotor blades turning, winding down.

Had they found him?

He didn't really care.

After a few minutes, Moeng shouted: "Come here. I've found something."

When they gathered around, he pointed to a single set of footprints heading into the bush.

"Constable, follow them for a few hundred yards," Mogale ordered. "Then come back. We can follow them with the chopper if necessary. The rest of you, keep looking around. See if you can see anything."

The policemen scattered again to search the area.

A few minutes later, Pikati found another set of footprints. He followed them toward a clump of small trees. Not much shade, he thought. Then he saw a dark mound. As he walked toward it, he realized that it was a body. It had to be Kubu, judging by the size. He shouted to the others and ran toward it.

"Kubu! Kubu! Speak to me!" There was no response.

Pikati felt for a pulse. It was very weak.

"Let's get him to the chopper. Quickly!" he said as the others came running up.

"Where's the nearest hospital?"

"Hukuntsi," Moeng said.

"Tsabong," Pikati suggested.

The four of them battled with Kubu's bulk as they carried him toward the helicopter. It was very difficult to handle three hundred pounds of dead weight. But they eventually succeeded—all dripping with sweat.

At the helicopter, Moeng soaked some bandages from the medical kit in water and wrapped them around Kubu's head. Then he tried dribbling water into Kubu's mouth, but Kubu didn't swallow.

"Careful you don't choke him," Pikati warned.

"How are we going to get him into the chopper?" Moeng asked.

"We'll just have to lift him. Come on, guys. We may not have much time!"

With great difficulty they managed to get Kubu into a seat, fastening the seat belt as tightly as possible to hold him in position.

"We've found him! We've found him," Mogale shouted into the satellite phone. "He's alive, but unconscious. Should we try to find Tau as well? Or should we take Kubu to Tsabong?"

Mabaku came on the phone. "Spend a few minutes flying around the area where you found Kubu. If you don't see Tau or Khumanego in five minutes, head to Tsabong. Then come back and search for the others."

"Okay. Please have an ambulance and doctor meet us at the airport."

The pilot took off, but five minutes seemed far too long to

stay in the area, so after one loop he turned toward Tsabong, gained altitude, and headed south as fast as he could.

"Joy? It's Mabaku. They've found Kubu! He's alive, but unconscious. They're taking him to the hospital in Tsabong. We'll know more in an hour. It looks as though he was left in the desert. Must have been there for several days without food and water."

"Will he be all right?"

"He'll be in good hands any minute now. He'll be fine."

Joy put down the phone and burst into tears.

Kubu was walking in a graveyard. In front of him was a gravestone with the name TAU engraved on it. Underneath were the words KILLED BY KUBU.

Kubu put his head in his hands and cried. It *was* his fault.

"Wake up. Wake up." Kubu felt a hand gently shaking his arm. "You're safe now. Wake up."

Kubu opened his eyes, and a white room slowly came into focus. A smiling face was looking down at him. Kubu blinked the tears from his eyes, but the image remained. Was it real? Was he indeed safe?

"Where's Tau?" he croaked.

From his side a male voice answered, "They've gone back to look for him. They'll find him quickly. His footprints are quite visible."

Kubu turned his head to see Lerako smiling at him.

"You're in Tsabong. We'll fly you to Gaborone as soon as we can. Thank God you're okay."

"Get me a phone, please," Kubu said weakly. "I need to make a call."

"No. We've already called your wife. You can speak to her tomorrow. You need to sleep."

But Kubu tried to sit up. "It was Khumanego. He must be one of the murderers. He tried to kill us. Drove away and left us there to die. With nothing. In the desert."

"We'll catch him. You can be sure of that."

"And once, he was my friend." Kubu's eyes burned with tears.

Part VI

Ta: /kaggən /ki k''auki se ‾ã: !kwi se
Θpwoin

For the Mantis will not let the man
sleep

Thirty-eight

On Friday morning Kubu woke up at the Princess Marina hospital in Gaborone feeling more like his usual self. The dizziness and incoherence of the previous days had faded, although he still felt lethargic, and a headache threatened in the background. Trying to roll over, he jerked at the drip. There was no option, he had to open his eyes and face the world. Then he saw Joy.

Vaguely he recalled seeing her the evening before between the flow of doctors and nurses. Had Mabaku been there too? He couldn't quite decide, but he thought so. Joy was sitting on the bedside chair, as lovely as always. But her mouth was tight, and she looked stressed. He could see that she'd been crying. For a moment he felt a mixture of guilt and fear. Had this pushed her too far? Then he relaxed. Despite it all, she was here.

"How are you, my darling? I love you more than anything."

She smiled. "I'm fine, my love." Then she was out of the chair and trying to hug him around the combination of his bulk, the blankets, and the drip. After a moment they were both laughing, which made Kubu start to cough.

Joy was immediately concerned. "Are you all right, Kubu? Shall I call a nurse?"

Kubu shook his head and motioned for his water glass, which she filled and held for him. The coughing subsided.

"I was so worried. When Mabaku called me on Saturday to say they hadn't heard from you, but they had two Land Rovers on the way, I was beside myself. In a way I wish he hadn't told me then, because I was worried sick the whole time until they found you, but I'd have killed him if he hadn't!"

Kubu tried to decipher this, but soon gave up. "It wasn't fun," he said simply. Then he remembered clearly that Mabaku had visited yesterday. He'd tried to avoid Kubu's questions, saying they would talk later. But eventually he'd told Kubu what he needed to know. Now he remembered every word.

"Detective Tau died out there," he told Joy. "They followed his footprints. But after a while they looped back and crossed each other. After that they became erratic. He must've known then what had happened. And what was going to happen." He turned his head away, and tears ran down his face.

Joy took his hand. "Darling, I'm so sorry. I heard yesterday. But you mustn't blame yourself. If he'd stayed with you, he would've been okay."

"No, it was my fault. He didn't want us to go into the desert in one vehicle. He said it was a basic survival rule. He was right. And I made him do it because I had a mission and nothing else mattered." And all the time, he thought, the murderer was sitting next to us in the vehicle. I have to live with that too. I was responsible for Tau's death, and my school friend used me to help him with his crimes. But why had Khumanego done it? What was behind it? Had he acted alone or was he part of something bigger? Kubu felt a flush of anger. Whatever it was, he would get to the bottom of it if it was the last thing he did. And Khumanego would pay for his crimes.

He sighed. *There I go again. Thinking that nothing else matters.*

He turned back to Joy. "Where's Tumi?"

"She's at the crèche. I'll bring her this afternoon."

"I love you both." Kubu smiled. "Nothing else matters." Then he drifted back to sleep.

A pleasant surprise was in store for Kubu that afternoon. He was bored and nagging the doctor to let him go home. So the doctor was happy to escape when Pleasant, Bongani, Wilmon and Amantle came into the ward to much talking and hugging. Even Wilmon clasped his son's hand more firmly and for longer than a normal fatherly handshake would dictate.

"How are you, my son? We have been concerned."

"I'm okay. How did you know I was missing?"

Amantle interrupted. "When you were rescued, it was on the radio and the television! Everyone knows about it." She seemed to feel this was some kind of achievement. Kubu nodded and smiled, but he wondered how Tau's family was feeling today. He knew so little about the detective. Was he married? Did he have children? Living parents? Siblings? He needed to find out and see them. Try to explain the unexplainable.

"Well, I'm fine now," he said. "If only this doctor would let me go home. It was a bad experience, but there's nothing wrong with me now. They're wasting taxpayers' money keeping me here!" Everyone thought this was very funny, but Amantle gave him a critical look. "You have lost weight," she said accusingly. "I can see it in your face. They have not been feeding you up after all the time in the desert with no food. I will speak to the doctor."

Kubu groaned. Losing weight was the one good thing that had come from the grueling time alone in the Kalahari.

There was much discussion, and Kubu had to explain exactly what had happened. Everyone agreed that he'd done exactly the right thing in the circumstances. They expressed regrets about Tau, but they were the meaningless condolences of strangers—genuinely sorry for the loss of others, but guiltily grateful the axe hadn't fallen closer.

At last the talk died down, and Bongani said they must soon get back to Mochudi to avoid the traffic. He had gone with Pleasant to fetch Kubu's parents in his car. Everyone agreed to this except Wilmon. He nodded, but then said firmly, "I need a few minutes alone with my son. Please wait for me downstairs." The others left without argument, as though this had been planned. Kubu was intrigued.

Wilmon sat. "My son, Pleasant's uncle and I have had discussions with Bongani's uncles. His father is dead, but the uncles are good men. They don't drink much, and they go to church each Sunday." He nodded firmly to emphasize the importance of this. "They were very respectful, requesting Pleasant for Bongani by asking for her hand in the traditional way. Of course, we explained that Pleasant has a brother, and he must be consulted too. They understood completely. But they made a reasonable offer for the *lobola*. We discussed it back and forth, and I think we have a fair amount. Then we had some tea." The old man was clearly pleased; it seemed he'd led a successful negotiation. Kubu was pleased too, especially as Wilmon had seemed a little vague and uncertain on a few previous occasions.

"How many cows?"

Wilmon leaned over and whispered the number to Kubu, who whistled. "That is very fair indeed! You have done extremely well, Father. Pleasant's family will be extremely grateful. And Joy too." He said it graciously, but he was a little put out that the number was two higher than he had raised for Joy.

Wilmon gave a big smile, patted his son on the shoulder, and took his leave.

Kubu had hardly had time to become bored again, when Mabaku arrived.

"How's the dehydrated hippo today?"

Mabaku's idea of humor, thought Kubu, trying to smile. "I'm fine. Get me out of here, Director. There's a lot of work to do."

Mabaku hesitated. "We'll have to be careful. You're involved personally again. Sometimes I think we'd have half as many cases if I just gave you to the South African police." He laughed to be sure Kubu realized he was joking. Then he sobered. "And there'll have to be an inquiry about Tau. You know that."

Kubu nodded. It would be a formality. Tau had disobeyed him, a senior officer. But that doesn't change the reality, he thought.

"That reporter wants to see you. I told her to wait."

Kubu was surprised, but he had no doubt which reporter Mabaku was talking about.

"Have they caught Khumanego?"

Mabaku shook his head. "He vanished. Joined up with his Bushman friends after he abandoned the Land Rover, I'd guess. He's not alone in all this, I'm sure. But don't worry, we'll get him. We've got Wanted posters everywhere; his face is all over the newspapers. Sooner or later someone will recognize him. We're watching his apartment building in Lobatse too, just in case, and we've applied for a search warrant. It's only a matter of time."

"I'd like to be in on the search. Knowing him and what to look for might help."

Mabaku hesitated again. "Kubu, you need to take it easy. Get your strength back. I've spoken to the doctor. It'll be at least a week before you can come back to work." Kubu spluttered with indignation and started to cough again. Once he'd swallowed some water and had calmed down, Mabaku continued. "I'm not saying you must stay here. You can be at home. And I'll take charge of the case myself while you're away. I'll get your input and keep you up to date with everything." Kubu had to be satisfied with that.

Then Mabaku wanted to go through the whole story of the fateful reconnaissance trip into the desert step by step. He asked questions and noted all the details. At last he relaxed. "Well, that's the story then. Pretty straightforward." He could see that Kubu was in the clear. At the same time, one of his detectives had died in the line of duty; that was not easy to accept.

"I've got some other news for you, Kubu. The breakdown of the vehicle out there was part of Khumanego's plan. It wasn't a mechanical failure at all; he disabled it. He must have known a thing or two about Land Rover Defenders."

"What did he do? He didn't have a chance to get at the engine, and we tested the fuel flow and so on."

"It was very clever. There's a feedback pipe from the fuel injection, as well as a supply pipe to it. Both come from the fuel filter, which is easy to get to from behind the back wheel. He switched the pipes around. Takes a minute. So no fuel went to the fuel injection. It took the mechanic hours to work it out, though!"

Kubu nodded. "So Khumanego was planning this all along." That hurt.

"Probably he hoped you would give up and go back to Tshane. Perhaps he would've disabled the other vehicle as well if we'd just sent out a replacement, but he decided he had to kill you once he realized you would never give up." He thought for a moment, and added more kindly, "I think he was trying to scare you off, Kubu. I don't think he wanted to kill you." He paused. "But I'm not taking any chances. I've ordered that you are to have a police guard at your house until Khumanego is caught. And one will be with Joy whenever she leaves the house."

Mabaku got to his feet. "Well, that's enough for now. Mustn't tire you out. Do you want to see that woman?"

Kubu nodded.

"I'll tell her on my way out," he growled.

"Oh, Kubu, we were all so worried about you. Are you okay now?" Cindy appraised him. "You look drawn."

"I feel fine. They're just keeping me here to finish the Kalahari's work and bore me to death, I think."

Cindy smiled and settled in the chair next to the bed. "Do you want to talk about it?" Kubu shook his head, and she laughed. "I'm not looking for a story. Actually, I just wanted to see that you were okay. And to say good-bye. I'm leaving for Nigeria soon. It's big and bustling and exciting, and there'll be lots to write about. But I'll miss Botswana. And I'll miss you."

"Why are you leaving so suddenly?"

"There's a big issue around oil and the local people. It's hot news now." She paused and looked down. "I'm very upset about Khumanego. In a way I feel responsible. Perhaps my pressure put you all on the wrong track. Now four people are dead. And it could so easily have been five."

"Actually I'm pretty sure it's more than four."

"Why did he do it, Kubu?"

Kubu shook his head. "I've no idea. But I'm going to find him, and I'm going to find out."

They chatted for a few more minutes, and then Cindy got ready to leave. They said good-bye, and she leaned over and kissed him on the cheek. At that moment, Joy came in carrying Tumi. *Why do these things happen to me?* Kubu thought. *I've been suffering on a diet all year, more dead than alive in the Kalahari, and now Joy has to choose this precise moment to arrive. Why me?*

But Joy was trying to keep Tumi entertained, bouncing her on her hip. So when she looked up from the baby she saw Cindy just standing next to the bed. She stopped, and her face was not happy.

Kubu tried to rescue the situation. "Hello, darling. Bring Tumi over here. I'm dying to hold her. Oh, this is Cindy Robinson. She's the newspaper reporter who was following the Bushman case. She was just leaving. Cindy, this is my lovely wife, Joy, and my beautiful daughter, Tumi." He hoped he wasn't laying it on too thick.

Joy passed Tumi to him and shook Cindy's hand, but without enthusiasm.

Cindy rose to the occasion. "I'm actually leaving the country shortly, Mma Bengu. I just had to come and thank the assistant superintendent for his help. He's been very patient with my questions and keeping my reports accurate. It's just terrible what happened to him in the desert. I'm so relieved he's okay."

"Yes, we all are," Joy responded coolly. Kubu kept himself occupied with Tumi, holding her above him at arm's length and making faces.

"Your daughter's lovely, Kubu," Cindy said to him. "Get well soon. Now I must be going."

"Good-bye, Cindy. I wish you all the best in Nigeria. It should be an interesting time for you."

"Yes, I'm looking forward to it. Good-bye now." She waved to Joy, and headed for the door.

Kubu held his breath.

"That was the reporter you told me about?" Joy asked.

"Yes."

"She's very pretty. Nice figure too."

"Yes, I suppose so. Have you started planning the engagement party for Pleasant? Did you know that my father helped with sorting out the *lobola*?"

Joy brightened. "Yes, and did very well! Pleasant told me." Soon she was explaining the plans for the party and the outline for the wedding. Tumi chortled and smiled. Kubu breathed a silent sigh of relief.

Thirty-nine

Khumanego had been walking for three nights. He was grateful that the moon would soon be full, making traveling easy. And the nights were cold, so it was good to walk hard and keep warm. In the early morning and late evening he would search for the cactus-like *Hoodia* plants. Once, he found *tsama* melons, which he collected and carried with him. After foraging, he would find one of the thicker bushes and hollow a spot under it where he could sleep and conserve water during the heat of the day.

Most of the water he'd taken from Kubu's vehicle in a large plastic Coke bottle was gone. He'd hoped to find a seep in an old watercourse, which he knew was about a night's walk from where he'd abandoned the Land Rover, but it had been hard-dry. He could have dug for water, but at that point he had three-quarters of the bottle left, and the *Hoodia* plants had been plentiful.

Apart from the water bottle, nothing of the Westernized man remained. He'd removed his shoes at the vehicle and carried them a short way into the desert, where he'd buried them along with his shirt and shorts. Now he wore only a Bushman leather loincloth and carried his hunting kit over his shoulder. When he met another Bushman group—as he would—he'd be one of them.

Sometimes he thought of Kubu and Tau. The other policemen would be fine; they had food, water, and shelter. He felt he had been weak. A quick poison added to their food would've killed them all and made a dramatic statement. But all along he'd hoped to persuade Kubu to turn back, to abandon his search, to let the frenzy die down. There would've been no more deaths for a while, and after that he would have had to deal with Lerako. He would have enjoyed that. But Kubu wouldn't back down. And more vehicles were coming, coming to attack The Place and its lone guardian. He'd had no choice.

But Kubu had been a long-time friend. Khumanego did not want his death as he'd wanted the deaths of others. But now it didn't matter. He'd done what needed to be done. That was all there was to it.

By Monday, Khumanego had become very tired. The day had been hot, but he'd tried to drink only a little water. He lay still and watched gratefully as the sun set. He waited until the evening cooled and then forced himself to go on. But when the moon started to sink and the dark closed in, he collapsed on the ground exhausted. He needed guidance from the ancestors, but he was too tired to dance, so he found the horn in his bag, swallowed some white powder from it, and closed his eyes to focus his thoughts. Then he slept—or seemed to sleep.

When he woke—or seemed to wake—he was standing in

the desert. There was no moon, but the sky was full of stars, not fixed, but moving slowly across the sky. There was only starlight, but the desert sand and its plants seemed to Khumanego rich with colors—the reds and greens and blues of much more verdant climes.

Khumanego looked down and saw himself lying on his back with his arms folded across his eyes as if trying to protect them from a blinding light. He turned away and looked around the spirit world, a world familiar to him from many visits, many revelations, but also strange, always different.

He saw the body of an old man, lying at rest surrounded by his few carefully arranged possessions—a bow, hunting bag, containers for poisons, arrowheads. Next to the circle, sitting on a white-dry log, was a man past his prime but still strong. Despite the years rolled back, Khumanego recognized him at once. He almost laughed with joy at the opportunity offered here that had been denied him in the gray world that people thought of as real.

He addressed the man in their common language in the most respectful way. "Gobiwasi, I am honored that you are here to help me, to guide me, with my mission."

"You sought guidance before. I was wrong to deny it. So I am here. Waiting."

"Are you not with the ancestors?" Khumanego indicated the stars moving above them.

Gobiwasi shook his head. "I am here. Waiting."

Khumanego didn't ask why the dead man was waiting, nor for what. Here was a man who would understand, a man who had walked the same path in the gray world.

"I have tried to protect The Place—as you did."

"The ancestors are angry with you. That was not your

destiny. You protected The Place through the deaths of others. That is not the way of our people, not the way of the Mantis."

Khumanego became angry. "You, too, protected The Place that way. You, too, killed a man."

Gobiwasi stared at him, neither accepting nor denying this charge.

Khumanego persisted. "People know you did this. It is spoken of quietly and in secret. It was about this that I wanted to ask you."

Still Gobiwasi stared, but now his eyes seemed to be following the moving stars as if he'd lost interest in the discussion. "It was necessary," he said at last. "The white man was there, going through the caves, taking things, destroying the paintings. He would have returned, perhaps with many others."

"I understand," said Khumanego. "The man wanted to steal The Place from us, desecrate it, anger the ancestors. You had no choice but to kill him. All such men must die. It is necessary."

"But now I have to wait."

Khumanego was frustrated. This was not the encouragement he had expected, needed. He'd had visions before with the ancestors showing him the way. Leading and supporting him. Encouraging him.

"These others had to die too. We used the weapons of our people, you and I: *knobkierie*, arrows, poisons. Soon people will learn that if they go near The Place and trample our sacred ground, they will die. Soon they will stop coming. Fear will form a fence that no one will cross. A fence built of fear is stronger than their fences of steel that can be kicked down. I am building that fence around The Place. The ancestors will be greatly pleased."

Gobiwasi looked down at his aged, dead body surrounded

by the possessions of the gray world. When he looked up his eyes were sad. "What about the *Bushman* you killed? Your own brother."

Khumanego struck at him, but of course there was no contact. "You are stupid, old man! He was the younger. He had no right! My father sent me away to a school with the black people and showed my brother The Place instead of me. How could he do that? The ancestors were very angry, and soon my father became ill and died. My brother wouldn't help me, even refused to tell me where to find The Place. But he would have shown it to others. You could buy him for money. He was a worm. I crushed him with my foot! And I found The Place myself, without him. The ancestors guided me, gave me this mission."

Gobiwasi said nothing, and Khumanego's anger grew until everything seemed tinged with red, even the bushes and the desiccated grass.

"You are a fool, Gobiwasi! You killed too for The Place. Long ago. Yet now you challenge me! What right do you have? Now you say you wait. What are you waiting *for*, old man?"

But now everything was blurred by the red mist of his anger, and Khumanego closed his eyes to clear them. When he opened them and moved his arms from his face, he saw that the red tinge remained. It came from the huge crimson sun climbing ponderously above the horizon in the east, temporarily coloring the gray world.

The next night as he walked, he smelled a whiff of a cooking fire long before he heard or saw any sign of the Bushman group. He smiled. Once more the ancestors had guided him. His plan would be to join the group, live with it, camouflage himself completely. No one would find him. He could move to another group if the police got too close. And he would keep watching The Place. Keep guarding against intruders. There would be other killings when the time was right.

When he came to the edge of the campfire's light, he saw that the ancestors had indeed been good to him. For the little group he found there was the very group that Gobiwasi had once led. They knew him and would be grateful for what he had done to rescue them from Lerako. He could have asked for no better meeting. Perhaps it was for this that Gobiwasi had been waiting?

So he strode into the light of the fire and greeted the oldest man warmly in the lGwi language. "Dcaro! I know you. This is a most happy meeting."

The man regarded him with natural surprise, but there was a trace of something else in his expression.

"Khumanego. I know you." It was a cold response.

"Indeed! I am here alone and wish to join you. I will help you hunt, gather *Hoodia* and melons, do whatever needs to be done."

"We do not need help. Neither do we need extra mouths."

Khumanego glared at Dcaro. "I am strong and have much power in the spirit world. Recently I saw Gobiwasi there. It was him who led me here."

There was much excitement at this news, but Dcaro held up his hand and the others waited.

"You tell us that. But how do we know it is so?"

"Because I say it!"

Dcaro just shook his head and waited.

"It will be good for us to work together. I have many powerful friends in this world too. Did I not save you and these two men from being hanged?" He pointed at the other two men whom Lerako had held. Although they regarded him with respect, there was also hostility. Still, it was an important reminder. The group started to talk again. Some space was made by the fire; clearly they expected Khumanego to join them. But it was Dcaro who led now.

"Those other people say we Bushmen are liars, that we steal, that we kill what is not ours to kill. That is why they chase us, even though we are honest, take only what is ours, and kill only what we need. But you have lied, and stolen, and you have killed a man. We know you killed the white man with a Bushman arrow and caused much trouble. We saw the posters. We had to leave. You have done great harm. The ancestors are very angry." At the end of this speech Dcaro was shaking, but gave no ground.

Khumanego glared at him. "Since you reject my friendship and help, I will go. But you will regret this night. All of you will regret this night!" His arm encompassed the whole of the small group, and he could see their fear and was glad. Turning back to Dcaro he softened his voice. "I need water for my journey. You cannot refuse a traveler in the desert when he comes asking for water."

"We have no water to spare. There is no water here. There is water in Hukuntsi. Go there."

"Then I curse you all! May you too be refused water in your time of thirst." Then he stood up and stalked into the desert night.

He felt their eyes on his back, watching him, but they meant nothing. He would change his plan. He knew now where he must go. He would go where he needed no one, where there was water, and where he had power.

Forty

When he arrived at the CID on Monday morning, Director Mabaku appeared calm. He had visited Kubu on the way and thought he was on the mend. More to the point, the doctor was satisfied. But underneath, Mabaku was bottling up an explosion of anger. How had this nasty little Bushman dared to mess with his CID detectives? Once he was caught, he was going to be *very* sorry. Yet Kubu's burning question kept coming back to him. Why? What was Khumanego's motive for these vicious and apparently pointless murders?

Mabaku's secretary, Miriam, stopped him at his office door to give him a document—the warrant to search Khumanego's apartment. They had managed to get authorization over the weekend. Mabaku brightened at once. Now they could take action, do something positive. Perhaps get to the bottom of this mess.

"Get hold of Zanele and her forensics team," he told Miriam.

"Tell her to get them ready as soon as possible. I want to take apart the suspect's home piece by piece until we understand what this is all about. I'll supervise it myself."

Khumanego's apartment was on the second floor of a building close to the center of Lobatse. The caretaker was expecting them. She was full of questions; the police presence over the last few days had caused quite a stir. Mabaku brushed her concerns aside, showed her the warrant, and waited for her to unlock the front door. He wasn't talkative. His mind was focused on whether the key to the Kalahari murders would be inside this modest dwelling.

When they went in, it looked like a typical Motswana apartment: two small bedrooms, an open-plan lounge/kitchen/dining area and a single bathroom. Zanele and her team went to work while Mabaku stood in the middle of the lounge area. He looked around, but touched nothing, trying to get a feel for the Bushman's life.

On one wall was a bookcase containing three shelves of books and two display shelves. Mabaku called Zanele over. He wondered how she could look so attractive swaddled in her shapeless white laboratory coat. He pointed at the top display shelf.

"Those look like Bushman arrowheads. They may be harmless, but they may be poisoned. Tell your people to treat them as if they are. Even if the arrows are just collector's items, those poisons can last a long time. Use forceps and put them in strong bags, not flimsy plastic ones. Remember Haake."

Zanele nodded. "Do you want us to collect them all?"

"Yes, do that. And those little containers with them, too. They probably used to contain poisons. Maybe they still do."

Mabaku examined the books. Most were textbooks concerned with human rights and legal issues. He spotted a copy of Ditshwanelo's report on the Maauwe and Motswetla affair, *In the Shadow of the Noose*. But there was nothing untoward, nothing to suggest that Khumanego was anything other than what he claimed to be: an advocate for the Bushman peoples. The second display shelf was more interesting. It was empty but for six pebbles of white calcrete laid out in a straight line, each separated by about an inch. Other than the arrangement, and the fact that they were free of sand and powder, there was nothing unusual about them. Except that they were there. Why collect nondescript stones from the desert?

"Zanele! Please get pictures of the arrangement of everything here and then collect these stones as well." She was talking to a man searching for fingerprints with an ultraviolet light, but she nodded.

Mabaku wandered around the apartment. He came across one of Zanele's men going through a desk in the second bedroom, carefully sorting through normal office items with latex-gloved hands. It appeared that Khumanego used this room as a study. They had already dusted and fingerprinted his computer and printer and packed them in boxes to be checked later.

"There's a GPS in here," the man told Mabaku. "A Garmin. I think we should take that."

"Definitely. Why would a Bushman need a GPS in the Kalahari? There's a good chance it's Haake's. Don't turn it on. We'll get the technicians to try to extract his last route."

Mabaku moved on to the main bedroom, which had a narrow balcony facing the back of the opposite building. The small area was crowded with a variety of plants growing in reddish Kalahari sand contained in unattractive plastic pots of the sort nurseries use. Mabaku unlocked the steel-framed glass door and stepped out. Prickly and scraggly, they were hardly the pot plants a garden lover would have chosen for a balcony. Were they a homesick Bushman's reminders of the Kalahari? Or something more sinister? He asked Zanele to collect them too. Carefully.

A constable searching Khumanego's clothes cupboard called Mabaku over.

"Take a look here, Rra. Look at the shoes."

Mabaku glanced at the floor of the cupboard, seeing a collection of shoes and boots neatly arranged in pairs. For a moment he didn't get the point, but then he whistled.

"That one pair of boots is almost twice the size of the others—I'd guess size ten. The rest look like kids' shoes. Let's see the soles of those boots."

The man turned them over displaying smooth undersides. Mabaku nodded.

"Take those. Definitely."

They found nothing else. Several hours later they packed up their stuff, carried out the items they wanted to test or examine further, and headed back to the CID in Gaborone. They didn't have much to show for most of a day's work, and nothing that pointed to the motive Kubu sought.

But Mabaku was satisfied. He was sure they had found the boots that had made tracks around three murders, and he had a strong hunch they'd found Haake's GPS.

Forty-one

For Willie Taro, the gas attendant at the Kgalagadi Filling Station in Hukuntsi, life had become one of constant fear. He did his job every day, filling cars with gas, but his enthusiasm and pleasure in it were gone. He dreaded seeing the Bushman who called himself Piscoaghu. That was a name from Bushman legend, and Willie didn't believe it was the man's real name. At first it had almost been a game, watching the travelers come through the gas station, chatting with them and asking where they were going. And the money Piscoaghu paid him for the information had been most welcome. But after Haake's murder by a Bushman arrow, all that had changed.

He felt guilt too. He would never have said a word if he'd thought Haake was in danger, but it was too late now. He wondered what sort of game Piscoaghu was playing. And was the game over? He hoped so. But he'd heard enough about murderers to know that they didn't like to leave people alive who could connect them to their victims.

He'd sought advice from an elderly Bushman who lived in the town and knew things. He had listened carefully to Willie's story, and his response was immediate. Willie must go to the police. They would be fair to him, and they would help him. But Willie was scared of the police, so he didn't take the advice. Then he noticed that Bushmen in the town started giving him odd looks and seemed to be avoiding him. Had the old Bushman spread the story? He was scared of that too.

And Willie wasn't stupid. When the news broke of the policeman who'd died in the desert so near where Haake had been exploring, he put two and two together. And when he saw Piscoaghu's face staring out of a Wanted poster, he was terrified.

Now it was Sunday. Almost two weeks had passed since Detective Tau's corpse had been found. His body had still not been returned to the family. People said doctors were cutting it up to find out how he'd died. Willie shuddered, thinking about what those doctors were doing.

After church, the villagers who had known Tau gathered in the courtyard of his modest home for an afternoon of prayers and speeches in his honor. Tau had always been polite to Willie, and he went to the prayer meeting, sitting on the ground near the back of the gathering. He was scared to be there as the house was in the police compound, scared that if he was noticed he might be chased away. And he was scared of *not* being noticed lest people felt his absence showed ill will to the late detective. Willie's life had become one of constant fear.

The afternoon dragged on as one person after another rose to speak well of the deceased or to call on Jesus to reward their departed friend. When at last a break came in the proceedings,

Willie stood up, stretched, and almost bumped into a tall, well-built man wearing an immaculate police uniform with a fine medal. Willie was in awe. This man must be a very senior officer. Perhaps even the commissioner of police! He looked down and muttered a humble apology in Setswana. Unexpectedly, the man stopped and spoke to him.

"There is no problem," he said. "We are all here together as children of God to honor our friend Detective Tau."

The policeman started to move on, but suddenly Willie felt this man would hear his story and be fair to him. He ran to keep up, fearful that his opportunity to speak might be lost.

"Rra, I beg your pardon for disturbing you. I know you are an important person with much to do, Rra, and this is the day of rest, and we must pay our respects to the departed. But I have information which may be important to the police." The policeman looked down at him, quizzically. "Rra, it is about the murder of a man called Haake," Willie gabbled on, scared that if he hesitated his courage would desert him. "Perhaps I know who killed him. Rra Haake was a man from Namibia . . ."

The area chief of police knew very well who Haake was. Without further ado, he steered Willie into the adjoining Tshane police station.

Forty-two

On Monday Kubu was happy to get back to his office. The hospital had been a trial, and in desperation the doctor had discharged him to still his stream of complaints. Then he'd been stuck at home, bored and alone during the day except for the police constable outside, and sidelined in the evening while Pleasant and Joy focused on organizing the engagement party. He tried to keep out of their way, playing with Tumi and Ilia, who both appreciated his attention. The weekend had been better; they had taken a trip to Mochudi to visit his parents.

His colleagues greeted him like a hero, which he found embarrassing. Edison was particularly effusive.

"All right, Edison, I'm fine now. What's happening with the case? Any sign of Khumanego?"

Edison shook his head. "But we searched his apartment a week ago, and I've got the reports back. How did he pull it off,

Kubu? How did he get to all those places in the middle of no-where? How did he know where the victims were?"

They were good questions, and Kubu had spent lots of time thinking about them. "Let's get some tea and go to my office and bring each other up to date. Also please find some muffins. I lost a lot of weight in the desert. I need to build up my strength." He was going to have a proper lunch too. There had been no more nagging at home about dieting.

Kubu settled himself at his desk. His in-tray was full, and his computer had a demanding air about it. He ignored them both and waited for Edison, who arrived a few minutes later with six muffins. They both set to work on them.

"So what's in the forensics reports?" Kubu asked through a mouthful.

Edison searched through his file. "The arrowheads were clean, but one of the containers held something possibly very toxic, perhaps even what was used on Haake. And the plants Director Mabaku found were indeed the source of poisons and hallucinogens, including the one that killed the two students. The boots we found in Khumanego's cupboard match the prints found at each of the three murder scenes pretty well, and the size is right."

"Anything on the fingerprints on Haake's vehicle?"

Edison nodded enthusiastically. "Khumanego's fingerprints were on the gun and on the back of Haake's vehicle."

Kubu was about to ask about the GPS when Mabaku came in and muttered something about everyone having a party. However, after enquiring about Kubu's health, he helped himself to a muffin.

"I'm feeling fine, Director," said Kubu, after swallowing the rest of his muffin. "We were discussing how Khumanego pulled this off under our noses. Under my nose, I suppose I should say."

Mabaku grunted. "I got an urgent message this morning to call Lerako about the case. I thought we could do it together." He tossed Kubu a slip of paper with the message in Miriam's handwriting.

Kubu dialed the number, reached Lerako, and put him on the speaker.

"Kubu! Are you recovered? You're lucky to be alive. The Kalahari is a dangerous place."

"I'm fine, Lerako. Glad to be alive."

"Detective Tau's body has been returned to his family now. Will you be coming to the funeral this weekend?"

"Yes, I need to be there. I want to tell the family what happened in person." He owed the man at least that much. "I've got Director Mabaku and Detective Banda here with me," he continued. "Do you have some news for us?"

"I do! I was right about the Bushmen. Perhaps I had the wrong ones originally, but yesterday I arrested one of the right ones."

Kubu's heart jumped. "You've got Khumanego?"

"No, but an accomplice. A chap called Willie Taro who works at the gas station in Hukuntsi. He's admitted everything."

Kubu felt some doubt mix with the elation. Lerako didn't have a good record with Bushman arrests.

Mabaku chipped in. "You'd better tell us the whole story from the beginning."

"Willie's been spying on people for another Bushman who called himself Piscoaghu and who paid him for the information. All tourists and visitors coming through Hukuntsi pass through the gas station where he works. It's the only place to get fuel in that whole area. He reported everything he could find out, but this Piscoaghu was particularly interested in people heading south, especially if they came more than once."

"What did this other man do with the information?" Kubu asked. "Why did he want it?"

"Willie doesn't know. I think he's telling the truth about that. He's been very cooperative." From the way Lerako said it, Kubu had no doubt cooperation was in Willie's interest.

"And this other Bushman, this Piscoaghu, was Khumanego?"

"No doubt about it. Willie recognized the picture of him on the Wanted poster right away."

"Who did he give information about?"

"Well, he doesn't know most of their names. But he knew Haake all right. And here's the punch line. Khumanego was in Hukuntsi the evening Haake was killed. And Willie told him where Haake was."

Mabaku gave a low whistle. "Good work, Lerako! How did you get on to this Willie character?"

There was a moment's hesitation. "Well, he turned himself in, actually. He approached the Tshane station commander at a prayer meeting for Detective Tau. Took his time, though. If he'd come forward earlier, Tau might still be with us."

"So what charge are you holding him on?" Kubu asked.

"Accessory to murder! He's an accomplice before and after the fact."

It seemed to Kubu that Willie had been used and may have had no idea what was going on. But he didn't feel like arguing. Willie might be safer in police custody than free, where Khumanego could get at him.

"Did he know where Khumanego stayed when he was in Hukuntsi?"

"He said he only visited from time to time. But here's something really important. Willie says that Khumanego occasionally arrived at the filling station on an off-road motorbike."

Mabaku whistled again, and Kubu's brain shifted into high gear.

Lerako covered a few other points, promised to send them a copy of Willie's statement, and said he'd see Kubu and Mabaku at the funeral. Then he rang off.

Kubu turned to the other two. "Now the puzzle pieces are fitting into place. Khumanego was behind all the murders. Let's see if I can tie things together.

"First of all, Monzo took the two students into the desert to collect plants. It seems they must have gone close to the *koppies*—maybe actually visited them—and after that Khumanego set out to kill them. He traced the students to Sekoma and poisoned them. We'll need to check Khumanego's movements at that time if we can. He made it look like an accident, and we fell for it.

"As for Monzo's death, at our first meeting Khumanego told me he was in the Mabuasehube area around that time. And the phone call that led Monzo to his death came from a public telephone near the Hukuntsi gas station. Either Khumanego called himself with the story about the Bushmen poaching, or he set this Willie guy up to do it. Either way, he headed out the next morning on his motorbike, waited till Monzo reached the place where he said the Bushmen would be and then killed him. After that he wiped out his tracks and went back on his motorbike, keeping the bike's wheels in one of the tire ruts in the sand, confident that the next car would blot out his tread marks. But he made two mistakes. One was bad luck—that a Bushman group actually *was* in the area and discovered Monzo. The other was throwing away the rock he used to disguise the *knobkierie* blow. He wanted the death to look like an accident, but when Lerako found that rock, we knew it was murder. That's when Khumanego came to me to help free the Bushmen—after making the fake boot prints for me to find." Kubu paused.

"We know Haake was looking for the *koppies,* and now we know Willie was keeping tabs on him. Just before Krige was murdered, Khumanego left me in Tsabong with an excuse about visiting some other Bushmen. Willie probably told Khumanego about Haake's trip south, and Khumanego followed him, planning to murder him, but came across Krige unexpectedly and killed him instead. Haake must've surprised him, and Khumanego—who had found Krige's gun—tried to shoot him but missed. After that he escaped on his motorbike, the same way as he did with Monzo. By then he knew we were looking for a murderer, so he tried to make Krige's death look like Monzo's, even to the extent that he had the same fake boot prints. This time, though, he didn't do it well enough, and Ian MacGregor could see the *knobkierie* crater under the blow from the calcrete rock."

Kubu took a deep breath. "As for Haake. I was the one who told Khumanego we thought Haake might be in the Hukuntsi area." Mabaku's eyebrows rose. This was news to him. "So he headed down there and waited for Willie to tip him off. Then he planted Krige's gun in Haake's vehicle—perhaps hoping we'd still believe Haake was responsible for the other murders. And then he killed Haake with a poisoned arrow he knew I'd guess was not a real Bushman arrow. No doubt to deflect suspicion away from the Bushmen, but also to make us keep looking for the man with the size ten shoes." Kubu shook his head. "And I fell for all of it."

There was silence as Mabaku turned everything over in his head. Eventually he nodded. "Yes, it all hangs together. It must've been something like that."

Suddenly Edison came to life. "I didn't get a chance to tell you some other good news. We know the GPS we found in the apartment was the one stolen from Haake. It's got his prints on it. And we've got the route for his last trip." He handed Kubu a printout of GPS waypoints.

Mabaku glared at Edison. "What's the use of that? Get the computer guy to print it out on the same sheet as the tracks we got from the students and the one from Krige." Edison hurried off to do that.

"What do you make of this?" Mabaku passed Kubu a photograph of the six calcrete stones from Khumanego's bookshelf.

"He had these in his apartment?"

Mabaku nodded.

Kubu counted the deaths he knew about. The two students, Monzo, Krige, Haake. That was five. Then there was Tau; but Khumanego hadn't been back since the desert trip, and he couldn't have known in advance that Tau would be with them. Kubu had a sinking feeling. Was the sixth stone for him?

"Six stones, six deaths."

Mabaku nodded. He had made that connection too. After a few moments he said, "We counted five murders. Who was the sixth pebble for? You?"

Kubu shook his head. "I don't think he really wanted to kill me. He kept trying to warn me off. I think it was for the other Bushman, the one who was stabbed to death and left in the desert. I've no idea why." He paused. "Actually, we still don't know what the motive was for *any* of the killings. Just that it has something to do with the *koppies*."

Kubu sighed, and continued, "And Khumanego? Any trace of him? What are we doing about it?"

"The usual. Border checks, posters, alerts to all police here and in the surrounding countries. But I'm sure he's still somewhere in the Kalahari. It's a big place. We tried to follow his footprints from the abandoned Land Rover, but we lost them after a few miles."

Kubu sighed. Khumanego had vanished into the desert. Perhaps he had joined a nomadic Bushman band. Who would recognize him? Who took note of one extra Bushman in any case?

They continued discussing ways to track down Khumanego until Edison returned with the GPS plots. Haake had stopped at a number of places, but comparing the route with the ones of Krige and the students, Kubu was pretty sure he could guess the location of the *koppies*. Once he had the coordinates, he could check Google Earth pictures to see if he was right.

Mabaku agreed, but the big question remained.

"Why?" he asked.

Kubu shrugged. "I really don't know, Director. I can only think there is something very precious at the *koppies*. Maybe it's the diamond treasure trove Haake sought. Maybe something else. But it seems that Khumanego desperately wants it for himself. Desperately enough to kill six people for it." He paused and sighed. "But perhaps that's not it. Perhaps it's the killing he wants, and the *koppies* are just an excuse." How had this darkness overwhelmed the enthusiastic boy he had once loved?

"We'll have to go back," Mabaku said with regret. "We have to find out what's there. It's got to be the key. And we have to find this man quickly. I think you may be right; he's a psychopath. He'll kill again."

"I could . . ." Kubu began, but Mabaku held up his hand.

"*You* are going to stay right here with Joy. You are not going back there again. That's final."

Forty-three

It took three days for Mabaku to coordinate the personnel who would go to the *koppies* that seemed central to Khumanego's killing spree. And, to his huge frustration, Kubu had not found a way to accompany them. Mabaku would lead the force himself, leaving Kubu in charge of communications in Gaborone.

So on Friday morning, two police helicopters and one from the BDF took off from the small airstrip in Tsabong.

"We're in the air, Kubu." The patchwork of police and air-traffic control communications made Mabaku's voice sound tinny. "We'll call you in about forty-five minutes."

Three quarters of an hour later, the radio crackled. "We're in sight of the *koppies*. Should be on the ground in ten minutes!"

Kubu picked up his microphone. "Read you loud and clear," he replied without enthusiasm. He leaned back, popped an antacid tablet into his mouth, and drained half a glass of water.

His stomach hurt. Anxiety, the doctor had said. You worry too much.

Kubu *was* worried. He had pleaded with Mabaku to arrest Khumanego, not kill him. Mabaku had agreed in principle, but refused to rule out force. "Kubu, you're letting your personal feelings interfere with your judgment," Mabaku had said. "I know he was a friend of yours. But he's a criminal now, a murderer. You have to let go."

Kubu saw the logic, but he was torn. He still hadn't come to grips with the reality that his friend had tried to kill him. What had happened to Khumanego? he wondered. I have to find out.

The helicopters circled the *koppies*, looking for any sign of people in the vicinity. But after a couple of circuits they had seen nobody. The only signs of human presence were the motorbike tracks crisscrossing the area, just as Haake had reported. They would follow those later.

Mabaku ordered the helicopters to land several hundred yards from the front of the middle *koppie*, far enough away from small arms fire but still in view of the cliff face, which was spotted with crevices and caves. If someone's here, Mabaku reasoned, it's likely that he'll use the caves to hide.

After they landed, Mabaku pulled out a copy of Haake's map and held it up. The drawing was a good representation of the *koppies*. Final proof, he thought.

The men assembled behind the helicopters and checked their equipment once again—rifles, bulletproof vests, tear-gas canisters and masks, powerful flashlights, and radios. When all were ready, Mabaku spoke to them.

"Let me repeat what I told you earlier. The man we're looking for, the Bushman Khumanego, is very dangerous. We think he's killed six people already. But we don't know why. We also don't know if he has any accomplices. We only know that all the murders seem to have something to do with this area. We think it's probably rich in diamonds or something else, and he's protecting it for himself. I want him alive, so we can find out what's going on."

The commander of the police SWAT team gave the final instructions. "We're going to see if we can get him to give himself up. If he does, our job's over, and we go home. If he doesn't, we'll flush him with tear gas. Going into the caves is too dangerous. He knows them; we don't. And we'll be sitting ducks as we go in. When you throw in the tear gas, back away and be prepared for him to come out firing. But don't shoot unless he looks as though he's going to shoot you. Kill him only as a last resort. As the director said, we want him alive." He looked around at the serious faces that were already dripping with sweat. "One more thing. Don't let him get close to you. He may have something dosed with a Bushman poison. There's no antidote." He paused to let that sink in. "Any questions?"

The men shook their heads. They'd been over all of this before they left Tsabong. At a signal from the commander, they spread out, covering the width of the *koppies*, still staying well away from them. Two sharpshooters went to the middle of the area, lay down, set up their rifle tripods, and calibrated their rifle scopes. When everyone was in position, the commander gave Mabaku the thumbs-up.

Mabaku nodded and spoke into his mike. "Kubu, the men are in place. I'm going to try and make contact now."

He took hold of a bullhorn. "Khumanego, or anyone else here, this is Director Mabaku of the Botswana police. I'm giving you five minutes to show yourselves. Come out from wherever you are hiding with your hands above your head. I guarantee your safety. If I don't see you in five minutes, I will order the SWAT team to flush you out with tear gas. If you show any signs of aggression, my men have orders to shoot." He paused. "We don't want that, but will do it if we have to." He looked at his watch. "Your five minutes starts now."

After each minute, Mabaku called out the time remaining. There was no movement from the cliff face. With one minute to go, he made his final call. "This is your last chance. In sixty seconds, my men will go from cave to cave with tear gas. Come out now, and you'll be safe. After that it may be too late."

The final minute passed with nobody appearing. The commander gave the signal, and the men split into two groups, each going to opposite ends of the *koppies*. The leader of the group on the left pointed to the cave at the far end. One sharpshooter repositioned himself to cover the cave's entrance. Another man, keeping close to the face, edged to the entrance, tossed in a tear-gas grenade, and immediately moved back, rifle at the ready. Nobody emerged. After waiting for about five minutes, the group repeated the process for the second cave, which was nearly five yards above the first. It took some time to maneuver up the difficult slope into a position from which a canister could be safely tossed. The result was the same.

Mabaku watched with increasing frustration as each cave yielded nothing. When all the caves had been gassed, Mabaku contacted Kubu. "He's not here. We've flushed all the caves, and we've got nothing. It's been a total waste."

"Director, I suggest you and your men check each cave. Maybe he committed suicide rather than being caught and tried. Watch out for any other cover. He may be hiding from you, but not in the caves themselves."

Mabaku spoke to the SWAT commander, who instructed his men to don their masks and check each cave. A few minutes later, one of the teams radioed that they had found a body. Mabaku and the commander climbed the rock face to the entrance, pushed aside the branches of the bush concealing the entrance, and went inside. The cave was so small they could barely stand up. On the floor lay a skeleton surrounded by various Bushman artifacts.

"Obviously not the man you're looking for," the commander said drily.

Mabaku looked around in awe. The walls of the cave were covered with primitive but beautiful paintings. Of animals, single and in herds, some that were not to be found for hundreds of miles, of men hunting, and even of fish. These need to be in a museum, he thought. I've never seen anything like it.

He pulled out a pocket camera and took dozens of photos.

The radio crackled again. "We've found water!" Mabaku and the commander climbed out of the cave and slipped and slid down to the bottom. Then they walked over to where one of the men was waving. Mabaku pulled out Haake's map. The arrow with a *W* pointed at the cave they were about to enter. Whoever drew the map certainly had explored the *koppies* carefully, Mabaku thought

Then they went in. Again the walls had paintings in red and black. The man who had checked the cave led them to the back, where there was a pool of water. In the light of the flashlight it was crystal clear. A miracle for Bushmen, Mabaku thought. Water in the middle of the desert. Again Mabaku recorded the scene.

As they emerged into the blinding sunlight, another man shouted. "Look what I've found." They saw a long crack splitting the face of the *koppie*. The man told them to take off their bulletproof vests because the entrance was so narrow. They did so, and he beckoned them to follow. They had difficulty squeezing through the crack, but when they succeeded, they were overwhelmed by the rays of colored light that shot from the wall, wherever the flashlight beams played.

"Diamonds," thought Mabaku. But when he examined the wall closely, he saw the crystals were violet. He tried to remember what Haake had claimed he'd found. Amethysts? He bent over, picked one off the floor, and put it into his pocket. He then spent a few minutes photographing the walls. When he finished, he took one final marveling look and turned to leave.

It was early afternoon before all the caves had been checked. Mabaku had gone into several—those with skeletons and artifacts, and those with wall paintings. This must be a Bushman treasure, he thought as he photographed each. Such beauty, such isolation, and with water too. It should be preserved for all to see.

He walked back toward the helicopters. After the shade of the caves, the scorching heat was almost unbearable.

"Kubu. Are you still there?"

The radio hissed. "Yes, Director."

"Khumanego's nowhere to be found. Nor anyone else. I'm going to get the helicopters to follow the tire tracks to see where they go, but I'm not optimistic."

"Was there anything in the caves?"

"Kubu, this is an amazing place. It's a treasure house of Bushman artifacts and paintings. It may also be a burial ground, because we've found more than ten old corpses—mainly skeletons. You'll be amazed when you see my photos. I'll have to show them to the people at the National Museum. They'll be very excited."

"I don't think you should, Director. They'll turn the place into a tourist attraction. It'll be yet another injustice to the Bushmen."

Mabaku thought this over. Eventually he said, "Perhaps you're right. We'll need to think it through. I don't see anything to indicate diamonds. There's a wonderful cave with a ceiling of crystals, though. Maybe amethysts."

"More reason to keep it quiet," said Kubu. Then his thoughts went back to Khumanego.

"Director, I'm really worried. Khumanego is very dangerous. We must find him. I wonder where on earth he is and what he's doing."

Director Mabaku had no reply.

In fact, Khumanego was watching Mabaku as he spoke to Kubu. When he'd heard the helicopters, he hadn't taken refuge in the caves, where he knew he would be trapped. Instead he'd faded into the grass and bushes several hundred yards away. The SWAT squad could have walked within a few yards of where he lay dead-still and not seen him. Bushmen were good at hiding.

Khumanego watched with growing anguish as Mabaku's men threw canisters into the caves and tramped in and out of sacred Bushman burial places. As the hours passed, he became more and more incensed. It was his duty to the gods to protect this place, but he could do nothing. If he showed his head, the police would kill him like an animal and then laugh about it.

As his anger built up, Khumanego's eyes lost focus and his mind began to swirl. He heard the Mantis groan in pain. And he heard the voices of his ancestors. They were crying out for vengeance.

Forty-four

Hukuntsi was a dangerous place for Khumanego. People knew him there under a different name, but they would recognize his face if they'd seen the Wanted posters. Still he needed to know what was happening in the physical world around him—the world outside the spirit world of his mind, the world of the Mantis.

It had been a long walk from The Place, so Khumanego rested until evening, and then slipped into the town. He wasn't worried about being seen making his way along the side streets. Bushmen sometimes visited the town to buy provisions for their settlements to the south.

He made his way to the small corrugated-iron shack that Willie had built for himself on vacant land. One day someone would drive Willie away, but he knew that and would move his belongings when the time came. The door was padlocked, and the shack in darkness. Khumanego prowled around it, looking for a way in, wondering where Willie was. He should have been home by now. Khumanego was distracted as he came back to the road, otherwise he would have seen the woman before she spotted him.

She was large and busty and had a basket of provisions balanced on her head. She was watching him with disapproval, and she didn't look friendly.

"What are you doing there, hey? You people are always sneaking around here. What do you want?"

Khumanego sighed with relief. She didn't recognize him. Perhaps she was the woman who lived nearby, who always gave Willie trouble. Willie was scared of her.

"I was looking for Willie. You know him? The Bushman? He lives here."

"And who are you?"

"My name's Piscoaghu." It would've been better to tell her something else, Khumanego realized, but he wouldn't back down in front of this overbearing woman.

"Willie's not here. The police took him away," she told him with satisfaction.

"The police? Why? Where did they take him?"

"He's in Tsabong. Good riddance. He was involved with killing that policeman in the desert." She stared at him. "Perhaps you were involved, too. Your face looks familiar."

Khumanego knew it was time to move on, but he was intrigued. He wanted to hear the details of how his work had played out. "What happened to the policemen in the desert?" he asked.

"It was Detective Tau from right here! From the Tshane police station. He was a good man. I knew him myself. A

Bushman left him to die in the desert. Horrible. A Bushman! Like you." She looked angry now, her anger directed at him.

"And the other policeman?"

"The other one? How do you know there was another one?"

Khumanego stood his ground. "I heard two policemen died in the desert."

"You heard wrong. They took the other to hospital. I don't know what happened to him after that." She gave a small shrug of her shoulders. "Go away! Get out of here! I've got no more time to waste on you." She turned and stalked off with the basket effortlessly balanced in sync with the movement of her walk.

Khumanego stared at her back. "He's not alive," he shouted after her. "He's dead! He must be dead. You understand?" But the woman ignored him and kept on walking.

Khumanego had to know for sure. He walked through the dusk to the edge of town, to the corrugated-iron shack he sometimes used when he was in Hukuntsi. His motorbike was inside, locked to a heavy U-bolt that protruded from the wall. He unlocked the bike and, ignoring the risk, rode to the Kgalagadi Filling Station. He approached the man serving there. A man he knew, and who knew him.

"Piscoaghu! We haven't seen you for a long time . . ." The man stepped back, his voice scared.

"Where's Willie?"

"The police took him away. They said he was involved with murdering Detective Tau."

"The detective died?"

The man nodded.

"And the other one?" Khumanego's voice rose.

"The other policeman? They found him and took him to the hospital."

"But he died there!" Now Khumanego was almost shouting.

"No, no, he was okay. He came to Detective Tau's funeral. He cried."

Khumanego lost control. "You lie! You lie!" he screamed.

"No, it's true . . ." The man backed farther away, now terrified of the mad Bushman.

Khumanego was breathing hard, but he realized the man was telling the truth. He pulled himself together. Now he had very little time. He needed to move quickly and disappear. Soon the police would be searching for him in the town and nearby.

But he wasn't really worried. Disappearing was something he did well.

Forty-five

Kubu sat in his office, frustrated and angry. Somehow, he felt, if he'd been with the team that had gone to Haake's *koppies* the previous week, things might have worked out differently. They had needed to look beyond the obvious, to see as a Bushman saw. Maybe he wouldn't have been good enough to do that either, but at least he could have tried. What chance did a SWAT team have? They'd never look beyond the obvious threats, noisily attacking empty caves. Khumanego would never let himself be trapped that way. Now he was sure that Khumanego had linked up with a Bushman group and was living perfectly camouflaged among them in the Kalahari. There had been no trace of him since he had driven off in the Land Rover leaving Kubu and Tau to the sun and thirst of the Kalahari. He thumped his desk with his fist, and noted with approval that the telephone jumped. More impressive, it actually started to ring. He grabbed it.

"Assistant Superintendent Bengu."

"Kubu, it's Mabaku. Get up here right away."

No questions were to be answered; Kubu was left with the dialing tone. But Mabaku had sounded excited. Kubu lost no time heading to his office.

Mabaku got straight to the point. He waved Kubu to a chair and said, "Khumanego's been spotted in Hukuntsi. Hukuntsi! Amazing, after all these weeks. Not a trace of him, and then he's in Hukuntsi bold as you please, pretending to be Piscoa-ghu, and pushing people around."

Kubu leaned forward, excited. "Did they catch him?"

Mabaku shook his head. "He questioned a gas-station attendant—not Willie, we're still holding him. He wanted to know about you. He seemed upset that you made it." Mabaku grimaced. He knew this news would hurt Kubu to the quick. "Then he disappeared. The local police are scouring the area. But one of them was smart. He asked about motorbikes. Sure enough, a man on a bike was seen heading out of town to the north. The witness didn't think it was a Bushman, but he was wearing a heavy jacket and helmet. So it could have been any-one. I'm pretty sure it was Khumanego."

"When did this happen?"

"This afternoon. Lerako phoned through a few minutes ago. They're still searching, but they won't find him."

Kubu nodded. Now Khumanego had disguised himself as a cross-country biker. A leather jacket and helmet. No one would realize he was a Bushman. But where would he go? Back to his people in the desert? Probably, but they couldn't take the chance.

"We should set up roadblocks. Reinforce the border post alert. He might make a run for it now. He must know how close we are."

Mabaku nodded. "Get onto it right away. I want him behind bars, the bastard. I won't forget Tau's parents breaking down at the funeral. They deserve revenge for this. I want them to have it."

Kubu was silent. Revenge was a harsh word and shouldn't be in a policeman's vocabulary. But he had spent an anguished time with Tau's family describing the young man's last days. He had told them that Tau had set off to get help, knowing that Kubu wouldn't be able to keep up. That he had taken the best chance. That bad luck had prevented him finding the others, but that he was a hero. Kubu hoped he'd been convincing.

"I'll do it at once, Director," he said, climbing to his feet.

As expected, they found nothing. A man on an off-road bike had bought fuel in Kang. Had he been a Bushman? The fuel attendant doubted that, because Bushmen didn't ride nice mo-torbikes.

Kubu stared at the topographic map he had used to link the murders with the *koppies*, thinking of Mabaku's pictures of the gems, the paintings, and the funeral sites. One day I must go there, he thought. Then perhaps I'll understand. But I'll never understand Khumanego. These murders don't make sense. He sighed. They don't make sense to me, but they must to him. That's the tragedy.

He checked his watch. It was getting late. Perhaps he would just check if Mabaku had heard anything and then head home. To supper with Joy and Tumi. That thought made him feel better.

But Mabaku seemed in a mood to chat. He invited Kubu

to sit and asked after the family. He commented on his wife's interminable shopping. Clearly there was something he wanted to say, but he was taking a long time to say it. Kubu felt uncomfortable. He didn't want to be late for dinner. At last Mabaku came to the point.

"I share your concerns about the Bushman cultures, Kubu. You know that. And those *koppies* were absolutely spectacular. Unbelievable. But now there's a problem. Perhaps Khumanego was living there. Maybe protecting them even in a strange sort of way? But now there's no one. And that gem I picked up *was* an amethyst. If someone unscrupulous gets wind of those . . ." He let his voice trail off. "It's a human treasure, Kubu. Those paintings weren't made by today's Bushmen, who, I admit, do some interesting work, but it's modern art. Nothing like what I saw. We have to save it for everyone. Not just a few Bushmen who know about it and venerate it as a relic of the past."

"You spoke to the museum people."

"Yes, I told them about it, and I showed them some of the pictures. They were amazed and wanted to know all about it. I told them it was a police crime scene. I didn't tell them where it was. So no one is going there anytime soon. And I suggested that they tell the Minister of Youth, Sports, and Culture about it. That he should make a plan to protect the place and preserve it. Not turn it into another tourist attraction. They agreed. I said I'd let them know when someone could go there. Let's see what they come up with."

Kubu sighed. Perhaps this was the only way. Preserve the past, do your best for the present, ignore the future. "I think you had no option, Director. I hope one day I can see it for myself."

Mabaku looked relieved. "Yes, I hope so too. Once Khumanego is safely behind bars."

But first we have to catch him, Kubu thought.

Mabaku checked his watch. "Well, we best be getting home. It's getting late."

Kubu nodded, and said good night. It *was* late, and he was hungry.

Forty-six

It was nearly dark when Kubu drove up to his gate. He was tired and discouraged. He knew how easy it would be for Khumanego to hide in a nomadic Bushman band. After all, that was how he'd grown up. Unless they got lucky, the police might never find him.

As he swung the gate open, he was surprised that Ilia wasn't there to greet him. But that happened sometimes these days. Whether her sensitive ears couldn't pick up his arrival over Tumi's crying, or whether she stayed with Joy to provide moral support, Kubu couldn't say. Or perhaps she was just having her supper. Kubu hoped the latter was the explanation.

However, when he wasn't greeted by the police guard, who was normally at the gate, Kubu stopped. He's probably having coffee with Joy, he thought. But I'd better make sure. He pulled out his cell phone and called his own landline. After a few seconds, he could hear the phone ringing inside the house. It rang and rang, but no one answered. Then he tried Joy's cell phone. It went straight through to voicemail.

A chill spread through Kubu. Something was wrong. Had Khumanego returned to finish his work? He dialed Mabaku's cell number. It, too, went through to voicemail. Kubu left a message explaining the situation and asked Mabaku to call him back as soon as possible. Then he tried Edison, who answered immediately.

"Edison, I'm outside my house. The police guard isn't here. Ilia hasn't come out to welcome me, and Joy doesn't answer my phone calls."

"Could they be visiting one of your neighbors?"

"I'm sure Joy would've let me know, and she wouldn't have taken Ilia. I've tried phoning the director, but he's not answering. I have to check what's going on, so I'm going into the house. If I haven't called you in five minutes, get hold of him immediately. No matter where he is, whatever he's doing. Tell him what's going on."

"Are you armed?"

"No."

"I think you should wait until I find him."

"I can't do that," Kubu snapped. "Joy and Tumi may be in danger." With that he hung up and walked toward the house.

"I'm home, my darling," he called, trying hard to sound unconcerned. "I'm home. Where are you?" Then he heard Tumi crying. At least she was alive. He took a deep breath and went in.

He found them in the dining room. Joy was sitting at one corner of the table rocking the baby, who surprisingly stopped crying when she saw her father. Ilia was next to them, standing aggressively, on guard. And they were not alone. Khuma-nego was sitting at the far end of the table, his hands crossed on the surface. In front of him was a hunting knife, the blade partly covered by a yellowish stain. The back of Kubu's neck tingled.

"Hello, David," Khumanego said. "We've been waiting for you."

Kubu put his briefcase on the floor and sat down at the table between Khumanego and his family.

Khumanego picked up the knife and pointed it at Kubu. "David," he said. "Put your handgun and cell phone on the table. I don't want you trying something stupid."

"I'm unarmed," Kubu responded, as he slid his cell phone toward Khumanego.

"Stand up."

Kubu did so, and Khumanego patted him down.

"Sit."

Kubu complied, and Khumanego picked up the phone and turned it off.

"What do you want, Khumanego?" Kubu asked quietly. "Why have you come here?"

Khumanego frowned, but it was Joy who replied.

"He said he'd kill us if we tried to stop him. Kill Tumi . . . with the knife with Bushman poison. I called off Ilia . . ." She was battling to keep her voice under control. She and Ilia had seen off a man with a gun in their time, but the horror of the slow-death poison was more than she could handle. And there was the baby now. Kubu nodded, but he kept his eyes fixed on the Bushman.

"What do you want?" he repeated.

"What do I want?" Khumanego mimicked derisively. "I want my people to have their lands back, to have their dignity back, to have their sacred places respected. I want the elderly to lead decent lives—free in their traditional culture—not herded into camps to die of disease and hopelessness. I want respect. I don't want to be laughed at. I want to be treated with dignity." He met Kubu's stare. "That's what I want."

"I've always respected you, Khumanego. Why do you come here and threaten my family? Of all places outside the desert, it's here you get the things you want."

Khumanego shook his head. "There's a line. A line you hold and defend, that no one is allowed to cross. My line is The Place. No one goes there. No one desecrates it. It belongs to me, and I guard it for my people." He hesitated. "I'm *The Guardian*. That's what I am. *The Guardian* of The Place."

Kubu was worried that he was losing the drift of what the Bushman was saying, and it was vital to keep Khumanego engaged.

"What place is this, Khumanego? Tell me about it."

"It's not *a* place. It's *The* Place. The home of the ancestors and the gods and the Mantis. I am its guardian."

Suddenly Kubu understood. "It's the *koppies*, isn't it? That Haake found? That we searched for together in the desert?"

Khumanego shook his head. "We didn't search for it together. I was there to stop you. I had to stop you. I'm sorry about that, David. Because you're not a bad man, and you were once my friend. But you can't go to The Place. It's not permitted. I don't permit it."

"And that's why you left us to die of thirst in the desert? I wasn't looking for a place, Khumanego. I was looking for a murderer."

"You didn't need to go so far to find him."

No, thought Kubu. I didn't.

There was a silence for a few moments. I must keep him talking, Kubu thought. "Explain to me, Khumanego. I don't understand. You know I respect your people, that I'd do nothing to hurt them or insult them. What did I do wrong?"

"The Place is sacred. No one goes there and lives, unless I permit it. People must learn that The Place is cursed. They will learn to keep away. Otherwise they too will die."

"Why didn't you explain this to me before?"

"Explain? Then you would go there. Like the team you sent there last week! They desecrated that sacred ground! I watched them: firing bombs, insulting the ancestors, angering the gods! You wanted me to explain that this shouldn't be done?" His voice was raised in anger.

Kubu tried to calm him. "I thought you would go back to the desert. Back to your people who still follow the old ways. I thought we would never find you."

"They have also been corrupted. All of them! They get water and food from the towns, then pretend they live from the desert. They are not worthy of the Mantis! Not worthy of me!"

"So why did you come here?"

"It was *you* who led the defilers to The Place. You were responsible. And you were meant to die in the desert. To be a sacrifice for The Place. But they found you too soon."

"So you have come to finish what you started? Is that how it is?"

Khumanego said nothing.

"Let Joy and Tumi go, my friend. They have nothing to do with this."

Khumanego hesitated, and for a moment Kubu thought he

might agree. But he shook his head sharply. "They stay. But if you cooperate, I promise I won't harm them when it's over."

"What do you want me to do?"

But again Khumanego didn't answer, and Kubu felt a surge of hope. *He has come to kill me, but he cannot say it. He doesn't really want to do it.* How long since he had called Edison? Fifteen minutes? Twenty minutes? Longer?

"They found nothing at The Place, Khumanego. And nothing was damaged permanently. It can become a national heritage site—like Tsodilo—preserved forever for your people and your culture. We can do this together. I'd like to help. To make amends."

"Like Tsodilo? Become a place of amusement for gawking tourists with their digital cameras? And of research for academics who've never even met a real Bushman?" Khumanego shook his head. "You don't understand, David. This is real. It is not about culture. The gods are real. The ancestors are real. You remember Gobiwasi?" Kubu nodded. "I spoke with him recently. His spirit lives. And I hear the words of the gods. I have been accepted into their world. The world of the Mantis. It is a great honor."

"I want to help you. Help you preserve this place."

"You can help, David, if that is what you really want. You need to complete the sacrifice. If you do it willingly now, the impact will be greater. The gods more pleased. And your family will live."

"I'm no help to anyone dead."

"That's only your perception of life. In your world, I've been dead for a long time."

There was silence. Kubu had run out of things to say. He thought he might be forced to accept Khumanego's deal—his life for that of his family. If he held out his arm now for Khumanego's poisoned knife, it would be over. That's what he wants, he thought. He wants me to do this willingly or to resist physically. He finds it hard to kill me in cold blood. Because of the past. Two boys learning about life together a long time ago. And that is my only chance. I must do nothing. I must wait for him to gather the courage to make the move. If he can.

The silence was broken by the telephone. Kubu let out a breath he hadn't known he was holding. "I think I should answer that," he said and was on his feet and had grabbed the phone before Khumanego could object. Joy and Khumanego stared at him, hearing only his side of the conversation.

"Yes, it's Kubu." He listened.

"Yes, he's here with us." He listened again.

"We're all right. We're talking things over." Kubu listened for a few seconds more, and then said to Khumanego: "It's the police. They have the house surrounded. There's no way out. They want to talk to you."

Khumanego was already on his feet, the knife in his right hand, moving the edges of the curtains to peek out. At first he saw nothing, but then he realized that there were cars blocking the street at each end. And there were men assembling floodlights. The first one came on as he watched.

Khumanego turned to Kubu, pointing the knife in his direction. "You called them, didn't you? When no one answered the phone here. That was you, wasn't it? I heard you arrive. Now you will all die. That is what you have done." He started to move toward Joy.

"Khumanego!" Kubu said loudly, moving in front of her. "I knew you were here. That's why I came in. I wanted to talk to you. To see what we could work out together. To preserve what you have achieved. To save The Place. To venerate the gods and the ancestors." He knew he was gabbling rubbish, but Khumanego stopped and turned to him.

"Tell them we are leaving. All of us. They must bring a car, and you will drive. We'll . . ."

But Kubu shook his head. "No, I won't tell them that. That will never work. They won't do it, and if they do, it'll be a trap. This isn't a movie, Khumanego. They'll never negotiate on that." He paused. "But what we *can* do is arrange for you to turn yourself in. I'll say that's why you came here. Then you can tell your story. The press will interview you. They'll see why you did these things and write about it in newspapers around the world. At the trial, you'll be able to tell the whole world everything you've told me. The world will support you like they did your people when they were thrown out of the Central Kalahari Game Reserve. They will force the government to change its policies. To give you back what is yours. It'll turn everything around, I promise. Everything!"

He glanced at Joy. By the expression on her face, she almost believed he meant it. Oh God, if only Khumanego thinks so too.

"Come, my friend, let's sit down and talk about it. They'll give us some time, but not too much." When Khumanego collapsed back into his chair, Kubu carefully put the phone down without disconnecting the line and sat down next to him.

More than half an hour passed as they negotiated. Kubu was glad that the phone line was still open; Mabaku would hear the discussions and realize there was no need for immediate action. There was to be a press conference. Various reporters were to be there, including Cindy. Obviously Khumanego didn't know she was no longer in Botswana. Eventually Kubu promised everything Khumanego wanted, but negotiated hard to appear convincing. But, in reality, none of the details mattered. Kubu had to engineer things so that all of them remained alive. And that would only happen if he could persuade Khumanego that his cause would be best served by giving himself up.

At last Kubu picked up the phone and spoke to Mabaku.

"We've made a deal," he told the director. Then he detailed everything, careful to cover every point, while Khumanego listened to his side of the conversation.

"We're not going to do any of that," said Mabaku, when Kubu had finished.

"Yes, I also think it's fair," said Kubu solemnly. "It's important for the Bushman culture, for all of us." He gave Khumanego an encouraging nod.

"Will he give himself up? Is he armed?"

"He'll come out with me. He has a knife, but no gun or anything like that. He'll stick to his side of the bargain."

"He comes out with his hands up. Not with you. Alone. No weapons. No sudden movements. He walks slowly toward us in the street. Then we grab him and handcuff him, and it's over. Make it clear to him."

Kubu explained it to Khumanego, who looked dubious. "I don't trust them."

"You have my word. We follow exactly what they say, and you'll be all right. Then we can work on all the other things you need."

Kubu picked up the phone again. "I've given him my word he won't be harmed. He'll follow what you've said." Mabaku grunted in reply.

Khumanego was silent for several moments. "I want to talk

to him myself," he said at last. With considerable misgivings, Kubu handed him the phone. For the next few minutes, Kubu listened to Khumanego question Mabaku about the details of his surrender. At last Khumanego was satisfied. "All right," he said, and hung up the phone. Then he turned to Kubu.

"You must come with me. I won't go alone."

Kubu hesitated. It was all wrong and contradicted Mabaku's instructions. But if he agreed, at least Joy and Tumi would be safe. He nodded and heard Joy gasp.

"Very well. Now let's go. Leave the knife on the table."

Khumanego shook his head. "It comes with me. I'll keep it in my pocket. I won't touch it." The knife was still in his hand.

Again Kubu was tempted to let him have his way, but the knife was deadly. If there was a scuffle, someone might be cut and die. He shook his head. "The knife stays here. Someone might see it and panic. It's not negotiable."

It was the wrong wording. Khumanego bristled, and Kubu could see that he was overcome with indecision. Kubu prayed he wouldn't change his mind. But after a few seconds, which felt like forever, Khumanego lifted the knife and stabbed it into the table. It stuck there, upright, vibrating.

Kubu breathed a sigh of relief. "Come, my friend. We'll go together."

Suddenly Khumanego seemed to lose interest. He started talking in a Bushman language Kubu couldn't follow, as though there was someone else in the room with them. He paused from time to time as if listening to a reply or a question. At last he stopped and turned to Kubu, relief in his voice. "They say that I will join them now. They say it will be all right. Come, let's go."

Kubu gave Joy an encouraging smile and walked out of the

front door with the man who had once been his childhood friend.

At first all was well. But as they stepped off the veranda, the floodlights hit Khumanego full in the face. For a moment he staggered, but then he recovered, and his face was transformed by joy. He gave an ecstatic shout of greeting, threw his arms out wildly and, eluding Kubu's grasp, began to dance.

That was when the sharpshooters shot him. He never heard the shots—the bullets came too fast—but Kubu heard them and threw himself to the ground. And Joy heard them too, and screamed as she ran out of the house to where Kubu was lying. He grabbed her and pulled her down to the ground with him.

Seconds later, Mabaku ran up. "Kubu! Are you all right? Joy, you should've stayed in the house!"

Joy began to sob. Kubu looked up at his boss, but said nothing.

Forty-seven

Kubu and Joy hardly slept at all, spending most of the night on the sofa. It took Kubu several hours to calm Joy to the point where she could talk coherently. When she was eventually able to recount what had happened, tears flowed down her face.

"He threatened to kill Tumi if I shouted for help," she sobbed. "He put that terrible knife under her chin. I was terrified." Kubu put his arms around her.

"It must have been awful," he said softly. "You were so brave."

"There was nothing I could do to warn you. I hoped you'd think something was wrong when Ilia didn't meet you at the gate. When I heard the car, I held her so she couldn't run to you."

"Of course I noticed she wasn't there, but thought she was

eating her food. I was quite late." He squeezed her tightly. "But when the guard wasn't there either, I thought there was a problem, and when you didn't answer when I called here, I was sure. That's when I called Mabaku. I couldn't reach him, but I told Edison to find him unless I called again. Then I came in. I couldn't leave you and Tumi in Khumanego's hands."

Joy smiled weakly and squeezed Kubu's hand. Words were hard to find.

They sat holding each other for some minutes, gently rocking back and forth.

"Kubu?"

"Yes, my darling?"

"When I heard those shots and saw you on the ground . . ." Joy's voice choked. She took a deep breath. "I thought they'd shot you. That you were dead." She buried her face in his chest, tears pouring from her eyes. A few minutes later, she whispered, "I can't imagine living without you."

Now Kubu's eyes grew moist.

He slowly detached himself from Joy and went to refill their wineglasses. When he returned, he handed one to Joy, snuggled next to her, and raised his. "To us, my darling. You and Tumi are the most important things in my life." Their glasses clinked, and they both took large swigs.

Joy turned away so Kubu wouldn't see that she'd begun to cry again. She said softly, "I was afraid you didn't want me anymore."

Kubu was astonished. "Dearest, whatever gave you that idea?"

"Oh, Kubu, I thought you no longer desired me. My body's changed so much with the pregnancy. Everything has drooped!"

Kubu held her and laughed. "My darling," he said, "I'm hardly in a position to begrudge you an extra pound or two."

"But my stretch marks!"

"Every single one reminds me of the miraculous gift you've given me—our adorable Tumi, the child we feared we'd never have."

Joy was silent for a moment, taking his words into her heart. "I thought you were seeing another woman," she whispered.

"What?"

"That Cindy person. The reporter. You liked each other. I could tell."

Kubu knew that if he lied to her now, their marriage would forever have a tiny crack in it. "Yes, but as friends only. Had I been single, perhaps I'd have been interested, but Joy, you must know how much I love you. I'd never look at another woman. You're my soul mate, my heart's companion. I've never been unfaithful to you and, on my honor, I never will."

With that, the floodgates opened, and Joy wept for a long time. Kubu had the good sense not to try to stop her, the tears cleansing the part of her that had doubted him.

Finally Joy blew her nose and turned so she could look at Kubu's face. "Could you be happy, not being a detective?"

Kubu had a sinking feeling. He knew how much his job was affecting her. And since Tumi's birth, she'd become less tolerant of it. He realized he'd been expecting this conversation even before the horrible events of the evening.

"Do you want me to leave the police?" he whispered, fearing the worst.

"I'm not sure I can take any more of this." She put her head on his shoulder.

Maybe I should resign, Kubu thought. Not only for Joy's sake, but also because Mabaku betrayed me today. He promised they wouldn't harm Khumanego. I'm not sure I can work for someone I don't trust.

They remained on the sofa for a long time, holding each other quietly, lost in thought. Each wondering how they would negotiate the future.

Kubu went to work after lunch the next day, but only because Joy had recovered some of her composure and Pleasant had taken the afternoon off to be with her. Under normal circumstances, he would have stayed at home with her, but now he had a mission.

He put down his briefcase and went to see Miriam.

"Is the director available?"

She nodded and told him to go in.

Kubu knocked and opened the door to Mabaku's office.

"I'd like to talk to you, Director. May I sit down?"

Mabaku closed the folder he was working on and leaned back.

Kubu pulled an envelope from his shirt pocket and placed it on the desk. "This is my resignation, Director. I'll wrap things up by the end of the month and then leave."

Mabaku's impassive face didn't change. He stared at Kubu without saying a word.

They sat in silence, each waiting for the other to take the initiative. Mabaku was an expert at silence, and prevailed.

"Director, this is the hardest decision of my life. You know how much I love what I do. But I can't continue."

Mabaku went on staring, his eyes a little narrower than before. Kubu began to squirm in his seat. He thought he was prepared for this meeting, but Mabaku, as usual, was proving him wrong.

"Director, there are two reasons for my decision." Kubu gazed out of the window at Kgale Hill. He summoned up his courage and looked into the director's eyes. "I have to work for someone I can trust. Last night, I guaranteed that Khumanego wouldn't be harmed if he gave himself up. And you knew that. But when he was shot . . ." Kubu bit his lip. "When he was shot, you broke the trust between us, and I broke my promise to Khumanego. You may not have any reservations about what happened, Director, and I'm sure you've good reasons for what you did, but I have to live with myself. And I'm finding it very difficult to do so at the moment. I can't and won't put myself in the same position again." Kubu sat up straight. "I'm sorry, Director. You've been very good to me in the past, and I appreciate that. I've always admired and respected you. You've always pointed me in the right direction, and I thank you for that too. But last night something very special between us was broken. I can't work for you without it."

Mabaku stood up and walked to the window. He always took comfort from the permanence of Kgale Hill, and from the baboons that frequently came down from it and foraged around the CID offices.

"So, I'm unworthy of your trust?" He walked back to his desk and sat down. "You know, Kubu, as smart as you are, sometimes you let your emotions get in the way of your brain. What do you *really* know about what happened last night? What orders did the sharpshooters have? Who gave the order to shoot?" He banged his fist on the desk. "You come in here and blame me for what happened. Do you really know that I'm at fault? Do you know what actually happened? You are letting your emotions come to a verdict without any evidence. I'm disappointed."

He stared at Kubu and shook his head. "How many years have we been working together? Ten? Twelve? I'm not sure I even know. And how often have I let you down in all those years?" He jumped out of his chair, grabbed Kubu's envelope, and waved it in the air. "And yet, without a scrap of evidence you now accuse me of violating our trust. Grow up, Assistant Superintendent."

He flung the envelope back on the desk and returned to the window. With his back to Kubu, he said: "You want to know who was responsible for Khumanego's death? I'll tell you." He turned back to face the detective. "You were!"

Kubu sat in stunned silence while Mabaku returned to his chair and sat down again. "My instructions to you were quite explicit. Khumanego comes out *alone*. But you came out with him." Kubu started to interrupt, but Mabaku stopped him. "You may've had your reasons. You were the person inside with a madman with a poisoned knife. But when you came out with him, the game changed. He'd already killed the guard, and we didn't know if the knife was inside the house or with him. He could have cut you with it in a second and you would have been dead. If he made any sudden movement, we had to kill him at once."

Kubu wrestled with the accusation. The knife was safely inside, but the police couldn't possibly have known that. But he *had* given his word!

He gave up the issue for the time being. "There's a second reason."

"And what's that?" Mabaku said tiredly.

"Director, last night was the second time in two years that

Joy's life has been in danger. And this time Tumi's was too. Had we lost her, I'm not sure how we would've coped, and had I lost either of them . . ." He couldn't finish the sentence and looked down. It took him several seconds to recover his composure.

"I know all about the stresses policemen's wives feel, and I know how high the divorce rate is. As much as I love this job, Director, I love my wife more. I can't risk my marriage."

Mabaku stared at him without sympathy.

"Kubu, my father was a policeman. Just a constable. When I was twelve, we were in Molepolole. One night he was called out to stop a fight at a bar. When he got there, both men were bruised and bleeding, but still fighting with their fists and feet. There was a noisy crowd around them. He dragged the two apart and told them to go home. The crowd got hostile because there were a lot of bets on the fight, and then someone threw a brick. It hit my father on the head and killed him. They never found who did it."

He took a deep breath. "My mother was left to raise me and my brothers and sisters. Five in all. On a policeman's paltry pension. Obviously it wasn't enough, so she had to go out and find a job. And then another. But what I remember most of all was how proud she was of my father. She felt he'd made each community he worked in a better place. Made the country a better place. She knew how important it was for him to do that. She never complained about his death. Certainly, she missed him. But to her, his death was for a good cause. Something to be proud of. Had she forbidden him to be a policeman, both of them would've withered."

He stood up and walked to one of the filing cabinets, unlocked it, and pulled open the bottom drawer. He reached in and lifted out a bottle of Scotch and two tumblers. "I'm not Ian MacGregor, but I see his point that a stiff drink sometimes clears the way."

Kubu gawked—in all the years he had been at the CID, he'd never known Mabaku kept a stash of whisky.

Mabaku poured two large drinks and handed one to Kubu. "To an ex-policeman!" He drained the glass in a single gulp. "Come on, Kubu, drink up! Drink to whatever you are going to be in the future. Security guard? Private eye? The Number One Man's Detective Agency?"

Kubu was taken aback by Mabaku's sarcasm and didn't feel like drinking. Still, he drained the tumbler.

Mabaku sat down again and stared at Kubu, glass in hand.

He picked up the envelope and flipped it at Kubu. "On your way out, see Miriam and make an appointment to see me a week from Monday. Take next week off and go home and think about it. Don't come back till you've made up your mind."

Kubu picked up the envelope and walked out. Mabaku had won this encounter. Kubu wondered who would have the last word.

Forty-eight

For the first time since he had returned home to discover his family held hostage, Kubu was happy. They had made the decision the night before. Only time would tell whether it was the right one. In the end Joy's view had prevailed. He sincerely hoped that she didn't come to regret it.

Tonight they were going to relax and, despite the unusual nature of the cooking arrangements for the evening, had invited Pleasant over to celebrate. Bongani couldn't join them because he was on a field trip.

Kubu brought Joy and Pleasant each a glass of inexpensive but good South African sauvignon blanc as they sat in the cool shade of the veranda. They looked at him with broad smiles and eager anticipation. This was to be the evening that Kubu had put off for so long—the evening he was finally going to keep his promise to cook a full meal. Tumi had been fed and was in her crib. Hopefully, she would sleep through the event.

"Remember," Kubu said, wagging his finger, "you both promised that you wouldn't come into the kitchen while I'm cooking."

They nodded in unison. "We promise," Pleasant said.

"It's six now, dinner will be ready at half past seven. I have some snacks for you in the meantime."

He disappeared indoors, followed closely by a curious Ilia, who was used to Kubu sitting on the veranda and Joy disappearing inside.

Now to work, Kubu thought as he walked back into the kitchen. One step at a time. It can't be that difficult.

A friend had told him always to soak the rice for an hour before cooking. So Kubu found a bowl, measured out a cup of rice and added two and a half cups of water. Not two, not three, his friend had said. It must be two and a half. He put the bowl at the end of the counter out of the way.

He pulled a folded piece of paper from his shirt pocket. This was the recipe he had chosen after a review of several on the Web.

Humming "La donne è mobile" from Verdi's *Rigoletto* while he worked, Kubu first cut the pork into cubes. At least that is what the recipe called for; for the most part, the pieces looked more like bricks. He chopped an onion, causing his eyes to smart, then turned his attention to slicing a ginger root. I assume you take off the skin, but how much to use? he wondered. The recipe didn't specify, and he had bought a large root, about six inches long—with arms! He decided to take about a quarter of the root, since he loved ginger so much.

Next the recipe called for a minced garlic clove. Now he was stumped. Obviously the skin had to come off the clove, but how did you mince it? Joy had a grater, but he was scared he would grate the tips off his fingers if he used it with something that small. *Perhaps I can chop it finely enough that it'll be the same as mincing?* His humming stopped as he concentrated on making the little pieces of garlic even smaller.

Kubu surveyed the small piles of ingredients and was satisfied with his progress. Glancing over to Ilia, who was curled in the corner observing his every move, Kubu said, "This isn't so hard, Ilia. I'll have supper ready in no time. And you can have some too." Ilia wagged her tail enthusiastically.

Kubu took the bottle of wine from the fridge and went to see whether Joy and Pleasant needed a top-up. They did.

"How is it going, Kubu?" Pleasant asked as he filled her glass.

"Fine, thanks. Everything's under control." He looked a little smug as he returned to the kitchen. *I know they think I won't be able to do this,* he thought. *I'll show them.*

He scrutinized the recipe again. "Toss the pork with one tablespoon of sugar and the soy sauce." He found sugar in a cupboard and took a tablespoon from the cutlery drawer. *Level or heaped?* Hmm. He compromised by taking more than a level tablespoon, but not as much as he could have piled onto it. *Now, how much soy sauce?* He looked back to the ingredients—one tablespoon. He pulled a soy-sauce bottle from the paper bag on the counter and carefully dispensed one tablespoon into a large bowl. Then he tossed the pork into the bowl, splashing soy sauce all over the counter and onto his khaki shorts.

"Damn!"

He found a rag, wet it, and rubbed his shorts. It only made the stain bigger. Then he wiped the counter. Better add some more sauce, he thought. He estimated that half had fled the bowl, so he added half a tablespoon to make up for it. He looked at his watch: 6:25 p.m. The pork has to stand for ten minutes. Remember to take it out, he admonished himself. At 6:35 p.m.

As he contemplated his next culinary step, he recalled his mother cooking for him as a boy. It had seemed to be a joy to her rather than a chore. He remembered the pride on her face as he and his father wolfed down her food. And a few times Khumanego had been there too. That thought brought back sad memories which, he was sure, would never leave him. Kubu shook his head, grateful to bring himself back to the moment and to the next step in the recipe.

"Dip the meat in the egg and cover with cornstarch." Kubu read the next stage of the recipe aloud. Gazing back at the ingredients, he realized that he had to beat the egg. He found a bowl, broke the egg shell on its edge and poured the egg into it. It took him a couple of minutes to fish some shell remnants from the bowl. It was very difficult to catch them with a spoon, so he removed them with his fingers. Nobody will notice, he told himself a little guiltily.

He threw the egg shells into the garbage, and paused as he watched them leak over the scraps of his torn-up resignation letter. I suppose Mabaku *will* take me back, he wondered. I suppose I owe him an apology too. But that is for Monday. Today I have work to do.

He measured out half a cup of cornstarch and removed a tablespoon's worth, again compromising between a level and heaped spoon, which he put in a coffee cup for safekeeping. He poured the rest on the counter so he could roll the pork in it.

"Kubu! Could we have some more wine please? And more snacks?"

Kubu took the wine bottle out of the fridge, poured a packet of chips into a bowl, and went to the veranda.

"How is it coming?" Pleasant asked. "I'm starving."

"Everything is under control. Thank you. I just wish people would write clear directions!" The two women had noticed that Kubu had stopped humming about fifteen minutes earlier.

"What's that on your shorts?" Joy asked.

Kubu didn't answer and stalked back to the kitchen. Joy and Pleasant looked at each other and burst out laughing. Kubu was not amused.

Kubu glanced at his watch. Damn! Ten to seven. He hoped it didn't matter if the pork marinated too long. He grabbed a fork, pierced a piece of pork, dipped it in the egg and rolled it in the corn starch. Then he had some difficulty taking the fork out and ended up using his fingers once again. About five minutes later, he had finished coating the pork, which was now in a large bowl.

"Let the meat stand until the starch is absorbed." How long was that? How would he tell?

How do you tell anything? Kubu mused. How do you tell if someone is trustworthy? How do you know what is fair and what is unfair when dealing with criminals? And had they made the right decision about his job? His stomach began to hurt. It needs food, he thought. I'd better get a move on.

"Fat for deep frying." The man at the butchery, noticing Kubu's bulk, had told him to use oil instead of fat. "Heat the fat to 360°." Fahrenheit or Celsius? The recipe came from an American website. What would they use? It must be Fahrenheit. So what is 360° Fahrenheit in Celsius? Kubu couldn't remember how to convert from one to the other, but remembered that 20° Celsius was about 70° Fahrenheit. How far off could he be if he divided by seven and doubled the result? If I make it 350, dividing by seven gives fifty. Fifty doubled is one hundred. Kubu frowned. There was something wrong. He knew that water boiled at 100° Celsius. That wasn't hot enough. Well if I double that to 200° Celsius, it should be hot enough, he thought in desperation.

Kubu poured some oil into a pot, hoping it was enough. He turned on the front element of the stove, but couldn't find a way to set the temperature. Perhaps he should put the pot in the oven to heat it—he could see how to set the temperature there.

Kubu was getting flustered. Now he understood why he preferred sitting on the veranda sipping chilled wine. There he could relax and ponder his cases. If he cooked every day, he'd have no time to think.

Where was a thermometer? He pulled all the drawers out but couldn't find anything that looked useful. He looked on the counter and in the cupboards. Nothing. So how do you tell the temperature?

After a few minutes, he swallowed his pride and went to the veranda.

"Everything okay?" he asked nonchalantly. "More wine?" Joy and Pleasant both accepted. "By the way," Kubu said as he headed back inside, "where's a thermometer I can use for the oil?"

"When you think it's hot enough," Joy said, "just spit on the oil. If the spit dances and fizzes, it's hot enough." Kubu gaped at her. Was she serious, or was she having him on? Perhaps he could use water?

◀▶ ◀▶ ◀▶

It was twenty to nine when a disheveled Kubu invited Joy and Pleasant in to dinner. They had already finished more than a bottle of wine and were giggling at everything. Kubu on the other hand had not even sipped a drink, though on several occasions he had wanted to take a large swig from the bottle of brandy in the liquor cupboard.

When the ladies were seated, he poured red wine into the three clean glasses on the table and proposed a toast: "To restaurants! We should visit them more often!" Joy and Pleasant laughed uproariously.

"To the chef!" Pleasant was getting very loud. The glasses clinked loudly, and Kubu was worried that they might break.

"To my loving husband!" Joy leaned over and kissed Kubu on the cheek. "I'm looking forward to more of your wonderful creations in the future." Kubu glared at her and drained the rest of his wine in a single gulp.

"Hear, hear!" Pleasant lifted her glass for another toast.

Kubu refilled his glass and raised it once more. "To us," he said quietly.

Hunger took over, and the three set about the sweet and sour pork. Kubu was so ravenous that he was pleased he hadn't insisted on chopsticks as the butcher had suggested.

Pleasant looked around the table. "Where's the rice?"

Kubu groaned. The rice was still soaking; he had forgotten to cook it.

Joy saw his discomfort and put her hand on his arm. "Darling, you've done a fantastic job. Relax and enjoy yourself. The pork is delicious."

Kubu looked at his wife and saw she meant it. He put his hand over hers. "Thank you, my dear. I didn't imagine cooking could be so stressful."

Sanity restored, the three ate in silence, the only sounds those of cutlery on plates. And an occasional growl from Ilia to remind them that she too liked Chinese.

It was now after 10:00 p.m. Pleasant had left for home, sternly admonished to drive carefully; the table had been cleared, and the dishes were stacked in the kitchen. Kubu and Joy strolled onto the veranda.

"Come and sit on my lap, dear." Kubu patted his leg as though Joy didn't know where his lap was. "Are you sure we've made the right decision, my darling? No second thoughts?"

Joy shook her head. "I watched you as we discussed it, Kubu. *We* can't be happy if *you're* unhappy. Apart from Tumi and me, your whole life revolves around being a detective. You love your work. And when you started talking about working in security for Debswana, I could see how much you'd hate that. The routine, the boredom, the admin! After all, I don't want you to change. I want you as you are."

"You are the most amazing woman in the world," said Kubu, wanting to say something much less trite, but finding himself suddenly tongue-tied.

Joy curled up, put her arms around Kubu's neck, and gave him a deep kiss. "You are amazing too," she whispered. "I never thought you would do it. Cook a whole complicated meal. And it was so good. Thank you, my love."

Hmm, thought Kubu. This cooking business has some payoff after all. With one hand he stroked her back; with the other he pulled her head toward him. As their tongues explored each other, their breathing became short. Kubu shifted his hand to stroke her breasts. Joy groaned softly and pushed herself against him. She kissed him on his cheek, on his forehead, on his eyes.

"I love you," she murmured.

Kubu felt his eyes moisten. He loved her so much. He took her face between his hands and kissed her gently on the mouth. "Let's go to bed. The dishes can wait."

They stood up, held hands, and walked inside.

They stopped just inside the bedroom for their third long kiss since leaving the veranda. When they could stand it no longer, they separated, giggled, and headed for the bed, shedding clothes.

At that moment, Tumi started to cry.

AUTHOR NOTE

Although this is a work of fiction, we have tried to depict traditional Bushman cultures accurately. This has not been easy. Much about the Bushmen is uncertain. The cultures are difficult to research, partly because the Bushmen have oral histories and, in some cases, contradictory traditions, so that even authorities disagree on many points. Furthermore, these are diverse cultures with their own languages. Some of the languages are similar; others are not mutually understandable. The multiple clicks and tonal emphases make the languages very hard for outsiders to learn, and thus much of the information obtained by researchers is through interpreters, opening the possibility of questions (and answers) being misunderstood.

We have chosen to use the word *Bushman* for the people of our story. Even this decision was not easy, because all the names used for the *Khoisan* peoples are controversial. *Bushman* has been commonly used for many years and is derived from a Dutch phrase, but some people regard it as pejorative. In academic circles, *San* is widely accepted, but it derives from a derogatory word used by the farming *Khoi* groups to describe their hunter-gatherer cousins. And *Basarwa*, which is commonly used in Botswana, also has negative connotations.

Unfortunately the Bushmen seem to have no specific name for themselves; they refer to themselves just as "the people," and all other groups as "the others," whether white, black, or even Bushmen. Political groups have sometimes used the term

"First People of the Kalahari," alluding to the Bushmen's long tenure in the area.

In the end we settled for *Bushmen* simply because it is easier for the Western reader, and because no other name is broadly accepted.

An important personality in Bushman mythologies is Kaggen (sometimes written /Kaggen), a god with awesome powers but with the character of a trickster. In some stories, Kaggen is described as a mantis, giving the latter a special role in Bushman mythology. The face of a mantis is said to resemble that of a Bushman.

We found the Bushman quotes at the beginning of each part in *Customs and Beliefs of the /Xam Bushmen*, edited by Jeremy C. Hollmann (Wits University Press). The quotes themselves are originally from the remarkable work of Wilhelm Bleek and Lucy Lloyd, who recorded the stories of /A!kuŋta (Klaas Stoffel), //Kabbo (Oud Jantje Tooren), Diä!kwain (David Hoesar), / Haŋǂkass'o (Klein Jantje Tooren) and ǂKasiŋ (Klaas Katkop) between 1870 and 1880 in Cape Town.

The story that Khumanego tells of the arrest of Maauwe and Motswetla is essentially true, although presented from his perspective, of course. The case is described in detail in *In the Shadow of the Noose* by Elizabeth Maxwell and Alice Mogwe.

The story of Hans Schwabe's search for diamonds and his lonely death in what is now the Kgalagadi Transfrontier National Park is also true and provided the idea for one of the strands of the plot. However, there was no suggestion of foul play or that he left behind a map.

Berrybush is a real bed-and-breakfast near Tsabong, and Jill Thomas is its amazing proprietor. The camels live there in peace.

The Place is completely fictitious. However, if it existed as described, it might well have become a sacred site. Tsodilo is just such a collection of *koppies* rising from the desert. It contains a rich variety of Bushman art—even including a drawing of a whale, although the nearest coast is hundreds of miles away—and is venerated by the Bushmen as the place of creation. It is a wonderful and moving place to visit.

✴ ACKNOWLEDGMENTS ✴

With each new book we have more people to thank for their generous help and support, because we keep leaning on those who have helped us before while finding new ones to impose upon.

We are grateful to Claire Wachtel, senior vice president and executive editor at HarperCollins for continuing to support Detective Kubu. We also thank Ellen S. Leach for her careful copyediting. Kendra Newton has provided friendly and valuable publicity support.

As always we are grateful to our agent Marly Rusoff and her partner Michael Radulescu for their efforts on our behalf.

We were very fortunate to have a variety of readers of drafts of this book giving us input and suggestions, and catching errors. Our sincere thanks to: Linda Bowles, Pat Cretchley, Pam Diamond, Pat and Nelson Markley, Kit Naylor, Brunhilde Sears, and the Minneapolis writing group— Gary Bush, Maureen Fischer, Sujata Massey, and Heidi Skarie. With all their comments, it is hard to believe that the book still has mistakes. But it probably does, and we take responsibility for any that remain.

As always, many people in Botswana have generously given us their time to make the book as authentic as possible. We are always amazed by the kind and helpful reception two authors get when they arrive with odd questions about Bushman poisons, police procedures, and the like. We particularly want to thank Thebeyame Tsimako, commissioner of police in Botswana, for taking time from his demanding schedule to give us comments and advice, and for helping with our requests. Andy Taylor, headmaster of the wonderful Maru a Pula school in Gaborone, has been extraordinarily patient with all our questions and requests. On the question of the status of the Bushman peoples in Botswana, we were most fortunate to meet Alice Mogwe, director of the human rights organization Ditshwanelo, and Unity Dow, former High Court judge of Botswana. Their input has been invaluable. Jill Thomas told us much about the Tsabong area and its past, let us stay at her guest farm nearby, and even let us use her as a character in the book.

Chief Inspector Ngishidingwa of the Windhoek police station was very helpful with Namibian police procedures, as well as with cross-frontier crime issues. Station commanders Marata and Modise of Tsabong and Tshane respectively also provided invaluable information about the Kgalagadi District.

Wulf Haake, an expert on the German explorers of Namibia, found us an early published version of the Hans Schwabe story in Afrikaans.

We were also most fortunate to spend time with Colonel Roger Dixon of the Forensic Science Laboratory of the South African Police Service, who gave us much valuable advice on forensic matters. Similarly, Botswana police pathologist Salvador Mapunda helped us understand the environment of forensic pathology in Botswana. Dr. D. J. H. Veale, director of the Tygerberg Poison Information Centre of the University of Stellenbosch, provided very helpful insights into the complexities of Bushman arrow poisons.

All of our books have benefited from the detailed reading and advice of our wonderful friends in Kasane, Peter and Salome Comley, and this one is no exception. It is a great sadness to us that Salome passed away at the end of 2010. This book is dedicated to her memory.

Michael Sears
Stanley Trollip

❈ GLOSSARY ❈

bakkie	South African slang for a pickup truck.
Batswana	Plural adjective or noun, e.g., "The people of Botswana are known as Batswana." See *Motswana*.
BDF	Botswana Defence Force.
biltong	Salted strips of meat, spiced with pepper and coriander seeds and dried in the sun.
braai/braaivleis	South African term for a barbeque.
Bushman poison bulb	Poisonous plant (*Boophone disticha*) with beautiful flowers. Used in small doses as a hallucinogen and for traditional medicines.
Bushmen	A race small in size and number, many of whom live in the Kalahari area. They refer to themselves as "the people" (see *Khoisan*). In Botswana sometimes they are referred to as the Basarwa.
Debswana	Diamond-mining joint venture between De Beers and the Botswana government.
donga	A dry river course with steep sides.
dumela	Setswana for "Hello" or "Good day."
eland	The world's largest antelope (*Taurotragus oryx*).

gemsbok

In southern Africa, the Cape oryx (*Oryx gazella*), a large antelope with long, straight horns.

Hoodia

A cactus-like plant (*Hoodia gordonii*) eaten for energy and as a hunger suppressant.

!Gwi

The language spoken by the Gwi Bushman group.

Khoi

Hottentots (see *Khoisan*).

Khoisan

The name by which the lighter-skinned indigenous peoples of southern Africa, the Khoi (Hottentots) and the San (Bushmen), are known. These people dominated the subcontinent for millennia before the appearance of the Nguni and other black peoples.

kimberlite

The host rock of almost all diamonds. It is an igneous extrusion from deep within the earth's mantle.

knobkierie

A short club made from hardwood with a knob on one end, used as a weapon.

Kola Tonic

A sweet non-alcoholic syrup from spices and the Kola nut.

koppie

Afrikaans for "small hill."

kraal

An enclosure for livestock, usually made from stones or thornbushes.

kubu

Setswana for "hippopotamus."

kudu

A large antelope (*Tragelaphus strepsiceros*).

Landie	Term of affection for a Land Rover.
lobola	Bride-price (originally in cattle) paid to the bride's parents in African tradition. Sometimes used to set up the newly married couple.
mankala	A popular game throughout Africa, often played using holes in the ground and stones.
Mma	Respectful term in Setswana used when addressing a woman. For example, *Dumela, Mma Bengu* means "Hello, Mrs. Bengu," or "Hello, Ms. Bengu."
Motswana	Singular adjective or noun, e.g., "That man from Botswana is a Motswana." See *Batswana*.
pan	A basin or depression in the earth, often containing mud or water.
pap	Smooth cornmeal porridge, often eaten with the fingers and dipped into a meat or vegetable stew.
pappa le nama	Setswana for *pap* and meat.
pronk	To leap straight up (to stot)—a behavior of springbok when being pursued by a predator.
pula	Currency of Botswana. *Pula* means "rain" in Setswana. One pula = one hundred thebes.

Rra

Respectful term in Setswana used when addressing a man. For example, *Dumela, Rra Bengu* means "Hello, Mr. Bengu."

sambal

A chili-based sauce used as a condiment, usually with curry.

San

Bushman people. See *Khoisan*.

scherm

A flimsy dwelling constructed from grass, often temporary.

Setswana

Language of the Batswana peoples.

springbok

A medium-size brown-and-white antelope (*Antidorcas marsupialis*). Has the ability to survive long periods without water. National animal of South Africa.

steelworks

A drink made from Kola Tonic, lime juice, ginger beer, soda water, and bitters.

thebe

The smallest denomination of Botswana currency. See *pula*. Thebe means "shield" in Setswana.

tsama melon

A yellow-green melon abundant in the Kalahari. A major source of food and water for Bushmen.

BOOKS BY MICHAEL STANLEY

A CARRION DEATH
Introducing Detective Kubu

ISBN 978-0-06-125241-9 (paperback)

"Delightful. . . . Plot twists are fair and well-paced, the Botswana setting has room to breathe and take shape as its own entity, and Stanley's writing style is equal parts sprightly and grave."

—*Los Angeles Times Book Review*

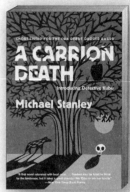

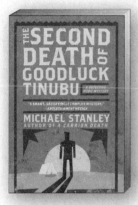

THE SECOND DEATH OF GOODLUCK TINUBU
A Detective Kubu Mystery

ISBN 978-0-06-125250-1 (paperback)

"[Kubu is] the African Columbo. . . . Like the first book to feature Kubu, *A Carrion Death*, this is a smart, satisfyingly complex mystery."

—*Entertainment Weekly*

DEATH OF THE MANTIS
A Detective Kubu Mystery

ISBN 978-0-06-200037-8 (paperback)

"*Death of the Mantis* is the best book yet in one of the best series going: a serious novel with a mystery at its core that takes us places we've never been, thrills and informs us, and leaves us changed by the experience. I loved this book."

—Timothy Hallinan, bestselling author of *The Queen of Patpong*

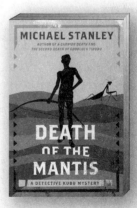